BINGE UNTIL TRAGEDY

A NOVEL

BEN D'ALESSIO

© 2017 Ben D'Alessio. All rights reserved. No part of this publication may be reproduced, distributed, or transmitted in any form or by any means, including photocopying, recording, or other electronic or mechanical methods, without the prior written permission of the author, except in the case of brief quotations embodied in critical reviews and certain other noncommercial uses permitted by copyright law.

ISBN: 978-1-48359-892-5 (print)
ISBN: 978-1-48359-893-2 (ebook)

ACKNOWLEDGMENTS

First, I'd like to thank my editors Samantha Gordon and Leah Wohl-Pollack of *Invisibleinkediting.com* for taking my fury of a manuscript that neglected the basic laws of grammar and punctuation and helping turn it into something coherent.

I owe a debt of gratitude to my high school creative writing teachers, Jessica Siegel and Suzanne Snyder, who not only inspired me to write, but told me I was a writer—I wish I had listened to you two earlier.

And lastly, although they are prohibited from ever reading this book, I'd like to thank my parents, for giving me the world.

Life is not a dream. Careful! Careful! Careful!
We fall down the stairs in order to eat the moist earth
or we climb to the knife edge of the snow with the voices of the dead
      dahlias.
But forgetfulness does not exist, dreams do not exist;
flesh exists. Kisses tie our mouths
in a thicket of new veins,
and whoever his pain pains will feel that pain forever
and whoever is afraid of death will carry it on his shoulders.

—Federico García Lorca, "City That Does Not Sleep"

PENNSYLVANIA

I FELT IT IN THE BACK OF MY THROAT, THAT DRIPPING bitter sting that only happens after a thick line courses through your nasal cavity and punches you in the face: *Pow!*

"How could you possibly think that?" a nasal voice insisted.

"What?" I said.

"What? I mean, how could you think that fascism could possibly be a creation of the Left?" the voice demanded.

What the fuck is he talking about? Kev cut up two thick lines on the cover of my LSAT practice book.

"Who the fuck are you, man?" I asked the voice.

"I overheard you talking to Riley about the concept of a neo-liberal fascist state, and honestly just cannot understand how you could think that would ever exist."

The dripping was still in the back of my throat, and when that happens I try to talk as little as possible—for at least a few minutes until it dissipates. But this voice had a political agenda and was destroying my long-awaited buzz: he must be terminated.

"First of all, chief, who the fuck are you, who the fuck is Riley, and why the fuck are you in my fucking room right now?" I responded to the voice, which now had brown eyes, a crooked nose, and thick black-rimmed glasses.

"Calm down," said Kev.

"Who, me?" I couldn't help but ask.

"Yeah, man. Just relax."

"I'll relax when this jabroni gets outta here," I said, sticking my finger right between the thick-rimmed glasses. The voice turned to leave and tripped on a beer bottle, catching himself on the doorknob.

I twisted the hundred-dollar bill into the tightest funnel my fingers could create (always do blow with a hundred—something my older brother Sal told me) and yelled, "Hey, Mussolini. Send Riley in."

Riley, contrary to what I told the voice earlier, was one of my close friends. Never had we slept together, but there'd always been a weird connection between us. She'd banged most of my friends by now. Similar to her insatiable gluttony when it came to my friends' penises, I indulged in my fair share of her girlfriends', well... everything, I suppose. We basically had an unwritten agreement of drunken sex, in which we traded our friends' genitals like produce at a farmer's market.

"Please don't tell me you're doing that guy all by yourself?" She nodded toward the cocaine, concern and humor fighting for dominance in her voice.

"There's room for one more," I responded. That thick line of blow waited on the cover of the LSAT practice book.

"I told you. I don't do that anymore."

"Is that why you've been so bitchy lately?"

"Fuck you."

"Kev?"

"Let's do it," he said.

Halfway through, I had to take a breather. My head hurt, my nose stung, the bitterness of the cocaine overwhelmed my tongue—I soldiered on. Once every granule was safely lodged in our nostrils, I unrolled the hundred-dollar bill and placed it back in my wallet. I snatched my sweating bottle of King's Natural and returned to the gathering that had matriculated outside of my bedroom door.

After weaving my way through a few drunken Gammas, a couple of basketball players whose heads were skimming the ceiling, and this goober wearing a bow tie—a fucking bow tie—I finally reached her. In typical Riley fashion, she had one hand on a guy's belt while the other gripped the thick shaft of a bottle of vodka. Her lips were seductively close to the right ear of Craig Jameson; I know, it's a fantastic name. Riley had fucked him before, of course.

"Riley!" I yelled over a blaring song with a catchy, repetitive hook by some new Swedish DJ everyone was crazy about.

"Hey, how's your nose?!" She smirked.

"Hilarious. Hey, so can you hook me up with Trisha?" I asked, certain that Riley would chat up any girl I was interested in.

"Give me a minute." She turned back to Craig Jameson to make sure she was all set for the night before making any advances in my favor.

My nose was sore and my right nostril was throbbing. It was Saturday night and by then we had already been up for three consecutive nights engaging in full-scale debauchery. While I usually limit myself to consuming only once a week, Thursday night was Josh Rosenblatt's twenty-first birthday, so offering shared lines between shots seemed like the only proper way for me to contribute to my friend's celebration. Last night—Friday night—was, well, a Friday night, and at this point in our college careers, we were hardwired to devour any liquid, powder, or pill we could get our hands on.

From across the living room, I could see Kev sporting a concerned look on his face. He was pale—paler than usual, pale like a ghost, Casper pale.

"Yo, Casper!" I belted as I waved my arm. He knew I was fucking with him, but walked over anyway.

"Dude, I think we're out," he said.

"What do you mean you 'think' we're out? Are we out or are we out?" I asked.

"We're fucking out!" He scanned the room like the NSA was watching.

"Well what the fuck do you want me to do about it, Kev? I want to hook up with Trisha tonight. I can't spend the whole night chilling with you and the white lady."

"Fuck, dude, you had more than I did," Kev alleged.

"Listen, I've been where you are now. I've had to chase it before. We all have. You need to relax and grab a beer." This was my attempt to relax my friend. I probably could've done more.

"You relax. You grab a beer."

"Okay, Kev," I said to keep him from getting argumentative. "Go grab us a couple of beers. I have some King's Natural in my fridge." I needed him out of my face. The kid had gone "skiing" plenty of times before. I didn't understand why he still got anxious like a fucking amateur. I was getting all riled up, and all I wanted to do was talk to Trisha. A tap on the shoulder relieved my stress.

"Hey there."

"Hey, beautiful. I wasn't even sure if you were here yet." She knew I was full of shit.

"Oh, no, I've been here. I was with Riley earlier. I think she's going to hook up with Craig Jameson."

"Great name, right?"

"Huh?"

"Anyway, how are the new pledges coming along?" Trisha was a Kappa Sigma and embodied every aspect of the sorority. The Kappa Sigmas were the stereotypical sorority. You know, the sorority that is in every low-budget college movie ever made. The sorority that has one hundred girls in it and they all fucking hate each other, but shout "Sisterhood above all!" or some stupid shit like that before they bang each other's boyfriends—that's the Kappa Sigmas, and they're my favorite sorority.

Trisha, brunette with golden streaks, had a wonderfully fit body. Unlike the numerous Kappa Sigmas who wore lacrosse pennies and neon sunglasses at every single party they attended, Trisha would take the next step. Jeans with rips at the knees, tight, low-cut t-shirts, and boots were all part of Trisha's "look." A girl's "look" is more than just what she looks like. It's her demeanor and her voice, her hand motions and her hair, but most importantly, a girl's "look" is how she looks at *you*. When Trisha and I made eye contact, it lasted a split second longer than with anyone else that night, and that's all I needed.

"What's your drink?" I asked, assuming it was vodka or tequila.

"Oh, beer is fine," she said, to my surprise.

"Okay, cool. I have some in my room. This way, *madame*."

I pulled the sophomore through the jungle of Gammas and chopped through a group of Zetas and softball players like my forearm was a machete. I like to believe you could tell how a party would turn out by what the situation was at midnight. Too many dudes and you're going to scare away the girls. Too many girls and the party is going to turn into a pop sing-along fashion shoot where you think gravity has increased due to the amount of "sorority squatting." This party had a solid representation of Greek life and sports teams, plus us.

"I only have King's Natural. Is that okay?"

"Oh yeah, that's fine. I've had about nine already."

My room was filled with people, a few I didn't know, so I looked at Kev to hint that I wanted the room to myself, and of course he got the message. After four years of college together, Kev and I were basically telepathic.

"Hey everyone!" Kev yelled. "We're playing Relay. Get out into the common room!"

Once my room cleared out, I sat Trisha on my bed, locked the door, and grabbed her face, pulling it just close enough to where our lips barely touched—like the cover of a Nicholas Sparks novel. I moved my hand gently up the small of her back and wrapped my fingers in her bra straps, pulling them back with one hand while the other was placed firmly on the back of her head. Our foreheads were pressed against each other and neither one of us went in for a kiss. Her hands rubbed my beard and playfully pulled my hair.

"Why should I kiss you right now?" she asked.

Not expecting this question, I threw out one of my lines I had loaded in the arsenal and hopefully hadn't used on one of her friends.

"Because after one taste, you'll realize you've been starving to death."

The floodgates opened.

She clasped my neck with one hand while the other scrambled for my belt. She clamped onto my bottom lip, which caused me to wince in pain and grab at her waist. I slid my fingers in between her jeans and body, making sure to get my hands caught in her underwear, which was something I stumbled upon one day, fooling around with a chick from back home who told me no guys do that and more really should—lucky me. I pushed her back on my bed, still locked at the mouth, and undid the top buttons and zipper of her ripped, tight jeans.

I've always said, when asked for advice on hooking up with girls, your mouth and hands should always be doing something—okay, that was my brother Sal's advice, too, but I advertised it as my own.

I threw off her pants, which slid down easily, and took a brief step back to admire what—at that moment in time—was mine.

"Can I help you?" she asked, with a petite smirk. In fact, everything about her was "petite," and the word itself was so perfect to describe her, I do not understand why I hadn't thought to use it earlier. That it was a French word made it that much more fun to repeat over and over in my head: petite, petite, petite.

"Oh, excuse me," I said. "I was just taking a moment to appreciate the most gorgeous girl at the party."

"My pants are on your floor. You can quit the one-liners."

"It's a habit."

I threw off my shirt by grabbing behind the neck with both hands and pulling over my head in one quick motion. Doing one arm at a time just looks silly, and God forbid you get your arm stuck in the sleeve. Plus, it usually messes up your hair just enough to give it a ruffled look.

Trisha grabbed my beard and bit my lip. I shuffled for my belt and whipped it off in one quick motion that snapped in the musk. I threw it around her lower back and pulled her in close to my body: a complete risk, but it worked. Still locked at my lips, she let out a dainty moan and mumbled something I didn't catch. She clawed down my back and nibbled on my earlobe and whispered something again. I caught it this time.

"Why isn't my underwear in your mouth?"

Starting between her eyes, I kissed the sophomore's body, moving a few inches down with each embrace, making sure not to go too quickly, because it was not the kisses that are enticing, it's the anticipation. The kissing, licking, and gnawing is fuel for a build-up to something all girls, if done correctly, adore.

Properly going down on a girl is an art. Never call it "eating out" or "eating pussy." Those are tasteless terms. They say that if you can make a girl orgasm, she'll never leave your side. I say that if you can do it with nothing but your tongue, she'll never leave your bed—yeah, yeah, yeah, Sal told me that one too; the guy's got a lot of 'em.

With my face down between her legs, I told her to keep her hands above her head and grab on to the headboard.

"If you move from this position, there will be consequences," I said.

"Ha, ha. Like what?"

I was at Trisha's midsection, right above her navel. I nibbled at whatever I could of her flat stomach, and she laughed and grabbed at my face.

"What did I say?!"

"How can you expect me to hold on when you do that!" she howled.

With both of my hands, I grabbed her wrists and threw them above her head. I put 'em together so I could hold them both with one hand, while my free hand tugged at her underwear. Looking her dead in the eyes, I said, "Don't move them." She stared back and didn't say anything. I waited a moment, looked down at her half-naked body, looked back into her eyes, and gave her a wink and a half grin.

"I fucking hate you!" she giggled.

"You're going to eat those words."

When Trisha finally understood that her cooperation was necessary, I made a quick move to her vagina and kissed right above her lips. I used my thumb to massage her clit while my four other fingers were snug inside of her. Still kissing, I grabbed her butt with my free hand. After a few seconds of her moaning and begging for me to use my tongue, I moved my thumb and gave into her wishes. I made circular motions around her clit with my tongue, and gently sucked on the upper part of her lips. As I moved my tongue faster, she became wetter; as she became wetter, she became louder; and as she became louder, I moved my tongue faster. Her moans became pleads and she covered her face with a pillow, and even though she moved her hands from her assigned position, I let it slide. Her lower back moved up and down, convulsing like a girl possessed.

I attempted to keep her pinned to the bed; her pubic bone hit my nose, which had been throbbing already from doing one too many lines with Kev. I winced and paused as pain shot through my nose and I could feel it in the back of my neck. The drips in my throat mixed with the tangy taste of Trisha rendered me unable to continue for a few moments. I lifted my head and looked up.

"That was fucking incredible," she said between breaths.

I grabbed a King's Natural from my mini-fridge, downed half of it, and rubbed the cold bottle on my forehead. The coldness from the glass was a relief and my nose had stopped throbbing. I had an idea.

"Flip over," I ordered.

"Huh? Why?"

I grabbed an unopened beer, walked over to the bed, slipped my forearm under the small of Trisha's back, and flipped her over. By placing my knee on her butt and using my hand to hold down her wrists, my free hand was able to slide the frost-glazed beer down her spine.

"Oh my god!" she screamed. I couldn't help but laugh. "Can we just fuck already?" she asked.

"What about me?"

"What do you mean?"

"I don't get anything in return?"

Her phone lit up and illuminated the dark room. She rolled over, checked it, and started to laugh. Unbelievable. I grabbed her waist and stuck my middle finger inside of her.

"Are we ready here?" I insisted.

"Okay, yes! Sorry."

I wasn't sure whether to make this quick and primal or elongated and passionate. The party was still going on. It was early. If I was on top of her and we started in missionary, I would kiss her neck and she'd probably pull my hair. As I bit her ear, her nails would tear up and down my back, leaving me looking like I got massaged by a man-o'-war. If I flipped her over into doggy style, it would be quick. I would palm her butt and grab the back of her head, pulling it toward me, turning it slightly to the side so she could see me. I had a decision to make.

"What are you waiting for?" she pleaded. I hopped on top of her bare body and wrapped my hand around the back of her neck. After laying a kiss on her lips, I pulled back and looked into her green eyes, which were prettier than I had thought. Green eyes only represent two percent of the world's population. When I find someone who has them, I'm immediately enamored and even jealous. People with green eyes are more mysterious, because their genes didn't pick a side: black or white, good or evil, blue or brown. Green eyes represent the medium of society; the centrism that keeps us afloat. We don't have to pick the Republican or Democrat. An issue does not always have two sides. Green eyes are a symbol of the nonconformity and individuality that reflects my generation.

Pressing my midsection against hers, I leaned in close until our noses were millimeters apart. I licked her top lip; she smiled. I peered deep and realized her eyes weren't green, they were hazel.

"Well?" she insisted. "I'm on birth control, so you don't need a condom or anything."

I placed my arm under her neck and worked my hand through her hair. I told her to wrap her legs around my lower back and lift up her hips. Thrusting my hips slowly, I made sure not to pull out of her completely. "Deeper! Holy fuck," she commanded. I continued until my thighs were weak, then pulled out and threw her on top of me. She placed her hands beside my head and started to bop up and down, her hair getting caught in my mouth. I moved her hands to my chest, which pushed her breasts together and made her look more in control. She did that thing girls always do, where they put one hand in their hair and throw their head back with the other hand pulling at your chest hair and their chin pointed slightly toward the ceiling. My fingers grasped her waist and slid up and down her stomach, back, and butt. I licked my thumb, pressed it against the top of her clit, and rubbed gently, trying to match her jazz-like frenzy. She fit me perfectly.

The view was spectacular. The sophomore had exceeded my expectations—she must've had a boyfriend in high school.

"How is it?" she asked.

"Fantastic," I said. "And yourself?"

She smiled.

She bounced and rocked her hips for five minutes or so and then I felt the rising tidal wave of orgasm. Without notice, I threw Trisha off of me and put her on her stomach. Grabbing her by the hips, I lifted her up and slid a pillow underneath her lower abdomen. I firmly grasped her butt, but slipped on the insertion and drilled her in the leg. She looked back at me but didn't say anything.

She kept her hands folded in front of her face as if she were in prayer. I crept my hand up to the back of her head and tightly grasped her hair directly at the scalp. I didn't pull; never pull, just grab. She leaned back her head, looking to the ceiling, and I kissed her on the cheek. Beads of sweat formed around my forehead and neck. I tasted the drips at the back of my throat and the bitterness made me thirsty. The light from Trisha's phone was bright on the bed. The text vibrations from the brick shot through the mattress and knocked me off course. I was over it. I needed to get back to the festivities.

"Where do you want me to finish?" I asked.

"Wherever," she said, as if she was over it too. "Just don't get it in my hair."

Trisha rocked her body to the same motion as my waist and threw her hair around her shoulder so it was out of reach. The sensation rose and I waited until the very last moment to pull out. My eyes rolled back in my head like a slot machine. I finished leaning forward over her, unknowingly pushing her body and face into the myriad of blankets and pillows I hadn't cleaned since winter break. ...

We lay next to each other not saying a word. I had managed to avoid her hair. My panting was the only thing breaking the silence. I was sticky with sweat and it felt as if all of the blood that was previously in my dick went to my face. My throat was dry and bitter. I kissed her on the temple and grabbed my pants off the floor.

"I'm going to go back outside. You want a beer?" I asked while looping my belt.

"Oh." Her eyes widened and she sat up on her elbows. "Yeah, okay."

BINGE UNTIL TRAGEDY

I grabbed a beer, opened it, and put it on top of the fridge.

"That was great, by the way," I said. "What did you think?"

Trisha covered her chest—which seemed unnecessary, considering I had just come on her back—and searched my room for her clothes.

"It was good. Where are my pants?"

"Was it?"

"Yeah. Why do guys always want to know if it was good? You were there too."

"I don't know. I'm not the spokesman for 'guys.'"

We found our clothes and got dressed. I put on a clean plaid button-down and rolled up the sleeves: four turns on each side, right below the elbow.

"I'll see you outside?" I asked.

"Yeah, yeah. Let me fix my hair. I'll see you out there. Thanks for the beer... and for the sex."

I walked into the common room I shared with my three roommates. There were about twenty or so people drinking and mingling and making plans for global prosperity. The music had switched from Nordic dance to Mad-Mannix, an incoherent, mentally unstable rapper who was the self-appointed "voice of our generation." I turned on my phone to check the time. It was midnight and the night was ripe.

I found Kev and Riley behind the bar, pouring shots of Hayman's whiskey for themselves and a pod of basketball players whose heads skimmed the ceiling. I usually hated to take shots late at night. But as usual, they put one in my face, and I sucked it down while attempting to smile, because it is just so damn hard to say no to Mr. Hayman.

"Yo, man. How was Trisha?" Kev asked. "You guys were in there for a while."

"Lovely," I replied.

"Nice. Where is she?"

"She was fixing her hair, not sure if she came out yet."

I turned toward my door, which happened to be opening at that very moment, and out came a clothed Trisha looking down at her phone with a smile. She traversed the pockets of partiers and met a group of friends in the far corner.

"Nice," he said, bobbing his head and awkwardly staring at the sophomore. "How long you gonna keep that thing?" Kev asked, snapping back to attention and pulling at my beard.

"Ehh, I don't know," I responded while stroking it from cheek to chin.

"We graduate in like a month. You keepin' it for graduation?"

"Nah, I'll trim it," I replied. "Even though it hurts to destroy something so beautiful."

"You're so gay. Want a smoke?"

"Yeah, I'll split one."

"No, have your own. I don't want to share one, because then I'll get sick."

"Wait. You're about to smoke a *cigarette* and you're worried about getting sick from sharing it with me?"

He paused a moment. "Yes."

"Oh my god, you are so fucking weird. Fine, I'll have my own."

"Love you, bro."

We stepped outside and onto the balcony with the life of the party at our backs. The amalgamation of music, cheers, and chants created a symphony of sounds that I knew I would soon miss, for graduation was nearly upon us. I lit my cigarette and dragged. I closed my eyes and exhaled and allowed a little bit of smoke to play in my mouth. I was at that level of enough drinks where all it would take was one tightly rolled cancer-stick to complete my buzz. The cocaine had virtually worn off.

The air was sweet and smoky, and the kind of breeze I adored swept over the balcony and cooled my face, which was usually sunburnt from hours of lying out behind our building and drinking only the finest beers for thirteen dollars a case. We would toss around that egg-shaped rugby ball, which had mud stains from fields across the state, while the girls covered their faces with oversized sunglasses and sported bright bikinis without a beach in sight. The grass was peppered with dried lime slices and cigarette butts. On slow nights, we would gather around a hookah, which a friend of a friend had brought back from Istanbul, and we smoked sticky strawberry tobacco, lounging in Adirondack chairs that could be mistaken for thrones.

I felt my phone vibrate as it lit up the pocket of my jeans. **Text from Queen of Campus <3<3: 12:28 a.m.: Where are you guys?** It was Riley.

Balcony, I responded. Within a few seconds, she came through the door and joined us for a smoke. She situated herself in between us and put her arms around our shoulders.

"So what's next?" she asked into the open air.

"What do you mean?" said Kev.

"After graduation, what are you two doing?"

"You know I fucking hate that question," I said.

"What crawled up your ass?"

"You."

"Bah! You wish, babe." And she gave me a wink.

"... Gross."

In the spring of my senior year, I had already been asked approximately one thousand times by one thousand different people what I was doing after graduation. Law school, med school, business school, or any other type of higher education that would plunge me deeper into debt, shackling my social freedom and rendering me a slave to student loans, seemed to be everyone's most desired topic of conversation. Or they just had nothing else interesting to say, I suppose.

The partygoers dwindled, and by four in the morning—the darkest hour of the night—there remained a bold few sitting on desk chairs, stools, and bean bags, sipping beer around a rectangular coffee table covered in liquor bottles, shot glasses, and beer cans—the alcohol graveyard. Parties changed, from who was invited, what the theme was, or which type of music was played. But the late nights? Those had a pattern; they fit a mold that after four years we all came to appreciate. If one of us was missing because we were in a girl's room or we were eructating our sins into the toilet, our absence was noticed.

I turned on my phone to find the Cavalry, my favorite band, staring back at me: no messages. I debated whether or not to text Trisha goodnight. It seemed aggressive. My eyes hurt, my nose hurt, my throat hurt. I undressed and collapsed onto my bed, covered in so many pillows that it would draw envy from a Moorish prince.

I woke up and checked my phone: 9:42. I went back to sleep until 11:57, and had three missed calls from **Mom** and a text that read: **Call me back ASAP. LOL mom.**

She always signed her text messages, and did so with "LOL," which meant "Lots of Love" in mom-text. When I read her texts, I always pictured her laughing, which made me smile. I had spoken to her yesterday or the day before. Dad had just gotten back from a business trip in Vegas and was doing fine. Carlo, my younger brother, was starting at shortstop for the high school baseball team and was playing exceptionally well. I was proud of him; I couldn't hit a baseball for shit.

Although he was only a sophomore, Carlo had grabbed the attention of some big universities due to his batting power—unusual for someone his size. At only five-nine, one hundred seventy-five pounds, Carlo was no prototypical power hitter. However, I've seen him smack the ball dead-center clear over the varsity fence at least five times since he was fourteen. The colleges knew they could make him stronger; it was his skill that excited them. The kid's got talent, that's for sure, and my dad made certain that Carlo only received the best training New Jersey had to offer. Twice a week, he was driven to private lessons with an ex-professional ball player from the Dominican Republic named Ángel Cortés Piazon. *El Angelito,* as he was known in the pros, won two consecutive World Series with St. Louis in the early 2000s before finishing his career with the Yankees. Like Carlo, *El Angelito* was also an undersized shortstop, and managed to have six seasons with twenty-five-plus home runs and a .310 career batting average while leading the league in stolen bases in '03, '04, and '06. I obtained the ability to recite these statistics on cue because of Carlo's constant reminders to the rest of us of who trains him. I vividly remember the 2003, game seven, ninth inning, two outs, cliché of a situation when Cortés pulled a ball over the left field fence, which barely stayed in fair play, for the title. It was at this moment that Carlo claims he knew he wanted to play shortstop and become a professional baseball player. Sal and I immediately reminded him that he was a mistake and that Mom wished he were a girl. My parents deny both of these statements.

Sal, short for Salvatore, is my older brother by six years. He's a successful financial consulting something-or-other for a company with three names: two Anglo-Saxon and one Japanese, none of which I could remember. He lives in Manhattan with his fiancée, and lives the life my parents always wanted for him. Sal is the "Alpha" I aspire to be. The dude is cool, and in an old-school, classy way that is rare these days. He taught me everything from what to order on a first date at a Lebanese restaurant to how to tap a keg.

When I visited him at college, I would watch how he acted with friends, with girls. The guy had an ethos. I witnessed him convince two girls he was Brazilian by using a mixture of Italian and Latin and claiming it was Portuguese—he got both of their numbers. Sal made it look easy. He was tall, dark, and handsome in the golden age of Hollywood type of way.

Advice from my older brother always carried a colossal amount of weight, despite his numerous mishaps, blunders, and straight fuck-ups that plagued his teenage years (he was the mastermind behind the hallway petroleum jelly Slip 'N Slide debacle of 2007). But Sal's incredible GPA, ACT, and SAT scores made it difficult for my parents to reprimand him in any meaningful way, considering he would be receiving a scholarship from virtually any university he wished to attend. He selected Stanford. His reasoning for the California powerhouse? "It's like Harvard or Yale, but with better weather and broads."

One of those "broads" became his fiancée. A California girl whom Sal convinced to move to the East Coast with him after college, Michelle loved my brother more than he loved himself. She was as sharp and witty as any tri-stater I've ever met. When I was introduced to her, it came as no surprise to me why Sal had decided to make her his girlfriend—blond and sarcastic was a perfect combination. When Michelle could recite the different wine regions of Italy with ease to my father, it didn't matter that a non-Italian West-Coast liberal was serious about his son either.

I received another text. **Text from Mom: 12:09 p.m.: Where are you? Call me. LOL Mom**

What's the matter? I responded.

Within seconds, my phone was vibrating. I was in no mood to talk, but I answered. I stumbled from my bed and leaned on the smooth wood of my dresser for support.

"Hey, Ma. What's going on?"

"Sweetheart, I need to tell you something." Her voice was soft. "I don't really know how to put this, so I'm just going to say it." It was that familiar tone that had nurtured me throughout my life. "Adam is dead." She broke. I broke. "He took his own life last night. Your father is on his way to get you."

Air left my lungs, but I could not speak. I could not walk and I could not drop to my knees like I should have, like the situation commanded. I just stood in a dopey paralysis and held my phone in the palm of my hand, below my chin, and listened through the speaker: "I love you, Joel."

NEW JERSEY

I'M JOEL LUPO, AND MY LIFE HAS IMPLODED AND caved in and I'm stuck breathing in the dust. I sat in the passenger seat of our gigantic black SUV and watched as life passed by. I watched people stand in line for coffee with their faces buried in their phones, reading mindless updates about some fucking kid-celebrity-moron who's only famous for God knew what reasons, I suppose. Is this really what has become of us? We stand in line, stare at a screen, grab our coffee, go to work, stare at a bigger screen, go to meals, stare at a bigger screen still, go to sleep, repeat, and then die. Was this the life that awaited me after graduation?

"Joel."

"Yeah, Dad?"

"Your mother and I know how close you guys were," he said. "Adam was like family."

"Yeah."

"You know he'd been struggling the past few years, and I don't think he could hang in there anymore. He just couldn't handle it, Joel."

"Yeah, I know."

"I wanted to tell you that your mother and I love you very much, and if you ever have any problems…"

"I'm not going to kill myself," I snapped.

"Okay," he responded, his eyes never leaving the road.

BEN D'ALESSIO

Adam, full name Adam Austin Reichman, and I had known each other since boyhood. We grew up on the same street and I long considered him my best friend. I had my brothers too, but Sal was older, more of a mentor, and Carlo was much younger. Adam and I, however, were the same age.

During the winter about five years ago, Adam was driving on Route 22, a godforsaken, menacingly designed commercial highway riddled with sudden merges and exits. A sedan sped out from a strip mall parking lot and Adam's truck—a behemoth of a vehicle—crushed its side in. After a moment of fuzziness, Adam dropped from the truck and in frantic haste, peered into the broken, spider-webbed driver's side window to find a screaming mother clutching her bloodied daughter.

Erika Tambor was only eight when she died. I choose these words purposely—she died—because what happened after the accident caused Adam years of grief and ultimately his demise, I suppose.

An eyewitness at the scene testified that Adam was driving at a reasonable speed. I had driven with him many times, and he was actually a cautious driver—something rare amongst my friends, and teenagers in general, I suppose. The witness called the police to report the crash. During the call, he said that Mrs. Tambor had her head down and seemed distracted, or something along those lines. An EMT found Mrs. Tambor's phone, miraculously intact, a few feet from the destruction.

Adam walked away virtually unscathed, but inside he was crumbling. We got drunk this one time in my basement, and he started rocking back and forth on the couch screaming, "My baby! You killed her! What have you done, you monster?!" as if imitating a woman.

Adam was not charged criminally by the state, but was brought to civil court by the Tambors for "wrongful death" at the loss of their daughter. The Tambors had hired a shrewd, slick, and expensive lawyer who slandered Adam in every way possible, slipping in the two times that Adam was suspended from school: once for fighting a kid in the sixth grade and once for smelling like pot. He labeled Adam as a nihilist with no regard for human life, claiming he was emotionless at the sight of a dead eight-year-old. In reality, Adam was far from emotionless. That day stuck with him and slowly, steadily, ate away at his core, I suppose.

His parents brought him to a psychiatrist, who put him on a prescription of "happy pills" that didn't do shit. They instead made him wildly irrational and irritable, with phases of, what seemed to me, intense depression. There were times when I would find him sitting alone, staring blankly at a black television screen.

Before the accident, Adam was motivated. He had dabbled in web and graphic design and was considering going to a college in the city. He was on the ice hockey team and the junior varsity baseball team, and every time winter began to fade and that first warm day in early April came, we would have a baseball catch in his backyard—it was a tradition. But we never had that catch that spring after the accident.

The next year, I had asked him a couple of times if he wanted to have a catch, but he always had different reasons to bail. When he told me that he had an appointment (he didn't give me specifics) and couldn't go out, I saw a few minutes later on Facebook that he had checked into *Robot Farm*, a mind-numbing online game. For the next four years I would attempt to get anything I could out of him, anything that might spark an interest or even a damn conversation, but he would just change the subject or not say anything at all, responding in grunts.

After I left for college, I rarely heard from him, and I always had to text or call him first. He was never good at keeping in touch, even before the accident, and oftentimes my texts would go unanswered. When I *was* able to speak with him, our conversations usually fell flat, ending after a **nothing much** or **how is everything?** Throughout college, I would try and see him when I was home for holidays and the summers, but he was distant, a shell of his former self. The first Thanksgiving I came home, I was ecstatic to share with him how incredible college was, with the hopes of spurring some excitement in him to start applying to schools, but nothing worked. He was cold. He was silent. Each time I returned home from school I would see less of him. Spring break of my junior year I didn't see him once—I was home for a week. I lost him before he took his own life, and looking back, I wish I would have just enjoyed the time I spent with him instead of trying to pry him open. I should have been a better friend.

"Dad, how'd he do it?" I asked. My father, born and raised in Newark, who I knew had seen some shit growing up, who was molded by the "old school," fidgeted in his seat, adjusted the rearview mirror, cracked his knuckles, and cleared his throat.

"You… you… don't want to know, Joel." He fumbled over his words, clearing his throat again. I could feel the phlegm vibrate.

"Yes I do," I said.

"Why? What good would that do?"

"I deserve to know."

"It was graphic, Joel."

"What do you mean?"

"I really don't think you want to know."

"Dad, you're the only one who is going to tell me. Please."

"When are we going to get some Yankees coverage? I'm tired of listening to the damn Phillies," he said to himself while flipping through the FM presets.

My mind started to wander. The liquids in my stomach sloshed, and a sickness came over me when I pictured Adam hanging from somewhere in his room. The Reichmans didn't own a gun, and I don't know where Adam would have obtained one, and since Dad said it was graphic, I didn't think it was an overdose. The second nauseating thought I had was that I even cared this much about how he did it. I didn't stop to think about his parents or about his older sister. *Holy fuck, how could they be handling this?* Mrs. Reichman was a delicate woman; she must be devastated.

After a few minutes of silence, I asked if he hanged himself.

"No," he said. As we sat at a red light, he turned to me, stuck out his arm, and made a slicing motion down his wrist. He then turned back and didn't say a word. We sat in silence for the rest of the ride home.

BINGE UNTIL TRAGEDY

I walked in the front door to a hysterical mother. With soaking eyes, she embraced me and wrapped her arms around my neck and whispered in my ear, "Oh, my poor baby. How are you holding up?"

I tried to respond, but my throat was closed and I couldn't make a sound. My mother's hair covered my face and caused a tickle in the back of my throat, and I began to cough uncontrollably. Any time I tried to say something, it turned into a cough. I pulled myself away from her shoulder and saw Carlo standing in the kitchen, unsure of what he should do. I kissed my mom on the cheek, walked past my brother (I didn't want him to see me cry—I'm older, after all), and grabbed a bottle from the liquor cabinet: straight bourbon whiskey. I went into my room without a word of resistance from anyone.

"Go take a shower, Joelie. Go take a nice hot shower, my sweet boy," she called after me as I disappeared down the hallway.

I sat on my bedroom floor. I had a bed and a comfortable recliner, but the floor fit my mood, I suppose.

I drank the bourbon straight from the bottle: no glass, no chaser. I had turned my phone off for the car ride home. I took a swig of whiskey, leaning against the side of my bed, my head tilted back. My throat was sore from the coughing and crying; the whiskey didn't help. I took a swig and turned on my phone. After a few seconds, it began to vibrate.

OMG Joel! Are you okay!?!?!

Hey bro, I heard what happened. Are you okay?

Holy shit dude. Sorry...

Joel babe, call me!! <3<3<3

☹

Yes, one of the texts was just a fucking sad face emoji. But my favorite was when someone I hadn't spoken to in years would say something along the lines of, "If you need anything, tell me," as if they would actually do shit had I asked.

As I sat on the floor of my room—bottle between my legs, head in my palms—I thought about Adam. I had resisted this long asking why because I thought I already knew, but I caught myself asking the question anyway. Had he not thought about his family? Had he not thought about how his death would kill his mother? I took a swig. Had he not thought about me? This last question scared me a little. A knock on the door startled me and I almost dropped the bourbon, but the stuff was so good I would've sucked it right out of the carpet.

"Joelie, can I come in?" asked my mom.

"I'm okay, Ma. I want to be alone," I said.

"Okay, honey. The wake is tomorrow; the funeral will be on Wednesday. If you need anything… just… anything at all, you call for me, okay?"

"Okay, Ma," I said, bringing the bottle down from my lips. I heard her back away from the door, as if hoping I would swing it open, calling for her to hold me, but I didn't budge. She finally turned and walked down the hall, making our old hardwood floor wail under her feet.

The first thing that went through my head was, *Which church did the Reichmans even belong to? Were they Lutheran or Episcopalian, or Presbyterian or Baptist? Fuck, were they Catholic? I can't remember the last time Adam stepped foot inside of a church.* There was only one time after the accident I remember him stating something about religion.

It was the following winter, so about a year after the accident, and Adam and I were sitting in his basement. We hadn't spoken a word to each other in about ten minutes, until he turned to me and said, "Life isn't always as simple as angels and demons, Joel." He didn't add anything. My spine tingled and my lip dropped; his words coursed through me like a drug. Except this drug skipped the high that is so desired by its users and immediately brought on a deflating feeling of sorrow.

Thinking it over now, Adam's statement wasn't very revolutionary. It was basically a different way of saying "not everything in life is black-and-white." But it was the way he said it, how he turned his head, how he looked me in the eyes—something he hadn't done in a long time, perhaps since the accident. His demeanor had been robotic or something possessed, and it was then that I remembered that his eyes were emerald green.

I woke up, head throbbing, to Sal knocking on my door. I fell asleep in my jeans and guinea tee: a term my father despises. If you haven't noticed already, my name is Italian. My surname, that is. In my father's eyes, if it was Italian it was better: the food, the wine, the cars, the art, and especially the women. Given the chance, my father would remind us how he had a girlfriend in college, an exchange student from Naples who "took care of him." With every ounce of strength, I tried not to visualize my hairy, olive-skinned, bowling ball of a father mounting some poor, innocent European girl who just wanted a better education—and yes, I believe he was just as rotund when he was twenty-one.

When his first son was born, my father refused to name him anything other than Salvatore, after my grandfather. My grandfather was a World War II veteran who witnessed the sky rain fire at Pearl Harbor in December of 1941. He later "island hopped" across the Pacific to fight the Japanese, who, in his own words, were "fearless yellow sons o' bitches who ate a sorry excuse for pasta."

He never went into detail about the war, but he was never amused by my generation's obsession with all things Japanese. Once, when I was seven, we went to his house for Thanksgiving, and I was carrying a binder filled with Pokémon cards, completely in Japanese. He took one look at them and then yelled something before storming into the kitchen and yelling at my father—I had to put my binder in the car.

However, for all of my dad's pan-Italianism, he did not marry an Italian girl. My mother was born and raised in Connecticut and has traced zero percent of her bloodline back to Italy—trust me, Dad had her take one of those genealogy cheek swab tests. She is a professed "mutt" and is a mix of Germanic, Nordic, and Celtic peoples. My father reminded her that Germanic tribes invaded Italy during the fall of Rome; he hoped she was a Lombard.

When she was pregnant with me, she demanded that she choose my name without any interference, so she went with Joel. Joel was the name of her grandfather, a man I never met. Supposedly he was funny and smart and very successful, but he died before I was born. Actually, I have never met another person named Joel.

More knocks hammered the door. "Joel, wake up, buddy. Breakfast in ten," called Sal.

I had to piss but needed to wait, because I had morning wood and couldn't walk to the bathroom with a hard-on. There was an empty glass next to a damp spot on the carpet. My mom must've come in the middle of the night and left the water on the nightstand because I hadn't left my cave; the bourbon—or what was left of it—was missing, too. I turned to my side and saw that my suit was hanging on my door, just back from the cleaners. My head pounded, again. I needed a good night's sleep. I swung my legs around the side of the bed, stared at the floor, and attempted to gather my thoughts.

Today is my best friend's wake. I'll dress in black. I'll shake hands and hold back tears. Every once in a while I'll glance over at the casket surrounded by flowers. God, I hope it's not an open casket. I'll see people I haven't seen in years. They'll ask me how things are going and what my plans are for after college and I'll smile. I'll make small talk but avoid eye contact; maybe I'll wear sunglasses. I wish I wore sunglasses more often and people knew me as someone who always wears sunglasses so today it wouldn't be so noticeable. I might wear them anyway. I'll stand next to the Reichmans and Adam's older sister, Olivia, who flew in from Dallas. I'll spend most of the time staring at the carpet as I listen to Mrs. Reichman weep. My palms will sweat and I'll get self-conscious about my handshakes, constantly rubbing my hands on my pants. Eventually a line will form and people will peer into their phones, looking at pictures of food they're never going to make or places they're never going to visit. They'll do this instead of thinking about what they're going to say to the Reichmans or to me.

BINGE UNTIL TRAGEDY

They'll reach us and stumble over a phrase or say something generic. Nothing original will enter the funeral home today.

When I got to the kitchen, the coffee was already brewed. I took it black with extra sugar—no milk or cream. My dad was sitting at the table in his robe, which was dangerously loose, both hands wrapped around his mug. He saw me come in and immediately threw on a smile.

"Hey, bud, what's the word?" he attempted.

"No one says that." I sat at the table across from him. ESPN played on the small flat-screen television mounted on our kitchen wall. It was always on in the background of our lives, like a piano that serenades the lobby of a four-star hotel. The *Star Ledger* was open and scattered across the table with olive oil stains seeping through the political section. The headline read: "Wright Accuses President of Being a Communist, Again."

Clayton Wright, the poster child of the Republican Party, was a common headliner in politics lately. His father served as Secretary of State in the nineties and Wright lost the 2012 presidential election. Wright was exactly what the right-wing population craved. He was young, attractive, bombastic, and white. As a Yale alum with deep-rooted family history in American politics, Wright had an unmatched pedigree and a witless, bland motto: *Wright for the Right!* The guy was an absolute nightmare, but the media ate him up. He made all those promises that tickle the voters' ears: lower taxes, hard on crime, cuts in spending, etc. He clean-shaved his baby face and parted his chestnut hair. He spoke with a Southern accent even though his entire family was from New England. He has appeared on the same talk show since I was in middle school. On the show, he demanded that voters have laser-eye identification screening before casting their ballot, and that Muslims must take a test proving their allegiance to the country instead of to "Allah." He accused President Meyer of being a KGB spy and claimed he had been a Black Panther during the Civil Rights Movement. The president denied these accusations.

Meyer was an anomaly in American politics. He was born in upstate New York to a Jewish father and a black mother from the lower middle class. He attended

Brandeis University for his undergrad and Harvard for law school. He eventually became a senator in Massachusetts and was virtually unknown to the larger American public until he took the country by storm when he ran for president.

Everyone was obsessed with Jerome Meyer, the mixed-raced young liberal who promised the national legalization of gay marriage and pot, the redistribution of wealth, the federal overtaking of the healthcare system, and the amnesty of immigrants already residing in the country. And by "everyone," I mean my college. Fervor burned through the school, igniting demonstrations and a handful of counter-demonstrations by the few Wright supporters.

Politics is nasty. Faux alliances are formed on beliefs that people possess for possession's sake. Accusations are flung like water balloons at a child's birthday party. Liberals view Conservatives as sadists: heartless and out of touch. Conservatives view Liberals as naïve, bleeding-heart pussies; no one gives a fuck about the Moderates. The war-thirsty "Hawks" are vultures. The pacifist "Doves," pigeons. Self-interest groups would spring up all over campus, promoting their "causes" and slandering all objectors. The gay rights group clashed with the religious ruffians; the environmentalist clan clashed with the "let them drill!" guild; the African-American, Asian-American, Latino-American, and any other group who couldn't be just "American" combined forces with the white guilt of our liberal arts colleges to create a formidable abomination of self-identity chaos. What's left are the apathetic, drinking our beer in the nooks and crannies. Did I mention I'm a politics major?

Well, not just a politics major—a politics–international relations double major with a focus in Middle Eastern studies and a minor in French. "Why?" you might be saying to yourself. Go ask Freshman Joel to find the answer. I considered going to law school after college, but decided against it because I'm not a masochist. So on the cusp of graduation, I was lost with my dick in my hand, probably having to work for some NGO who think they're God's gift to the putrid earth. I sipped my coffee.

"I don't know how you drink it like that," said Sal.

"He studied in France, remember? That's what they do over there," my father added. "Right, Joel? Isn't that right?"

"Yeah. I mean no. Sorta," I responded with the intention of not explaining the difference between a drip and French press, espresso and filter. It was a conversation I could've sworn we'd had before. I ate a piece of burnt, dry toast and excused myself from the table. Again, no one stopped me. I went back to bed.

I woke up to a pool of drool flowing from my pillow to the mattress. Adam's wake would begin in a few hours and I could barely think. I stared at the grooves and cracks on my ceiling that I had studied since I was a child. As a kid, I was often sent to my room. I had already read all of my books, and without a television, computer, or smartphone, I was confined to those grooves and cracks to kill time. I counted twenty-seven cracks, six blots, and a greenish-blue dot that completed the constellation that kept me company.

When I closed my eyes, all I could see was blood. Blood on white tile, blood on white marble, soaked into the carpet that hugged the toilet. I imagined Adam in gym shorts and a t-shirt. Does one dress for such an occasion? I could see him sitting on the floor against the tub, one arm at his side, the other draped across his lap, both open, both bleeding out. When I pictured his face, I didn't see his eyes. I didn't see his nose, ears, or chin. I only saw a smile; probably the first smile he had in a long time.

I set the shower to scalding. My forehead rested against the tile; the water beat the back of my neck. I hadn't showered in two days. I needed to clean myself but was immobile. I watched as the water ran off my nose and mouth, hitting the floor of the tub with a thud. I could feel the water trapped in my beard, which after a few months had grown to a respectable length. I was surprised Mom hadn't told me to shave it. She was probably hesitant to be demanding. *You'll stay a little longer, my friend.*

When I got out of the shower, my neck and shoulders had crimsoned. I looked into the mirror and realized I needed to start working out again. My once chiseled abs had turned into a gut, due to the copious amounts of beer and whiskey and vodka and tequila and rum and gin and Rumple Minze. The tattoo on my right side, right on the ribs, read *Survive* in black ink. I was eighteen when I had it done, when I thought that's all I needed to do: survive. Survive my youth and everything would be okay; I was such a pussy.

As I stared at myself in the mirror, contemplating attempting a sit-up for the first time in weeks, I received a text. **Text from Chloe: 10:15 a.m.: Hey Joel, hope you are okay. Txt me if you need ANYTHING.** We never were an *official* couple, but we were virtually together for most of my senior year. She's two grades below me and decided to go to school locally, which ensured that she was always around when I came home.

On command, she would send naked photos, and on nights when I returned to an empty bed, I would text Chloe and she would tell me she missed me. Sometimes I wondered why I didn't just make her my girlfriend. She was good to me and seemed to actually care. There was also that time I had a girlfriend for a couple of months at school sophomore year, and when Chloe found out, she sent me an armada of texts about how upset she was and posted on my Facebook wall four or five times about it. I had to call her to tell her to stop. She said she never wanted to see me again. I texted Chloe when we broke up. We fucked that Thanksgiving break.

Then I thought about how easy it all was with Chloe, and if it was this easy for me, how was she with the other guys? This was always at the back of my head, I suppose, and therefore Chloe was always on the back burner.

I cranked out a few sit-ups and push-ups and went to change into my suit. I hated wearing suits. The neck size on my shirt was always off and I'd get those red bumps where I'd have to shave; at least I was avoiding that this time.

My family was waiting for me at the bottom of the staircase—solemn and dressed in their Sunday best, they looked like the cover of a Christian rock album.

The five of us packed into our SUV and headed to the funeral home. My dad turned on the radio; he flipped through a few stations and after finding nothing he could tolerate, turned it off in frustration. We sat in silence for the ten-minute ride. Halfway through, I realized this was Carlo's first real experience with death. When our neighbor Mr. Tomasello passed away, Carlo was at baseball camp and didn't attend the funeral. And when my uncle died, my dad's brother, Carlo was so young that my mom sent him to her sister's house in Connecticut—that was still the only time I'd ever seen my father cry.

It was in the pew at church. I sat next to Sal, who was next to Dad. The priest had been in the middle of a sermon on the frailty of life and was reciting a line from the Gospel of Matthew: *Blessed are those who mourn, for they will be comforted*. I can remember it in such detail because as I was following along in the flimsy, paperback Bible, I heard a deep groan. I turned to see my father with his thumb and middle finger plugging his eyes. His chest pulsed and contracted, and he was gasping for air. My mother rubbed his back and Sal leaned against his shoulder. When he took his hand away from his face, I could see his bloodshot eyes and glistening cheeks. I felt awkward. I looked down at my Bible and randomly thumbed to a page and pretended to read it. I didn't look up from the Book for the rest of the funeral, but was trapped by the brutal sobbing of the toughest man I knew.

I stared out the window but didn't really look at anything. *What am I going to say to Adam's parents? Will I shake Mr. R's hand or give him a hug? What about his mom? Definitely a hug, perhaps a kiss on the cheek? No, that might be weird.* Then I remembered my uncle's wake had had an open casket.

I had been petrified at the sight of my overweight uncle snug in the casket, surrounded by my weeping family, Nonna covered in black, holding a gold handkerchief, delicately blotting her wrinkled cheeks.

We arrived at the funeral home quicker than I had anticipated. I hate that. My timing was off. *I'm not ready for this.*

At the front door, I scanned the room. I saw familiar faces but couldn't remember many names. Some were sad; others, neutral. Before I could enter, a hand grabbed my elbow.

"Hey Joel. It's Mr. Green, Josh's dad." I nearly jumped out of my suit. "Aren't you a senior this year? Any plans for after you graduate?" I felt my face flush and overheat. My hands instinctively formed fists and I bit my bottom lip really fucking hard. Mr. Green stared at me as clueless as a Labrador. My mom, who was only a few steps away, diffused the potential disaster.

"Joel just lost his friend, Glen. He doesn't want to talk about that right now."

"Oh, yeah, of course. We'll talk later, Joel."

With her hand on my shoulder, I stepped into the funeral home. The electric red carpet clashed with the black suits and dresses of the mourning. In the back of the main room, I could see an array of flowers, a cacophony of colors pulling me closer. As I approached, I heard my name whispered amongst the small groups of people; I ignored them. I was transcending toward something larger. In a place frequented by the dead, I felt alive, drunk in color. The violets spoke to me and the tulips made me smile. The lilies sang while the roses called my name—perhaps it was the roses I could hear. In my sober stupor, I stumbled upon Adam, snug in his casket.

I froze. His somber appearance made me wilt. He was in a suit and tie, black with a white shirt. I couldn't remember the last time I had seen him in a suit.

Another hand grabbed my shoulder and squeezed gently. I turned to see a puffy-eyed Mr. Reichman holding an envelope while holding back tears. In a defeated voice, he said, "Hello, Joel. I'm happy that you made it. Adam left this for you." His hand remained on my shoulder. "He told his mother and me not to open it and to give it directly to you." He started to lean on me; his breath was putrid and he had white crust in the corners of his mouth. "Adam was a good boy. You know that, right?" he asked, as if he had been asking the same question all day.

"Yes, of course I do," I responded.

"Yes, yes you do. He loved you, Joel."

At this point, I was physically supporting the man. As he pushed his weight onto me, I looked over his shoulder and saw people beginning to notice the scene.

"I could have done more, Joel," he pleaded into my ear. Mrs. Reichman came over and hugged her husband, relieving me of his dead weight.

"Honey, come with me," she said.

Mr. Reichman turned to see the silent mourners staring at him, stumbled backward a few steps, and gathered himself. He buttoned his jacket and fixed his tie as if he were about to begin a business meeting, then handed me an envelope and walked away. *Joel* was written in sloppy script on the front. I turned toward Adam, and there was my father, looking down into the pillowed box. *What if this had been Carlo's wake, or mine?* Would the toughest man on Earth crumble in front of staring mourners? Would sorrow overtake him? The kind of sorrow that makes a man's knees shake? I watched as he rubbed the side of the casket and took a deep breath. He absolutely would; the fear of great men is to outlive their sons, I suppose.

I walked to the casket. After a moment of mutual silence, Dad said, "Say whatever you need to now. This will be the last time you see him."

I kneeled in front of him, hands clenched at my waist, eyes closed. I listened. I could hear banter float across the room, along with the occasional sniffle of a runny nose. I pictured Adam six years ago, baseball glove on his hand, the sun burning the backs of our necks, and I prayed. I prayed for the first time in years. I asked God to look over another lost soul, to welcome him into the flock. I didn't speak like that, but it's what came out. Then a thought came to me, and I felt my stomach turn and I became nauseous—I even clutched the side of the casket for support, which might have appeared like I was in deep prayer, but I was really trying to hold down vomit: *What if Adam went to Hell?* Maybe it would be better if there wasn't a God. I said goodbye to my friend, walked out of the funeral home, and sat in the car. My family members left the funeral home one by one, first Carlo—who still hadn't shed a tear—then Sal, with my mother following not far behind, and then my father. No one spoke when they took their seats in the SUV, and we drove home in silence; my father still couldn't find anything adequate on the radio.

I lay on my bed and ran my hand over my jacket where the letter still sat snug in the inside pocket. *When did Adam write it? The night before? Hours before he ended it?* I held it in my hands, my palm sweat smearing the ink in which my name was written. The edge had a tear in it; someone had begun to open it and stopped. I unfolded the loose-leaf paper and read the note quietly to myself.

Joel,

If you're reading this, then it means I did it. I killed myself. It also means that my parents aren't as gutless as they seem. My decision was not rushed. I will not regret what I am going to do. I'm lost, Joel, a limping lamb, a whimpering sheep. My final years on Earth have not been living. Instead, I suffocate inside of a blood-filled shell. I will ask Erika for forgiveness. Hopefully her smile brings light back to my soul. Please don't worry about me. There was nothing you could do, I promise. One day we'll see each other again. Until then, I'll be up there kissing angels.

I love you, Joel.

Your friend,

Adam

P.S. Don't forget to put coins on my eyes, heaven isn't free

I read the letter three times over with a pit in my stomach. I had questions that would never be answered.

Dinner was quiet. Dad asked for the rice. Sal asked about the wine vintage. It was a vacant meal that filled nothing but our stomachs. Mrs. Reichman called my mother and asked if I would speak at the funeral. Mom said she would ask me and get back to her. In bed, I recited Adam's letter in my head. I already had it memorized. I had never heard him speak that way before—profoundly, metaphorically. I went to sleep without drinking a sip of alcohol. It was the first time in weeks I didn't drink whiskey or wine; I couldn't stomach the stuff, I suppose.

That night I didn't dream about Adam. I didn't dream about death, darkness, or despair. Instead my dream was nonsensical, meaningless. In it were people I barely knew. Friends? No. Acquaintances? Sure. There was confusion. People introduced themselves with different names than I had known them by. Rick was Mark, Steve was Joe, and Caroline was a girl I used to fuck freshman year. They say dreams focus on the last things you are imagining before falling asleep. This cannot be true. I wanted a nightmare. I woke up warm and cozy, feeling guilty.

THE FUNERAL

IN THE MORNING, THERE WERE NO BANGS FROM Sal on the door. Instead, the delicate pattering of rain on the roof pulled me out of bed with a glib melody. Usually I enjoyed listening to the rain; I found it soothing. There was a time for thunderstorms too—nighttime, when I was tucked into couch cushions with my feet stretching out the last fibers of the blanket so my bare toes weren't naked and I could listen to the pounding drums of the war gods. And sun showers, Mother Nature's display of serendipity, my favorite form of precipitation that only occurred in rare New Jersey Julys. But the weather today was typical of any hackneyed scene when everyone seemed to have a black umbrella on hand—the funeral umbrella, I suppose.

The Reichmans insisted I give a eulogy. They asked my parents, not me. I didn't understand why they wouldn't ask me. They had barely spoken to me since they found Adam; however, they had never been that warm anyway. Mrs. Reichman has always been uninviting and properly bitter. She's condescending in a wealthy suburban housewife kind of way. It is difficult to fathom the devastation that confronts someone who witnesses their child dead on the floor. I queased at the thought of the bloodied tiles.

I had to change into that damn suit again. Instead of wearing the shirt my mom put out for me, I snagged one from Sal's closet in his old room—it was probably one of his from high school. This time the neck hole was too loose, but I didn't really give a shit; at least I could breathe.

I met my family in the kitchen. I slugged a cup of lukewarm black coffee and went out to our SUV sitting in the driveway. They followed, as if waiting for me to make the first move. We headed downtown to the Church of the Holy Light. I'd never stepped foot inside the place before. The green-wooded building stuck out in the heart of the brick jungle. We traversed the parking lot and found the priest greeting the mourning at the door. His white cloak contrasted with the parishioners, who were painted in black. His toothy smile clashed with the faces of the solemn. He shook my hand and welcomed us into the church. Following my family, he pulled me aside, looked into my eyes, and said, "It will all be okay." I thanked him and continued into the church, dabbed my index and middle finger into the cup of holy water, crossed myself, and repeated, "It will all be okay." I took refuge in the simplicity.

There was a pew reserved for us, second row. The priest greeted the congregation and gave the opening prayer. He insisted that we not worry for Adam. Eternal life is guaranteed. There was no doubt in his weathered voice, which emanated from his dominating frame, that Adam was in heaven. His words seemed genuine, as if he knew Adam personally. I sat between Sal and my mother. During the sermon, a man I recognized but couldn't remember kneeled beside our pew. He whispered that Mr. Reichman would give the first eulogy, then me. Before I could ask if anyone else would be speaking, he left.

When it came time for the eulogies, Mr. Reichman rose from his seat and paused for a few moments. No one spoke, no one coughed—it was pure, dead silence. He kissed Mrs. Reichman on the cheek and placed his hand on the tawny casket before ascending the podium steps. He unfolded a piece of paper from inside his jacket and looked up with those same defeated eyes. And he read.

"Adam was a struggling soul. He was a good boy; he was my boy. He had been fighting depression for some time now. He used to tell us how much he wanted to work with computers, perhaps become an engineer. But all of that went away after the… the accident. He didn't want to go to school or leave the house. We tried to help him, his mother and I… We really did, but nothing… nothing seemed to work. We are deeply… saddened by the loss of our son." He bit his clenched fist. "Look what you've done, Adam. Look what you've done." He became louder. "Look what you've done to your mother! You idiot! Look what you've done to your mother, Adam!" He was pointing at the casket. Mrs. Reichman was hysterical. The priest gently pulled Mr. Reichman down from the pulpit while the rest of us sat in silence.

I was irate. I could've hit him. Seriously, I could've fucking hit him in front of his wife. I clamped my teeth with such ferocity that a cramp began forming in my jaw muscles. When I looked at Sal, he had a similar disgusted look on his face.

It was my turn now, I suppose. With the pressure collapsing my shoulders, I made my way to the pulpit. The priest greeted me with a smile and motioned his hand up the few steps. The half-filled church looked up to me, many squinting against the light flooding in from the stained glass windows. I had a panegyric in my jacket pocket, but didn't take it out.

I looked at my family, each one propped up in the pew, supportive as usual. My mom straightened her back and raised her eyebrows at me; she would do the same thing when she attended my debate competitions. I put my shoulders back and my chest out. I looked to the Reichmans. Adam's sister was holding Mrs. Reichman, both of them crying. Mr. R had his head down. I wondered if he'd even hear what I was going to say. I forget how long I'd been standing, silent. There were a few coughs that snapped me back to attention, and I spoke the first words that dropped from my mouth—over the wails of Olivia and Mrs. R.

"Adam was a gorgeous soul." I decided not to read what I had written. I continued, naked, "I met Adam when I was five or six… and… we were best friends ever since. When I look back on our friendship, I'm overwhelmed with memories of baseball in the spring and riding our bikes to Antonelli's Italian Ices. I would always get lemon… He would get cherry. We were inseparable, always needing to be on the same team for everything. I… I remember staying up till four in the morning… the darkest hour of the night… playing video games until our eyes froze in their sockets. The things I would give for a younger us, but time dances by, I suppose."

I paused and scanned the church. The same mourners were present: no one went for a cigarette or to take a phone call; no one was checking their emails or biting their nails. I had their full attention—I liked the way that felt.

"When I learned of Adam's passing, I was devastated. I have questions that will never be answered. All I want is one final conversation with my friend, to tell him to take care, to wish him all my best."

I accidentally shot a look to my family and saw my mom crying—that was a trigger for me. I didn't even watch movies with her if there was a chance a dog died at the end. I clenched onto the podium wood, and my forearm muscles tightened as tears poured down my face.

"Instead I'll tell him now. Despite all of the confusion, Adam, I am not angry. I miss you already… but I am not angry. Anger corrodes the soul and will serve no purpose here. Anger is weakness, and weakness is not an option." Gazing up, I concluded, "Goodbye, my friend. There will be no more suffering." I left the pulpit and embraced my family and I didn't look at the Reichmans. For a few moments, silence hovered around the sniffles and coughs. Nobody spoke, not even the priest.

The priest read the final prayers, ending with John 3:16. Adam's uncles wheeled and carried the casket to the graveyard behind the church—Mr. Reichman didn't lift a finger. The black nebulas of mourners followed and covered themselves with black umbrellas. Outside, a few different people came up to shake my hand or pat me on the back, but I was fixated on the brown hole of fresh earth surrounded by wet green grass. We all held a flower; mine was a red rose. I laid it on top of the other flowers—a mélange of red, white, and yellow roses—knocking some off into the grave. After all of the flowers had been placed, forming a bed of color, Adam was lowered into the ground, where he would remain forever. Mrs. Reichman crumpled to the grass as if her joints were made of paper. She screamed in a crackling voice, "Goodbye, Adam!" her husband holding her by the arm. My chin dropped to my chest and I cried violently, catching my breath between coughs. I thought, *When I die, I want to be cremated.*

My mom hugged me while I nestled my face between her neck and shoulder. She rubbed the back of my head. Dad stood next to us, holding the umbrella over us so it barely covered himself. I lifted up my face to watch Adam's descent into the earth. A fist of nausea punched me in the pit, but I didn't puke. Dad asked if I had any final words for Adam. I didn't, but asked if we should we tip the gravedigger.

THE DELICATESSEN

MY PHONE HAD BEEN OFF FOR A DAY. I FELT NO reason to compulsively check it, nor my Facebook. I lay in bed, paralyzed, listening to the sweet piano acoustics of Chopin. I was in a wine mood, a red wine mood. I opened a Sonoma Coast Cabernet and glugged it straight from the bottle. It was young and rough and dried my throat, but it was exactly what I wanted—something untamed, unrefined. It contrasted beautifully with the eloquence of the Polack's fingers.

Halfway down the bottle, I begrudgingly turned on my phone and received a bombardment of messages—I knew it was a mistake. I checked the texts, skipping to those from Chloe.

Text from Chloe: 3:45 p.m.: Joel baby, I really want to hear from you, please text me. Xoxo :)

Text from Chloe: 3:56 p.m.: I can make you feel better! Xoxo

Text from Chloe: 3:58 p.m.: Text me if you want to see me tonight babe <3

I considered it, but didn't text her back. I wasn't sure if I could perform, anyway, and the Cab would keep me company tonight. My parents asked if I wanted to watch a movie with them and Carlo, but I declined.

Sal had left for the City after dinner. We had a talk after the funeral. He told me not to hesitate to call him and to value the time I spend with my friends. Enjoy each girl you see, but be respectful and don't burn your bridges. He said he'd come down for graduation and warned me not to get too drunk the night before—I didn't make any promises there.

My parents checked on me every hour or so throughout the night. I caught on to their system and after the third round I yelled, "I'm fine!" before they tapped on the door. I had become one with my bed and one with my wine. I fell asleep to pass the time. I still didn't dream about Adam.

Coffee the next morning was a roasted Ethiopian black. Dad couldn't understand why I didn't drink Folgers. "This is the good stuff!" he would say.

Mom had the TV on her standard news channel. It's biased, ignorant, and superfluous, and it's the highest-rated news channel in the country. The anchors make outlandish remarks like "No more student visas for Middle Eastern students!" and "Pornography is deteriorating the moral fabric of the American household."

As I delved into my jam-smothered English muffin, they were replaying Clayton Wright's speech to a crowd in Virginia. He insisted that we not only *maintain*, but *increase* our nuclear arsenal because of uprisings taking place across the Middle East and North Africa. The fiercest protests were the student-led in Algeria, Palestine, Syria, Tunisia, and Iraq.

About six months ago, in response to government corruption, an Algerian carpet shop owner walked into Martyr's Square in Algiers with a sign tied around his neck and set himself on fire. The sign, translated from Arabic and French, read: "Without freedom we are cattle. I will carry out my own slaughter." Since his self-immolation, a wave of movements had been born—some with surprising success, others that had been brutally quashed. Here in the West, we watched perplexed and gobbled up whatever luscious garbage was force-fed to us through the media.

Tanks crushing compact cars and Molotov cocktails illuminating the smoke-filled sky kept Mom glued to the sixteen-inch flat-screen mounted on our kitchen wall. A teenager in the streets of Damascus hurled a rock at shielded police, his face covered with the black-and-white scarf or *keffiyeh* that had become the symbol of the movement. Many over here associate the *keffiyeh* with a terrorist symbol—it isn't. Many claim that the protesters want to impose Sharia law and live under a banner of radical Islam—they don't. An interview from a fringe media source with an Algerian student quoted him as saying, "We want the same freedoms found in America, Europe, the rest of the world. That is why we fight, and that alone is worth dying for." You won't find this quote in our mainstream media. We're bored without enemies, I suppose.

In Israel, in Palestine, in Israel/the West Bank/Gaza, in Heaven/Hell—however you'd like to delineate it—tensions were sparking, the embers of revolution were burning, American interests were being tickled. The night before, Israeli tanks and Humvees steamrolled a village in the West Bank, killing six. Two were children. Wright was going off on how Islamic fundamentalists had leaked into the West Bank and were training and arming teenagers for war. Dissenters offered that the protests are secular and exist in the name of survival and identity. My mom asked me what I thought as she turned away from the screen, her hand on her chest. I told her I wouldn't have minded some 2% in my coffee.

Breakfast had left me with a void in my stomach. I lounged around until lunch. Around one o'clock, I had an epiphany about the sole thing that would be able to fill my pit: the Millburn Deli. This sandwich sanctuary was a few towns away, a twenty-minute drive or so, and worth every damn second. I ran the idea by my dad and he shot out of his La-Z-Boy recliner—the two of us pranced into the car like children on the way to the ice cream shop. For tunes, he threw on Clyde Stevens, aka the Kid, aka Sly Clyde, aka the Jersey Clutch, and we rode down Bloomfield Avenue as if we owned the street. We passed pizza parlors, Greek diners, kosher delis, and Jersey bagel shops. But nothing, not a single one of those joints, could quench my craving.

Mr. Stevens was belting one of his classics: "Live Fast, Live Tough" from the late seventies, and Dad was eating it up. Clyde Stevens, originally Clyde Stavinsky from Brick Township, *is* New Jersey. During the summers, his concerts were sold out in seconds. Drunken fifty-year-olds wrapped in American flags sang into their bottles of beer in an attempt to imitate the raspy, rough, epic voice of Clyde. It was between "Born to Love" and "Dirty, Easy Money" that I remembered the last time I was at the deli was with Adam, during winter break.

BINGE UNTIL TRAGEDY

He would always get the "Godfadda," a chicken cutlet–based concoction with mozzarella cheese, Russian dressing, and bacon on a sub roll. It was created by a sixteen-year-old kid and instantly became as classic as "Dirty, Easy Money." I am more adventurous with my selections, however. Oftentimes I needed something warm and juicy, but who didn't every now and then? A "P-Ray," a meaty slathered-in-barbecue-sauce confection, was a staple of my deli order. If I was in an avant-garde mood, a macaroni and cheese griller would suffice.

But today I was craving a classic, something comfortable, something stoic. I needed a sandwich that stood for something, so before I stepped foot inside that delicatessen Mecca, I decided I would order a pastrami sloppy joe grilled. Let's set the record straight. This isn't your Manwich ground-beef-on-a-burger-bun sandwich. We're talking about a Jersey-style sloppy joe, which entailed your selection of deli meat, Russian dressing, and coleslaw on Jewish rye. If I ever got the chair (or I suppose we're killing our criminals with injections these days) this grilled, dripping delight would be my last meal.

We marched through the door and the attached bells rang. It was lunchtime, rush hour—between twelve and one thirty it was a madhouse. I elbowed my way to the ticket dispenser and lunged for a ticket: 96. They were on 84. *Son of a bitch.*

"96," I said to Dad.

"Son of a bitch," he replied.

We stood, backs against the racks of potato chips, arms crossed; I admired the beautiful mayhem. The Millburn Deli is of the New York City style, attitude included. Colorful signs and stickers plastered the walls with phrases like *10% surcharge for complaining, Love Him Like a King, Train Him Like a Dog, Your Village Called, Their Idiot is Missing*. The same handful of workers that had run the joint since I was a kid called out order numbers and ingredients. Less experienced customers fumbled with their orders, asking questions about cheese types and for more detail on the roast beef.

89. We were cruising. I recognized a few customers who knew what they were doing. They would be quick and easy. We frequented the establishment, especially

on Sunday mornings, when a "Monster-Joe" (that's *two* types of meat) and a half gallon of their homemade iced tea was pure hangover nectar.

93. Almost there. My dad was looking at the mac and cheese and jerk chicken spread. I hoped he had his mind made up when our number was called; no pussy-footing around here. I scanned the grillers—premade sandwiches on top of the counter, numbered one through ten. These were all classics, and many had been in the lineup for years. Chicks always liked the number eight: white-meat chicken, tomato, mozzarella, and pesto on ciabatta bread. It didn't do it for me, and with the obligatory side of cock, it was just too much food.

The door opened, and of course I turned to see who it was, and of course it was someone I went to high school with, and of course I made eye contact immediately and looked away. Julie Colombo. I probably only had three conversations with the girl my whole life. Was I really obligated to say something to her? I mean, if I was going to say anything, it should be, "Sorry for puking into, and then knocking over and breaking, a flower pot on your front porch during that New Year's Eve party… No hard feelings?" She caught my eye and I looked down at my nonexistent watch. I squinted at something dead ahead of me and turned as if my dad had called me.

95. I was popping up and down on my heels like a schoolboy waiting to ride the new roller-coaster. A suntanned township worker in a navy-blue sleeveless t-shirt placed his order at the counter: twelve Monster Joes consisting of various specifics. "Motherfucker." I said it loud enough for the mother with three kids in front of me to do a half turn in disgust. I moved up to the counter, my knees crunching the New England Crab–flavored potato chips, my elbows resting on the glass. Sandwiches and subs were sweating in the panini presses, their gooey extracts seeping onto the grill. The tall, calvous, baseball-capped worker called out "Ninety-one!" Clearly he had not been listening, and no one behind the counter had pressed the button to change the number. "Ninety-two!" he shouted. Ninety-two was back in her oversized truck, cramming her way out of the inadequately spaced parking lot. "Ninety-three!" *Oh, for fuck's sake.* "Ninety-six!" I blurted.

"You ninety-six?"

"Yes, I am," I said as I placed my crumpled-up ticket stub into the basket on the counter. "Yeah, can I have a pastrami joe grilled, and a chicken parm for…"

Before I could finish the sentence, my dad interrupted, "I don't want a chicken parm. Italians eat veal parm."

"They don't have veal here. We've gone over this."

"Okay, fine… a… a Black Forest."

"That has sweet apples on it."

"Oh god, no."

"Then what do you want?"

"Who puts *sweeeet* apples on a *sangwich*?!"

"Dad, hurry up!"

"What did you get?"

"A pastrami Joe grilled."

"Okay, a Friday Joe."

The worker, irritated, asked, "Is that all?"

"And two sides of mac and cheese."

At home, we tore into our lunch. Mom watched like an onlooker at a safari witnessing the demise of the slowest gazelle. Bits of coleslaw dropped from our mouths onto the translucent sandwich paper. We washed down the salty-sweet meat with homemade iced tea, the third greatest drink on Earth after coffee and wine, I suppose.

My phone gave three powerful text vibrations that were accentuated on our wood dinner table—they were all from Chloe. My fingers, greasy and saucy, were in no condition to answer. "Who's that?" asked Mom.

"It's Chloe," my dad replied.

"Fuck, Dad," I responded.

"What? It says right there," he said, pointing to the screen.

"Oh, I always liked her, Joel. Such a sweet girl, and *smart*. Where does she go again?"

"Drew," I responded.

"That's not far at all! Give her a call."

"No one calls anymore."

"Okay, text her then. Jeez, I don't know. Send her a hologram like in Star Wars. Remember that, honey?"

"Text me, Joel. You're my only dope. Ha!"

"Good one…" I said.

"That was one of our first dates," said my mom, staring off, back in time.

"1977, I remember it well. How couldn't I? Your mother had an ass…"

"Oh, stop it!" She wrapped her arms around his thick shoulders and clenched his mouth shut.

"Fucking gross. I'm taking this downstairs before I lose my appetite." And I lifted the sandwich paper by the sides and hovered it down the stairs to the basement like a stork delivering a newborn.

I was headed back to school the next day, so I decided at last to respond to Chloe after lunch; she came over that night. She bounced out of her car and leaped into my arms and I could feel her ribs against my chest. There was a stud in her nose so big it looked like something out of an African diamond mine. And she was blond—I'd never seen her blond.

"You changed your hair?"

"Yes! I can't believe you noticed!"

"Well, you used to be a brunette. Now you're blond, Chloe." She didn't say anything and continued to kiss me instead.

I pulled her by the hand into the basement and we plopped onto the couch. Hopefully my parents, who would have heard the garage door open and close, wouldn't come downstairs, for in a few minutes, Chloe's clothing was on the floor and she was on top of me, in the raw.

We attacked each other like Rottweilers, like I was Edmond Dantès freshly sprung from the Château d'If. She'd bite at my neck and I'd toss her under me, firmly placing two fingers on her clit; she'd "overpower" me and hop on top, pressing her hands into my chest and shoulders in an attempt to portray a mean look, but constantly cracking toothy smiles. We kept at it, and in between the gnawing and gnarling, I'd throw her head into my lap. I'd situate her on her knees; I'd sit on the couch. Her butt and back plateaued out from her neck, and her blond hair mopped my thighs. I reached forward, grabbing her butt, spreading it apart and smacking her cheeks until they were an equal rose. When she came up for air, spit ran down her chin, her eyes teary and gorgeous, illuminated by the television light.

"You okay?" I asked.

"Of course, bae" she said and returned to my depths. It was at this pre-climactic moment that my perfectly timed mother decided to yell down the stairwell, "Joel, is Chloe down there with you?!" Well, thank God it was *her* and not somebody else. Chloe pulled her head up and my penis popped out of her mouth like uncorking a Barolo. "Hi, Mrs. Lupo!"

"Hi, Chloe. How's school?!"

"Oh… it's going so well!" Her hands rested on the insides of my knees.

"Hey Ma, can you guys talk later?!"

"Okay, okay. Talk to you later, sweetie. I want to hear all about Drew!"

"Sounds great. Talk to you later, Mrs. Lupo!"

And immediately we were back to it. Back to ripping at each other, her heart deep in the fire, mine just enough to pull it out when I needed to. I had always kept Chloe at a distance—emotionally, that is. I could tell it hurt her a little, perhaps more than a little, but when I looked at her, I saw a beautiful smile, a stunning body, big brown eyes, and a coy tongue. I saw a partner in bed, a partner in crime, but I didn't see love—only a lover.

Of course I felt guilty. I felt guilty that I didn't invite her over or text her back right away. I turned her around so I could peer through the little gap between her thighs below the plumps of her butt; my heart thumped and thumped and thumped. I lunged at her and she let out an adorable cry and giggle. I had her pinned and warned her not to move unless she wanted her bottom beaten. I thrusted from behind; she was on the tips of her toes. Her hands began to move, so I held them tightly by the wrists and bit her earlobe—she started to come. The warmth made it difficult not to finish, but I punctured my desire and allowed her to enjoy herself, at least for a moment. When I couldn't control it any longer, I pulled out her hips, pressed her shoulder blades forward, and finished on the small of her back. I stopped the cum from running down into her butt crack and cleaned her up with a paper towel.

We plopped onto the couch; she rested her head on my shoulder and ran her hand through my chest hair. Our breathing returned to a normal pace. I flipped through baseball highlights (the Yankees won in eleven), celebrity tabloids, and Middle East protest montages with fire and dirt. She checked her phone; I peeked and saw missed texts from Bill, from Andrew, from Greg Cornelli. Guys were always chasing Chloe; she left them with brutal hearts. She put her phone down and asked if I wanted to talk about Adam. I excused myself from the couch, steamed past the rattling dryer, and pushed away the hanging t-shirts and baseball jerseys for Carlo's many All-Stars uniforms like I was security pushing through the paparazzi. I pulled the string that hung from the naked soft white light bulb with a miniature Giants football helmet tied to the end so there was something to grab, sat on the toilet, and wept like a child.

THE GRADUATION

THE TWO-AND-A-HALF-HOUR RIDE BACK TO SCHOOL was standard; Dad would ask about school and I gave one-word answers. He'd tell me about a cousin I'd never met who was getting married, or that my great uncle was back down in Florida. I swear there must be five hundred Lupos between Belleville and Boca Raton, each one leathery and olive with dark brown or hazel eyes.

We tried talking about something other than the Yankees or Carlo's All-Stars, but whenever we discussed politics, it usually fizzled into shriveled nothing. Neither of us gave two shits about the upcoming election; however, our shits weren't given for different reasons. My father was a working man—what kind of work I was actually never certain, something with construction and contracts, I think—but a working man nonetheless. So long as he was employed, the "issues" didn't matter to him. I viewed politicians with contempt and believed they were snakes, the harbingers of ill fate and broken promises. Humanoids who applied ad-hominem tactics to what was once considered debate.

My peers at my liberal arts college were ever so swooned by members of both parties, by the slick-tongued, the fire-eaters, the silver foxes, and the Cleopatras of American politics. Students displayed posters and yard signs on the front lawns of "Greek Street" and "minorities of minorities for minorities" row. Arguments erupted during parties where the words "communist" and "fascist" were *de rigueur*. I'd sit by and appreciate the fervor; I found it more entertaining than my apathy.

Sometimes I'd throw in my two cents in passing before ripping another line with Kev or Riley. Because where one saw a hawk, I saw a vulture, and where one saw a saint, I saw a sinner; and to call me the antichrist would be too extreme. To call the world a place of dualism would be too simplistic. It all comes with being a middle child, I suppose.

On campus, everything was in its right place. Fraternity brothers tossed footballs; the Asians, Frisbees. The single girls wore sundresses and let down their hair, while those with boyfriends wore t-shirts and sweats. I found Riley and Kev in the dining hall at the usual table where we usually procrastinated, sipping coffee until closing.

"Hey guys," I said.

They both got up from their seats and gave me a hug. They didn't ask how I was doing, nor if I "wanted to talk about it." They just sat by my side; they are good friends. We delved into school gossip and sports banter. I smiled, perhaps for the first time in days, at the way Riley described the "uber-sexiness" of her seventeenth-century poetry professor. It was then that I realized how much I appreciated them, how much I appreciated normalcy, and I was warmed in their solace.

"Have you seen what's going on in Algeria?" asked Kev.

During my weekend of mourning and fucking, I hadn't paid too much attention to my usual news sources.

"No," I replied. "What's changed?"

"Oh, it's intensified. People are getting violent and shit."

Before this conversation, I hadn't thought Kev knew where Algeria was on a map, let alone the status of their uprising.

"Oh, fuck," I said. "Do you know how big their military is? No way they don't use it on the people. It's going to get ugly."

"Yeah, true. But when someone is cornered, they will fight claw, tooth, and nail to liberate themselves," he responded. I sipped my coffee. Black, extra sugar.

"This is what we have now: the people are sick of persecution, they're tired of poverty. It's revolution, it's revolution!" shouted Riley.

"You've been talking to Marcel again, haven't you?" I said.

BINGE UNTIL TRAGEDY

"He called me last night."

Marcel graduated last year. He'd joined our group after dating Riley for a little at the beginning of junior year. After their rupture, we decided we liked him too much to cut him off—to Riley's protests, of course. After a few weeks, they were comfortable enough to be around each other as friends, although there were a few instances of weakness where they would slip into each other's pants after a half dozen raspberry vodka shots.

Marcel was born to a Sudanese, Muslim mother and a first-generation French, Christian father whose father was a refugee from the Happy Republic People's Free Democracy of the Congo. He spent most of his life in Paris, but also traveled to the UK and the US for his education. This offered him the chance to develop fluency in three languages and a palpable identity crisis.

Hanging with Marcel was a great way to strengthen my French and sharpen my tongue. Depending on the political climate, Marcel possessed two different styles. The first was the well-dressed European who knew he wasn't in a European country. This entailed scarves in balmy weather, shoes instead of sneakers, and more jackets than I could keep track of. The other, more exciting style was what I nicknamed "Marcel X," which gave us camo fatigues and aviator sunglasses, military boots, berets, and various colored *keffiyehs*. When he found out about Adam's suicide, he sent me a simple text: **Stay strong, brother**. I read it in his French accent.

"How's he doin'?" I asked Riley.

"Oh, ya know, he's fired up over this and that."

"He's in France now?"

"Yup, in Paris. I'm so jealous! Could you imagine living there? The City of Lights, the City of Love," she gushed, closing her eyes to better conjure the city on the Seine.

"It's kind of dirty," I interrupted. Kev laughed.

"Shut up. Don't ruin this for me," she said, eyes still closed.

"You miss him, don't you?"

"No, I don't," she answered defensively with a reddened face. She took out her phone and started to type.

Kev didn't even look up from his bowl of chocolatey cereal. The crunching of refined sugar and slurping of sweet milk made me crave a bowl for myself, so I got up to grab one before the staff put the cereal dispensers away for the night.

When I returned with my overflowing bowl of cereal, a dude in cargo shorts and a "vintage" t-shirt was sitting in my seat. He was leaning into Riley; his moppy brown hair bounced against the side of her head. He would "whisper," but it wasn't even a fucking whisper. He just spoke in a normal voice really close to her ear.

"Excuse me," I said.

"Hey man, sit down. Join us," he said.

"You're in my seat."

"There's a chair right there, man."

"Yeah, I can see that, but that's my seat. My bag is leaning up against it."

"It's all the same, man."

"Riley, who the fuck is this?"

Kev came up for air from his cereal and leaned back in his seat.

"Oh, this is Robin. He's a junior," she said.

"Okay, first, Robin, jabroni, get out of my seat. Second, go shave whatever the fuck you call that off your chin. It's making me lose my appetite." Robin immediately grabbed and pulled at his sorry excuse for a beard. Riley glared at me, shaking her head.

"Jesus, man, fuck, here. Lighten up," he said, pushing back the chair. "I'll talk to you later, Riley." Then he left.

"Why do you have to be such a dick, Joel?" she asked.

"Really? That guy?" I said. "His name is *Robin*."

"He's really nice," she said.

"Did you see his chin? And since when are you attracted to 'nice'?"

"And he really likes me."

"Riley and Robin, ha! It sounds like a lesbian sitcom." I almost got her to crack a smile on that one.

"You just texted him after I mentioned how you missed Marcel, didn't you?"

"No," she said sheepishly.

Usually I would prod her on the topic, but I wasn't in the mood today. I poured myself a second cup of coffee and sat contentedly with my friends. We bitched about finals and discussed television shows—many of the best series were heating up. I preferred the one about Rome and Carthage called *Punic*.

It took the perspectives of each city and played them against each other, objectively. There was no "good vs. evil" narrative that we have fallen in love with. Instead, it showed both cities vying for power in the Mediterranean, both sides filled with lust, blood, and wine. The Carthaginians, located in modern-day Tunisia, and the Romans each had their respective man-candy—chiseled men with hazelnut complexions, ravishing their equally tasty concubines, who were draped in claret cloth and golden bands. *Punic* takes place before Christianity and Islam, when the greatest of men were viewed as gods. The show took off with such conflagration that everyone who watched it picked a side to support.

I was well aware that Rome eventually slaughters Carthage. However, there were still two wars and trekking across the Alps atop war elephants before Rome could be victorious.

"Spoilers!" yelled Kev. "I'm not caught up yet."

"Oh my god! Is that the show with Damien Rogers? Ugh, I love him. *Such* a dreamboat," Riley gushed.

"Yeah, he plays Hannibal," I said.

"Who?"

"Hannibal Barca. He was the general," I said.

"Italians are so hot," she said.

"Hannibal was Carthaginian."

"Them too."

"But Damien Rogers is Welsh."

"Whatever, Joel, he's fucking sexy."

After finishing our coffee, we went back to the apartment and caught up on *Punic*. I had to finish a presentation for my Tuesday and Thursday afternoon class,

Apocalypse in Film. Kev needed to study for his baseball statistics final, and Riley went to meet with a partner to finish their Russian doll-making project. Ya gotta love that liberal arts education.

I finished my politics major my junior year with a focus in Middle Eastern studies and a minor in French. My senior year two-semester curriculum consisted of classes titled: Icons: Remembering the Timeless; History of Jazz; the Arab–Israeli Conflict; What is Life? A Discussion on Life; Epics—where the "epics" of history are read and discussed—the Potential of Turkey (not the bird); Arabic 101; Apocalypse in Film; and French 401.

I coasted through much of college, beginning papers hours before they were due. I enjoyed the pressure. At first I was just lazy, but then I became addicted and put off all work for as long as possible. Kev and I would buy a bottle of vodka, lock ourselves in a basement classroom, and "Kerouac" essays until the sun started to peek through the blinds—repeat for four years and you have your college degree.

The night before graduation is a carnival on campus. It's one last shot to hook up with that person you've been flirting with in class during the semester, before we're shipped off to our unpaid internships—the white-collar, modern American slave labor, I suppose. It's that last taste of the place for the crazy-hearted wild horses, the reckless, the untamed dreamers who sweat sweet honey and spit simple sugar. Since the late sixties, the tradition on campus has been to, throughout the night, gather and give an offering to Dr. Siegel, whose statue stands erect outside the humanities department building—the building of his tenure.

Adored by his students and colleagues, Dr. Frederick Siegel was known for his outlandish style of "guiding," a phrase he would often use in place of "teaching." He is famous for leading a protest against police abusing students demonstrating against the Vietnam War. Ironically, the police beat him up so bad that he spent two weeks in the hospital. Over fifty years later, bikini-clad girls kiss his feet and fraternity boys pour out single-malt Islay scotch—his drink of choice—in tribute. It is believed that making an offering to the professor brings good luck in the world after graduation. Kev and I bought our bottle and headed for the statue to meet Riley.

She was already drunk, dressed in a pink polka-dot bikini, red roses in one hand and a plastic pint of vodka in the other. Behind her, flowers were tucked in between Dr. Siegel's legs, and a pile of roses, lilies, and snapdragons had formed around the base. We made a circle and passed around the vodka, smiling after each swig. It was a rule we made, smiling after the shot. One night freshman year, we took a double shot of spiced rum and Kev gave an ear-to-ear grin. He had recently broken up with his high school sweetheart and none of us had seen him smile in two weeks. I asked him why he was smiling and he said, "Fuck her. I'm here with friends and rum. What more do I need?"

From then on, we made a rule that whenever the three of us did a shot together, we had to smile afterward, no matter how putrid the spirit.

We wrestled our way to the front of the semi-circle and placed our liquor offerings at our feet. I received a text.

Text from Trisha: 7:37 p.m.: Look up

She waved to me from across the semi-circle in a silver bikini with matching fluffy boots—little was left to the imagination.

Text to Trisha: 7:37 p.m.: Find me later?

Text from Trisha: 7:38 p.m.: sure ;)

Amongst the chatter and music, I heard a tiny bell. Omega Delta, a fraternity known on campus for their liberal drug use, was coursing through the crowd with a goat and a bucket. They reached the statue and the fraternity president pulled out a knife, which caused many gasps and a few screams. Riley, a contributor to PETA, grabbed his arm and pulled it down from above his head. The fraternity brothers started to laugh, and Riley, after grabbing the knife, realized it was plastic. She smacked the president in the shoulder and returned to the circle, red as a tomato. The goat would live.

Kev and I prepared for our sacrifice. We stepped up to the bed of flowers, unscrewed the scotch cap, and poured three shots. We placed one at his feet and raised our glasses to eye level. Kev yelled, "*Sláinte!*" and we downed the water of life. An unknown voice from the crowd asked, "Joel, party at your place tonight?" I gave a thumbs-up high above my head.

Before Adam's death, I'd sent out an invite for the sacrificial after-party to be held at our apartment complex. It only made sense to me that the class of hedonists who would soon adopt the world would finish college at the opium den we called our home.

Our apartment complex, completely occupied by students, surrounded a grassy courtyard with tables and chairs. On warm nights, we gathered there, tucked away in our corner of the earth, uninterrupted by campus safety or police. We drank, smoked, snorted, and popped our way through four years of lectures and deadlines. After my last class on Thursdays, a frisson of delight would tickle its way down my back, for Thursdays were sacred.

Hordes of imbibing soon-to-be graduates stampeded their way into the courtyard, carrying with them the acrid smell of desperation. We hugged and kissed as if we were being sent off to war. After a couple of hours of beer pong, flip cup, and relay, Riley, Kev, and I found ourselves at our usual spot on the balcony, smoking cigarettes.

"I can't believe it's over," said Riley, leaning on the balcony railing, a cigarette between her fingers.

"Weird, right?" I said.

"Did you guys take anything tonight?" asked Kev, attempting unsuccessfully to light his own cigarette.

"No."

"Nope."

"If I go pick it up, will you guys pitch in for some molly?"

"I can't think of a better way to go out," I said.

"I'm on it!" said Kev as he swung open the door to go back inside.

BINGE UNTIL TRAGEDY

Riley and I stayed on the balcony. The lamps, surrounded by mindless flies and mosquitoes, shed light on what we fell in love with four years ago: an ephemeral life. We looked at each other, and four years of memories came crashing into my chest. The four years of soft-core boot camp had come to an end and I felt unprepared. I'll admit it: I was nervous. I was anxious. Riley wasn't anxious at all; at least she didn't show it. She had a job lined up in Philly—something in social media—and would make Kev and I promise that we would visit her after we graduated.

Kev returned to the balcony in fifteen minutes. I didn't ask him if he did any coke, but the kid was humming. He opened his palm and three little white capsules lay embedded between the creases of his hand. We each took one, holding them vertically between our thumbs and index fingers, and raised them out in front of us.

"To us, you guys!" shouted Riley, and we chased 'em with beer. "Guys, this can't be the end of this." She wiped beer foam from her mouth.

"Graduation is tomorrow," said Kev. Seeing that he completely missed her point, I asked her what she meant.

"Let's go somewhere! Anywhere, I don't care! England, Australia…"

"Thailand," said Kev. "No, Brazil."

I could not attribute their enthusiasm to the molly. She takes at least twenty minutes to kick in and we'd just popped her—this must have been the alcohol talking.

We threw out countries like they were poker chips. "Ireland. We could hit up Dublin, Galway, and Cork. You love Irish whiskey, Joel. We might be able to stay with my cousin, he has a place in the countryside," said Kev, smiling as he imagined the possibility of endless Guinness and Jameson.

"Wait, wait, wait," I said. "Don't you guys have jobs that start after graduation?"

"Mine doesn't start until September. My dad says it doesn't make sense to start until then," Kev responded.

"I've always wanted to go to Kenya or India or… Hong Kong," said Riley, as she looked up into the smoky night.

"Riles?" I said, attempting to pull her back to Pennsylvania.

"No, I'm fine. My parents said they'd give me a grad gift. It was probably going to be a cruise or something anyway."

"Oh… well, my parents did tell me they'd send me back to Nice as a graduation gift if I wanted to go. I must've forgotten, I suppose," I said. "So let's go to France. I speak French, it's a beautiful country, and we could easily get to Amsterdam and London from Paris." Riley knew what I was going to say next, I knew that she knew, but she didn't stop me, and I didn't stop myself. "Plus, Marcel is there. He was always telling me to go to Paris and see his family when I was studying in Nice. I'm sure he'd be down for us to crash there."

"You had me at Amsterdam," said Kev.

Riley, with a coy grin, stumbled and stuttered a few words before saying, "France it is, then. Fly into Paris?"

"I'll look up flights tomorrow," I said, and we clanked our beers and succumbed to the night.

I woke up with glass-shattering red eyes and a pain in my pit. On my way to the bathroom, one of my sandals stuck to the dried beer on the floor. As I hopped around the living room like a frantic flamingo, I began to replay parts of the night over in my head. I didn't think Trisha was in my bed when I got up, but I might just not have noticed her, she was that petite. I remembered doing shots of cinnamon whiskey with the basketball team, and having to stop Riley from taking her bikini top off to her favorite song. Our enthusiasm for our newly decided trip grew as the molly kicked in and the whiskey flowed.

I hugged the toilet, dry heaving. I could feel the veins protruding from my temples and my skin gripping my ribs. The problem wasn't that I drank too much, it was that I had eaten too little. My cough scratched my throat like sandpaper and my eyes were wet and sticky. I wasn't even sure of the time, just that the ceremony began at eleven. Kev knocked on the door and asked if I'd make it.

"What time is it?" I called, removing my head from the toilet.

"It's ten," he called back.

I was frustrated with my body. I knew if I could pull the trigger I would feel better, and that's what I did. I put my middle and forefinger together and craned them down my throat. Green and yellow bile splashed into the bowl. I wiped the sweat from my forehead and tears from my eyes, rose from my knees, and crashed into the shower. I suffered through an ice-cold shower to wake up—it didn't help my hangover. I threw on my gown and shoved a few stale pretzels that had been sitting in a plastic tub since February into my mouth.

I checked my phone and had three unread texts from Trisha. I didn't see her last night after all: **Text from Trisha: 12:56 a.m.: Come to Jack's.**

Text from Trisha: 1:29 a.m.: Where are you????

Text from Trisha: 2:22 a.m.: Fine, see you NEVER.

These didn't bother me all that much. Trisha lived three hours away from my house and still had two more years of school left. She didn't strike me as the girlfriend type anyway. I knew too much of her history. However, I considered mending things with her so I had a place to stay for homecoming.

"Alright, let's go," Kev said, busting out of his room.

"Where'd we go last night?" I asked.

"The basketball house, remember? You told Tyler Lichner he was a pussy."

"I did?"

"Yup. Riley diffused the situation."

"How?"

"By making out with him."

"Well, he is a pussy."

"I didn't disagree with you."

We strode down Main Street. The sticky breeze that carried pollen from the blossoming pink Japanese trees that lined the road smelled like semen and agitated my gurgling stomach. It didn't help that I had forgotten to take my allergy medicine. I began to sneeze uncontrollably and told Kev to stop walking.

Families fought for parking, cramming themselves into spots that were too tight and would inevitably give them a problem when they left. But fuck it—Dad popped out of the minivan, camera draped around his neck, and Mom downed the last of her diet soda while searching for her sunglasses.

"You gonna be okay?" asked Kev.

"I… I… I… *achoo!*" Splat. A translucent snot rocket splattered onto my sleeve—at least I didn't have a sinus infection. I wiped my sleeve on the grass. We got in line, following the orders of the professors who had yet to receive tenure. I waited between Lily Lumley and Isaiah Luthor, and used every fiber of my being not to throw up into my cap.

Under their gowns, pockets of guys wore t-shirts from the Buzz for every picture they took with family, they would pull down the collars of their gowns with both hands like Superman breaking out of his constricting suit. The Buzz is a website that launched two years ago and achieved immense popularity on college campuses by combining drinking culture with sports and girls. It served as the perfect time-killer for lecture classes.

The "Broad of the Day" was what initially made the site unlike any other competitors. Every day a new co-ed, chosen from thousands of submissions, had her picture, along with her name, year, and school, put on the site. Each Friday, a ballot was also put up and a vote would take place. All the votes had to be in by four.

Every day during Arabic 101, I watched as all the guys in the class voted from their laptops. The winning girl would get a special "Weekly Challenge" t-shirt and free stalkers. The girls' shirts are pink, while the ones that anyone could buy, the ones my fellow graduates wore today, were turquoise. Both had the recognizable bee mascot dead center—no, I didn't own one.

As I scanned my peers, I began to notice numbers in white tape on the tops of their caps: 34,000; 28,000; 31,000; and so on. I asked Isaiah, who told me these were their awaited student loans.

"Who doesn't have student loans?" I asked.

"Shit, we all do. They just feel the need to share theirs," he said.

"I like the way you think, man."

I peeked ahead in the line and saw Riley on her phone. I wondered if she had told Marcel about our plans. I wondered if she remembered our plans. My phone vibrated.

Text from Queen of Campus <3<3: 10:48 a.m.: Hey drunky pants you okay??

She found me in the crowds and I gave a thumbs-up. I scrolled through my newsfeed on my phone to take my mind off my pounding hangover and went to the thumb-marked section titled "Arab Spring." It sounded like an ethnic-themed junior high mixer. A photo of two young Syrian boys headlined the first article. One was holding his fingers in a peace sign while the other held the new Syrian People's flag—green and black with a crescent moon in the center. The article described the protests taking place.

The president ordered the army to use any force necessary to quash the dissidents. They jammed their tanks and Humvees through the streets of Homs and Aleppo, and demolished anything that stood in their way. Cars were flattened and entire apartment buildings, suspected of housing students sympathetic to the "cause," were decimated. Damascus had protests in the early stages of the "spring" that mirrored those in Algiers, Tunis, and Baghdad, but they were promptly quashed and had yet to reincarnate. Six students had been confirmed killed in Aleppo and ten in Homs. Many others had gone "missing."

Hassan al Baqir, the president and self-appointed general of the military, was quoted as saying that he "will not let Syria succumb to terrorism awakening in the urban centers of our hearth. My men will use force on all enemies of the state like we always have done. Our students will not be poisoned by Western parasites."

The line finally started to move, but only at a crawl. I scrolled through the rest of the photos. Most were of protesters no older than me looking into the black hole of what they knew as government, masked in berserker screams. Meanwhile, I stood in pollinated Pennsylvania, hung over, marching to my debt. When I finally reached my seat, I plopped into the chair, testing the strength of the metal, and hovered my head between my legs.

"You okay, brother?" Isaiah asked.

"I'm dying," I said.

The tent for the ceremony wasn't large enough to hold all of the spectators. The school had requested that at a maximum three family members attend, but clearly more had shown up, baking in the sun. I heard laughter coming from the far side of the tent and looked up to see a beach ball being bopped around the crowd of students. The president of the class, a Korean from LA with a diamond in his ear and a 4.0 GPA, began his speech. He touched on camaraderie and sacrifice, sleepless nights studying and getting coffee with professors—all things to which I couldn't relate. I held my head in the web of skin that connected my thumb to my index finger, carefully breathing, praying I didn't choke on the air.

The president finished his speech, and an alumnus from the class of '66 began with his own. He was an activist, anarchist, and engineer. He praised the liberal arts education, calling it food for the heart and energy for the unknown. He told us to grasp life by the tusks, by the fangs, and pull. He told us to drag life down to the very dirt where we build. He told us life is full of regrets and to try and minimize them. He said "fuck" at least once, which made the parents uncomfortable. He said, "If I could go back, I… I wouldn't go back. Life is daunting, but it's life's shadow, it's life's darkness that makes it worth exploring. Go into the night, and never look back." Applause.

And so began the never-ending list of names. Ahmad Aboushi led off, and by the eighth graduate, I would have gratefully ingested arsenic or snorted anthrax. Mild laughter emanated from the crowd. Some kid named Berger was strutting along the stage with sunglasses and an unlit Churchill cigar in his mouth. "You fucking asshole!" someone in the Rs yelled. The student section of the tent erupted.

By the Cs, I was ready to keel over and die; the whiskey pit in my stomach had turned into an energy-zapping black hole. I needed to save my energy for Kev and Riley. Luckily Kev would be soon. I checked my phone and had a text.

BINGE UNTIL TRAGEDY

Text from Sal: 11:41 a.m.: Congrats bud! Welcome to the real world! lol. As if I wasn't sick enough already.

"KEVIN CALIGAN," they announced.

Kevin Seamus Caligan is a fellow Jersey boy, but instead of the sprawling New York City metro area overtaken with Lupos, the Caligans are from the magical land colloquially referred to as the Jersey Shore. Like anyone from the Shore, Kev craved the slow months, the winters and the rainy Aprils. He is a self-declared pluviophile who is at his best under the cracks of thunder and the melody of rain. He is the youngest of five and an "Irish twin," having been born within a year of his older brother Mickey. His father was born in Ireland, and his mother is third-generation Irish herself. I'd seen his father drink; it was inspiring.

During Christmas break sophomore year, I went down to their house for a few days. The six of us—me and his four brothers—made perfect teams for day-drinking games in the basement. One afternoon, Mr. Caligan came down to join us, just for a few minutes, and made us all feel like pussies. He grabbed the bottle of whiskey, which was some cheap bourbon, and called it shit. He grabbed six shot glasses in one callused hand and cracked them on the table. Each shot overflowed onto the wet wood. He made eye contact with each son and one by one, slugged down the liquor. Without blinking, he turned toward me and asked how my family was. Then he went back upstairs. Even Kev's older brother, Padraig, at six-four, two forty, and a former tight end at Boston College, wouldn't dare mess with his dad. The man's forearms could crush a human skull. His sons showed him the utmost respect.

Mr. Caligan talked about his homeland in a critical, honest way that immigrants from other countries didn't. Always, *always*, it was India, Mexico, Brazil, places of wonderment, where the food tasted better, where the women were more voluptuous, where the coffee was bolder. Every fruit was an aphrodisiac and the medicine worked faster with fewer side effects. But Mr. Caligan didn't entertain such notions about Ireland. He grew up in a militant Ireland, in Cork—the "real capital" of the island. Cork, in the south of the country, was known for its grit, unlike the Cork of today, which was recently recognized as a "cultural capital of Europe."

Once in a while, Mr. Caligan would share anecdotes of his upbringing with Kev acting as translator. Although Mr. Caligan spoke English, his accent was so quick and thick that I rarely comprehended full sentences. I would just bob my head up and down, and judging from his tone and body language, would laugh when I didn't hear something clearly. He denounced the IRA on several occasions, but I didn't have to understand every spoken word to see that in his reprimands there was loss, betrayal. Perhaps he was a broken patriot, a man exhausted of his passions. Only once did he share his experience with political violence.

He told us about the firefight in the streets of Cork, urban warfare, something unheard of outside of Northern Ireland. It was 1974, and the Irish Republican Army was splintering into factions. Some had wanted to become totally political and leave the paramilitary for good; others sought to reclaim the entire island, to take back the North and end the repression. Mr. Caligan was eighteen at the time and had been heavily recruited by those who wanted to maintain their arms. IRA troops had covertly slipped in and out of the North, into Derry and Belfast, planting bombs inside of car tires and as close to government buildings as possible. Upon completion of the training, he and four other boys would head to Belfast under the guise of a "stag party"—the English/Irish equivalent of a bachelor party—with the intention of bombing a pub known to be a Loyalist and British military watering hole.

The plot was to place homemade water-resistant bombs in the tops of the toilets. They would enter the pub with two bombs tucked away in their jackets. They would have a pint, have a shot, place the bombs, stay long enough to have another pint and another shot, and then leave the pub and continue on their crawl about town.

BINGE UNTIL TRAGEDY

But Mr. Caligan never made it to Belfast. Instead he witnessed the shooting outside a local Cork parish of a sixteen-year-old boy who was a suspected up-and-coming drug dealer. The IRA had zero tolerance for drug dealers and believed pestilence followed drug usage—they looked to London and New York to prove their point. As it turned out, the boy was not a drug dealer, not even a drug *user*. He had been mistaken for a similar-looking boy who had started selling his father's pain-relief pills to his friends in the neighborhood. The assailant, a masked member of the IRA, shot the boy once in the back and then once in the head as he lay on the ground. Three months later, Mr. Caligan was in Brooklyn, starting a new life.

When Kev was eleven, he watched as his father argued with another fan at a Jets game. The fan was probably around twenty-five, drunk, and disrespectful to everyone in that section. Mr. Caligan—in his early forties, but strong as an ox—kindly asked the guy to calm down and stop using such crass language around families with children. The fan made the mistake of impersonating Mr. C's accent. Kev, who loved telling this story, would then act out how his dad grabbed the guy by the throat and lifted him off the ground until his face went purple. It was the only time Kev ever saw his father act violently; he talks about it like the man conquered the Gauls.

Unfortunately for Kev, he doesn't have his father's build, nor that of his older brother Padraig. He is tall, but lacks the work ethic to ever add serious muscle to his frame. He swam in high school and was always too preoccupied with his girlfriend, Genevieve, to focus on anything else. He met her his junior year and they quickly became high school sweethearts. Her parents didn't approve of Kev; not because he drove too fast or because he didn't get into Dartmouth, but because he was Irish. I mean, these people were WASPs to the nth degree. They would insult him right to his face about being Irish, too, and all he would do was smile and laugh it off, but he couldn't deny it hurt. Genevieve, a year younger than us, would visit campus on occasion—I hated it.

Kev wasn't my freshman roommate, though. That was Josh, a fat kid who partied too much, worked too little, and didn't make it past winter break of sophomore year. But Kev was my best friend from day one. Genevieve's parents would seldom let her visit Kev at school, so for the first few months, he would drive back to Jersey on the weekends. There was a pattern to this, you see: Monday they were fine, Tuesday they would fight, Wednesday was still heated, Thursday was a crap-shoot, but by Friday they were young lovers again, wet for each other's embrace. The few times she was allowed to visit, I could tell she didn't like me, probably because I smoked cigarettes and made Kev do shots of whiskey. But the girl had an arrogance about her that made her pretty face negligible. I swear the first two times I met her she called me "Joe." As in Joseph.

She was so paranoid about getting pregnant that she made Kev wear a condom, pull out, *and* use spermicide all while she was on "the pill"—that was, when they actually had sex. When the two of them did actually come to parties, they'd be gone by eleven and back to the bunk bed, dry humping until she was "in the mood." Riley and I called her the Blond Bomber because of her ability to decimate our friend's self-esteem. He would never admit it, but the girl was a succubus. If Kev ever had a picture on his Facebook with me or Riley or anyone else where it looked like he was having a modicum of fun, she would throw a fit. By early December, she would tell him she'd "text him in the morning" and "don't bother me for the rest of the night." That kind of shit. I knew what this meant, Riley knew what this meant, but Kev didn't. He couldn't admit that she was cheating.

When Kev went home for winter break that year, Genevieve was distant. They exchanged gifts on Christmas. He bought her a necklace from a jewelry store that was out of his price range, and she bought him some shirts that he would "*actually* look good in," but she made excuses not to see him after that, and she even went days without responding to his texts or calls.

When we got back to school in early January, he was in a funk. Three days later, she sent him a text:

Hey Kevy, look, I don't think that I can do this n e more. I feel like we have been growing apart for some time now. You're probably at college hooking up with the sorority sluts and that's OK. I understand! I've been seeing Miles, the guy from my drama class, we have a real connection Kevy.

BINGE UNTIL TRAGEDY

You have to understand that, right??? You wouldn't want to get in the way of true Love would you?? You will always have a special place in my heart and we can always be friends! please text me if you are feeling sad. ☹ ☹ ☹ xoxo.

I could've murdered her after reading that.

The kid was humiliated. He didn't go to class for three days. I would drop by his room multiple times a day, leaving energy drinks and snacks in his fridge. Riley and I finally got him to come out one Saturday night when he insisted on telling every girl he met at the party that he was single. He ended up getting way too drunk off cinnamon schnapps and puking on the lawn of the fraternity house. The next morning, Kev swore off girls and alcohol for good.

Like any good friend, I tried my best to put Kev in social situations with the loosest girls on campus—I even brought him to Kutztown, the undisputed sluttiest girls in Pennsylvania—but he was rusty. He had been faithful to Genevieve for two years and barely spoke to another girl while they were together. She would get mad at him if he joked around with Riley too much; trust me, Riley had zero sexual interest in Kev. Kev is quiet; his whole affinity for drugs is a recent phenomenon. He crammed four years of experimentation into one and a half with surprisingly few mishaps.

There *was* the time he did do too much blow and went missing for a couple of hours—Riley and I finally found him strolling down main street with a tie wrapped around his head, hailing himself the "White Wizard." The fraternity houses he passed cheered him on from their porches, offering him more blow. Luckily we found him before he collapsed a nostril, and we threw him in the back of Riley's car. He had never been so happy to see us.

Occasionally he brings up Genevieve; frequently I catch him texting her. We made an agreement that whenever he said her name I was allowed one punch in the arm, and when I caught them texting, I'd knock the phone out of his hand—he never agreed to that part. Since Genevieve, he never gave another girl a chance. If he ever felt himself getting too close to someone, he'd make some bullshit "mistake" and ruin the prospect. He asked me how I did it, how I could fuck a girl Saturday night and not text her Sunday (or at all).

"I'm completely numb," I would say. But I wasn't numb. Far from it, actually. That's what the drugs and alcohol were for. Kev was better than that, I suppose. Kev is a good guy. You'll like Kev.

By the Js, my neck was crunched atop the backrest of my metal folding chair. *Breathe 2, 3, 4, 1, 2, don't puke,* I repeated. They changed the name caller to a nasally, high-pitched statistics professor from Taiwan. Her voice cut straight to my temples. I could scream, I wanted to scream, I was going to scream. I coughed and vomit shot up my throat; I caught it in my mouth and it burned as it dropped back into my pit.

Riley stumbled in her heels when she went to get in line. They make her awkwardly tall, and combined with her curled hair, she looked almost unrecognizable. She whispered to the girl in front of her and began to laugh. Her laugh floated across the sweaty tent and dissipated shortly after reaching my ears. Her parents nicknamed her Aphrodite; I called her a siren. Her laugh made you happy to be alive; it made the world a better place.

"Riley Johansson," announced the professor.

Riley Abigail Johansson is from the Main Line suburbs of Philadelphia. Both of her parents are rich, stinkin' rich. Recently divorced, her dad lived a penthouse lifestyle in downtown Philly while her mom bred horses with her new boyfriend out in the country. Riley is an only child, which always surprised me, because she didn't act like a selfish brat.

BINGE UNTIL TRAGEDY

We met during the first week of class freshman year. We lived in the same dorm, just down the hall from each other. She hated her roommate and therefore sought refuge in my room, playing video games and smoking weed with us on uneventful Tuesday evenings. Unlike Kev, Riley and her high school sweetheart broke up the summer before she went to college. He was a clean-cut ROTC guy who was a control freak—if she sneezed, he would want to know what brand of tissue she used. She disclosed, one drunken night, that she had tried to break up with him on two occasions, but he wouldn't allow it. The first time he told her that she had lost her mind, that she was hysterical and he couldn't let her make such a drastic decision under the circumstances.

The second time, they were standing outside of his car in front of his house and she told him it was *over*, that she needed to be single and wasn't in love with him anymore. He grabbed her head and slammed it against the windshield, holding it there until she took back everything she had said, and then pulled her by the arm into his living room. Her body froze from shock, and when she tried to scream, all that came out was a muddled whimper.

When she finally could eke out a few words, she told him she was wrong, that she was just nervous about them going away to different schools. But Conor—I think that was his name—he didn't hear any of it. Riley had been Conor's first. He lost his virginity to her, but Riley had been with a couple other guys before him and he never let her forget it. They had been having less and less sex since graduating high school, because of Riley's genuine loss of interest. He had this fixation that the other guys she had been with were better lovers, with bigger penises—Riley never once entertained this idea, but it consumed him and he became obsessed. If a guy took his shirt off in a movie, he would rampage up and down the stairs, screaming, "Did you fuck him too?!"

He held her on the couch, his veins bulging from his forehead, neck, and biceps. "Fuck me like you fucked them!" he yelled. He jammed his forearm against her throat and covered her mouth with his other hand. She bit it until he let go. She looked out the window; the landscapers were mowing the lawn across the street. If she could just make it outside, they would surely see her and she would be safe.

She slipped out from under his waist, missing the opportunity to take a shot at the groin. She banged her shin on the coffee table as she ran toward the door, the big brown gateway that ensured her liberation. He was coming after her. She heard him slam his shin into the coffee table too, and yell, "Fuck!"

She reached for the wrought iron door handle and pulled—it opened, but stopped after a few inches—the chain-link lock above the handle had done its job. She didn't have time to shut the door and slide off the chain, and she knew this, but before she could turn around to throw up some kind of defense, it was too late. He yanked her by the hair and pulled her to the floor. The hardwood quake made the China cabinets shake and quiver.

"Conor, stop. I'm on my period," she pleaded. He knew she was lying. He swung once, open-fisted across her cheek, which erupted with a *pop!* He pulled her up by the back of the head and tossed her back onto the couch. She stopped the fight. Crying, she undid her jean shorts and slowly pulled them down. He stood above her, staring without emotion, tugging on his penis outside of his gym shorts. As she pulled down her underwear, he stopped her and looked out the bay window. There was a brief moment of calm. Maybe he had come to his senses and realized what he was doing. Maybe one of the landscapers, like *Don Quijote*, had heard her torment and was coming to rescue her and would lance the ghoul right there in the living room.

"Hurry the fuck up!" He ripped down the underwear and they remained tangled around her ankles. He turned her over, depleting her of human emotion. The lawn mowers from across the street drowned out the noise of the smacking of flesh—smiling family members observed from picture frames. She tried to leave, mentally; she searched for a safe place like she had seen in a movie, but every few seconds he would smack her on the butt or grab her around the chin, sending her crashing back to reality. It lasted for a little more than six minutes. She kept track on the clock mounted on the wall in front of her. He finished inside of her, hoping to get her pregnant, and told her she was a whore for fucking those other guys and that she disgusted him. He told her that he better not have caught anything from her, and that if she told anyone about this, he'd upload all the naked pictures she sent him onto porn sites and then send those links to the college.

She left his house. Charges were never filed against Conor; he got away with it. She didn't even tell her parents. She tried, and it almost came out on several occasions, but she bit her tongue, her lip, her cheek, anything to keep it in, anything to suffocate it. In the late spring weather, she had to wear sweatshirts to hide the bruises—she wore a smile to hide the pain. She screamed into her pillow every night, leaving make-up stains caked onto her Egyptian cotton pillowcases. Lightning bugs illuminated the night and the cicadas sang her to sleep. They never asked why she was crying.

She went to the pharmacy to buy a morning-after pill. The sleeping pills were right there on the shelf; she doubled back as she passed them. She fantasized about ending it. It would be easy: pills, vodka, sleep. She would never need to see him again. Perhaps she would leave a note, describing in extreme detail what he did to her. She would become famous, and he'd go to prison. They would be poster children: the corrupt, privileged white youth. She had loved him—not then, not for a while—but at one point, she did. She even said it first, on a Saturday summer night. They had been together for about a year already. She was aching to tell him how she felt but had held out, hoping he'd get the hints, that it was time. She was uncharacteristically squeamish that night, and she kept fiddling with her pink lip gloss, applying it three times in thirty minutes. He asked her what was wrong. "Nothing" she'd say. He knew her better than that.

"Babe, what's going on?" he asked.

"I don't know… Do you love me, Conor?" she said, to relieve herself of the pressure. But it didn't work. Before he could answer, she caught herself leaking, "Because I love you." They kissed and transcended time.

Butterflies fluttered in her stomach when they embraced in the hallway. She wore his jersey to his football games and baked his family brownies on Fridays. Now the thought of him made her sick, a harrowing emptiness that stole the air from her lungs. How about that vodka? What about those pills? Would it hurt? It wouldn't hurt her, but her suicide would kill her parents. "Suicide doesn't end the pain. It just shifts it to someone else"—she had read *that* somewhere. Without another child to lean on, Riley was the sole thread holding together her parents' marriage. But once she had left for college and her parents were alone, together, in that gigantic empty house, divorce was inevitable.

Her first year at school was tough; her pain was ineffable. She experimented with love and drugs, seeking fulfillment where she once felt alive. She attended every meeting on campus that was offered: on happiness, on perseverance, on God—nothing worked. Her parents were too busy with their divorce to see how much she was struggling, and to Riley's credit, she held it in pretty well. She didn't tell me about Conor until two years after we met. Once in a while she would randomly start crying. I figured it was the whiskey or the tequila or the gin. The devil's swill will do that to you.

I think I told you this earlier, but let me reiterate: Riley and I have never hooked up. We've never made out, sucked face, French kissed; engaged in mouth play, hand play, ass play, or foreplay; we've never role-played or fooled around—we've never fucked. She slept in bed with me a few times, on particularly rough nights, but I never made a move. Riley is gorgeous, intelligent, and has an excellent sense of humor. She was the president of the campus PETA chapter and is a surprisingly formidable poker player. One time she was at the lacrosse house and witnessed a girl Kev had been dating flirting with another guy. Riley went up to him and whispered that his current dalliance had herpes and was known for using too much teeth. The midfielder did a spit-take and almost fell off his stool. She's protective of us; we're her boys.

Without Riley, Kev and I probably wouldn't have made it—we were two lost souls punching in the dark. There were times even I would've written me off, like when she left a party early to fuck an exchange student from Estonia and I wouldn't stop pounding on her door. She made him leave so she could handle me; I don't even remember why I was irate. But Riley never held a grudge. She was better than me, I suppose.

BINGE UNTIL TRAGEDY

I crossed my bedroom to get my laptop, avoiding scattered boxes and bags of my belongings like landmines. I couldn't unpack right away; I was in denial college was over and I was back in my childhood room, I suppose.

I clicked and clacked at the computer, mindlessly surfing through articles, updates, and photos: "Best Bars in Paris," "The World Economy and How It Works," Mad-Mannix's new music video, a trailer for *The Crusher 3*. I would do this, I would catch myself lost in the interweb. I'd go on to check the score of the baseball game and end up on a list of Byzantine emperors.

I clicked on the tab at the top of the page that cuts directly to my Facebook. As I browsed my feed, a spark shot through my body that tingled the back of my skull and made my armpits sweat. Adam's name appeared, along with comments like **R.I.P. bro, R.I.P. love, R.I.P. Adam**. No one had deleted his account. *Is Olivia or his mom keeping it up?* I scrolled down his page, which was littered with R.I.P.s and anecdotes that weren't *really* for Adam at all. They were for themselves, written to show artificial generosity. They oftentimes started with something like **You were in my bio class and we barely knew each other, but**... or **We used to be friends in school**... I had to delete it.

I searched "how to delete a deceased person's Facebook" and was directed to another page that asked ten different questions about the person and why you wanted to delete the page. There were no numbers to call or any answers in the FAQ. Basically, if I didn't have the password, I was shit out of luck. *Are they fucking kidding me?* I smacked the top of my laptop screen.

An hour later, I received a message saying that they had contacted Olivia and she wanted to keep the page up for the time being, that she wanted to "memorialize it." I told them it was wrong to keep it up. They told me it wasn't their decision and all decisions on deletions are deferred to immediate family. I told them to fuck off.

I attempted to guess the password and after the ninth try or so, I gave up. I reread the same comments and stories by people who barely knew him, over and over, and scrolled insanely, clicking on each person, getting a more thorough glimpse of who they were. My eyes, like gnats in the summer, were spiraling aimlessly. I texted Olivia without thinking: **You should take that down.**

Text from Olivia Reichman: 2:45 p.m.: What?

Text to Olivia Reichman: 2:45 p.m.: His profile page. You should take it down. It's not right that it's still up there those people don't know him.

Text from Olivia Reichman: 2:46 p.m.: That isn't your decision to make Joel. Leave me alone.

I slammed my fists on my desk and screamed. No one came running to the door. Dad had brought Carlo to a baseball tournament in South Jersey and Mom was having brunch with a friend. I closed all of my tabs and opened a new page. I ran to the bathroom and grabbed a wadded up handful of toilet paper and snatched three tissues, *one, two, three,* in swift succession. I plopped down into my swivel chair and typed **www.pornacopia.com** into the naked browser. Rows of thumbnail images flooded onto the screen: **Teen railed by duo of dudes, Latin beauty guzzles cum, Milf goes anal**, etc., etc. They have everything, anything you could ever want (the legal stuff, that is). Having to decide is more difficult than drunkenly choosing from the menu at the twenty-four-hour diner on Route 10. An olio of categories lined the top of the screen, narrowing down your desires into sinful tabs. I clicked on **Russian** to get started. **Russian seduces stepdaughter's boyfriend**—sounded promising. The circular loading symbol rotated in front of me; I was hypnotized while unbuttoning my jeans.

A dangerously skinny bleach blond and a guy who looked like he went to the University of Alabama were nestled into the leather couch. A voluptuous darker-blond woman with an exaggerated Russian accent slid in next to them, and the "stepdaughter" gave her a hug.

"What a long day I've had. I'm going to shower. Enjoy the film, you two," the mother says.

"Thanks again for letting me stay here, Mrs. V."

"Oh, you're so welcome, Tyler."

BINGE UNTIL TRAGEDY

Why is Tyler there? What did he do? Is he hiding from someone? The plot thickens. The stepmom lathered in the shower, touching herself after the long day at the office. Tyler turned to his girlfriend. "I'm going to take a shower," he said—she thought nothing of it. Quick cuts of them in the shower were layered with shots of the daughter on the couch, ponytailed, all in pink.

The stepmom was on her knees blowing Tyler, who had an average—at *best*—penis. *How does someone get this job? He isn't good-looking, he isn't buff or well-endowed, and yet here he is on my screen, banging two beautiful blonds and getting paid for it.* I fast-forwarded on the timeline at the bottom of the screen; I wanted them out of the shower.

Fuck! I forgot the lotion. It was in the bathroom. I swiveled my chair around until I was staring at the door. *Fuck it, I've come too far.* When I turned back, the stepmom was on all fours atop the bed, holding the back of Tyler's head, forcing him to go down on her from behind. Tyler said something, but it was muffled and incoherent. "Oh yeah, right there, right there, baby," Mrs. V groaned in her Soviet accent. Tyler stood up and nailed her from behind; the wrinkles on her ass gyrated as she smacked against his hips.

I used the tissue instead of lotion—it was better than going dry. My bare hamstrings were sweating and sticking to the chair. The leather squeaked. Finally, the girlfriend had grown suspicious enough of her absent boyfriend to go looking for him. She meticulously walked up the stairs, following the sound of the bed post smacking against the wall. The camera cut back to Tyler, showing no remorse for his actions, not skipping a beat in his thrusts. The little blond threw open the door right when Tyler smacked her stepmom on the ass.

"What are you doing, Tyler?!" she said, standing at the edge of the bed, her hands on her cheeks like Macaulay Culkin in *Home Alone*.

"Babe! It's… it's not what it looks like," he said without a shred of believability.

Tyler took his time to pull out of his girlfriend's stepmom, who didn't move from her prostration: "Relax, honey," she said reassuringly. "He's *only* a boy. Why don't you have some fun?"

It took the girlfriend all of three seconds of contemplation and a pull on the arm to be convinced to engage in a threesome with her boyfriend and stepmother. They laid her on the bed, stepmom at the head, holding her legs up by the calves, as Tyler leaned over her and thrusted.

The tissue I used as lubricant was deteriorating, but the sensation crept up my dick as Tyler pumped his girlfriend, leaving me no time to swivel around and snatch another tissue from the night stand. The tiny blond was in the reverse cowgirl position, moaning, while Mrs. V sat on Tyler's face. I was at the point of no return. You could pour hot acid on my chest, smash a board across my back, you could stab me with a ballpoint pen or set my shirt on fire, but I would come, and have a cigarette after.

As my knees jerked and neck snapped, I came into the little indent I made in the balled-up toilet paper and covered it with a tissue so it wouldn't spill. I sat sweaty and sticky and watched a few more seconds of the clip as I sobered up from my orgasm haze—the moaning and grunting and smacking of skin made me queasy and depressed. There was always this wave of guilt waiting to crash over me after I snapped one off, as if I had been given the task of recruiting the impressionable young blonds the second they stepped off their bus from Phoenix or Des Moines.

I shut the top of my laptop and stared out the window, watching the mailman drop a chunk of letters into my neighbor's mailbox. I waited for my penis to return to flaccid, walked to the bathroom, flushed my sickness down the toilet, and went to bed.

Something told me to go to the window. Not a voice, not actual words, but a feeling, an impulse. Out in the yard, a brown-suited man stood with a briefcase, not moving. I squinted to get a better look—he didn't have a face. I tapped on the glass: nothing. I waved to him: nothing. I didn't think much of it and went to the kitchen for a glass of water. The one I kept next to my bed had spilled onto the floor. I tried to jump over the puddle, but midway through the air, it expanded to an impassable length and I crashed into the black waves. I swam to the door, punching the current, gasping for air. Someone grabbed me by the arm and pulled me out of the water; it was Adam.

"I've been waiting for you," he said.

"Am I dead?" I asked.

"Um, no, dumbass."

"Then where am I?"

"You don't recognize your own house?"

I looked around the room and hallway. It was my house, but nothing was in its right place. The walls were blue and the floor was changing colors: red to green to black, in that order. There were web-like patterns of light floating in the air like snowflakes.

"Did you drug me, man?" I asked.

"Still no. I want to show you something. Follow me!"

Adam took off down the corridor. I hopped up and sprinted after him. He looked back and laughed and separated from me even more. Pictures of my family lined the walls, but they weren't my family at all. I mean, they *were* my family; I recognized them as my family, but they were not my family. One picture had five kids, two of which were girls, my sisters. *My sisters?* In another picture, my dad was unusually pale and my mom had a long, stem-like nose. I continued to sprint after Adam, but the faster I moved my legs, the less distance I covered—it was like running in hummus.

"Don't go!" I yelled into the darkness, down the deep unknown. I could hear the faint echo of his laugh in the distance.

I woke up.

THE CITY

I MET SAL IN NEW YORK CITY. HE WANTED TO TAKE
me out for dinner and drinks for my graduation, so I hopped on the 3:04 NJ Transit and watched as waves of New Jersey passed me by. Everyone sat apart from each other, one-seat spacing. The kid behind me had his headphones plugged in, but I could still hear his music. It had a deep bass with a pop; his lips smacked together as he mouthed the lyrics. An Asian girl with blond hair followed a Latino wearing a yarmulke, students got on with tourists, and businessmen treaded behind cleaning women. As we flowed from west to east, the suburbs blended with the city fringes. Everyone dawdled on their phones; the window seat has no value anymore. We tore through the Meadowlands and stopped at Secaucus Junction, where a group of high school kids dressed in neon and nothing else rambled into their seats. Festival season had come early, I suppose. A girl in a lime-green fishnet top popped a molly capsule into her mouth and sucked down her bottle of water so hard even the kid with the blaring headphones turned to the crackling of plastic. We passed under the Hudson River, the divide between us and the City, and arrived at Penn Station.

There was a rush to get off the train. Minor pushing and shoving occurred; the protocol of letting those in front of you off first was broken. We crammed onto the narrow escalator and dispersed into the ugly station, overlooked by Grand Central, and rightfully so. I darted for the subway and passed police officers with drug-sniffing German Shepherds. I pictured the dog snapping at me because I forgot about a little bag of coke or weed in my pocket. The officer would search me, the dog biting at my arm. I would cause a scene. Foreigners and commuters would watch as I was brought to the ground and put in cuffs. I'd be humiliated.

When I passed the dogs, one tilted its head as if to say "Come back." A woman, the same woman as always, with frizzed hair and a high, angelic voice, sang before the portal to the subway. She was too good to be singing there. She should have lights on her and an attentive audience—I dropped a dollar in her box.

At the turnstile, I swiped my MetroCard that I had left over from a few months back when I saw the Cavalry at Hammerstein Ballroom with Kev. Insufficient fare. *Are you fucking joking me?* I knew I had at least two more swipes; I made a note of it last time. The girl behind me, whose five seconds of time I had wasted, was breathing down my neck. I swiped again—it worked. Dreadlocked men played drums on the platform; one was reggae rapping incoherently. I put my back up against a support beam; I didn't care if it was filthy. I had seen the videos of people being pushed in front of the train at the last second by some lunatic, but I wouldn't let that be me, no way; my "savior" running to my aid, only to snap a selfie before my guts are strewn across the 34th Street platform.

I hopped on the 3 train, which coursed down the West Side spine of Manhattan. I hated holding on to the railing on the subway, and luckily found a seat next to a tiny Asian lady who was holding a bag of something stinky, like fish and vinegar.

14TH STREET: the great divide between Downtown and Midtown, the skirt of the City, I suppose. The doors convulsed three times before we got moving again.

"Excuse me!" I heard from a few feet away but didn't look up. "Thank you. *Damn*," a skinny black man said to a student whose backpack was taking up precious space on this worm. We made eye contact. *Shit.* There was no one to my left. The bare seat was calling to him. I whipped out my phone and pretended to check something important—it didn't take.

"Hey, man, I'm Derek," he said, holding out his hand. I shook it. His hand was dry and mine was sweaty. I didn't have time to wipe it off on my jeans, I wasn't expecting that. He probably thought I was nervous because he's homeless or because he's black. But that wasn't it, I just wasn't expecting that.

"Hey, how's it going?" I said, but I didn't really want to know how it was going. I wanted to be left alone; it's just a phrasal reaction.

"Not too good, brother," he said—he called me "brother" and I felt cool. "I'm homeless and I've got AIDS." My eyes widened; I could feel everyone else in this part of the car turn away. He said something about being from Brooklyn and asked me where I'm from.

"Jersey," I said, but really all I was thinking about was the handshake. Is that stupid? Yeah, yeah, yeah, I know AIDS is only contracted through bodily fluids, like blood and cum, but come *on*. There I was, trying to avoid touching the railing, and I end up shaking hands with a terminal guy? Go ahead and judge; at least I'm being honest.

CHAMBERS STREET: The little Asian woman next to me got off the train. I contemplated getting off with her, pretending we were together.

"My cousin lives in Jersey. Irvington. You live near Newark?" he asked.

"Kinda," I said.

"You ever go to Newark?"

I wanted to say, "Fuck no, why would I go to Newark? Getting shot or stabbed isn't on the agenda." But instead I said, "Sometimes. My dad is from Newark."

"No shit?! I knew we were brothers."

He moved closer and I could see he was younger than I thought, probably not a day over thirty-five. He was barely wrinkled and his teeth were surprisingly white. There was a pause in the conversation; the sweat from my hand smeared the screen of my phone. The subway careened downtown like a black mamba in the brush. It hugged the tunnel, showing how truly trapped you are when you're down here.

PARK PLACE: *One more stop.* I turned so I was facing straight ahead. I shot glances at his hands. I knew he wasn't going to pick-pocket me or anything. What a stupid thought to have; how inconsiderate of me. It was wrong and I hated myself for thinking it, okay? But I kept eyeballing his hands like we were in a standoff at the OK Corral. On his wrist was a rufescent wood bracelet with tiny images of the Virgin Mary, an assortment of saints, and Jesus Christ. In the pit of life, one needs faith, I suppose. He spotted me looking at his bracelet. "Some kid gave this to me. Also a Jersey boy like yaself."

"It's nice," I said, fantasizing about vanishing into thin air.

"Hey Joel, I'm hungry. Can you spare anything for me, brother?" Yeah, I saw this coming, one stop away too.

"What are you going to eat?" I asked.

"A chicken sandwich," he said.

"Burger Barn?" I asked.

"Hellllls no. I don't want that crap. I want the good stuff, from Jimmie's."

"Jimmie's?"

"You def not a Brooklyn boy," he said with a grin.

"I suppose not." And I gave him a fiver.

FULTON STREET: I told Derek good luck and left the train. I emerged from the depths of the City into the Financial District. Even though I'd been coming to Manhattan since I was a child, those steel behemoths still amazed me. The City dwarfs its residents. This is what foreigners talk about; this is the city you see when you type New York City into a search engine, the city in aerial shots of hackneyed cable cop shows.

Sal lived in one of those towers, on the twenty-sixth floor of a metal monstrosity on Pine Street. It had one bedroom, one bathroom, an L-shaped kitchen, a living room, and—of course—the breakfast nook. Pictures of Sal and Michelle scattered the walls and shelves: from college, in the City, on the white beaches of South Africa where they went on their honeymoon (Dad said he would've paid for it if they'd gone to Italy, but Michelle comes from money). Everything was new and clean as if arranged for a catalogue.

"Hey Joel!" Michelle always gave me a big hello. "Congrats on graduating. What are your plans now?"

I poured myself a glass of water from the tap. "Oh, use the Cleansa in the fridge," she insisted. "The City water is so hard." I finished the glass to avoid the question.

"Joel and I are going out for dinner and drinks with Tom!" Sal called from the living room. He marched into the kitchen and gave me a bear hug. "How ya doin', buddy? Lovin' the beard."

"Sounds great, you guys. You should take him to Father Time," Michelle said.

"For dinner?"

"Why would you take him there for dinner?"

"That's what I'm asking," said Sal.

"For drinks," said Michelle.

"Why there?"

"He'd like their beer selection."

"I was thinking the Knight's Head."

"Why there?"

"Best Manhattan in Manhattan."

"Where did you hear that?"

"I read it."

"Where?"

"In the West Village."

"No, I mean, where did you *read* that?"

"I don't remember."

"That's a reliable source."

"Shut it, babe."

"Don't say that to me. You're only acting like this because you want to look cool in front of your brother."

"What are you *talking* about?" They both looked at me—I poured myself another glass of water from the tap.

"Joel, use the Cleansa," said Sal.

Sal hurried to change and we took a cab—the yellow wasp cut through the City like butter. Three times I thought we'd get into an accident and three times we escaped unscathed. The taxi had a little TV built in to the seat, running the news 24/7. A pretty blond with big lips was reporting on Syria, on Iraq, on Tunisia and Algeria. The Iraqi president was calling for all student-led demonstrations to cease or the universities would be shut down indefinitely. Syria's president had already unleashed the military police on "any and all forms of demonstration." In Tunis, a wave of self-immolations in front of government buildings had caught on as a form of protest throughout the region, confusing police and causing many to lower their weapons; some officers even defected.

In Algiers and Oran, the two largest cities in Algeria, the protestors called for lower food prices and for the dissolution of the military police, but their cries were met with tear gas and batons. Most of the protesters wore kelly green, the color of the Algerian flag, but amongst them were pockets of what looked like students dressed in red and black, which had become the de facto colors of the anarchy movement. These were the guys at the front who wanted to be seen. Some had even acquired gas masks; they hurled rocks back at the police.

A student with a green bandana covering his face spoke on camera to a Western reporter. His French was translated at the bottom the screen. He called for French and other European nationals to come to Algeria and join them in the liberation movement.

"*Vive l'Algérie, vive la liberté!*" the crowd echoed behind him.

We arrived at the Knight's Head, an English pub in the West Village. I pulled out my wallet to pay the $17.50 fare and Sal just laughed. "Are you serious? Don't even think about it. I got you taken care of all night."

Sal's college roommate Tom sat in a dark corner at a beat-up round wood table. Tom is a financial consultant for one of the Big Boys in town and makes Big Boy money. I have never asked how much Sal makes, but Tom, being single and tumid, was much more visible with his cash. One year for Christmas, Tom bought our father such an expensive bottle of Scotch that my dad blurted out, "My first car didn't even cost this much!"

Tom comes from old money, Long Island money, and was never timid to remind Sal of his Jersey roots. Michelle hated Tom. I'm putting that lightly, I suppose. In college they were adversaries in contention for Sal's attention. Tom knew Sal before Michelle did, and he never let her forget it. When they all got together, Tom would reference Sal's crazy days in school, before he was "tied down," as Tom liked to phrase it. He would do this thing where he'd start to tell a story about Sal, "realize" it was before Michelle was around and therefore probably contained a different girl, and then make a big deal about not finishing the story so as not to embarrass them. I would always sit back and count the steps as they played out.

When Tom saw us, he hopped up from his seat, and with his arms raised at his sides, said, "Salvatore, the big guy! And Joel, how's it going, buddy?" and rubbed my head like I was in junior high. "You guys ready for a few brewskies? Hey sweetheart," he called to the waitress. "Three Stellas, *si vous plait*." *Ew.* "Joel, you speak French, right?" I don't fucking like Tom either. He's the epitome of douchebaggery.

"*Oui*," I responded.

"Fantastic. So, Sal, you hear about the McDuffie merger?"

They went on about business for a few minutes, giving me a chance to check my phone.

Text from Chloe: 5:31 p.m.: Joelie, what are you doing tonight???

I didn't respond.

The waitress plopped our first round of drinks onto the chestnut table. Stella Artois: the international asshole's beer.

"Shots?" Tom proposed to Sal. "Shots?" he asked again, turning to me.

"Eh, I don't know, we just started," said Sal.

"Don't be such a pussy. Three Patrón shots, sweetheart." The waitress was not amused by her new nickname.

We sat around the table drinking beer and eating burgers, and the more alcohol I poured down my face, the more tolerable Tom became. I really didn't like tequila, but it was top-shelf shit and it was free. Sal kept checking his phone as Tom droned on about this broad in his office with the tight ass, or that trip he took to Brazil or Australia. I could see Sal was getting calls and texts from Michelle, but he would only answer some of them, pressing the button on the side of the phone to ignore the others. I sat there and nodded, gave the occasional "That's cool, man," and drank my beer.

After we finished our greasy pub food and slugged one more round of tequila shots, Tom took care of the check, even though Sal insisted he pay for our part.

Tom said, "Let's get *into* something tonight." He didn't specify. Sal said he had to call Michelle real quick and stepped outside. Tom made the *wha-tish* sound of a whip.

"So Sal told me about your friend Alex. That sucks, man."

"Adam," I corrected him.

"Oh, right. The quiet kid who lived down the street?"

"Yeah."

Where the fuck is Sal? I peeked out the window and could see him making typical "I'm a fed-up Italian-American" hand motions like he was conducting an orchestra. They had been together a while, so I suppose it was normal. The one stuck at home gets jealous that the other is out having a night on the town—especially with someone they hate. Not answering the phone, not texting back quick enough, not sending a smiley face emoji with the text: it all adds fuel to the imminent fire. That fire was exploding into an inferno of every fight they had had in the past couple of months. He hung up, took a couple of breaths, and reentered the bar with a forced smile on his face.

"Where to next?" he asked.

"Cannito's?" said Tom.

"What about the Thirsty Turtle?" asked Sal.

"Where's that?"

"Brooklyn."

"*Egh!*" scoffed Tom. "I don't *do* outer boroughs."

I got out of my seat, which I hadn't left for two hours, and had to immediately grab on to the chair to keep from falling over. I was shitfaced but didn't want to let Tom and Sal know it. I played it cool and headed to the bathroom to "break the seal."

We sauntered through the West Village like drunken baboons. I could tell Sal hadn't gotten sloppy in a while, and that he was enjoying every splendid second of the liquid haze.

The City is like a sundry assortment of miniature cities within the giant metropolis, I suppose, and the West Village represents the pinnacle of urban success. Residents of this neighborhood will argue that it's the single greatest neighborhood on Earth. Tucked away in the southwest of Manhattan, its streets jut and mingle with each other at angles in direct contempt of the larger New York City grid—representative of the beat bohemian past that made the neighborhood famous, I suppose. Independent coffee shops rattled from the inside to keep this neighborhood alive, awake, and thriving. But I didn't need the caffeine; I felt a frisson bolt up my spine simply by walking the tree-lined streets that provided shade for the brownstone and red-brick homes. Don't get me wrong, the place is expensive, as in need-money-coming-out-your-ears expensive. But that's Manhattan. You want to pay less for something comparable? Try a borough; try Park Slope, Cobble Hill, Brooklyn Heights, or Astoria. But this is Manhattan, the new Mediterranean, the center of the world.

I had to piss again. Sal and Tom were arguing over the starting rotation for the Yankees, so I undid my zipper and leaked on an iconic brownstone. "You see, that's why we don't let Jersey trash into the City!" Tom yelled and slapped Sal on the back.

I checked my phone again.

Text from Chloe: 6:58 p.m.: ???

That's all it was. I should've responded, but I had my dick in my hand and didn't want to get arrested.

We crashed into an unsuspecting bar with girls in oversized scarves and guys wearing knit hats, in late May. "Three Stellas," Tom shouted at the female bartender.

"We only have *local* microbrews," the bartender scoffed.

"Well, fuck me then," Tom replied. "Three microbrews of your choosing, my bartendress."

Sal was outside on the phone with Michelle again. I poked my head out the door and heard a lot of *fuck that*s and *I never said*s. When he was about to say something about her father, I stopped him. "Yo Sal, come inside. Let me talk to her." He just hung up.

BINGE UNTIL TRAGEDY

We were given dirty looks by the patrons of the bar who had been having a delightful evening before our arrival. Tom was the only guy within three blocks wearing a suit, and Sal was all fired up from arguing with his wife.

"Fucking can't stand it. You're smart, Tom. You stayed single." Despite the fact that Tom probably wasn't single by choice, I agreed with Sal, who was beginning to slur. "See that, Joel, never get married."

"What's going on, big guy?" Tom asked.

"Stupid shit, ya know? It's *always* my fault."

"I think I've got what you need." He pulled out a little pouch of coke and cupped it in the palm of his hand like he was holding a wounded bird. "This is good stuff. *Peruvian*. That's the new coke capital. Colombia hath been dethroned!"

The annoyed bartender dropped a second round of hoppy beer in front of us. "Tab?" she asked, with a pinch of attitude.

"Yes, ma'am," said Tom. "How about a smile, sweetheart?"

A few seconds later, a bearded burly bartender in a tight black t-shirt approached us. "If you don't stop annoying her"—he pointed to "sweetheart"—"I'm going to have to ask you guys to leave." Tom laughed awkwardly and said, "Sure, whatever, three tequila shots, then."

"We don't have tequila."

"Vodka?"

"We actually don't *do* shots."

"You don't do shots?! This is a fucking bar!"

Needless to say, Tom's outburst got us kicked out of the bar. He chugged his beer on the way out, which was actually pretty cool. "Fuck them and their phony hippie asses. Let's go back to my place and party with the white lady!"

We hopped in a cab, and my phone began to vibrate repeatedly. Six unread texts messages, all from Chloe.

Text from Chloe: 7:46 p.m.: 1 of 6: What the fuck Joel?!?! How come you can't answr me back?? What have I done? What didn't I do?? I've fallen for you but you treat me like a child. What more do you want?? Tell me TELL ME!!

2 of 6: You cannot love me. Can you even love??? Here I am. All day and all night. I try not to text you. I try not to go on your Facebook. I think maybe you'll come to me. But you ignore me. You used me.

3 of 6: I knw I should just give up. But I can't, okay? I can't. I know you fcck all those girls. You've even fcked some of my friends. My closest friends. I DON'T CARE. Why can't you just answer me? I knw you check your ducking phone.

4 of 6: fucking* phone.

5 of 6: You havn't felt anything? All those nights 2gether must have meant nothing to you. Well they meant something to me. I thought that we shared something special. I figured once you graduated we could be together. I guess I was wrong…

6 of 6: I'm broken. You broke me. You drug.

I should've responded to that. The girl was hurting. I should've texted her, maybe given her a call, something reassuring to mend her self-esteem, but I didn't. I ignored it, put my phone back into my pocket, and crammed cocaine up my nasal cavity, numbing all feeling that leaked from my pores.

You're probably on the fence right now, uncertain whether you like me or not—don't worry, I understand. Hopefully you've at least found this story of decadence and despair interesting. Know this. You don't have to like me. I'm okay with that—I'm not certain I like me either.

We nosedived into the blow: Tom, Sal, me, Tom, Sal, me. Like a hyperventilating men's softball lineup, we took turns bumping off Tom's apartment key. Sal was humming. Clearly he hadn't indulged in quite some time, and we both knew Michelle would be furious if she was aware of tonight's extracurricular activities.

We ascended to the roof, where a few small groups of young thirty-somethings were eating finger foods and drinking Chablis. We carved out our own corner of the balcony, where Sal and I deliberately spoke with delicate voices, hoping Tom would follow, but he didn't catch on.

"Look at that shit. New York fucking City. I fucking love it." Despite Tom's crass lack of detail, he shared the same sentiments of so many who called this place home. The skyline spires glittered under May's cotton-candy skies. So many of the beasts that form the concrete jungle of Manhattan are unrecognizable to the ignorant eye, but there are, at the very bottom of the island, two behemoths that even the most remote goat ranchers would recognize on a postcard—the Twin Towers—the poster children of American capitalism. "Can you believe those towel-heads tried to knock those down? Could you fucking imagine it?"

Tom was referring to the plot uncovered in 2000 to destroy the towers. Supposedly, Saudis based out of Afghanistan and Pakistan were going to fly hijacked planes into the Twins, destroying them completely, and relish in all the chaos that ensued. The plot was discovered before they could execute their plans, and international coalitions led by the Marines raided their safe houses in Islamabad, Kabul, and the warring states in the North, which resulted in the arrest and detention of thirty soldiers, commanders, and even a few politicians. If the plan had succeeded, conservative estimates believe the carnage would've been no less than five thousand deaths; others calculated double.

Many don't believe the plot, doubting its very existence due to the convenient uncovering right before the 2000 election. The president had abysmal approval ratings weeks before the plot was spoiled, but after project "Crippling Wind" (as it was translated) was neutralized, he was virtually canonized in American politics, sliding into his second term like it was a Ho Chi Minh City prostitute. The plan was never published to the public, which only legitimized the doubters. How could a bunch of psychos dwelling in the caves of BumbleFuckistan destroy the symbols of Western capitalism in New York City? It's not like they would be able to get guns onto the plane. Was a pilot behind it? Some of it just never added up. There were a few demonstrations in front of mosques in the City, but the protestors were viewed as crazies who didn't have anything better to do with their lives. Once in a while, it would come up in class, the argument stuck in limbo, with one side saying what could've happened and the other saying that nothing *actually* happened. But that paranoia never quite went away, at least not near the City. You'll still see patrol cars on Fifth Avenue and bereted soldiers with M16s walking down Wall Street.

BEN D'ALESSIO

Clayton Wright wants US soldiers in every country in the Middle East. He believes preemption should be a promise, part of the party's platform, that proliferation is for pansies. He's one of those hawks who eats and drinks INVADE—invade the brown people who worship Allah, invade everything east of Israel, if they're not with us they're against us—his words, not mine. Well, that bozo might be the next president of the United States; he turns fears into votes. Gallup polls have him as the favorite to win the primary, and then, who knows? The guy would wage war on the sea if the waves got high enough.

Tom poured out a few shots of top-shelf vodka—Russian water, the clear cretin. That was it, the end of my night, the knockout punch. But just then, as if he had had an epiphany, Tom shouted, "Strip club!" Sal and I just looked at each other and sort of laughed.

"No, I'm serious. Candies. It'll be my graduation present to Joel." I looked to Sal for approval. He was down. *I* was down.

"It's settled then. To the titties!"

We took another yellow wasp headed toward Chelsea, because Tom said the Uber we hailed was taking too long. Fifty-dollar cover at the door. Tom took care of it—that was part of the deal: we go, Tom pays. There was no way Sal could tell Michelle about this either. They weren't in their mid-twenties anymore, the inevitable father of their unborn child wouldn't be cramming dollar bills into Mercedes' ass crack with her blessing.

We sat beside the stage, and a girl who looked like she'd been in my French literature class asked if we wanted massages with our drinks.

"That guy does," Tom said, pointing at me. "He's the new grad."

There I was, getting rubbed like Xerxes, watching a tall Ukrainian elegantly strip down, down, down. Her face was emotionless, her eyes were dead, just like her "American dream," I suppose. She strutted across the stage, not making eye contact with a single guy in the joint, as if wearing a mask on another ragged Saturday night. We got a round of beers and I put the cold green bottle to my forehead. I was hot and needed to cool down, and the electric lights of the club made me nauseous.

BINGE UNTIL TRAGEDY

"Look at her, look at *her*. Mother of sweet baby Jesus." Tom liked the stripper. "You like this one, Joel?"

"Yeah, she's hot," I said, lacking any color.

"Hot? I'd *pay* to sniff her ass. Hey, big guy, you want me to buy you a dance? I know Joel wants one, right, Joel?"

I nodded.

"Hey!" Tom called out to the girl massaging my traps. "Get a few girls over here so my bromigos can start the selection process."

"I'm sorry, I don't handle that," she said professionally.

"Then how do my boys get their dicks tugged around here?"

Sal diffused the situation by grabbing the nearest cocktail waitress and asking how we paid for a dance, and then told my masseuse she was in for a nice tip. Within five minutes, three top-notch girls approached us, asking, "Who is the graduate?" I raised my hand and the tan brunette bent over, her hands on my knees, and said, "I'm going to take care of you tonight, baby." Tom and Sal gave me the go-ahead.

"Why don't you come with me to the Champagne Room." She took me by the hand and we traversed the seedy club, past suited drunkards and big black bouncers, past Latinas in G-strings and a Thai girl in a cowgirl hat and little else. I was no stranger to strippers; when Kev turned twenty-one we took him to a highway joint. They brought him on stage and spanked him twenty-one times with a comically large wooden paddle. When I was seventeen, this rich kid on my hockey team had two girls put on a show in his basement. I licked whipped cream off of the one that looked like Joan Jett and the other one picked a dollar off my face with her vagina—best one hundred cents I ever spent, I suppose. But the Champagne Room, that was the big show, where lonely businessmen blew their money at the end of the rainbow.

There was a pounding in my nose and the drips were sliding down my throat, but I had a mile-wide smile on my stupid face. "Sit there, baby." I sat. She began to slide up and down the pole facing me, spreading her legs as her ass hovered inches from the ground. The wall of mirrors multiplied her by ten; I felt like I was in an

X-rated fun house. She crawled over to me from the pole and rested her elbows on my knees. "No touching. I touch you, got it?" I got it. I sat and watched with my tongue unraveled on the floor.

She pushed off my knees and walked back to the pole, her ass cheeks bouncing with each step. She started with splits, spins, upside-down falls—the works. My dick was bulging in my jeans so hard it hurt. What was proper etiquette? I mean, that was her job, right? To get me hard, to turn me on—why hide it? Why, because I had been hiding erections since the seventh grade, behind European history textbooks in the hallways of Brewer Junior High. Go Bobcats!

So I sat back and enjoyed the show. She was good. Well actually, I'm not sure if she was good, but she was hot. Her outfit, which barely constituted underwear, clung to her curves to the dismay of all manhood. She smiled at me and I almost bust right there in my pants. Maybe she liked me. I had to ask for her number. I'm pretty good at sexting. It wasn't that bad of a commute. I'd get jealous, though, those freaks drooling over her perfect chest and stomach. I would pay one of the bouncers to keep a special eye on her.

She strutted over to my lap as I finished my beer. She bent over, palms on the floor, her butt staring back at me. I wanted to smack it, but I stopped myself. *Don't do it, don't ruin this, you guys could have something special.* Another song began, dirty R&B, it was slow. She wrapped her arms around my neck and threw back her hair. I was sweating and I reeked. She was thin; I wondered if she had blow. "So where'd you go to school?" she asked. Her C-cups were skimming the tip of my nose.

"College," was all I managed to eke out. It was an inferno, and if it weren't for the demoness on my lap, I wouldn't've tolerated it.

She flipped around, and in the process her knee jabbed my stomach. It turned over. My stomach, I mean. Well, she turned over too, I suppose. The tequila, beer, whiskey, and vodka were awake. *Oh no. Oh no.* Her half apple caressed my lap, her hands were folded behind my neck, her hair got caught in my mouth, and I started to cough. *Oh no. Oh no. You're not going to do it. You're not going to blow.* This inner monologue was the only thing keeping me from committing the up-chuck heard round the world. My mouth was sweating, the enamel was coating itself around each tooth, preparing them for imminent doom.

"Your friend, the pedantic one, he paid me for you to finish," she said.

Pedantic? Did she just use 'pedantic'? Tom wasn't so bad after all, I suppose. She kept rubbing my dick with her butt and would use one hand, wrapped around her back, to stroke the base. My eyes closed; the sensation in my pants, which started as a feeble ember, torched into a full-blown scorcher. I was past the point of no return.

"You there, sexy?" she asked.

Here it comes.

"Are you gonna finish?"

I'm gonna blow.

"Baby, you don't look so good."

I splattered her back with chunks while simultaneously finishing in my pants. She ran out of the room screaming, calling me "a fucking psycho" and other colorful terms of endearment. A bouncer who ate weights after he lifted them grabbed me by the collar. If it weren't for Sal calming down the staff and for Tom slipping them a few fifties each, I would've gone flying through the front doors like I was in an Old Western.

"You idiot, Joel," said Sal while trying to hail a cab.

"I think it's hilarious," said Tom. "You make it worth my money?"

"My jeans aren't full of jizz for nothing," I said. Sal was trying not to laugh.

The City had chewed me up and puked me out, along with its dinner, happy hour, and afternoon snack. Like so many other reckless fools who get abused by this city, I had a short memory and would come crawling back just in time for another beating. I drank too much, ate too much, snorted too much, and made a complete ass out of myself, covered in puke and cum, sitting on the Chelsea pavement under that clogged New York City sky that is never forgiving. But we shouldn't be forgiven, not for what we've done.

The cab dropped us off before the behemoth, and instead of stampeding inside, Sal and I sat on the steps of his building. We both needed to let the drugs wear off and Sal needed to fabricate a story to tell Michelle, who would most likely be in interrogation mode upon our arrival.

"Mom tells me you're going to Europe?"

"Yup."

"Where to?"

"Flying into Paris. Then probably Amsterdam and Berlin. I'd like to make it back down south, too."

"Sounds great. You still talk to that girl you had over there?"

"What?"

"Oh, don't play stupid. You were upset for weeks when you came home from France. You were miserable at Christmas!"

"… I haven't spoken to her."

"What have I told you? Don't burn your bridges."

"Yeah."

"What was her name?"

"Fantine."

"That's pretty."

"How're you and Michelle?"

"Married."

"Yeah?"

"Nah, I'm just kidding, we're good."

"You guys fight a lot?"

"Like gladiators."

"You guys fuck a lot?"

"… Like poets."

"I suppose they go hand in hand."

"I suppose," he said.

They call her "the city that never sleeps" due to the night life, the underground world, the 24/7 eateries. But I always thought of her differently. I never pictured the drugged-up club fiend probing to score, or the tireless writer, jabbing away at a laptop in their studio on the Lower East Side. No, instead I pictured the paranoid schizophrenic, the conspiracy theorist peeking out their window shade in a Queens basement full of automatic weapons, waiting, waiting for the signal of revolution, engulfed in the zeitgeist.

"You want a cigarette?"

"Michelle doesn't let me smoke."

"You just did blow off a Ukranian stripper."

"Are they menthol?"

"Fuck no."

"That's my little brother."

Sal took a drag and sat back on the stoop like he just finished fucking Marilyn Monroe.

"Ya know what, Joel?" he asked. "If you go to Paris, Amsterdam, Berlin, fuck it, *Russia*, and you love it, and you find a girl who… when she looks into your eyes, the world seems smaller…" He took another drag from the cigarette. "If you feel when she looks at you that each and every atom in each and every muscle latched onto your bones is shaking, simultaneously, to the beat of your heart, and… and… that if you step foot outside of her sphere of love that those muscles and those atoms will wilt and decay… and your heart will cease to pump not from exhaustion, but from apathy… well… then don't come home."

SALIM: SAVIOR OF ALGIERS

THE CALL TO PRAYER BURST OUT FROM THE Ketchaoua Mosque and slithered its way through the white-washed Casbah of old Algiers, waking Salim gently like his mother did when he was a child. The Casbah, which was once distinguishable on the Mediterranean coast, had been lost to the peddlers, the deranged, and the forgotten. The winding, romantic streets held fear when they used to hold mystery, and getting lost, once a blessing, was now a curse. What the old neighborhood did offer was cheap housing for students, which is where Salim made his home while attending university.

He rose from the thin mattress, glanced at the window that was so dirty the light barely trickled in through the filth, and unraveled his prayer rug. With his palms facing the heavens, arms bent at the elbow, he whispered his morning prayer to the rising sun.

Having missed the last three morning prayers after staying up late and studying for exams, Salim felt guilty. That day he would honor all five prayers. He needed it, his friends needed it, Algeria needed it.

Salim was tall and slim with almond eyes and a year-round tan complexion that Northern European tourists envied. For the first time in his life he had let his hair grow so long, it now curled around his eyebrows. When he would return home to Tebessa, his mother would say, "Salim, Salim, my boy I barely recognize, what has Algiers done to you?!"

BINGE UNTIL TRAGEDY

The "Unchained Generation" was the self-appointed nickname for the younger group of demonstrators, the North African millennials, who had been gaining momentum, pulling followers from the large cities, especially from the universities. Salim needed to be a part of it and wholeheartedly believed in their message of freedom of expression and fundamental human rights. He and his roommate Omar even started their own faction of University of Algiers students who named themselves *La Liberté* or *Al-Hurriya*—"freedom." They wrote this on their clothing and on their bandanas, they graffitied it on crackling walls and even made a Facebook page, which they used to communicate with students throughout the country.

Salim, like much of Algeria's youth, was fluent in French and Arabic and used them both regularly. Most of his classes were in French, and it was usually the language of choice amongst his friends. Because Salim was studying medicine at the university, he had an affinity for English, and wanted to learn enough to explore the UK—he wore his beat-up Newcastle United jersey every game day. For him, the dreariness of Northeast England's weather seemed like an exotic change from the persistent Mediterranean heat. Omar, however, preferred Arabic, and would change midway through a fluid conversation, which got on their friends' nerves and led to many arguments.

"This is the language of our people. Why should we use the tongue of our incarcerators?" he would say, to which Salim would point out that Berber would be the language of indigenous Algerians, and since it was still spoken by a quarter of the population, then why shouldn't they speak that?

"Arabic is the language of Islam, our people, the spoken word of God," he would contest. And when Omar began this banter, the group would scoff and continue on with their previous topic.

Omar had grown out his beard in the mustacheless style common amongst conservative Muslims, and the Amish. He wore his *taqiyah*, a white skullcap, whenever he left the apartment. He recited the Quran in the living room every day, oftentimes to Salim's protest, and denounced many of the US and UK programs that Salim watched on his laptop to strengthen his English. Three times a week,

Omar met with an imam at a small, neglected mosque, where he practiced his recitations and interpretations of the Quran. Omar had a deep-seated hatred for the "Godless Hannachi regime" and would refer to the president as the "Apostate."

Despite their differences, Omar and Salim had remained close friends since attending university, where Salim studied medicine and Omar, Islamic studies.

Omar was glad to hear that Salim had woken up early for prayer, and after he put away his own prayer rug, he waited in the kitchen, stirring his morning tea. He had barely slept that night because of the planned protest the next day. One more push for liberation. And with more police defecting to join the protestors, the movement seemed stronger than ever. But for each police officer who left the force, a soldier was put in their place. The military clashed with the police when it came to methods of suppression, and since the military was much more loyal to the regime than the police, they were given the unchecked authority to conduct themselves with force.

Hamza Hannachi had been in power for an unprecedented twenty-five years; his father, twenty; and his grandfather, a general during the war for independence, the first six years after defeating the French. Hannachi made no effort to fell any dictatorial stereotypes. He was known for having new concubines adorn him every night, many of them only girls. Rumors spread that he had a lustrous taste for virgins. His obsession with purity was well known throughout the country, and it is believed that after his concubines bled on him, he would make the other naked girls, those he had already deflowered, clean his body with warm water and goat's milk.

Although he only "served" in the military by title, Hannachi insisted on wearing full military regalia, complete with medals, a cap, and a shimmering sword. He had a fondness for all types of "toys"—tanks, jets, helicopters, RPGs, you name it, he's purchased it—from the French, from the Russians, from the Americans. The "Green Eagle," a self-appointed nickname, bought so many goodies for his military that it started to rival Egypt for the largest arsenal on the African continent.

The uprising to Hannachi's regime began when a carpet vendor set himself on fire in Martyr's Square, borrowing the tactic from Tunisian demonstrators. The disillusioned crowd rushed with buckets of water and carpets from the man's own shop to put out the flames, but all efforts were useless. His crisped corpse remained in the Square, legs folded, for an hour before it was taken away, enough time for pictures to be plastered all over the internet. A handwritten sign that stood a few feet away from the embers read: "Without freedom we are cattle. I will carry out my own slaughter."

After the self-immolation, the Hannachi regime put the country in an immediate state of emergency. This gave the military police full autonomy—if you demoralized the president, baton to the head; if you spit at an officer's feet, arm barred and thrown in a cell for "questioning." They responded to stones with rubber bullets, but to Hannachi's surprise, the people were relentless. The unexpected response confused the regime, which looked to Egypt for riot control tactics.

The Egyptian government responded to its own uprisings with direct military intervention and suppressed all demonstrations taking place in Cairo and Alexandria with force. But Algeria feared sanctions that would be detrimental to an already struggling economy. It was rumored that ex-military thugs were put in law enforcement positions, which flew right under the noses of the European human rights monitors. Although demonstrations were growing, the country was fixated on Martyr's Square, which became the epicenter of the movement. That is where Salim and Omar were headed after prayers and breakfast.

In the past few months, their numbers had increased tremendously, and much of the gains were because of their presence on Facebook. They made a group, with anonymous accounts of course, to organize and spread their message. Salim set up and ran the *La Liberté* Facebook group—Omar was removed as an administrator after Salim caught him denying Europeans and women from joining the group. Their message was clear: Overthrow of Hannachi, NO to military rule, NO to Islamic rule. (Omar wasn't completely supportive of the last prong). The hope was that their desire for liberty would strike a chord with followers on the other side of the Mediterranean, into the homes of France, Switzerland, and Belgium. The one-time colonizers would become the chain-breakers, if only the students could hang on and put enough pressure on the regime to make them slip up and do something costly. The "free world" would come with missiles, with troops, with magic wands, and dethrone the long-lived tyrant. The truth, which is never so bright, was that France and the rest of Europe didn't care all that much about this world. To them, it was the Arabs' world, and as long as the tourists were safe, the Islamists weren't in power, and the petroleum was flowing, Algeria remained a geopolitical debate instead of a humanitarian crisis.

The leader of France, President LaGrange, made a statement at the onset of the protests, urging Hannachi to "proceed with caution in all matters concerning the Algerian people." The "Green Eagle" snubbed his ally, responding in a nationally televised speech with bogus statistics about the growth of the Algerian economy. He added that the "Happiness Meter," a poll created by the regime in the early nineties, had never been higher. He ended his speech by lambasting LaGrange with more statistics, this time about the French people, and how they were one of the largest religiously apathetic countries in Europe, and that French neighborhoods were disgustingly segregated.

At the protest that followed, police beat a young man in the street and dragged him by his scalp. His offense? Giving the *bras d'honneur* to the line of police.

Then there was *La Peste*, Hannachi's secret police—the plague. Some were ex-military, others were thugs getting put to good use. They asked questions and monitored groups of students; they crept through alleyways and crashed into apartments, showing up unwanted and uninvited, like death itself. There was little doubt that during the protests *La Peste* were speckled throughout the angry crowds, taking pictures from cell phones, surreptitiously gathering information on possible threats to the regime. They would stare at you and take notes, but the moment you blinked, they would vanish.

The civilians of Algiers gathered in the streets that funneled into the square like arteries. Green-and-white national flags swayed gently in a breeze choked by the Casbah's narrow streets, the sun drenching their red crescent moons. Chants, constant and fervent, came from the rooftops, for much of life in Algiers was lived above the streets. The rooftop was an Algerian treasure. Salim and Omar trudged through the streets below, the buzz from the rooftops like calls to gladiators before entering the arena.

Once they reached the Square, they met with a group of friends from the university and shared a portion of naan and hummus, discussing what awaited them that dry afternoon. The General would speak to the crowd on behalf of the president—the coward couldn't even address his own people.

Salim had overheard a fellow medical student at a café telling a friend that after he was pulled aside by police during an earlier demonstration, he was taken to cells underneath the police station, had his wrists and ankles bound, and had to swear his "allegiance" to Hannachi. He was warned not to attend any further protests and to inform his friends what would happen if they continued to disrespect the regime. While saying this, he held out his wrists to display the bruising from the restraints.

Another student Salim recognized from university showed up to one of the cafés near campus in a makeshift sling and a fat lip, black eye, and ruby scrape on his calf. Salim prodded at the matter.

"What happened to you? Who did this? Come on man, speak!" The other café patrons stopped talking and turned toward the scene occurring at the counter. But the student just broke down in tears, paid for his coffee, and stumbled back into the faded bustle of the streets.

"You see!" Salim screamed. "This is what they do to us. We are the people, we are Algiers." And then he left, just in case *La Peste* was watching.

The demonstration grew; Martyr's Square was flooded with the sweat of the masses. The police looked on from a distance, like vultures circling wounded prey. They were dressed in full riot gear, many wielding batons and shields, some carrying guns loaded with rubber bullets—not lethal, but dreadfully painful.

For the middle-aged protestors, the onlooking police force was no new sight. In the late nineties, Algeria went through a wave of protests that began peacefully, with protestors carrying olive branches throughout the cities as a sign of peace, thus earning the nickname the Olive Protests. However, by the fourth month of the movement, there had been two car bombings outside of government buildings that left twenty-eight people dead and fifty more injured. The government blamed the bombings on Islamists and immediately shut down all further protests with force, in the name of national security.

The legitimacy of the movement had been usurped and jettisoned for the dreamers to collect and make whole once again. Detractors lamented that this time it would be no different, that although the cause was good and pure, the wicked would rise to fight the wicked once again, and it was the innocent who would suffer the most. But these lamentations were too few to be taken as policy. The supports were broken. You can only beat a dog so many times before it takes a chunk out of your hand. The regime had to fall, Hannachi had to fall—dead or alive.

The crowd, the men and women, the students, the children of the city vibrated with each devout shout. Some had tears in their eyes, tears of anger, tears from aviated dirt clusters of stampeding sandals that formed a tan film on sweaty brows. Salim and Omar were locked at the elbow with other members of *La Liberté*, their reflections bouncing off the riot shields of the police, who started to get overwhelmed by the surging masses. The police, leftover regime supporters and soldiers given new uniforms, stood their ground. One rock, one pebble, was all they needed to unleash chaos. The threshold of martial law whittled down to virtually perceptive threats, anything considered less than peaceful.

A burly officer, whose belly was testing the button capacity of his shirt, stepped out from the line of police with a megaphone, shouting at the crowd to back up, calm down, go home.

"We will never back down!" Omar shouted from the middle of the pack, which made those around him echo in solidarity. They screamed and screamed until their vocal chords were strained and there was a crackle in their inflections.

The officer repeated, "We are warning you. Back down. Go home. We don't want to hurt you."

"Hurt us? You're supposed to protect us, you're the police!" Salim shouted back.

A short, elderly woman in a green hijab traversed the crowd, handing out bottles of water to the dusty demonstrators. They called her *La Petite Mère*—the little mother. Known throughout the city for her unparalleled kindness and gatherings at her home, every day she would cook for hungry students whose own mothers lived far away, and in return, the students would help clean, plant, and crop in her overflowing rooftop garden. It was odd to see her at her full height—she still barely reached the chest of the other demonstrators—because she was always bent over a pot of tea or potted plant. During the demonstrations, she never screamed or said a negative thing about the regime. Instead, she bobbed around the crowd, tending to nicks on knees and bloody elbows.

She spoke with a notably Occitan accent instead of the typical Algerian-French of Algier's natives. Students who gathered in her apartment rarely spoke a word to *La Petite Mère*. They were too busy discussing—more so, arguing—over current events, trends, and classes. She would refill their tea or sing to herself in the garden. When they did ask for her opinion, sometimes in jest, knowing she carried no such opinion about a singer in London or new food craze in New York City that had overtaken the internet, she would respond with words of wisdom: "Love unconditionally, but first, finish your tea."

However, there was one occasion when Salim and a group of hungry medical students were with *La Petite Mère* unusually late at night, and perhaps it was the balmy air that whipped through the Casbah or the herbals of her famous tea, but the little mother sat with the students and told them about Jacques, her childhood sweetheart from Toulouse.

The students were enthralled the moment she left her garden to sit down with them, but when she mentioned a childhood love, their jaws dropped in astonishment. Not a single one of them spoke nor stirred their tea, just in case the clanking of silver on porcelain should shake her from the nostalgia.

Her story began with her as a young girl during the French occupation; she would help her parents sell spices in their tent at one of the largest bazaars in the city. Arabs, Berbers, French, Spaniards, and tourists would all come to this particular bazaar because of its location and quality.

When he approached the shop, she was the only person at the front; her father was in the back helping unload fresh sacks of jasmine, and her mother was home taking care of her new born brother. Jacques timed the encounter perfectly, making it appear to be chance, when in actuality, he had been scoping out the tent for the past week, making mental notes of when the brute would depart for deliveries. He couldn't get through a sentence without wiping sweat from his forehead; he wasn't dressed for the Algerian heat. Unlike many of her friends, she enjoyed practicing her French—it didn't hurt either that Jacques was the most beautiful boy she had ever seen.

He was coy, with a smile that somehow made his eyes a shade darker, and when he asked, "*Quel est votre parfum préféré, car il sera le mien aussi,*" she told him it was Scottish heather, without hesitation. He was surprised by the answer and asked her where it was that she had smelled heather, for it was not native to North Africa and not terribly popular anywhere else.

"I was walking past a café and a woman had it in a bag." All of a sudden becoming more aware of her accent, she spoke slower. "I suppose she was a tourist from Britain."

"Was she inviting?" he asked. "The English can be so crass."

"She was very kind and seemed lonely. She invited me to have tea with her."

"Did you join her?" he asked, leaning across the wood counter to appear genuinely interested in the story.

"I couldn't. I wanted to, but I couldn't. I had to return to the shop. I did ask her what it was that was in her bag, and 'heather' is what she told me." She paused. Jacques politely but awkwardly left a moment for her to finish the story. "… And there it is. That is why heather is my favorite scent."

"What a delightful story!" he erupted, throwing his arms into the air, forcing her to jump back in surprise. It didn't matter that his face was sweaty and red from the heat. It didn't matter that he was one of *them*, an offspring of the "invaders." She loved him, deeply, and right then and there, she knew he would be the single greatest thing to ever happen to her.

As time burned on, the two young lovers fell deeper and deeper into each other, meeting clandestinely in the nooks of the Casbah. They became disinterested in past pleasures and in school, and in the market she would think of him and only him, and what would be and what they would become. Her mother noticed her reading less and leaving more—leaving in the afternoon and before their evening tea—and that she would take food with her, but not just food for *her*, enough food for her and another.

They would find a spot and meet there, two, three, four days in a row before they were noticed by a shopkeeper or perhaps by someone who, God forbid, would alert her father and ruin all life and everything in existence like a swath of locusts on a naked field. She would tell him to dress down, to not wear such dashing clothing because he stood out... well... like a French lad in the Casbah. She would take dirt and rub it on his cheeks and forehead and tell him that his complexion just would not do—she giggled every time she stepped back to look at his dirtied face.

He told her, one night when they were sitting on a piece of unspoiled beach, that he wanted to take her back with him to France. He would show her the splendors of Paris and his hometown of Toulouse. She blushed at the thought of it and told him she had never left Algeria, that she had barely left Algiers.

He had lived in North Africa for the past four years, bouncing through Morocco, Algeria, and Tunisia with his mother and sisters, following his father's work. His father set them up in gorgeous villas on the Mediterranean coast in the gems of the Maghreb, and in fountain-filled mansions shaded by palm trees in Marrakech, but never, not once, did one of these surrogates feel like home. He missed his pink brick home in the heart of Toulouse and meeting with childhood friends in plazas and cafés to discuss whatever was worth their time discussing. But most of all, he missed the autumn and the way the trees sacrificed their beauty every year just to fill his world with shades of orange and red. So when he told her to come with him and leave Algiers, he meant it.

He was getting ready to attend a premier university on the European continent and promised her all of the magic of Paris or London or Rome. Surely his father would understand his love: it was true and it was pure and his father was quite the romantic himself, plucking his mother from a small village in Provence while she was still ripe and in her teens. His father had told Jacques that not even the greatest war on Earth could keep him from her. He had always admired his father's daring bravado. When Jacques would tell her these promises, his eyes would widen and he'd forget to blink; he would rise up, as if making a sweeping declaration, which she would then hush, without demeaning his enthusiasm, of course.

She was flattered by it all, but each time she had to tell him she could not leave. "Why don't you want to see Europe with me? There is more to life than Algiers."

She didn't take offense to his statements because she understood his frustration. He loved her and she knew it and she took solace in it, but she told him it didn't matter if she *wanted* to go with him. Of course she did. She wanted to see the world and look into his eyes in every great city it has to offer, but she couldn't leave her family. That was out of the question.

What neither of them knew was that Algeria was on the verge of extreme changes. France had ruled Algeria for over one hundred years, and with economic disparity ever growing between natives and Europeans, long-winded talks of revolution were beginning to take form. In the South, Saharan towns were already being run by self-appointed Algerians who neglected French-made law. The phenomenon was reaching the hearts of intellectuals and leaders in the big cities of the North, and since France had just suffered the abuses of World War II, the time to arm and strike was soon, while their colonizers were still recovering.

Jacques's father knew that North Africa was a tinderbox and had been in the process of having the family removed from Algiers. Jacques had heard his father talk about returning to Europe for the past couple of years, and regarded such statements as nothing more than wishful thinking. As soon as he would allude to taking the family to Paris or back to Toulouse, he would receive a job opportunity in another French colony that was just too damn lucrative to pass up.

His father believed that they still had at least a year before tensions became too strained to bear, and the family would need to relocate for safety. But in a surprise ruling that had been garnering attention for the past few months, a *pied-noir* who shot and killed an Arab on the beach was acquitted entirely. The judge found there was a lack of evidence, lack of a motive, no reliable witnesses, and that the defendant did not have a history of violence. The acquittal cast a schism between European and non-European peoples, which only amplified the calls for revolution.

On the night of the judgment, Arabs, Berbers, and black Africans marched in the streets in solidarity. French-owned businesses, the wealthiest businesses in the city, were targeted for destruction. Their front doors were smashed in, broken glass covered the sidewalks, blood from cut feet spattered throughout downtown. Police units responded with force—three more Algerians and a Malian were killed.

Jacques and his family stayed in their home with two armed officers stationed at their front gate. His father was pacing around the house like a mad scientist on the verge of his *Eureka!* moment.

"*Ceci est la limite!*" he would shout between incoherent muttering. "Those animals have done it. They want this country to burn? Well, I say let it burn then! We're leaving this godforsaken place immediately." Jacques knew his father would have their family out of the city by tomorrow and back in Europe by the weekend—he was serious this time. Jacques had to get her, in any way possible. He would throw money at her, make promises he wouldn't be able to keep, but he couldn't let her go.

His bedroom was located on the second floor of their three-story home. This wouldn't be the first time he left the house from the window, so when he dropped down from the ledge, he latched on to beams and protruding stones like a spider monkey. He dashed across the backyard and jumped over the fence, to his surprise, with ease. Usually when he attempted this part of the escape, he would bang his ankle or his shirt would get caught on the fence on the way down. But this time it was silky and smooth and he didn't even break pace, blasting across the street far enough away not to attract the attention of the guards outside the gate entrance.

He ran through the wide tree-lined streets of the rich neighborhoods approaching the borders of the Casbah, past pockets of angry natives who didn't pay him any attention, and across the boulevards where taxis buzzed methodically in both directions like bees back and forth from the hive. As he hit the bank of the Casbah, the little sunlight that had guided his sprint vanished, and he had to traverse the tiny, suffocating streets to the orange glow of lanterns.

He reached the front of the house and in his haste, realized he should not have stood so close, for their relationship had been hidden from the very beginning, and having a well-dressed French boy at the front door in the Casbah at this hour, on the day a French *pied noir* was exculpated of his ruthless crimes, would thicken all suspicions that her father already held. So he turned the corner and grabbed a handful of pebbles, scraping his knuckles on the ragged stone. He knew her bedroom was the top right window, and he could see through a hole in the wood a flickering candlelight barely surviving the zephyr. He launched the first pebble with reckless abandon; it smacked the wood of the windowpane and hit the ground with a *tisk tisk tisk*. He threw another and another until he was out of ammunition. He dropped to his knees and violently searched for more pebbles, until the front door opened and her father jutted his head out into the stuffy night in irritation. Jacques did a reactionary leap onto the cascading stairs like a frog out of water, and luckily remained hidden from the suspicious man. There he stayed, motionless, for the better part of a minute, waiting for a signal of safety. He was scraped and battered and bruised but he couldn't feel any of it, so he crawled to just below the top step and peeked up at the wood-paned window so only the top of his head and eyes were visible, like a crocodile. And he stared at the window and his eyes filled up with water, because if he blinked he was afraid it all would vanish like a dream.

There was movement behind the curtain, the window opened, and her dark flowing hair dropped farther than he had ever seen before. He jumped to his feet in excitement, but before he could call to her, she put her index finger in front of her mouth and glared down at him, not in an angry way, but in a way that showed him the seriousness of him being there right then. She closed the window and the light in the room went out. He waited. He knew she would come down, she had to, that could not be their goodbye. There couldn't *be* a goodbye. A few seconds turned into a few minutes, and then ten, fifteen, and he was getting cold and those scrapes and bumps and bruises were starting to come to fruition and it hurt to stand so he knelt; but it hurt to kneel too, so he sat on the ground, and that fire in his belly had turned down into a flickering ember. Then she appeared.

BINGE UNTIL TRAGEDY

From around the corner opposite where Jacques sat, she knelt beside him; he was confused at first because it was dark and her head was covered and he wasn't expecting her to come from around any corner but instead through the front door, which after a second of thinking about would be a rather silly thing to anticipate, given that he himself had climbed out of his bedroom window and jumped over a fence to reach her that night. And then she touched him right above the wrist and he knew it was her, he was certain about it, because the ember in his stomach had morphed into fluttering butterflies, bees, and dragonflies pushing up his throat. She grabbed his hand and they went down the stairs, around a corner, up a little hill, and into a nook that was usually the hangout of a group of football boys, but it was late and they were surely in bed.

"You shouldn't be out this late, my dear," she said, stumbling over the French because she was nervous. "It's very dangerous tonight."

"Listen to me," he said, looking over his shoulders like an escaped convict. "My father is going to make us leave Algiers tomorrow. You need to come with me."

She was confused but gathered from his tone that when he said "leave," he meant as in permanently, never coming back.

"I cannot go, Jacques, my dear, you already know this."

"Why not?!" he blurted and right then, gunshots rang out from not too far away.

"Quiet yourself," she said sternly. "I cannot leave my family and go to France with you. I live here. I am Algerian, not French, and if you leave I will miss you and would hope that one day I would see you again." A single tear ran down her cheek and when she said, "Now it's time to go before you get hurt," her voice cracked and she let go of his hand.

A string of gunshots broke the silence. He had so much more to say; he could offer her so much more than Algiers. But he didn't say anything more, and instead he kissed her. But it was dark so the kiss landed around her nose instead of on her top lip where he always kissed her. But maybe because of its significance or maybe because she was stern with him for the first time ever, this was his favorite kiss, and not just with her, but of all the kisses he had ever placed on young lips.

He said, "I love you deeply," and she nodded, but this whole time, since the moment he approached her at her family's spice stand, she knew he would hurt her and this love would end. But their time together had become more frequent and her feelings unending, so she let her guard down and for one brief, beautiful moment she believed, naively, that perhaps this wouldn't end. Her thoughts became selfish—or at least to her they were, because she had never felt this affection before, so she thought they were selfish—and during that brief, beautiful moment, she believed that Jacques would stay in Algiers and remain, unconditionally, forever hers.

The gunshots continued until dawn, and that night would become known as *La nuit du début*—the night of the beginning—because it was this night that "started" the Algerian War of Independence; and seven years, four months, two weeks, and four days later, Algeria won its independence from France.

He never visited Algiers again, never even crossed the Mediterranean back to Africa. He never wrote her, not once. He drafted a letter three days after reaching Toulouse, but never sent it. He drafted another in a drunken stupor two years after leaving, but passed out at his desk next to an open bottle of cognac. His fiancée found the letter when she found him, tore it to pieces, and sprinkled the bits of paper on top of him like snowflakes. He married in Paris, moved to London, and died in New York City in 1965, where he was hit by a taxi while illegally crossing Fulton Street in the early morning rush.

She never discovered how Jacques died, but then again, she never discovered how Jacques really lived. As the years passed, he became more of a fantasy than the reality he once was. He didn't leave her a photo, or a letter, or even a callow trinket to remember him by. Her family survived the war by leaving their home and finding refuge in the fortified city of Constantine with her aunt. She married a kind man who was also from Algiers, but he died of cholera five years later. They had two children—one lives in France, in Reims, where kings are made, and Champagne, too. The other, a boy, was stillborn.

She never said it out loud, she wouldn't dare, but she thought to herself that that boy wasn't meant for her husband, and when she hummed in the garden and when she sang while making tea, she was singing to her lost child, and to herself, she called him Jacques.

"Back up! Back up!" blared the megaphoned soldier. Shortly, the General would be making a public service announcement to the people, the first communication of any kind from any official in weeks.

The crowd inched its way closer to the platform and to the row of police standing between the speaker and the people. As the military-regaliaed man took the microphone, the jeers grew louder, forming a consistent hum of dissent.

"Please, my fellow Algerians, be still." The General was in his mid-forties, with dark features in every sense of the word. His brow was demanding and his chest protruded like it was chiseled from solid rock. He stood out, erect, fearless of a thrown stone or sniper bullet. "I ask you not as your general, but as a citizen, to go home and be with your families."

The General's words appeared sincere; he personified the father figure of the country. The president was scum and everybody knew it, but the General didn't have the same reputation of hedonistic extravagance. He was a family man, a religious man known for visiting the city's mosques and for meeting with French officials for coffee or tea.

"To the many students here today, are there not exams to study for?" he posed to the crowd.

But underneath the façade of paternity, the General was just as sadistic as the president. The Algerian prison system was notorious for being one of the worst in Africa. Very few people knew the military was actually behind the creation of interrogation techniques used by police, and the General, being the micromanager that he was, personally visited and advised the prisons of the country to note how his creations were being implemented. Breaking phalanges for "lying," wrapping electrical wire around toes for not cooperating, and if an officer had been assaulted (a term that should be used very broadly here, similar to what many would call "resisting arrest"), it wasn't uncommon for the interrogatee to have a broken jaw, nose, or eye socket.

"I speak to you today not as a soldier, but as a father, a brother, a fellow citizen. I implore you, my fellow countrymen, to return to your homes in peace. We do not want to hurt you."

Salim and Omar were in the dead center of the amorphous crowd. With each word the General spoke, Omar grew visibly more unnerved; Salim masked his frustration with more restraint.

"Listen to him spew that filth!" Omar directed to no one in particular. "I don't trust him and neither should any of you." Those in earshot started to turn toward him. A police captain pointed at him from the line, giving directions to nearby officers to keep an eye on *that one*. Salim, very aware of the escalation, wrapped his arm around Omar's shoulders in a fashion that resembled two varsity linebackers in the hallways of a high school. He wanted it to appear like he was calming his friend down, but his real intention was to hide him from on-looking authorities—the tactic was useless. Omar nudged off Salim's arm and continued with his rant.

"This pork-eater, this drunkard, would rather be dining in Paris than protecting his own people." The harsh throatiness of Omar's Arabic cut through the General's French, which seemed unnecessarily forced and formal. Salim continued to attempt to calm Omar down, but with each pat on the back, he became larger, his demeanor brooding as his shoulders broadened. He yelled and spit spattered the air. That unbecoming white crud accumulated in the pockets of his lips. Salim put a bottle of water in front of his face, but he pushed it away with more force than necessary, not realizing it was Salim holding the bottle.

The General had paused his speech and was giving orders to an officer to the side of the stage when an airborne shoe smashed into a folding chair that made a clacking sound like a gunshot. The officer talking with the General immediately jumped in front of his superior, acting as a human shield. The rows of police unsheathed their batons and lowered the visors on their riot gear helmets like knights before a joust. The General was red. He ripped the megaphone from the fat officer's hand and shouted in Arabic, which caused the megaphone to crack and emit an ear-splitting screech. He scolded the entire lot and demanded the perpetrator be arrested. The unarmed protestors grabbed each other, a natural reaction to impending violence, as the police beat their way through the crowd. Plain clothes officers on side streets who were waiting as reserves flooded into the Square and hit the protestors from all directions. They indiscriminately began plucking out young men from the crowd and tossing them into trucks. Their friends grabbed on to arms and legs, their bodies suspended in midair, being yanked by opposing forces like human magnets.

Salim saw that he and Omar would be easy targets. Breathing became difficult in the kicked-up dirt.

"Omar! Omar!" Salim yelled over screams of panic. The General continued to bellow from the stage, his voice bouncing off the buildings and surrounding the protestors like that of an omnipresent demigod. The entire group was getting pushed back, and Salim was ready to give up and move to a side street—hopefully Omar would do the same.

Just as he was clawing his way to a shop where he was friendly with the owner and would surely be given refuge, an elongated call cut through the crowd: "Saliiiiiiim!"

Omar had been pulling a classmate by the ankle as police pulled him by the arms, until Omar himself was being contorted by the officers and dragged to a truck. Salim rushed back and grabbed at his ankle, but slipped and tumbled to the dirt with his friend's sandal in his hand. Two officers had Omar by the shoulders, neutralizing the power of his arms. Salim rushed up from his knees, racing blindly toward his friend without the slightest idea of what he would accomplish when he got there, and as he reached out, close enough to get hit by the spit of Omar's screams, a baton cracked him across the face, and the screams silenced as it all went black.

THE SUMMER

THE TRIP WAS BOOKED: NEWARK INTERNATIONAL to Paris-Charles de Gaulle. From there we had rooms booked in Amsterdam and Berlin. The rest we'd decide as time caught up with us. My parents would be partially funding my trip, the big costs—plane tickets, hostels, trains, etc. The rest, that shit was on me. They felt some sort of guilt with Adam, I suppose. I don't think either of them had ever lost a friend at a young age and this was their way of supporting me. I heard it in their voices—every time the trip came up, Mom would lower hers to a comforting level and Dad would pat me on the back or some equally masculine gesture. He'd say, "Joel, go to Italy, you've got to go to Italy, I had a girlfriend from there once..." and this is when I'd remind him that I'd been there, spent the week off during study abroad traveling through the boot—Milan, Florence, Rome—did it, did it, did it, and it was lovely and such. "Yeah, but you've got to go down *south*. That's where your ancestors are from, you know that, right?"

How could I *not* know? We had a blown-up map of Calabria proudly framed in the kitchen, hanging below block lettering that read *In bocca al lupo*, an Italian idiom similar to our "break a leg." He'd point to it and say, "At least we're not Sicilians," in a nostalgic sort of way that made it seem like that shit really mattered.

My phone vibrated.

Text from Queen of Campus <3<3: 10:09 a.m.: Can't wait! I'll b over Wednesday morning. PARIS!!! <3<3<3.

BINGE UNTIL TRAGEDY

She was staying over the night before our flight, and Kev would meet us at the airport. Our flight was set for 11:35 a.m. We would land at 1:05 in the morning, then taxi from the airport to Marcel's place, where we had an apartment to ourselves for an entire week. He was more than welcoming about putting us up; his parents were on business trips in Africa—Gabon and Cameroon—so they would be gone until late June. I bought one-way and neglected all thoughts of post-travel life. At dinner, Mom said she didn't know what she'd do if I wasn't home for Uncle Tony's Fourth of July barbecue. She was nervous, the inflection of her voice belying the calm cutting of the braciole strings, but I didn't respond, didn't acknowledge it. Instead I buried my face in the penne, hoping the starch would gorge my conscience of a mother's guilt. I hated the guilt more than anything; Mom was raised Lutheran but she guilted me like a Jew.

Riley came early Wednesday morning. I was packed, found my passport in the sock drawer, and had already bought ten Hayman's whiskey airplane bottles for the flight—Kev was bringing ten of his own. We went to Starbucks because we're sell-outs, and Riley got a vanilla soy latte and I got a double espresso. When the barista asked for my name, I told him it was Jackson—he rolled his eyes.

"*Jackson?*" Riley asked.

"Yeah," I said. "Today I'm Jackson."

"Why? What?"

"I give a different name to the same barista every time. Sometimes it's Xerxes, sometimes it's Dan."

"Oh my god, you're still doing that?"

"It keeps me off the grid."

"You're so weird."

We discussed the trip, which led Riley to sharing every single list and every single article about "Arbitrary # of things to do in City Name" she could get off the Buzz. Despite Riley's family wealth, she had never been to Europe. They took trips, but those were limited to fruity-drink-resort-where-brown-people-serve-you type of island vacations. This way her mom could expedite the leathering process of her skin and her father could drink morbidly without being judged by their neighbors or live-in maid.

"You excited to see Marcel?" I asked, cutting her off from finishing a list on "19 *Poffertjes* you NEED to try in Amsterdam before you Diiie!"

"Well… yeah… of course." I didn't say anything and waited to see where she would take the conversation. It's amazing what people will say when they're overwhelmed by silence. "I mean… no… yeah… like… why wouldn't I be? I mean I am, but not like *that*. Of course I am. I haven't seen him in forever. Aren't you? I'm not going to fuck him if that's what you mean…" She was spinning her coffee cup in circles so the sloppily written *Riley* would face me every four rotations. "I couldn't, it would mess everything up. I couldn't, ya know? I couldn't." She looked up at me from the coffee cup for some sign of understanding.

I raised my eyebrows and said, "I suppose we'll see."

"Yeah, I guess."

The sun broke through a cloud and blanketed the coffee shop with light. She turned to me and away from the giant window that faced Main Street; her eyes sparkled as if they were filled with pixie dust.

"Hey, what color are your eyes?" I asked, surprised I didn't know already.

"Oh my god! How adorable, look at the little pickle!" she shrieked, forgetting to answer my question.

A tangly-haired brunette with oversized sunglasses carried her rat in her arms with the leash dangling, smacking against her knee with every step. The thing had all its hair shaved except for a lion's mane around the head and the hair around the ankles that made it look like it was wearing boots.

"Ew, you like that thing?" I said.

"Um, you don't? Ugh, he's so cute, I want it."

"I've taken dumps bigger than that thing."

"Gross, Joel!" And when she said this, she smacked my arm and gave the "Riley cackle." I named her laugh because it made her sound like a giddy wicked witch. But in all honesty, her laugh was more than just a dramatic guffaw; it was my first memory of her—I heard it from across the sticky hallway of an otherwise unmemorable fraternity party in August of my freshman year. It drew me toward her, if for no other reason than to discover what on earth could possibly make a human being emit such a noise. It was tantalizing, alluring, and kind of annoying; it captured my interest and has yet to let it go.

Something told me to go to the window. Not a voice, not actual words, but a feeling, an impulse. Out in the yard, a brown-suited man stood with a briefcase, not moving. I squinted to get a better look—he didn't have a face. I tapped on the glass: nothing. I waved to him: nothing. I turned around and Adam was standing in the doorway, soaking wet. He told me to follow him. A gust of wind knocked me down. I scrambled to my feet, but Adam had already taken off; he darted down the hallway and rounded the corner. I followed. His laugh was growing fainter. I was in a full sprint, my feet barely touching the floor, and as I passed the living room, I glimpsed a boneless body draped over a cushioned chair, the skin melting under the ottoman.

I turned the corner and could see him in the distance; he wasn't too far. *I can reach him.* The walls shot up into the air like emerging skyscrapers and from them, flowers bloomed, but just as quickly as they grew and bloomed, they died and withered. Their petals fell to the floor and I slipped on them and tried to regain my footing. The flowers were screaming as they died, high-pitched blood-curdling screams. The snapdragons were the loudest, the tulips were shy, and the roses were too proud—all of them, all of the roses were proud—the pink ones, white ones, yellow ones, purple ones, and of course, the red; red roses died with courage, they set themselves on fire and fell around me. It rained fire, fire and glass. I heard thunder crack but didn't see lightning. I saw Adam in the distance; he wasn't too far. *I can reach him.* I got closer. A gust of wind knocked me down and then another and another, but I scrambled to my feet. It became harder to breathe; it was humid and I was sweating and my sweat pooled and I had to swim into the sea of sweat—I dove in, the salt burning my eyes, but I kept going. *I won't stop. He isn't too far, I can reach him.* I looked up and the sky was gone, the fire-rain had stopped, and if I didn't wake up, I'd suffocate. The pops and cracks weren't thunder; I was mistaken. They sounded like conjoining bones, tendons, and muscles forming above me. I looked up and Adam was standing on the island, out of reach. The liquid was thick blood. The metallic taste coated the inside of my jowls. I yelled to him, frantically waving my arms—he waved back.

"I'm sorry," I said, right before drowning.

"But it wasn't your fault," he whispered, as if he was swimming right beside me. I woke up.

My parents dropped us off at the airport. Terminal C, direct flight on United. A hard finger tapped my shoulder and I turned around, anticipating one of those guys who hurry people up on the drop-off line, telling me to, well, hurry up, but it was Kev flashing his doofy, wide-eyed smile. Dad couldn't get out of the car, so he reached across my mother and gripped my hand with unassuming strength, the kind of strength you get after years of being a father—dad strength—and he looked me dead in the eyes and said, "Italy." Mom was tearing up, and although I had seen her cry on a regular basis, practically every day after school growing up when she'd be deep into her second glass of Pinot Noir and watching *The Light of Our Lives,* it always got to me. I started taking the long way home with Adam. She told me to be safe, to be smart, and to remember that I'm still her little boy and that she will worry about me every day because "that's just what moms do."

We said goodbye to our parents. Riley had her mom on video chat from her phone and Mr. Caligan got out of his car to greet my dad—no one bothered them to hurry up, they looked like they could move mountains—and the three of us headed to security. Kev and I threw our bags of whiskey minis into the provided bins while the overweight ground crew member asked if I had any of the prohibited items on "my person," which was an unusual thing to say for someone who, moments before, referred to the full-body scanner as "the swirl thingy." I stood in the full-body scanner, hands above my head, imagining this was a time machine and where I would go; where would you go? Past or future?

I like to believe I would go backward; history had always interested me and I had a question that needed answering—how *really* racist were the Founding Fathers? What made Hitler—the ultimate nature vs. nurture debate. Jesus? What if what you found wasn't at all pleasing or insightful? Would it ruin the present because we are molded, through education and social activity, to uphold the ideals created by men, real, actual, men who existed? But what if these men didn't actually live or were real, but were real-life motherfuckers, or what if the motherfuckers weren't as dreadful as they had been perceived? I should note here that when I say "men" I am using the word to represent humanity, human beings, not so much those with a shaft and balls. Like, what if George Washington personally whipped his slaves and he fuckin' smiled when he did it and got a rush from the dripping blood that resembled the legs of a full-bodied red wine dripping down the side of a crystal glass. Or what if you went back to Rome during the time of a prepubescent Caligula, who after all, won the hearts of the Romans by being such a darn cute little kid, and he was kind to animals and other children and would say things like "Hand me my sWord, Uncle Germanicus," placing emphasis intentionally on the "W," making it all the more adorable. But this is Caligula, the poster-child (no pun intended) of evil, the harbinger of nightmares, the one who would declare himself a different god on a different day and order the beheadings of statues of the chosen god to have them replaced with a marble sculpture of his own—not to mention the beheadings of his subjects, regularly, for no sufficient reason besides boredom. But sword is *gladius* in Latin, so that doesn't really work… but you're getting the picture, right?

And what about forward to the future? No thank you. You've read the books, and if you haven't, you've seen the movies—the future will SUCK. We're talking Orwellian America here, people: cameras in every room of your house, microchip implanting, brain-wave monitoring, so hard on "the grid" it hurts, can't take a shit without the government analyzing your wiping habits (this one's back-to-front, keep an eye on him) United States "Land of the Surveyed, Home of the Enslaved," where 2+2=5 and any deviation from politically correct Newspeak will lead you straight to a Joycamp—better go check that tweet from 2012. You laugh now at those people who have manmade bunkers under their backyards somewhere in a rust-belt suburb, packed with food rations and semi-automatic weapons. But trust me, those hicks will have the last laugh, because with what this country is in for, that shitty, gritty bunker will look like a glimmering Valhalla.

My arms were still raised above my head as the fat TSA agent lined the inside of my belt with his sausage-link fingers. Ever since that foiled plot in 2000, the one where some cavemen were going to fly planes into the World Trade Center in the name of God, airport security had become brutally thorough at the expense of self-respect and dirty socks on the airport floor. Riley already had her shoes back on and was waiting by the electronic gate table while Kev had to go through the "time machine" again because he forgot to empty the loose change from his pocket and was wearing a titanium watch.

Everyone hurried when it came their time to undress and shove their belongings into the sliding trays. Nowhere else in the world will you see so many people from so many different cultures come together to be pissed off than in the security line at a major metropolitan airport. I liked to call it "silent infuriation." After I was finished being sexually accosted and after Kev managed to make it through security without setting off the metal detector, we searched for our gate and waited to board.

Large flat-screen high-definition televisions lined the expansive hallways of Newark Liberty Airport. They all played the same news reel with the stone-cold blond from the taxi TV reading from her teleprompter. CHAOS IN THE MIDDLE EAST lined the bottom of the screen while a montage of destruction flashed before apathetic travelers. Syrian protestors getting shot with tear gas, Iraqi Shias clashing with Iraqi Sunni "police," the Algerian military crushing protestors with batons and dragging unconscious students through the dirty public square.

BINGE UNTIL TRAGEDY

I stopped to watch the carnage at every television we passed; Kev and Riley got fed up and continued to the gate without me, but I couldn't help it: I was enamored with the brutality, not in a sadistic kind of way, more so in the purity of it all. It's political perfection, the good guys (students and workers pushing for political reform toward liberal democracies) vs. the bad guys (military dictators who carried themselves as demigods). This was the real deal, the grassroots shit; this wasn't whiny Vassar students having a sit-in because they disapprove of the American flag being flown on their campus. Students in Damascus and Algiers were taking batons to the chops just because they showed up, and I admired that.

We didn't say much at first while we sat at the gate. We were all amazed that it was happening—what started off as a drunken promise was actually taking shape. I put my bag under my legs to simulate a recliner-like function and cracked open my fresh copy of *On the Road* by Jack Kerouac. Ya know, that book where he goes back and forth across the country like twelve times, gets sick in Mexico, and writes the whole story on a single typewriter scroll fueled by coffee and Benzedrine. Kerouac, man, he was something. The balls he must've had to hop in a car and just go with it, ride to wherever the fuck it was. This was the forties, remember; there was no GPS or smartphones or Twitter and Facebook or the internet, not any of that shit. He and Dean Moriarity and that girl, Marylou, (well, those weren't their real names), the one who jerked them both off at the same time in the front bench seat of an old Ford, they got in the car, scrapped for whatever coinage they could scrounge, and hit the road—see ya in Denver, Des Moines, New Orleans, San Fran. Made me feel like such a pussy. Kev was wearing $300 headphones, Riley was reading a book on a Kindle, and I need a GPS to get to my cousin's house in Montclair.

"Whatcha readin', Riles?"

"I'm not telling you," she said, trying to hide a smile. "You're going to give me shit for it."

"Come on, tell me. Kev, what's she reading?" Kev was deep in the new Colossus album (a pioneer in South African trap music) and didn't hear me.

"Does it have a sweaty shirtless hunk on the cover?"

"Nope," she said.

"Does it have two white people *almost* kissing?"

"Nope."

"Is it about a fierce, possibly lesbian protagonist who is going through an early twenties life crisis and just *can't even* seem to find her fit in this cruel world of ours?"

"Not at all! Where do you get this shit?"

"I'm going to keep bothering you until you tell me."

She smirked.

"Wait, don't tell me. No *way*. It's that sex book, isn't it? The one where the girl gets off by getting her ass beat by some rich dude?"

She laughed and remained defiant in her choice.

"That isn't literature, it's porn! How come you can read that in public, but if I were to load a pornacopia.com video on my phone right now, I'd be escorted straight to the no-fly list"?

"It's actually really good," she said, curling her legs up onto the seat and tucking her Kindle tight.

"Ya know, if that was some average schmuck in a split-level from like, Piscataway or something, it'd be a horror story." She ignored me. "I thought you were above that, Riles."

"I want to get *under* that, if ya know what I mean."

"Well done. Well done."

The gatekeeper announced: "All Gold members only can begin boarding at this time, thank you."

Immediately, more than half of those seated at the gate stood and weaseled their way to the boarding area, forming a line of fabricated uncertainty. They knew they weren't Gold members, so they stood in a serpentine part line, part hodgepodge clusterfuck assemblage. This made the rest of us anxious, because if we didn't stand fifteen minutes early like they did, we'd get seated last, have to check our carry-ons, lose our seats, miss our flight. So we joined the amorphous gathering, checking our folded printed-out boarding passes with each row announcement, because apparently, the three of us have the memories of goldfish.

BINGE UNTIL TRAGEDY

An obnoxiously persistent little man continued to roll his bag to the front of the, well, whatever the fuck we're calling this gathering, bumping into ankles and the heels of boots. He didn't care that they were calling for rows 29 to 20 and he was seated in 11C. He needed to board the plane first, because if he did, he'd get there faster and his life was more important than ours, I suppose.

As I waited, I did what everyone else does: I picked out all of those I hoped I wouldn't be sitting next to. Here's the breakdown: people who look smelly; any guys in knit caps during the summer; women who look like they have more pubic hair than I do; anyone with dreadlocks; the kid who's been taking up three seats at the gate sleeping and snoring and will probably be doing the same on the plane; any fat people; the girl whose music is too loud; the crier; the singer; the salesman; the businessman who didn't shower after his afternoon with a call girl; the six-member family coming back from a vacation and the parents have given up on controlling the kids, on trying to be happy, and on God himself; the Jesus freak; the human rights activist; the lesbian human rights activist; anyone from the Midwest (Pittsburgh is my cutoff); the Australian surfer; Australians in general; the NYU study abroad student who only wants to speak in their rudimentary Italian and asks the flight attendants if they have any "international newspapers"; the flamboyant gay guy, not because I think he's gonna hit on me or anything, but because he's going to judge my sense of style and snicker when I eat the in-flight meal; Texans (see: fat people); anyone from anywhere who eats curry on a daily basis; the body-builder; the girl who's scared of flying; the guy with too many nose hairs; the creepy existentialist; the morbid pessimist; the giddy optimist; the puker; the lady who checked her cat; the wannabe guitarist; the uncomfortably open atheist; the cowboy; the Cowboys fan; the sick man; or the self-entitled housewife. You don't do this before a flight?

Kev and I were sitting next to each other, with Riley a few rows back. It's him and me and this guy who looked Greek or Syrian or Armenian or something fun like that. He was actually seated between us, but was more than happy to switch to the aisle seat so Kev was in the middle and I was at the window. We each snapped open our Hayman's nips and Kev offered one to our new friend. He politely declined, but I knew in some cultures it's customary to decline anything from a stranger at first, even if you really want the item, so I leaned across Kev and gave an assertive "You sure? Please take one, take one." He declined again and grabbed the *Sky Mall* magazine from the pouch of the seat in front of him and pretended to be enthralled by the glow-in-the-dark toilet seat.

The flight attendants patrolled the aisle, moving oversized bags under seats and telling passengers to "please turn off your phone, thank you." You could hear it every few rows, getting louder as they approached us. I shot Fantine a quick message—**À bientôt madamoiselle**—before the attendant reached our row. Her words dissipated as she passed, but I counted sixteen more times "please turn off your phone, thank you" before they went over safety precautions.

I probably should've touched up my French beforehand. Mom and I tried to use it around the house in everyday conversation. She studied it for years and it had always been one of our little things that she didn't have with either of my brothers nor my father. We usually exchanged a greeting or conversed for a sentence or two before reverting back to English. My dad thinks French is for sissies and considers it a throaty aberration of Italian. He's never said it, but he was disappointed when I decided on France over Italy; we barely spoke during my semester in Nice.

We hit the runway and our friend muttered to himself in a language I couldn't place. Kev looked dead ahead and was surprisingly nervous about the flight, which explained why he suggested the superfluous amount of booze. I assumed Riley was okay; she flew somewhere with her family every winter break and spent her summers in California, Cabo, or St. Croix. She was probably deep in a crop-whip chapter of her "book." I've used one of those before, the crop-whip; it was underwhelming at best. She was a junior and liked to get beat up, the dyed black hair, all black clothing faux-Satanist total stereotype, and she insisted that I welt her ass and *then* insisted that I take pictures on her phone. I never asked what she wanted with them, but the girl was deep-fried crazy with a side of daddy issues, so I'm sure they didn't go unappreciated.

The monster roared down the runway. My eyes were trying to count the various airline logos displayed on the fins as we sped by: *Delta, JetBlue, British Airways,*

BINGE UNTIL TRAGEDY

Open Skies, TAP Portugal, US Airways, Lufthansa, shit, what was that one? Virgin Atlantic, Air Canada, fuck, missed another, Southwest, United, Aer Lingus—ending on my personal favorite. And there it was, the rush, the butterflies beating their wings against my pink innards, the rush I had been missing and attempting to duplicate, no, replicate with drugs and liquor and loose women. I felt the roaring of the engine and sat back in my seat with a cheesy smile plastered across my jaw. I was going back to Europe; I was going back to the land of Charlemagne.

PARIS AND THE HEDONIST'S HILL: LIFE ON THE MONTMARTRE

WE DESCENDED INTO THE EVER-EXPANDING Parisian lights, our plane landing with a thud that caused my stomach to pop and my heart to skip a beat. I was drunk and my mouth was dry to the point where my tongue did little to heal my cracked lips. My throat was itchy because I fell asleep with my mouth open like a Venus flytrap. The cab took us as close to Marcel's apartment as physically possible, but the dwelling is located toward the top of a typical Montmartre hill with the corrugated shelf-like feature and arduous flight of steps crackling down the hummock's spine. The cream-white shops and blocky homes glowed orange in the flickering light from lanterns. It was past one a.m., but Marcel still greeted us from his balcony, with a glass of wine in hand.

"*Bienvenue à Paris!*" he shouted, raising the glass above his head, drops of red wine plopping onto the cobblestone below. I looked down the steep steps, past the trees and miniature garden plots, the streetlamps providing the only light besides the lit cigarettes that illuminated and disappeared like lightning bugs on a summer's night.

BINGE UNTIL TRAGEDY

Marcel buzzed us up and handed each of us a fat glass of wine as we walked through the front door. He assured us that "this isn't that shit we drank from the box at school."

The apartment was modern with an international flair; dispersed throughout the place were statuettes, carvings, and masks from Africa. A pair of crossed swords was attached to the wall above a seldom-used fireplace. Framed pictures of geometric designs shouted in prolific purples, indigos, pinks, and turquoises, with Arabic script lining the edges. A dramatic mural took up a large portion of a solid white wall; in it, a man lay lifeless in a bathtub, his head and arm leaning off the edge, and a mourner in red robes sat by the deceased man's side and covered his own face as four onlookers stood idle. The mural's title: *The Death of Seneca*.

"My father loves that painting," said Marcel, snapping me to attention. "He says Nero ordered Seneca, that old man, to take his own life after he was the blame for… *conspirer* in a failed attempt of assassination. Seneca… how would you say… stoic… stoically cut his own veins, hoping to bleed to death. He drank poison too and was put in a tub with hot water to increase the bleeding. And after all that *auto*-mutilation, it is recorded that he died a slow and painful death, but remained stoic with every drop of blood. My father says that *stoïcisme* is something lost with my, with our, generation."

"I know who Seneca is," I said, looking back at the shriveling bloodless man.

"Well, now I don't want this wine…" said Riley. "What's the WiFi password?"

The painting had been addressed, and Marcel was eager to hear what we had researched about Paris and what we planned to do in his home city.

"But why celebrate suicide?" I said, which caused Marcel to turn back in surprise.

"Celebrate?" He put his wine down on a glass table. "Should we… how would you say… *diffamer*, instead?"

"Like… vilify? Of course not."

"Then what should we do when a man is made to take his own life in the most *macabre* of ways, Joel?"

Kev and Riley watched like spectators at a UFC fight.

"Mourn," I said, hoping he'd get the message. His intentions were anything but malicious, and he could have made me feel like a real jerk, but he didn't do that. Marcel was cool and humble in ways we weren't accustomed to in college. Riley broke the scene by asking for the vintage of the *Côtes du Rhône*.

He grabbed his glass of wine from the table and showed us to his sister's room. She was off completing her journalism thesis on the role of women in three distinct Muslim majority cities: Fez, Istanbul, and Tehran. The room had one queen-size bed. There was also a couch in the living room. "You guys can fight it out," he said, leaving the room so we could drop off our bags and set up our spots for the week. I immediately began to take over the desk, unpacking my toiletries and unraveling my towel. I had shared a bed with both Riley and Kev on numerous occasions in college, drunk and sober, so I had no qualms about doing it again.

I plopped onto the bed, which was half covered in white lace pillows, and put my arms behind my head. I figured Riley would eventually be sleeping in Marcel's room, probably by tonight if we popped open another bottle of the ruby elixir, so I made a "come hither" gesture toward Kev and said, "Why don't you join me, big boy."

"Wait, why do you guys get the bed?" she asked, sincerely.

"Oh, please. If we weren't here your pants would've been off so fast they would've put a hole in the floor."

"What? No…"

"Come on, Riley. You get to Paris and you're the same smitten co-ed who met him junior year."

"We'll see," she said.

"Exactly. Till then, Kev and I will share the bed, unless"—I winked at Kev—"you want to join us?"

"No way!" she laughed and threw her Paris guidebook at us.

"Are you not familiar with the *ménage à trois*?"

"… I'll take the couch."

"We *are* in France!" I yelled as she left the room.

As predicted, we opened more wine and Riley spent the night with Marcel. Kev and I stayed up smoking cigarettes on the tiny balcony that looked out on the fabled *arrondissement*.

"Crazy it's over, ya know?" said Kev.

I blew out the smoke from my last drag before I responded, "It's crazier that we're in fucking Paris right now."

"With Marcel," he added. "Never thought I'd see that dude again."

"Fuckin' Riley tells me two days ago she *isn't* going to fuck him. We got here three hours ago."

"Probably a record for quickest bang by an American."

"I don't know, this is Paris and he *is* a Frenchman."

"Sorta," he said.

"What do you mean?"

"Well, his parents aren't from here."

"Yeah, but he is. Marcel is French as shit. Just because he's black doesn't make him any less French. They don't all wear berets and sport silly mustaches."

"No, I know, but…"

"And your dad isn't from the States. Does that mean you aren't as American as I am?"

"Yeah, but…"

"Marcel is French. I know he likes to portray that Pan-Africa nonsense, but he's European. Fuck, Africa is the most diverse continent on the planet, but in the States and Europe, they all get lumped together."

"I saw *Hotel Rwanda* too, man…"

"Like, a guy from Senegal and a guy from Mozambique have very little, if anything, in common. But we just call them 'African.' But God forbid you confuse a Serb and a Croat."

"Have some more wine, Joel."

"We're out."

"Marcel said we can open anything from the first two rows in the cabinet."

"Oh? What do you want then?"

"I don't know dick about wine. Give me something that will get my clothes off."

My mouth was dried out from the tannic wine. I checked the fridge and grabbed two Kronenbourgs. There was an unnatural stillness in the apartment; the pristine countertops and tables, stools, and chairs all had ninety-degree edges that clashed with the curvatures of the African and Arab statuettes. I handed Kev one of the beers and he attempted to claw off the cap, grinding the soft web of skin between his index finger and thumb.

"Motherfucker!" he yelled in agony, grabbing at his wrist.

"Oh yeah, most non-American beers aren't twist-offs."

He held the bottle at a slight angle, leaned against the railing of the balcony, and smashed down on it with a closed fist. The cap ricocheted off the metal, then the balcony, and then hit the ground with a few modest *pings*.

"Don't do that, man. This isn't college."

"Thanks for reminding me." He took a swig of the beer, which sloshed around in his mouth. I watched as he let it sit in his gums and cheeks. He analyzed the bottle like it was the product of a recently completed scientific experiment and swallowed the mouthful. "This is French?" he asked.

"Yup."

"It sounds German, Kro-nen-bourg," he said with a stereotypical German accent.

"It's made in Alsace."

"Where's that?"

"Near Germany."

"Well, there ya go."

"This is all I drank when I studied here. Well, this and wine."

"Oh, true, you gonna hit up that girl, the one you…"

"Fantine? Yeah, I did before we left. She hasn't answered yet."

"We *did* get here super late."

"Right."

"She live here?"

"She does. She moved here from Nice shortly after I left."

"Nice looks great. I remember stalking your pics on Facebook every time you put new ones up."

"It was the best four months of my life."

The familiar sound of my vibrating phone woke me from a sweaty slumber. The neighborhood was bustling with Sunday brunchers and colorful street artists, men walking their dogs, and girls in oversized sunglasses texting as they struggled with the steep, cascading Montmartre steps. Through the open door I could see Marcel and Riley already up and contorted on the couch, their legs intertwined like vines, her head rested on his shoulder. Two spilled espressos clanked on the coffee table as they half attempted to hush their laughter so Kev and I could get some sleep. I checked my phone. It was Fantine—**The Riviera Queen**. She texted me from a messaging app I hadn't used since studying abroad: **Bonjour Joel. Welcome back.** I read it over three times and felt the weight of uncertainty lift from my chest, transform into a fiery mirth, and swan-dive into my pit. She sent two more: I **wish to see you soon. Which hostel are you staying?**

I scrambled to text her back.

Text to The Riviera Queen: 9:31 a.m.: Bonjour mon amour, I am staying with a friend. I am in the Montmartre.

I stared at the phone. The screen said the text had been **received**, but not yet **read**. Kev rolled over and his hand gracefully stroked my back. I jumped from the bed, tangled in the white sheet, and stepped on a renegade shoe, tumbled forward, and crashed to the floor. I could hear jeers from the two reunited lovers: "What're you guys doin' in there? Should we leave?!" yelled Riley from the couch.

I was still holding my phone as I lay tangled on the floor. I checked it: still the text had been received, but not yet read. Of course Marcel had a French press. The aroma alone made my testicles swell. As I looped my belt, I noticed that the giggling had stopped. I threw on a wrinkled t-shirt that was hanging out of my bag and went into the living room. Marcel had the television on and turned up to an uncomfortable level. Riley was off his shoulder and sitting upright with her arms wrapped around her knees.

The newscast showed clips of shattered buildings with missing walls and electrical wires dangling from the rubble like headless snakes. The headline read: "Missile Attack Leaves Children's Hospital in Ruin." Marcel was up and pacing around the room, swearing fervently in a trilingual firestorm of French, Arabic, and English. "*Ya ibn asharmoota!*" (You son of a whore.) "*Va te faire enculer!*" (go fuck yourself.) He was really heating up. "*Nique ta* mère*!*" (fuck your mother) "*Kul khara!*" (Eat shit—one of my personal favorites.) "Motherfucking bastards, I'll murder your fucking families!" No translation necessary.

Riley's ephemeral expression of fear transformed into one of penetrating attractiveness as she realized the cynosure of her appeal in Marcel, and to a greater extent, the appeal of men. The passionate yelling; the ardent support for sports teams, political movements, and in Marcel's case, justice; veins bulging from tight-skinned foreheads; and necks pushing up stubbled growth put in her in that natural salacious state of desire everyone deserves to feel at least once in their early twenties.

The footage was grotesque. Government forces had rocketed the building, believing it was holding militant protestors who had been charged with assaulting police officers during a rally. The shots were grainy and recorded from cell phones, which were subsequently uploaded to YouTube. Disfigured little bodies were strewn across debris-filled rooms while men screamed incoherently, tossing pieces of fallen cement through the dust-filled air. Their faces were perfect horror, the kind of shit directors try to pry out of their teenage slasher-film actors.

A new heading swept across the screen: "*Guerre Civil.*" Syria was falling into complete chaos without a safety net. Western human rights monitors interviewed doctors from the hospital and fathers of dead children. Some spoke broken English or French, while others, too distraught to function, screamed and cried in muddled Arabic, waving their fists toward the sky, begging for answers to the suffering.

BINGE UNTIL TRAGEDY

A doctor with thin-framed glasses sat on a block of cement that previously served as the base to the west wall of the hospital. His dark complexion peeked through the white soot that covered his face and arms, and he sat uninterested in the debris that was falling from the exposed slanting floors. He lit a cigarette—not a hand-rolled cigarette, but a prerolled cigarette with the burnt-orange base and filter—and as a reporter from the London-based Human Rights Monitor asked him questions about the "events that unfolded here today," he kept his head down and responded, "We will not forgive them," in perfect English.

"Watch, you will see. They will do the same shit in Algeria and Tunisia, Libya, and Egypt, and everywhere," Marcel asserted. "And if the Sudanese march in the street, they'll kill them too. Children, fucking children. It is the fascist pigs who kill and do not show remorse in the killing. They kill you and you and you..." As he said this, he pointed to Riley, Kev, and me. "These people do not have voices, they are smothered in blood and ash." And when he said "ash," his voice cracked ever so slightly, as if he were about to cry. "*Les enfants sont morts.*" He repeated *Les enfants sont mort* as he sat on the couch with his face in his palms.

Riley hugged him ferociously and whispered in his ear. Kev looked at the floor. I poured myself a cup of coffee: black, extra sugar. I checked my phone; the message had been **received** but not yet **read**. We had plans to wander the Montmartre and make it up to the Sacré-Cœur, which sat high on the martyr's hill, offering smog-filled views of romantic Paris. We then had a gratuitous traditional French lunch planned, where we'd sip wine by the Seine before returning to the apartment to nap, rest, and dress for the night. But Marcel, our local and de facto guide, had yet to lift his face from his hands.

I grabbed the remote to change the channel. Kev and Riley watched me, neither giving me nods of approval nor stares of caution. I clicked up one channel, which was showing highlights of last night's soccer match between Paris Saint-Germain and Lille—it ended in a scoreless tie. Marcel didn't budge. Kev stood by the door and the three of us sat in silence for five minutes before he gathered himself and suggested we start the drinking part of the day earlier than planned. We all concurred and each had a glass of *Mâcon-Villages* while we got dressed.

Although it wasn't the high season, tourists packed the main streets with thick camera bands slung around their necks, ogling redundant souvenir shops and slabs of apartment buildings. As Marcel put it: "In Paris, the high season, it never subsides." I wasn't able to check my phone unless we stopped at a restaurant or café that offered free WiFi, but I carried it with me anyway to use as my camera and to check the time. In Europe they use the twenty-four-hour clock, a.k.a. military time, for most lists and schedules, which used to confuse me when I first came to France last spring. They teach you that it's quite easy, just add an hour after 12, so 1:00 p.m. = 13:00, 4:00 p.m. = 16:00, and so on—but after five Kronenbourgs, a bottle of Merlot, and two shots of Pernod, you sound like an idiot telling a Vietnamese exchange student that "we should totally meet up tomorrow at seventeen o'clock."

We trekked our way up the hill, dodging and ignoring vendors selling bottles of water and the same key chains of the Eiffel Tower mass-produced in a loveless Taiwanese factory. At the beginning and end of every set of steps, I just lifted up my bottle to avoid giving a hardened *non*. The first time I climbed those steps I was hung over and miserable. The night before we had gone to Wayne's Bar, which is the well-known foreigner bar in Nice where a little blond sings Blondie and Maroon 5 and everyone dances on the tables. Fantine hated this place, but would go with me on Thursday nights if I went to the market with her the next morning for fresh fruit and *socca*. When my friends and I decided we were going to Paris for the weekend, we chose to leave early Friday morning because we never had class on Fridays. I took those days for granted, I suppose.

The church, or *basilica* (don't say "cathedral" because it's not a cathedral and if you call it one they will correct you, and being corrected by a Frenchman is worse than it actually sounds, it's similar to the feeling you get when being yelled at by a German), is a polished alabaster due to the constant exuding of calcite, with breast-like domes and an arched façade, Byzantine rose windows, and a tall bell tower in the back that makes the whole structure appear more Eastern than Western.

I'm not sure if it was the Paris air or Marcel's temper tantrum earlier, but Riley was open with her affection unlike any time I had seen her before. She pointed at the Notre Dame, which was recognizable enough to stand out in the city's skyline, and begged Marcel to take us to see it first thing in the morning. "I want to feed the birds and breathe the love of the place," she said while hanging off him like a spider monkey.

We descended back to the tangled streets of the Montmartre and had lunch at the Café Bruant, which was situated on the corner of a café-lined street. We sat outside, squeezed into little tables covered in plates, crumbs, and glasses, and I asked for the WiFi password, but that never came. I'll be honest and tell you I was frustrated. I rushed my meal and sucked down the wine, showing no interest in coffee. "We can fucking get coffee back at the apartment," I said, and when I said "fucking," the waiter holding a tray of glasses with his palm facing the sky and towel draped over his shoulder wagged his finger and said, "No fucking." I was embarrassed because I did the most "American" thing that we Americans can do, and that is to be crass in public. So I dropped a silly red 10€ note on my plate and excused myself from the table.

I turned left and followed the slumping street and heard Kev say, "Well, that escalated quickly" to the table. I knew where we were in relation to the apartment and had no problem finding my way back, so I walked until I hit a hostel with a bright, flickering sign that said "Free WiFi" hanging from a wood block in the window. There was an inviting couch with an even more inviting brunette, so I sat down next to her and asked her in French for the WiFi password. She gave me a blank stare, so I repeated myself in English. She told me to ask for it at the desk, and I explained to her that I wasn't actually staying there but needed the password to get in touch with a "friend" who I was supposed to meet that very evening. She was sympathetic to me and handed me a slip of paper with an eleven-digit combo of letters and numbers.

"They gave me two by accident," she said, and asked if my friend was a girl, and I said no, like a liar. She wrote down her name and told me to find her on Facebook. I said I would, and did, after I put in the eleven-digit combo of letters and numbers and waited for those three little bars in the top left corner of my phone to burst into life. I checked the conversation on the app and it said my message had been **read**, but there was no response. *I should play it cool. I shouldn't* *message her anything and just wait until she messages me back.* But of course I didn't do that. I sent the **???** that is symbolic for "Are you kidding me?" or "What the fuck?"

Just one **?** is genuine concern, while two **??** is kind of like saying "Are you there?" But those three **???** are universal and are never lost in translation. I skipped those first two sets of questions marks, which might have been coming on too strong, but we had a thing last spring that was more than a fling, and I'm not some schmuck who doesn't deserve to have his messages **read** and not responded to.

Back at the apartment, Riley and Marcel were curled up on the couch while Kev lay shirtless in bed, eyes closed, drifting off to trap music on oversized headphones. I checked out the girl from the hostel on Facebook: **Jane Hagenberry.**

From: Winnipeg, Manitoba, Canada.

Jane graduated: McGill University (Class of 2015)

Jane majored in: Marketing & Feminist Studies

Jane interned at: Inventa Marketing Group, Toronto, ON

Jane speaks: English (fluent), French (fluent)—*yeah, fluent my ass*—**Chinese-Mandarin (intermediate), Italian (beginner)**

Jane likes: TV shows—Girls, Gilmore Girls, Arrested Development, Punic Celebs—Ryan Gosling, Lena Dunham, Damien Rogers, Chad Kroeger

Music—Coldplay, Nickelback (gross), Avicii, Swedish House Mafia, Adele, Dixie Chicks, Kendrick Lamar, Oasis

Jane recently visited: London, England, UK, Edinburgh, Scotland, UK, Calais, France, Paris, France

Despite her awful taste in music and questionable fluency self-accreditation, I scrolled through her profile pics, which changed with each new city she had visited, making the most recent, from Paris, her from the bridge that offers the most excellent view of the Eiffel Tower, holding a purple umbrella with big yellow dots. Before the one from Edinburgh, her first of her **Euro-Adventure!!!** album, she had a photo with a guy named Brennan, and the one before that, and the one before that, and the one before that, and each one was of her and Brennan until October—*recent breakup, explains the strong come-on.*

Her cover photo was her in a group of girls walking across Abbey Road in London, imitating the cover of the Beatles album of the same name. Besides Brennan, a cat named Leo was the topic of virtually every other photograph on the girl's profile: Leo rubbed up against her face, Leo in a stupid little hat, Leo soaking wet and sporting a vicious set of ragged teeth on the tiled bathroom floor. We never had cats and I don't really like them. One time my mom wanted us to get a cat or at least adopt one that her friend Sue Ellen had told her about, which came from an abused home. I said no and am also pretty sure I'm allergic to cats, but even if not allergic to them, I'd at least want a pet that actually does something—you can teach a parrot to swear, for example. But I was thankful for Leo because this entire time swiping through this Canadian's photos and contemplating the epicness of talking birds and which words, exactly, I'd teach them, I'd forgotten all about the flake that is Fantine. Then my phone vibrated.

It was her, Fantine: **The Riviera Queen**. My neurotransmitters bolted shots of dopamine to the synapses that entangled and created the web formation of my brain.

Text from The Riviera Queen: 2:34 p.m.: Bonjour Joel. How are you enjoying Paris? It is just as lovely as you remember, no?

I wanted to tell her off but couldn't get myself to do it. All the mush from last spring came flooding back—she had a spell on me, you see. Someone call the witch doctor.

Text to The Riviera Queen: 2:35 p.m.: Find me tonight in the streets of the Montmartre and we'll share a bottle of Burgundy or Chablis, si vous plait.

Fantine didn't have a Facebook. Too cool, I suppose. The first time I saw her it was on a dripping day in the resort city of Nice. I was with my study abroad group on one of the few mandatory sight-seeing walking tours—Fantine was our guide. I was the only guy from my school who was studying abroad in Nice during that semester. I never understood the popularly shared logic of France as the epitome of the homoerotic nation of "pussification" that so many of my peers held. With gooey cheeses, the cultivators of the most succulent wine, and the pioneers of the *mé*nage à trois, France had appealed to me since I inadvertently masturbated for the first time during an episode of *Three's Company* in the basement. So I gravitated toward a group of guys from the University of Iowa, who all seemed to be from Chicago suburbs.

Although "advanced French" was a requirement for the program, very few of the other students could carry on a conversation in the beautiful tongue, and even fewer attempted. Fantine, as a native of the city, was hired by the program to give tours during the day and to take us out at night. Since the drinking age is like thirteen in France, the term "reign of terror" took on a new meaning when the U of Iowa guys crashed into Wayne's Bar. I, on the other hand, needed the tall, skinny *Niçoise* in my life and had learned from experience that drunk Joel is a rude, easily agitated Joel with few morals and a small vocabulary, and to bag a girl like Fantine, we needed a lubricated, not saturated, Joel.

At twelve, Fantine had been considered "gifted" as an artist and was put in some of the most prestigious art schools in Paris, Barcelona, and London. At nineteen, she had paintings featured in galleries that attracted esteemed collectors and fat-cat connoisseurs. She even managed to sell quite a few of them, which is more difficult than creating the damn things. And her art, her style, her works' *raison d'*être is like that of a love-child created during a summer dalliance between El Greco and Braque. This wasn't that "throwing paintbrushes at a giant canvas while heavy metal rips through your eardrums in a Brooklyn loft" avant-garde bullshit cheap imitation of art; she was the real deal, baby.

Only a week after her twenty-first birthday in deep October, the ecstasy of the art world came crashing down like sweaty Icarus. Her father was diagnosed with bronchial cancer, underwent treatment in the hospital, and passed six months later. Fantine smoked a pack a day (these are the ten-cigarette European packs, but regardless), which made her friends shake their heads in disapproval. But that was Fantine, the prototypical "coffee and cigarettes for breakfast" type of girl we Americans see in the movies and drool over, and I think that's what I was attracted to most—the banality of it all. We didn't lock eyes and fall into a drunken stupor of love right there in the romantic old neighborhood of Nice. At first she was disinterested and gave off a pretentiousness to which I should've taken offense, but instead found enviable. When I did get to know her, I quickly realized she wasn't the least bit pretentious—more so guarded to whom she opened up. She didn't like swearing either and was put off by the casual cussing of American undergraduates—I definitely would've been scolded back at the café: "Joel, why always 'fucking'?" Around the U of Iowa guys, she'd roll her eyes so often I'd rarely see the chroma of her iris.

I could hear the two reunited lovers jostling around on the jam-colored couch. I took *On the Road* to the balcony and picked up at the beginning of part two where Dean has a hankering to see Marylou and drives from New Mexico to Denver so they can make love—for ten hours. I know what you're thinking, and no, I didn't come all the way to France for a warm bed. I just find the extent to which some guys go for box fascinating. I mean, one time I did go vegan for a week to impress this chick from the YMAAC (Youth Movement Against Animal Cruelty), which is a more militant offshoot of PETA, but she got arrested the morning before our date protesting the pesticide use at a local pumpkin patch, so I met Kev for a bloody steak and a hoppy beer instead.

Riley came out to the balcony with staticky hair like a mad scientist. She said Marcel was in the shower and we were going to the Eiffel Tower. Her juvenile, bubbly exuberance contrasted with the cooler-than-thou part of the city we were making our home base. Kev was passed out on the bed and only woke up after hearing the perfect pop of an uncorked wine bottle. I asked Marcel what we were doing for dinner, but I said it in French, to which Kev and Riley simultaneously eye-rolled.

"What?" I said. "Are we *not* in France?"

"It's obnoxious," said Riley.

"Ugh, remember when he would get drunk and speak to Marcel in French and dabs of Arabic?" said Kev.

"It was so lame," said Riley.

"I've taken French for the past *eleven* years and plan to use it WHEN I'M IN FRANCE."

Marcel poured four glasses of a full-bodied Pommard that his parents were definitely saving for a more special occasion. Riley and Kev smirked at each other from across the kitchen island.

"So what did you take?" I directed the question toward Riley.

"When? What do you mean?"

"What language did you take, in college?"

"One year of Mandarin."

"Ha! Why?"

"Because China is going to take over!" Kev interjected from an open-doored bathroom.

"What a bunch of crap," I said.

"Here we go."

"No, listen. I don't get why everyone has their panties in a bunch over China. They're an industrial economy with a rudimentary military."

"Yes, but there are *many* of them," Marcel added.

"Yeah, and *a lot* of that place is a third-world shit-hole that would be obliterated to smithereens if they went to war with the US and the West. Don't get me wrong," I said. "We're fucked, but China isn't going to be our rapist."

"Oil the War Machine!" Kev yelled from the bathroom.

"How long is that piss?" Riley asked.

"Hoorah!"

We took the subway to Trocadero, which offers the "sexiest view" of the Eiffel Tower, according to Marcel. After dodging perched trinket vendors selling the same indistinguishable key chains of the Eiffel Tower as the vendors at the Basilica, we turned the corner, and there stood the world's most recognizable phallic symbol in all its illuminating glory.

Riley shrieked an "Oh. My. God," pronouncing the three words separately and with equal emphasis.

Kev said, "Oh, wow," as if he weren't expecting such a gargantuan structure.

Riley had Marcel by the extended arm and was pulling him down the steps. "It's not going anywhere, ya know!" I yelled after them. It was crowded, and every twenty feet people posed for pictures—groups of Asian girls with identical smiles were set in the backgrounds of couples kissing with the tip of the tower crowning over top. Isn't it funny to think that somewhere on the internet, you're probably in the background of someone's profile pic?

We were bombarded by dark-haired girls holding pieces of paper and pens, shoving them in our faces to "sign here sign here sign here."

"Don't sign there," said Marcel. "Ignore them."

"Holy shit, these are Gypsies, aren't they?" said Kev as they held out the paper and pens.

Marcel explained that the scheme here is that they print out crap petitions for causes that pull on tourists' heartstrings, like money for the blind and deaf, and after you sign the paper, they stick out their hands for a "donation." But in actuality, you could sign it "Mickey Mouse" or put an X through the entire paper and they couldn't care less, because the entire time, one of their friends is pulling out your wallet with their long fingers.

"I've heard about these. I fucking hate Gypsies," said Kev.

"They're right in front of you," said Riley.

"I don't care. Get a real fuckin' job."

A "Champagne" vendor insisted to us that an experience like this could not be complete without a bottle of Champagne, which Marcel vehemently scolded and then asked, rhetorically, if he looked like the kind of idiot that would pay 50€ for "Champagne" without the *Champagne* designation needed to verify its status and separate it from the cheap imitators in California or Australia.

The air was balmy and pleasant, and I'd like to tell you that the stars glittered across the Napoleonic sky, but I'd be lying. Paris is one of the most polluted cities in Europe, despite the paintings with bright white dotted stars swimming in inky black and blue—I suppose that's a drawback to the City of Light, or is it "Lights"? Anyway, people come here with the expectation that it's the Elysian Fields. It has a name—the Paris Syndrome—which is experienced by tourists who come to the destabilizing realization that the streets don't smell like Dior and the women are not all long-legged in nether-provoking skirts, and the men are not all thin in berets (actually, no one wears fucking berets). The Japanese embassy even has a hotline for their citizens to call when they've fallen victim to the debilitating symptoms.

The truth is that Paris is everything it needs to be—nothing more and nothing less. It's artsy, edgy, and the epitome of cool without flaunting it. Actually, for a Parisian to call herself "cool" is anything *but* cool. Paris doesn't want to be Europe's NYC; London can have that title. This is the center of Europe if there ever is to be a center, and if you disagree, well, the Parisians don't really give a damn.

Marcel was apprehensive as Riley grabbed him by the collar to reel him in for a kiss. Kev held Riley's phone and snapped three quick pictures while she tried to make them look candid. The whole thing was sort of awkward, but Marcel went along with it because he was a good host. I went over and grabbed the phone out of Kev's hands.

"What are you doing?" Riley yelled, still grappling Marcel's shirt.

"Scrolling," I said.

"What? No!"

"What do you have to hide?"

"What the fuck, Joel?!"

I didn't see anything scandalous, but I had heard rumors at school that Riley was fond of drunkenly sending nude pics to guys after hooking up with them for only a couple of weeks. I wanted to see if it was true, I suppose. She snatched the phone from me and called me a "fucker."

"Take 'er easy there, Buck," I said, to which she flipped me off and Kev laughed.

"Taker 'er easy there, Buck" is Larry's catchphrase in *Buck and Larry Get Stuff Done*, a stupid movie about two friends who, after a series of coincidental and profiting events, come to be the heirs of a famous BBQ joint in South Carolina: hilarity ensues. I had often used the catchphrase to ease tense situations with comic relief, which to no one's surprise, often led to the tense party(ies) becoming angrier and the situation more tense. I yelled it when some freshman slipped and fell into a puddle of spilled milk in the dining hall, his vegan ramen covering his head like a mop. We usually say it to Riley when she starts to get thirsty over Damien Rogers or one of the other god-resembling actors from *Punic*. But I must admit that Kev said it best when Campus Safety busted through the front door like coked-out firemen and Kev was ninety degrees upside down in a keg stand and delivered the most beautiful "Take 'er easy there, Buck." He was cited and had to meet with the student council.

After Riley was content with her seventy-five pictures in seventy-five poses at the front of the tower, the general consensus was that we needed a drink. Marcel took us to a bar in the Crimée—a visibly Jewish and Muslim part of the city in the Northeast. The authentically European buzzing sound that came from the Vespas had a therapeutic effect on me. Although this wasn't the swankiest section of Paris, the smells from emptying bakeries and the groups of young friends sitting along the *Quai de la Seine* sharing inexpensive food and wine couldn't be replicated anywhere else. However, there was one thumping sore thumb of a building plopped right down in the middle of it all.

The part hotel, part hostel was a modern glass monstrosity filled with the traveling youths of the world. As we walked by, a group of Australians smoking on the front steps asked, "Where's the next party but?"

I could see through the windowed-walls young travelers from every corner of the globe crammed shoulder to shoulder, three rows deep at the bar. At the bar was a group of girls celebrating what looked like a birthday, and they were getting sloppy. One tall blond wore a crown and pink boa—the birthday girl, I presume.

"They have rut tables set up," Kev pointed out.

You see, Kev and I were champions at the game, gunners really, and I would've bet that had we gone up against any Aussies or jabronis studying abroad from Alabama, we would've smoked 'em out of the hostel. Kev jumped down the few steps and pressed his face and hands up against the glass. But I was in Paris, after all, and the whole getup, even the fresh memories from only a few weeks ago of sticky, beer-stained floors, seemed below me, I suppose, and I insisted that we continue over the bridge, over the Seine and deeper into Europe; Riley grabbed Kev from the window, kicking and screaming.

Marcel led us to a different bar for an after-hours gathering. Riley and Marcel maintained a ten-foot lead ahead of us. They sort of fit together, Riley and Marcel, and I was happy for them, I suppose. They held hands, and his sat on top of hers, fingers interlocked—whoever is on top "wears the pants" in the relationship, that's what Sal always told me. I suppose Kev and I were too loud, because Marcel turned back and gave us a look like, "Come on, guys, don't make me regret this."

A small girl with round cheeks and a button nose warmly greeted Marcel at the entrance of the bar. She held her cigarette with such comfort that it looked like she had been smoking since she was a child. She had chestnut hair in a short style that never really appealed to me on girls, but it worked on her, I suppose.

The bar was dingy and industrial-looking with a small steel bar-top that had two beers on tap. The walls were bare; the lone decoration was an Algerian flag hanging behind the bar. Black tables stood in disarray. There weren't any windows, so the smoke floated around the bar, trapped inside the lungs of its patrons. Riley broke out in coughs, the rough kind that sound like congealed clumps of hair shooting up a coarse throat.

A guy popped out from under the bar. With clay-colored skin and onyx hair, he epitomized the term "tall, dark, and handsome." He hopped over the top of the bar and hugged Marcel like a long-lost brother returning from war. He introduced himself as Mehdi, putting stress on the "h" like he was clearing his throat. I said *Salaam* when I shook his hand, which made him chuckle. "Your name?" he asked.

"Joel."

"It's a pleasure to meet you, Joe."

"It's Joel."

The only other occupants of the bar were two old men speaking a rough Slavic language, which I assumed to be Polish, and a group of Senegalese smoking at a corner table, bursting into incoherent mixtures of laughter and French, which made Riley jump in her seat. Kev and I both had Kronenbourg on tap.

Marcel and Mehdi switched in and out of French, sometimes to English, but when they desired to be covert, to Arabic—I envied how insouciantly they could switch tongues.

BINGE UNTIL TRAGEDY

Mehdi is third-generation French; his grandfather came to Europe from Algiers in the sixties to work on the docks of Marseille. Despite his Maghrebi pride, Mehdi had only been to the motherland twice in his life—the most recent time was five years ago for his eighteenth birthday.

After she was finished with her cigarette, the petite girl who greeted Marcel at the door signaled Mehdi over to pull down the gate to the bar, which had been our sole source of fresh air. Riley was annoyed and coughed uncontrollably to display her dissatisfaction to Marcel.

We sat at the tables that were covered in writing—markers and pens were dispersed throughout the bar, encouraging self-inflicted graffiti. Rudimentary cartoons were covered in tags, and intimate floral patterns spread across one of the tables and crashed into a Technicolor spider web design in the corner. The tables, the human element embedded in the woodwork, gave the bar character when it would otherwise be indistinguishable from any other neighborhood dive.

Marcel, Mehdi, and the petite brunette talked like they hadn't seen each other in years. I tried to keep up with their conversation, but they spoke so quickly that I was only catching bits and pieces, mostly coming from Marcel, whose accent I had grown the most accustomed to. Kev asked me something, but I ignored it. I wanted them to see that I could join. It was something I always had back home, that "Joel could speak another language that wasn't Itanglish," but this happened all too often when I studied here.

The natives with whom we were friends all spoke English, and it became a custom to defer to the language of the least proficient speaker, and since there was never a French speaker whose English was worse than an American's French, the de facto conversational language was English. Only on occasions when I would go out with Fantine and her friends would I be able to use my French for more than a *Ça va?*

Eventually the petite brunette noticed me staring at her lips and mouthing their sentences, so she introduced herself. "Oh, how rude of me. I'm Jeanette. It's a pleasure to meet you."

"*Enchanté, Jeanette. Je suis Joel.*" I could hear my friends snickering behind my back as I leaned in to give her *deux bisous*.

"Ahh, you speak French? Is this your first time here?"

"*Non, j' ai étudié ici, eh bien, à Nice. Il y a un an et demi,*" I said. She acknowledged that I spoke French, but continued in English.

"How fantastic! I love to go to Nice. I went there as a little girl. It is a very nice place."

Mehdi asked, "Joe, have you seen…"

"Joel."

"Yes, yes, JoeL. Excuse me, JoeL. Have you seen Marseille?"

"Yes, it's a hectic city."

"It is interesting, no?"

I figured Mehdi had a connection to the city, so I bit my tongue in order to trap the reply "Well, it's dirty and crime-ridden, but it's where the French national anthem comes from… so there's that, I suppose," and instead said, "*Oui, c'est amusant.*"

"My uncle lives there. Next time you go, you meet him. He will take you out, show you the city authentic."

I gave up on using my French. Eleven years of schooling plus a study abroad and I couldn't even get one response in the tongue—I wasn't even going to try the Arabic. Riley kept fidgeting and peeked over at the table of Senegalese every few minutes. Kev and I went to the bar, where Jeanette told us to pour our own beers. She charged us less than 4€—the cheapest beer I'd ever find in Paris.

Jeanette had a tight body, the kind you definitely didn't maintain by drinking beer and eating melty, stinky cheese. From the bar, I could see what appeared to be a large black sun on her shoulder blade. Kev whispered, "I'd hit that," under his breath.

"Then go for it," I said, knowing full well that Kev didn't possess the chestnuts to even approach a girl. "Genevieve ruined you, man. Don't let her. She's across the fuckin' Atlantic and she's still got a vise grip on your nut sack."

"Not at all."

"Yeah, she does, and I can't stand it. That was what… four years ago? You still talkin' to that bitch?"

"Hey!" he said. "Don't say that shit, man. She isn't a bitch."

"You see? Why do you stick up for her? Do you even *remember* what she did to you?"

"I really don't want to talk about this. Leave me the FUCK ALONE."

Riley came over and stood between us, her arms wrapped around our necks. Marcel hadn't done so much as look at her since we walked in the place, and the three of us were picking up a bad vibe from the Senegalese.

"I think they're talking about me," said Riley in a concerned tone that made them appear like velociraptors.

"They said they'd take you all at once," I said, fueling the fire.

"Stop. Don't scare me."

"They initially were discussing who would go first."

"Stop."

"The one in the blue was ardent, he wanted first or not at all."

"Shut up."

"The one in the hat was fine with going last."

"Shut up, Joel."

"He's a team player, ya gotta admire that."

"I'm going to murder you."

"Eventually, they resolved their differences and will have you all at the same time. Now it's just a matter of who's in which orifice."

"Ewwwwww."

"The whole jambalaya!" added Kev.

"I would *never* do that. Anal is fucking gross."

"You've never done butt stuff?" I asked.

"Hellz no," she said. "Have you?"

"How so?"

"How *so*?"

"Well, I'm not gay, so I've never caught, if that's what you are alluding to."

"Boys' G-spots are in their buttholes."

"Really?" said Kev.

"Yeah, yeah, yeah, that's an old wives' tale to give bored housewives an excuse to stick something in their husbands' butts, probably in retribution for years of neglecting dirty diapers and overflowing trash cans."

"No, it's true. Remember when I was seeing Ricky?"

"Nope! No. No. No," I said.

"Huh?"

"We don't want to hear about this."

"Why not?"

"Because, Riles, most of the guys you've 'spent the night with'…"

"Oh, *now* we're censoring this conversation."

"Happen to be our close friends. And *even if* Jack or Eddie or Luke or…"

"Or Ricky."

"Yes, *or Ricky*, enjoy your little fingers in their sphincters, we don't want to know about it. Right, Kev?"

"Right."

An eruption came from our table. Mehdi had slammed his fists onto the wood, and a glass of beer spilled over and shattered on the floor. Marcel and Mehdi were yelling, gesticulating above their heads and smacking their hands together. "What's happening?" Riley asked. "I can't tell if they're mad at each other or if it's one of those arguments where you're both agreeing but get heated anyway."

It was the latter. Marcel had brought up the scenes from the protests in Algeria and Syria that we had watched this morning, which struck a chord with Mehdi. He still had family in Algiers, but lost contact with his cousin a few days ago, and on his Facebook it said that the last message to him had been **received**, but not yet **read**. Mehdi was speaking loudly enough that I could translate pieces of his French tirade:

"If that bastard Hannachi hurt my cousin, I'll cut his fucking balls off and shove them down his fucking throat. I'll kill that motherfucker. I'll kill him." (Directed at Jeanette) "No, I won't calm down. Would you calm down? Don't you have a younger brother?" He turned back toward Marcel. "You would do it with me? I love you like a brother. We will do this. Hannachi won't know what hit him." (With pointed fingers in the typical machine-gun fashion, spitting the noise with his lips) "*Thththt... ththt... thtththt...* just like that! *Thththt...* We'll light him up, Marcel, you and me, together we'll liberate Algeria," he shouted, and laughed like a Maghrebi Tony Montana.

"That's ironic," said Kev.

"What is?" I asked.

"That we watched those clips this morning and he's talking about it now."

"It's not ironic, it's a coincidence."

"Whatever."

Marcel waved us over to rejoin them at the table. I finished pouring myself another beer and hadn't realized that one of the Polish guys was standing behind me, waiting to serve himself. "We are going to Algeria to kick ass. Are you coming, my friends?" said Marcel, bouncing on the balls of his feet and shaking out his hands.

"Fuck that," said Kev, who hadn't comprehended the importance of the protests to Mehdi, who then sat up a little more in his chair and glared at Kev. "I mean, it just isn't my fight," he said, trying to salvage the moment.

"And why is that?" Mehdi said. "You mean that human life is not *your fight*? No, of course not, not when it is inconvenient for you Americans."

"Whoa, that's not what I meant."

"So when—let me straight this out. So when the scary Communists attack Vietnam, America sends their army entire, but when the same happens in Algeria, they do nothing? Hmm?"

"What I meant was…"

"Only send the army to help the Europeans."

"Weren't we helping the French in Vietnam? Aren't you French?"

"*That's* ironic," I said.

"Or, how about this… hmm… when a country in South America has a leader, or wait, Cuba—when Cubans fight against fascist pigs and win, America calls them 'terrorists.'"

"If you let me…"

"Never want to help Muslims. Only Israel and Europe."

"What about Afghanistan, when the Soviets invaded Afghanistan?"

"Bahh! Only for oil. America only helps Muslims who will give them oil."

"There's no oil in Afghanistan," I said.

Jeanette shot me a look, a warning not to get involved, as if Mehdi was a strong current but this would pass nonetheless. He kicked back his chair and stood up, tears in his eyes, and shaking from nerves. His passion, although unwarranted and misinformed, was refreshing, to the point that I was excited for what he was going to say next: "I promise you, with *Allah* as my witness"—he pointed to the sky—"I am going to kill Hamza Hannachi, or I am going to die trying." I felt like I was in a fucking movie.

"Wait, is he serous?" asked Riley.

"Yes," responded Marcel, staring at his friend with admiration.

"Well… what about you? Are you going to Libya?" she asked.

"It's *Algeria*, and I don't know," he said while lighting a cigarette.

The three of us sat there feeling out of place, like the white players on the Don Imus–dubbed "Nappy-Headed Hoes" Rutgers women's basketball team. Jeanette brought over a few beers and told us they were "in the house." We all knew what she meant. Her accent drove me *crazy*, it fit her figure perfectly, but I was set, finally, to have lunch with Fantine the next day, so I felt guilty imagining my face between the thighs of Amélie with tattoos.

"You gonna shave for your date tomorrow?" asked Riley.

It hadn't even crossed my mind. When I was in Nice, I didn't have the behemoth growing on my face, and thinking about it, Fantine didn't like beards. She called them "barbaric" and would roll her eyes when the U of Iowa guys would stick pens and pencils in their face ivy.

"No way," said Kev. "That thing is like Joel's child. He's been growing it since November."

"It sorta bothers me how you know how long Joel's been growing his beard for."

"Not really. He started it for 'No-Shave November,' we both did, but he just kept growing his. I shaved mine because it grew in patchy and gross."

"This really does put me in a pickle," I said, twirling my beard at the bottom. "I mean, I have been—well done, Kev—growing my beard since November, and didn't shave it for Christmas, Easter, graduation, or Adam's funeral, all to my mother's protests, and shaving it now would go against everything I stand for, every time I defended my beard when I was told I looked homeless…"

"Didn't you name it?" asked Riley.

"The Visigoth," Kev and I said simultaneously.

"Great name."

"I know. And if I shaved it now, for her, well… I just wouldn't feel right. But…"

"But she fucks you," said Kev.

"But she fucks me," I said.

"Oh my god," said Riley. "Give me a break. You know that by lunchtime tomorrow that beard is going to be shaved off, clogging a drain somewhere."

"Don't clog my drains," said Marcel, turning around in his chair.

Mehdi returned to the table and dove into the bristly discussion. "In my culture, to grow a beard is a sign of manhood."

"In French culture?" asked Kev.

"No, no. Islam," he responded.

This time, Jeanette shot Kev a look not to broach the subject, a subject that needed to be broached.

"Do you know that in this country it is *illegal* for a woman to wear a *burqa*?" he persisted. Everyone at the table knew he was not finished, so we sat silent. "The government takes my rights as a human and as a Muslim. I am not part of *that* culture." He was getting worked up again, and a chair kick was in the foreseeable future. "When I get the chance, I am leaving this place. They target us, the Muslims, and want to kick us out. There will be a war. I would welcome it."

"It says here," Riley spoke while looking down at her phone, "that the ban is of all face coverings and doesn't specify Muslims. It says that…"

"I know what it says," Mehdi interrupted.

"Wait, how do you have WiFi?" I asked.

"Actually, most Muslim women here don't…"

"It is lies!" He cut her off again. "We don't care what they want."

"Okay, this is bullshit," said Riley, turning toward Marcel, who gave her a look of indifference.

"I wouldn't wear that shit," she said. Mehdi jumped up from his seat.

"Would you?" she directed at Jeanette. "We went over this issue in FEM Studies 206 and…"

"It's tradition, it's in the Quran. In the Quran it says…"

"I don't care what it says in your book."

"Freedom is the veil!" Mehdi began to scream in incoherent Arabic that even Marcel had a difficult time understanding.

"Women only *want* to wear that shit from societal pressures. It's gender subjugation. It says here that even *Muslim* countries ban it in public places. Look, it says Turkey and Egypt and Tunisia…"

"Marcel, it's time for you to leave," Mehdi said.

"Are you kidding me? You can't even ask *me* to leave?" Riley said, then, looking toward Jeanette, "I hope you don't put up with this shit." Jeanette had sunken down in her chair to avoid what had started to become obvious, a common theme.

"We should go," said Marcel.

"Eww, fuckin' chauvinists. I'm outta here anyway." She stormed out the back of the bar to much protestation from the Senegalese at their back table. After exchanging words of understanding with Mehdi, Marcel followed her. Kev and I awkwardly finished our beers while Mehdi went behind the bar and Jeanette lit a cigarette. Marcel and Riley argued the entire cab ride home and we could hear them through the walls as we tried our best to get comfortable next to each other in our undersized bed.

"You know he has a couch," said Kev.

"With your name on it," I said, and went to sleep.

I stumbled from the sweaty bed and did not acknowledge any other forms of existence until I was sucking down sweetened black coffee. Riley and Marcel must've made up, judging from the swishing sound of sheets jostling on naked skin. Each squeak of metal springs and bang of headboard on the blanched walls irritated my hangover, and the skin of my temples stuck to my skull. It was bleak and wet, but the pitter-pattering of the rain never got old to me. Isn't it interesting that we skip over thousands of songs on our iPhones and iPods and iPads, but can sit and listen to the percussive solo of the rain?

I was still stuck in the beard conundrum, Fantine's condescending remarks about my classmates' facial growth replaying in my head. I'd brought an electric shaver with me for the sole intention of using it on my neck and dick and balls. A wood-carved statuette with cartoonish bulging eyes and pointed lips sat on the mantle of the seldom-used fireplace and peered into my soul. It followed me as I paced around the shiny black-topped island in the kitchen, sipping coffee and debating the pros and cons of going stubbled.

"Don't do it."

I jumped.

"Jumpy today, aren't we?" said Kev, leaning against the island in the kitchen.

"You scared the fuck outta me."

"I can hear them from here, fuckin' creatures. Dude must run on diesel."

"I'm gonna shave."

"No! Don't do it."

"She *hates* beards. I have to."

"Fine, then I'm taking this." He held out his index finger and thumb like a bouncer asking for I.D.

"Come on."

"Nope, if you shave I'm taking your 'Man Card.'"

"Baloney. I once saw your jeans rolled up past your ankles and a periwinkle shirt with a polka-dot bow-tie because Genevieve told you it was 'totally in this season.'"

"I looked dapper and you know it!"

I locked the bathroom door and put on my headphones to avoid listening to Kev's objections. I put on the Cavalry's debut album: *The Cavalry*, my personal favorite, recorded in 2006 before their launch into superstardom that really came with their lesser fourth album, *Bushwackin'*.

They hailed from Keansburg, New Jersey, and their sound has been compared to the mega-star Clyde Stevens, who is also a Jersey boy and the face of not just New Jersey rock 'n' roll, but everything cool and everything right with American rock 'n' roll. Stevens even endorsed the band by having them open at one of his shows last year. That same summer, they began a tour of Europe, and I would've ridden cargo on a coal train to Bratislava if it meant I'd see a show on international soil. I'd seen them at the Stone Pony and a couple of times in New Brunswick, but their best show was at the Hammerstein Ballroom in the City, where Kev and I skipped our afternoon class to drive from Pennsylvania and stayed with Sal and got so drunk off half-priced rum and Cokes that Kev ate a cigarette and we almost—*almost*—got matching tattoos.

It took fifteen minutes of pulling clumps of hair from the sink and tossing them into the toilet and holding back tears when the trimmer would rip out hairs from my neck. I'd have to blot the blood with a wad of toilet paper. In the end, I looked like a different person. I stared in the mirror at the guy I hadn't seen since before Christmas, bouncing between contentment and "shaver's remorse."

"You look like a child," said Kev, shoving his face into the bathroom.

My phone vibrated on the kitchen sink.

Text from The Riviera Queen: 11:21 a.m.: Bonjour mon ami lunch today still? Remember Au bon temps. I will see you there. Be hungry! Xoxo

Marcel emerged from his bedroom shirtless and glistening. He gave me the simplest directions to the bistro and sprayed me with a pungent cologne. He pulled out a tulip from the vase on the kitchen table, insisting that it is customary to be a lover when in France. Water dripped from the stem as I walked down the stairs. I opened the umbrella while still standing in the apartment building's foyer so the spring rain wouldn't ruin my perfectly disheveled hair.

Because of the rain, parts of the Montmartre that were usually packed with tourists scrambling from café to bistro during the lunch hour were bare, as if the *arrondissement* had emptied for my special occasion. I didn't even bother hiding the stupid smile on my face and gave toothy *bonjours* to every shopkeeper or dog walker I passed on the street. The scent of crackling fried fish clogged my nostrils and I was instantly transported back to Nice, to one of those afternoons where I'd stroll through the old city and photograph the pastel teals and tangerines of buildings that appeared more Italian than French. I reminisced about mornings spent on rocky beaches that lined the Côte d'Azur, where Fantine and I would sunbathe before returning to my apartment to make love before lunch. Wine intermingled throughout those days, and I'd drink that pink stuff that's so popular in Provence because she liked it, and she liked how my openness to trying new things juxtaposed the other American boys.

I'd hoped she would already be there when I arrived and I'd see her smile through the window that faced the street. She'd giggle while I struggled to close my umbrella, and two glasses of wine would already be poured—she'd remember that I love Burgundy and she'd playfully criticize how I drink too fast, that I don't appreciate the *terroir* enough, whereby I'd dip my nose deep into the glass, pull it out, and say "Ahh, and a swell vintage it is!" We'd embrace at the table, and the waiter, too busy to wait for us, would come back in a few minutes, and she'd kiss me and tell me that she missed me, and that I must stay in France—for good this time. Eventually, she would convince me to stay because I wouldn't be able to say no. I never had been able to say no to her before, and under the pitter-pattering of Parisian rain, I wouldn't be able to start.

Lost daydreaming, I stumbled onto the bistro. I peered through the wet glass and didn't see Fantine. I assumed if she was not at a window table, she wasn't in the restaurant at all. Not wanting to wait alone, I considered doing a lap around the block and then return to peer through the window again—repeat until daydream is fulfilled. But before I could make it down the street, a finger tapped me on the shoulder.

"*Bonjour,* Joel!"

I was nervous. I had successfully prevented the nerves up until that point, and I stuttered over my greeting, but she didn't seem to notice, or care. She grabbed my face in her hands, which sent a cold shock to my newly exposed skin. All I had thought about were those gorgeous eyes and her tight figure, but I caught myself, again and again, looking toward the ground, bashful, like our whole past had never existed.

We took a table by the window and in my line of sight, a puddle was forming where a stone was missing in the sidewalk. We fumbled over which language we should use. I pushed the French, trying to make up for my earlier blunder, but we conceded to English and switched to the beautiful tongue only when speaking with the waiter.

"How about wine?" I asked.

"Oh no, not for me. Only café."

"Okay then, how is your work?"

"How is school?" she asked.

"I'm finished now."

"That is it? It is over?"

"Yes."

"Then what will you do now?"

"Well, I am here." I fidgeted with my knife and fork.

"Yes, silly, I can see that. But for work? You Americans love your work."

"That's a commonly held misconception," I said.

"Huh?"

"*Comment est la peinture?*"

"I don't do that anymore."

"But… you're a painter."

"I do not paint anymore."

I'm still not sure why these words dug so deep into me, like a jagged dagger of disappointment; I suppose I was enamored with the idea of loving a French painter more than I loved the painter herself?

"I don't understand."

"I work now. I work for, how would you say, *bureau?*"

"Bureau."

"I know, how would *you* say it."

"We say *bureau* too, we use the French word."

"How magnificent. Well, I work for a bureau advertising in La Défense, you know it? It has the interesting-looking building…"

"So you don't make art anymore?"

"No, Joel. I do not have the hours."

The bistro was beginning to fill up with a mix of local Parisians and confused tourists who crawled inside to escape the rain, which had picked up its pace from a pleasant pitter-pattering to a pounding on the gray stone that matched the color of the sky. I turned back to her and our eyes met, my chest tightened, my heart thumped; she was more beautiful than she was in the few photos I had saved on my phone from Nice. She had demanded that I not upload any photos of us to Facebook, because that was something you did with serious boyfriends, boyfriends who would become husbands—*fiancés*—they invented the damn word. So I needed these photos on my phone to show off to my friends when I returned home. Otherwise it was doubtful that they would have believed I could bag such a beauty.

We ordered our lunch: I had sausage *d'auvergne* and she had the *soupe du jour*, which had an odor that reminded me of my Nonna's house and warmed my insides from first sniff. We talked about the times we spent together, but more frequently, we talked about the times we didn't. If I even hinted at a love-making afternoon after a morning on the beach, or a wine-induced argument that led to make-up love making, if that's what we're calling it, she would skirt the subject and ask about "university" or my family—she was always interested in Carlo's athleticism and would joke about him playing for the Yankees: "I see those hats everywhere," she would say. When the check came, she insisted that she pay.

"You are a guest in my country."

"Okay, then let me pay for drinks tonight."

"Oh, no, I cannot allow that."

"I insist. I'll bring over wine and watch you paint, like I used…"

"I don't paint anymore," she snapped.

"But why not?! I don't understand."

"Because I had to continue. Life is not just *la bohème,* Joel."

"…"

"And I cannot see you tonight. Or again here. I cannot. You see… I *have* a man now."

A punch to the gut doesn't do it justice. I felt the torrents of passion expel from my lungs. I wanted to get angry, nice and good and mad, throw a tantrum that would make Hemingway proud, but I composed myself and dropped my clutched fork onto the floor.

"That's a bummer" was all I could muster, and I put on my jacket and left the bistro, and she watched me from the window that faced the street as I fumbled with the umbrella while the warm rain messed up my hair. I took the first turn I could find and then the next and the next, pacing down the street like she was following me, even though obviously she wasn't. She had a second cup of coffee and met with a friend shortly after. I deleted her number from my phone, so as to avoid the drunk texting that was bound to ensue otherwise. *This isn't right, none of it.*

I could smell her flowery perfume stuck to my jacket and it made me nauseous, so I didn't say *bonjour* to any of the shopkeepers I passed, because if I opened my mouth I would projectile vomit onto some innocent baker sweeping the front of his *brasserie,* and I didn't want eructated missiles to become a "thing" for me. *I can't believe I shaved for this.* I felt like fraud, a fake, a phony! All that I'd built was gone and all I could see were beards—hipster beards, tourist beards (probably Australian), beards of the Book—Orthodox Jews and Conservative Muslims—goatees, lip caterpillars, fuck, I'd even take a sleazy soul patch. I felt rejected and naked and although the sun was taking a break that day, the city was perfect. It must be the only city in the world that is more beautiful in the rain; every roasting soul should experience Paris in the rain, I suppose.

They heard me come in and waited at the top of the stairs, and when I didn't say anything they knew nothing was in its right place. "How'd it go, love?" asked Riley.

I was embarrassed to the point I considered lying, but instead let it spill: "Awful… Not happening… Don't want to talk about it."

"But you were like, in love with her?" she said.

"She's nothing but a fading paramour now."

"We were thinking about spending the rest of the afternoon in the Louvre. Want to…"

"No. No thanks," I said. "I think I'm just going to hang here."

"I'll stay with 'im," said Kev, having no desire to be the third wheel.

"Alright then, take care, *mes amis*. Please do not make a big mess," said Marcel, and then he and Riley went out into the rain.

"Wine?" posed Kev.

"No thanks."

"Man, you must be hurtin' then."

"Ya know, it's such a crock of shit," I said. "She knew *exactly* why I wanted to see her. She could've told me…"

"Told you… what?"

"Told me… that she had a boyfriend. Ya know? Like, why the fuck couldn't she have texted me that? Why can't we just be honest with each other? We had something legitimate. She knows it and I know it."

"I know it."

"And she's already got a new guy? Ya know, we used to Skype every day the first few months I was home."

"I never saw you do that."

"I would go to the library, find an empty room on the third floor during the day."

"Why?"

"I didn't want anyone to find out."

"... Why?"

"Because, man, it was fuckin' cliché. And it would've ruined my chances with girls at school. Point is, we weren't just some fling."

"How 'bout that wine?"

"Sure, fine. It takes one text message."

"Sing it, brother," he said, uncorking the wine.

"One fuckin' itsy-bitsy, teensy-weensy, cunt hair of a text message." He handed me a glass of something red. "Ya know what? Wait, what is this?"

"*Chate-oo-neeuff duh pApe*. Did I say that right?"

"Not even close. Anyway, ya know what? I'm going to hit up that Canadian girl."

"Explain."

"Oh yeah, remember the other day when I freaked out at lunch and stormed off?"

"How could I forget?"

"Well, I found a hostel and needed a WiFi signal to check if I got a text from… her… and I met a Canadian girl who is *definitely* down to fuck."

"DTF!"

"Bingo."

"What's her name?"

"I don't remember."

"That's a good start."

"Let me check my Facebook search history." I took a sip of the freshly opened wine. "Dude, this shit is rough. You didn't let it breathe at all."

"Breathe?"

"And this is expensive juice. Marcel said we could drink this?"

"…"

"…"

"So you find her yet?"

"Trying to. It was a stupid fucking name with "berry" in it, but now all I can think of are strawberries."

"Cranberry?"

"No, it isn't the name of a fruit itself. It just had "berry" in it. Like… like… Thornberry?"

"Blackberry?"

"You're not helping."

"Boysenberry?"

"It definitely began with a T. Or an L…"

"Loganberry?"

"Seriously?"

"Papaya?"

"Hagenberry! Jane Hagenberry. That's it."

"I was close."

I searched her name and showed Kev her profile pic, the one from the bridge with the view of the Eiffel Tower and the purple umbrella with the big yellow polka dots.

"Total babe," he assured me.

"Right? I had complete tunnel vision when I first met her, I suppose."

"Hit her up. Right now. Invite her over for some wine and some sex."

"Yeah, that'll work."

"Fine, leave out the sex part, but hit her up now. You need this. Every second you've lived has led you to this moment."

"You could say that about anything. That's just called 'the present.'"

"Jeez, just do it already."

"Okay, okay."

Hey Jane, you might not remember me, but we met the other day in the hostel. You gave me the WiFi password and told me to friend you. Anyway, we've got an apartment here in the Montmartre if you wanted to come over later and hang. Just let me know. Joel

"You signed it?" he said. "I've seen you charm a girl's pants off by just using quotes from *Punic*. You could've done better than that." He made a motion with his finger like he was fixing the imaginary glasses between his eyes. "*If you'd like to come over later and hang,*" he started in a nasally voice.

"Fuck off. I'm out of my element. I just had my heart broken, man."

"Sack up. Drink your wine."

And we sat and talked and got drunk off wine that was too complex for our palates, but the alcohol numbed my pain receptors and our banter took my mind off Fantine, the Riviera Bitch, if only for a few hours.

Jane responded quickly:

Heyyy! Yeah of course I remember you. I'm with a couple of friends but we'd def come over if that's okay. Give me the address and I'll check the nearest subway stop.

"Ya see that? Three Ys, she wants to fuck," I said, sitting back in my seat with my hands behind my head.

"*I can* see that," he said, "and *I'll* have two to choose from."

By the time they arrived, we had already finished the *Châteauneuf-du-Pape* and were on to something cheaper and easier to drink. Marcel and Riley had not yet returned from their rendezvous, which meant we had been unsupervised for the better part of the day and had left the apartment a mess. We sat on the balcony, and I would lean over the railing to check if I could see them approaching the building. The rain had subsided and the sun peeked through the clouds, casting an ominous glow over the wet city.

"Is that them? No way," I said.

"What?"

"Dude, she brought two *guys* with her."

"Seriously?"

I checked the message again and reread it out loud: "I'm with a couple of friends…"

"Power move," said Kev.

"Hey!" I called down, waving my arm in the air like a sailor returning from voyage. I buzzed them in and waited by the door. Kev sat on the couch with his glass of wine and feet resting on the coffee table. I checked and could still smell residue from the cologne that Marcel sprayed on me earlier. I didn't wear my jacket—that smelled of *her*.

"Hey, wow, this place is really nice," said Jane. "I didn't think Airbnb had places like this."

"Oh, it's our friend's apartment. He's just not here right now," I said.

"Hello, it is a pleasure to meet you," said one of the guys standing behind Jane. "My name is Enrique."

"Yeah, so this is Enrique and this is Iago. He's from Portugal and he's from Spain."

"Actually, I am from Portugal," said Iago. "And *he* is from Spain."

"Oh, I always confuse those two. It's like the same thing anyway."

The two Iberians rolled their eyes in disgust, but didn't correct her—hot chicks can get away with murder.

They brought gin and tonic, which they unpacked on the island and poured into plastic cups.

"They're also staying at the hostel. We're roommates. Usually I stay in all-girl rooms, but those were already booked. We already went to the *Notre Dame* and I want to go to the cathedral up here. It looks gorgeous. You can see it from the top of the Eiffel Tower, which I already did but would do again, it was *that* gorgeous."

I resisted the urge to correct her Cathedral-Basilica mishap and instead asked, "So where in Spain and Portugal are you guys from?"

"I am from *Sevilla*. Do you know it?"

"I am from Lisbon."

"I haven't been to either of them. Actually, never been to Spain *or* Portugal."

"How long since you have come to Paris?" asked Enrique.

"We've been here a few days now," I said.

"This apartment is so gorgeous. I can't get over it," said Jane, spinning in a circle, admiring the artwork.

"I think we've got Amsterdam next, then Berlin. Right, Kev?"

"You will go the wrong way," said Enrique. "You must come to Spain after Paris. We have the best food in Europe. This I promise to you."

"No, no, you will come to Portugal. If you have time, then go to Spain," said Iago while grabbing Enrique's arm.

"Eww, why is there a painting of a dead guy in a tub?" called Jane from the living room.

I couldn't tell them, but Spain and Portugal had never appealed to me. In middle school, my French teacher had the mentality that "Africa begins at the Pyrenees," and from then on my focus had always been to the east of France. My only experience with Portuguese was when we went to the restaurants in Eastside Newark for *rodizio*: all you can eat meat brought to the table in rounds and sliced straight from skewers and washed down with pitchers of cheap sangria, which led us, more than once, to get caught in the Brazilian Day Festival a.k.a. "Chopfest." My mother would shield Carlo's eyes from the voluptuous, barely covered asses of Ironbound's finest.

"Where are you and your friend from?" asked Enrique.

"The States," I said.

"Yes, of course, but where? Which city?"

"New York."

"Seriously?" said Kev, to which I gave a Gallic shrug I must've picked up earlier.

"I have always wanted to go there. I have never been to America," said Enrique.

Enrique had short amber hair with both sides and the back buzzed skin-tight, with the back of his neck tapered. He wore his khaki pants with the bottoms rolled up past the ankle and a t-shirt that had Old Glory and the Union Jack melting into one. On his wrists were brown leather bracelets and on his middle finger he had a black ring. He rarely stood straight up, always leaning on something: the counter, the island, a chair. His jaw line was chiseled and it looked like he was never able to grow any facial hair. If I had to guess, he was about twenty-one. He was comfortable enough with English that he rarely needed to say the word in Spanish and ask for a translation. He would instead pause for a moment and find a synonym, even if that meant the sentence didn't flow smoothly. He was clearly educated in the UK or by a British teacher, because he would use words like "rubbish bin" in place of "garbage can" and "mate" for "dude" or "man" or "chief." He was one of those guys the rest of us guys hated for no reason, but I was drunk and chipper and decided to give him a shot anyway.

Iago didn't speak much until after his second or third gin and tonic. His English, to my surprise, far exceeded Enrique's in both proper sentence structure and vocabulary range. His skin was parchment-white with blots of scarlet where he had failed to apply lotion and was tinged by the sun. His eyes were a gorgeous cerulean, and I caught myself sneaking glances at them when he was in conversation with Enrique or Jane. What I would soon find out was that Iago is a stellar guitar player who specializes in the hauntingly beautiful musical genre called fado, which is genuinely Portuguese with its provenance in Lisbon. He had come to Paris to play in a few shows at "fado bars" located in the traditionally Portuguese neighborhoods of the city. After Algerian, Portuguese is the second largest minority population in Paris—I know, you can find these people everywhere.

"The guitar is my lifeblood and my best friend. I would be lost without it," he said when Jane asked, "What would you do if you didn't play guitar?"

Marcel and Riley finally returned around ten, and I suppose the place was in shambles compared to what Marcel had grown accustomed to, because he immediately began cleaning and muttering to himself.

"Hey guys and new friends. Love it. This is what it's all about, right? Let me guess, Australians?" Riley said, holding out her hand to Jane.

"I'm Canadian. He's Spanish and he's Portuguese."

"Oh, I'm sorry. Canada is cool too! You guys have free healthcare!"

"We will too, if Meyer gets what he wants," said Kev, perking up from the couch.

"And that's a bad thing?" said Jane, with support from Riley.

"You guys don't get it. The US *isn't* Canada. It's not just one equation fits all. This is one-sixth of our economy going to the federal government…"

"Guys, guys, guys," I said, "cardinal rule being broken here—no politics or religion talk while drinking. I think we learned that last night… Now someone take this shot with me."

Marcel, who for the past several minutes had been frantically picking up wine and beer bottles and scrubbing the dirty dishes that had been piling up in the sink, whispered something to Riley and went to his room. The rest of us stood at the edges of the island, forming a casing of inebriated mirth. Here, we pointed across the granite countertop, sharing travel anecdotes and insisting that one city had better street food vendors than the other, that the beer in Germany outperformed that of the Czech Republic, and that Barcelona was the most cosmopolitan city in Europe, despite dissenters for London. We only left the island to take a leak or have a smoke on the balcony, returning to find someone lining up a row of shots of something that burned our throats.

Marcel emerged from his room and hurried out the door. Over his shoulder, he said, "I will see you later. Please clean up, Joel, Kev." Riley was visibly distraught and chugged the gin and tonic Enrique had made for her, unscrewing the cap to the gin bottle before pulling the cup down from her lips.

"What was that?" I asked.

"He's going to see that psycho from last night."

"Mehdi?"

"Yeah, the one who wants us all in chains."

"End women's suffrage!" yelled Kev.

Riley positioned herself at my side and spoke into her cup, "So this chick here for you?"

"Yeah, I suppose."

"That was fast."

I took a shot of tequila. I hate tequila.

"I'll talk you up to her," she said.

"Don't sweat it. How was the Louvre?"

"Oh. My. God. Incredible! The sculptors are alive, huge pieces of perfectly cut marble…"

"And perfectly cut man butt," said Kev.

"Ha, ha, but seriously, it blew my mind. Have you heard of… hold on, I wrote his name down… Anne-Louis Girodet de Roussy-Trioson? My new favorite artist. *The Entombment of Atala* spoke to me. I wanted to spend more time in the Renaissance and Roman and Etruscan sections, but Marcel kept pushing the Islamic art. Oh, and the *Mona Lisa*! Tiny! Could barely see it. This group of Chinese tourists just crammed their way to the front of the thing and snapped like four thousand pics. It was insanity."

"They're like locusts," I said.

Enrique held a plastic grocery bag in the air and plunked it down on the granite countertop. We all swung to face him like he had shot a bullet into the air. "My new friends, for you, I have a gift." The glowing bottle was a shamrock green. "Absinthe," he said.

A barrage of cheers and jeers stopped all conversations as the Spaniard lined up the shot glasses. "No excuses. I know you like it, Iago."

I was already shitfaced, and it occurred to me that Kev and I skipped dinner to get straight to the good stuff—rookie mistake. He was also shitfaced, and this shot of the "Green Fairy" was sure to send us over the edge. The sociable, witty Joel that we've all come to love would drown and decay after this shot. Kev and I looked to each other for a shred of sanity: perhaps one of us would cast a line, fall into the safety net that hung below roller coasters filled with hats and sandals.

"Brothers in arms," he said.

"Brothers in arms," I echoed.

"This has the wormwood," Enrique assured us. "It's hard to find. I have a friend."

From then on, the night was a tumultuous blur of sundry conversations and photo ops. In lieu of my warning, Kev and Enrique argued over Cuba's role in the Western Hemisphere and whether or not "cultural revolutions" were masked by despotic agendas or naturally occurring events that were destined to occur in all parts of the world with the acceptance of liberalism. "Examine Algeria," said Enrique. "What could Hamachi, or whatever he calls himself, hide his intentions to hurt people?"

"Brother, I have no idea what you're saying here," said Kev as he mixed another gin and tonic with his finger.

I caught Riley texting in the corner several times. I snatched her phone from her hand and tossed it around the room, to Kev, to Enrique, to Iago—Jane gave it back to her. I finally made a move on Jane. I pushed her into the bathroom with me and told her, "We need to talk. It's a matter of life and death, I suppose."

"I'm not going to have sex with you," she said immediately, as if throwing up a laser beam force field grid. We kissed and I unbuttoned my shirt; she took off hers. "I'm serious. I'm not *like* that."

"To what are you referring?" I said.

"I'M. NOT. GOING. TO. HAVE. SEX. WITH. YOU," she iterated. "I mean it."

I went for her pants and slipped on the bathroom rug, smacking my head on the sink countertop. "Oh my god!" she shouted.

"Is everything okay in there?" said Enrique as he knocked against the door.

"My fucking head! Am I bleeding?"

"No." Jane stood up against the wall with her shirt clenched against her chest.

"Fuck, that hurt."

"I'll give you head," she said, an offer I should've taken. But instead I transformed into some machismo asshole who only wanted one thing.

"Fuck that. Kev can do that for me. I want to fuck." See above: transformed into some machismo asshole.

"You're vile. I'm outta here."

"No, don't..." And I lunged at her, and I promise I wasn't going to rape her, it was a mere drunken cry for help: I wanted to kiss her and I know it doesn't seem like it and everything leading up to that pointed to the opposite, but I'm not like that, I swear. I was just really fucking hurt by stupid Fantine and I didn't want any more rejection and I could tell you it's a childhood thing, but I don't really think it was. I just felt shitty and alone and I felt like the biggest pussy, so I lunged at her to keep her in the bathroom, which I know was so very stupid, but just do me the favor and believe that my intentions—well, I wouldn't say they were *pure*, but they weren't as abhorrent as you must be thinking.

Jane screamed and bolted from the bathroom, shirt still in hand, and beelined it for the stairs, snatching her clutch from the island on the way out. Iago went after her while the three others hurried into the bathroom to witness the pathetic, blubbering cretin named Joel Lupo.

"What the fuck happened?" said Kev.

"Get out," I said. "Get the fuck out!"

My stomach slow-churned like Amish butter. Enrique brought in a glass of water and Riley patted my back.

"No. Get off. No. I'm fine." I retched into the porcelain bowl and vividly remembered (the only thing I could vividly remember from that night) Kev commenting on how "green" my creation was.

"Joel is an alien," he said.

"Fuck her, man," I said, five, ten, thirty times over.

"Dude, what happened?"

"No, not her. The other one. Fountain… Fantine." More green liquid splashed into the toilet.

"Oh, Joelie, let's get you to bed."

"No. I'm fine."

"You're wasted."

"Why don't you go suck that black dick."

"Oh shit, dude," said Kev, covering his mouth with his hand.

"FUCK YOU, JOEL! Fucking asshole." And she left.

"Sssadam in ell," I mumbled.

"What?"

"Sssadam in ellll."

"Dude, what are you *saying*?"

"Adam's in Hell! Adam's in Hell!"

"I'm going to leave now," said Enrique. "Nice to meet you, mates. Find me on the Facebook, Kevin."

"Oh fuck. Okay, man. Let's get you up and in bed. Drink the water."

"You drink the…" I stuck my face back in the toilet; the vomit stuck like a string attached to my lip. My hand gripped the flush handle.

"Get it out, Joel. Get those demons out."

Fuck Absinthe.

My stomach was eating itself like a trapped fox gnaws at its own gnarled foot. I smashed into the kitchen and devoured an entire baguette while sitting on the floor. No one else was awake, so I just lay in my filth; my bare back froze and jumped when it hit the cold tile. Nothing much came to me from the previous night, only mortifying snippets of embarrassment left to piece together my torment. On the subject of torment, I pictured Fantine wrapped around my midsection, moving in for a kiss, and suddenly vanishing into clouds of tan dust, only to reappear under her thrusting French lover, Antoine—I named him because, like I said, I was tormenting myself.

I had set up a time to Skype with my family later that day and spent the rest of the day nursing myself back to a presentable state. Mom didn't like how grouchy I was when hung over. Marcel and Riley were cracking the headboard against the wall shared by his sister's bedroom. Kev, unable to sleep, moseyed over to the couch and retold what had transpired last night.

"I said that?"

"Yeah, man, it was pretty fucked up. You should def apologize to her. She loves you, man."

"I suppose… You think she told Marcel?"

"Doubt it."

"He's going to hurt her."

"I know. She's going to pull something for sure, the way they go at it," he said, listening to the cracks against the wall.

"No, dude, not like that. Like, *emotionally*."

The sunlight beamed through the windows and illuminated the partly cleaned apartment, mocking me as I wrapped myself in a static-inducing blanket and hissed at the outside world. I received a text.

Text from Sal: 10:12 a.m.: Hey bud. Remember today is father's day. Don't forget to say happy father's day to Dad when we Skype. See you soon!

BINGE UNTIL TRAGEDY

The door to Marcel's room opened and I was nervous to see Riley, something I had never felt before. She had always been on Team Joel, regardless of how shitty I treated her friends. For instance, there was the time I sharted while I was on a date with a chick from the all-girls college nearby, and Riley drove to the restaurant and met me in the men's bathroom and airdropped the clean underwear and cologne into the stall and saved me from what was—until last night—the most embarrassing moment of my life.

Or the time when Riley and Jessica Zurn were joining me for mid-party coke lines in my room and Campus Safety Officer Jack—Little Jack, who was a total dick, unlike Big Jack, who was a six-foot-six teddy bear—banged on the door because he was getting noise complaints from our neighbors. Campus Safety rarely bothered us, so we must've been extra rowdy that Wednesday. Little Jack was set to come in and demanded we open the door or else he would unlock it himself—the man had a ring of jingling keys that could sink a canoe.

Riley told me to turn off the lights and get in my underwear while she and Jessica did the same and jumped into my bed and held the covers just over their boobs, then she instructed me to answer the door, respectfully, but sort of in a rush, like, "Brother, come on, look what I got going on here," and guess what? It totally worked. Little Jack took one look at the blushing girls, asked if they were drunk, and winked at me after insisting we turn the music down.

Riley was my partner in crime, and I'd been a shitty Clyde. So when she came out of the room, she said, "Morning," and poured herself a cup of coffee and stood at the counter, facing away from us. She waited, to give me more time to say something, I suppose. She even opened the refrigerator again to add cream—Riley is lactose intolerant. But I lay on the couch, cocooned in the blanket, and didn't say boo. She went back into Marcel's room and huffed "unbelievable" under her breath before shutting the door. I lost my shot, I suppose.

I Skyped with my family on the tablet my aunt gave me for graduation. When I heard that ring, the bubbly chime of the outgoing call, I thought of those afternoons I'd spent tucked away in the corners of the third floor of the library, waiting for Fantine to answer from the shores of the Mediterranean. I snapped from my daydreaming once the ring stopped and my father answered, sitting at his laptop with my family hunched over, forming a semicircle around his bulbous head.

"There he is! The world traveler," he said.

"Heyyyy, Dad. Happy Father's Day."

Aunt Maria, Aunt Lena, my mom, my Uncle Vito, my cousin Maria, my cousin Ottavia, my Uncle Nico, my cousin Angela, Sal, and Michelle all crammed for eye space and shouted incoherently at the computer, my aunts believing the closer their dyed lips were to the screen, the better I could understand them.

"Joel, where are ya?"

"You eatin' enough?"

"He looks thin."

"He shaved! There's that face I love."

"Doesn't he look thin?"

"Is he in Italy?"

"Vito, don't touch that, it's for dessert."

"Remember when we went to Positano? Nico, are you listenin' ta me?"

"Tell him when he goes…"

"Joel, your Aunt Lena says when you go to Verona to try…"

"Why are we talking to him if he's only in Verona?"

"Not Verona, New Jersey, you meathead."

"Joelie, how are you on money?"

"Joel, did you hear that? Your uncle thought you were in Verona, New Jersey!"

I can't do this.

"Have you met any French girls?"

"Shhh, that's a sore subject."

Mom took the laptop from the kitchen and went alone into the dining room.

"We all miss you so much here… How's Paris?"

"It's good."

"It's the City of Lights! Or is it Light? Anyway, how could that *just* be good? I remember when I first went there in 1975… or was it '76?… This was before I knew your father…" She checked to see if anyone was listening from the kitchen.

"Well, it was so… romantic. I know, I know, it sounds cliché, but… ugh… wow… *Paris*." She stared off into another time of her life that, given her animalistic noises, I'd rather not know the details about. "Anyway, how are Kevin and Riley?" she said, returning to present-day New Jersey.

I turned the tablet so it faced Kev. "Hi, Mrs. Lupo," he said, waving like a doofus.

"I spoke to your mother the other…"

"Mom, he can't hear you, I'm wearing earphones."

"Oh, right. Where's Riley?"

"She's… busy." Kev gave me an odd look, like "you're more clever than that."

"Okay then, I'll put more money in your account if you need it. Be smart. Be safe."

"I will."

"I love you, Joel."

"Love you too, Ma."

"Oh! Your brother has something to tell you. He didn't specify. Sal! He's ready for you!"

My big brother plopped down in front of the laptop, sporting that million-dollar grin that won him "Best Smile" for his senior yearbook superlative.

"What is up, mah man?"

"Hey, Sal."

"Long night?"

"You could say that."

"Hey, so I got Dad this contraption for Father's Day. It's for when he's on the toilet and reads his mags—you know how he spends forever in there. Well, this thing is like a stand for the magazine so you don't get those pins and needles in your legs. Looks pretty funny. Now he'll never want to leave!"

"That sounds pretty good."

"Yeah, I put your name on it too."

"Oh, thanks."

"So, where to next, big guy? Rome? London?"

"Amsterdam."

"Amsterdaaammm. Very sweet."

"Yeah, I've been there before. This'll be round two."

"You meet with that old crush yet? Ya know, the one from your semester abroad?"

"No… Haven't seen her."

"Bummer. Okay, well, I have some news, and I haven't told anyone yet, not even Mom or Dad."

"Promotion?"

"No, no. Joel… Michelle is pregnant."

"… You sure it's yours?" I still don't know why this was my response.

"Shut up, dick!" he laughed. "Yes, it's mine. I'm gonna be a father!"

"That's nuts, man. Congrats."

"What happened?" asked Kev.

"Thanks so much, bud. Hope it's a boy, fingers crossed." And he made crossed fingers in front of the camera.

"Karma's a bitch."

"Gee, thanks, man. Hey, lemme know if you need anything while you're over there. I asked Mom to set it up so I can direct deposit into your account. Have fun. I'm going to tell the fam the news now. Love ya, bud."

"You too, Sal."

I lay on the couch face up, eyes closed. My headache had subsided, but I could feel cramps forming in the arches of my feet. Kev asked what happened, so I told him Sal was going to be a father, but if we continued this conversation I'd literally die.

Marcel and Riley crept out of their dwelling and asked us if we wanted to go to the Père Lachaise Cemetery: "It's where Jim Morrison is buried, along with Proust, Chopin, Edith Piaf, and Oscar Wilde. Most visited cemetery in the world," said Marcel.

"Already did it," I said. "Last time I was here, I took a split of Côte de Beaune with me and had a drink with Oscar."

"So that's a no," said Riley. "Kev?"

"No, thanks, I'm cool. Cemeteries give me the heebie-jeebies."

"Zombies?" asked Marcel.

"Yeah, man, say what you want about us Americans, but when the apocalypse happens, I'll be down in Texas where they have Hummers and worship the Second Amendment."

When Riley and Marcel left, I yelled, "I'll clean any puke that didn't make it into the toilet, Marcel!"

"Thank you, Joel!" he called back, already walking down the stairs.

I looked at Kev, who shook his head and stared into his phone, and I closed my eyes and took a deep breath and fell back asleep.

THE WHITE CITY ON THE COAST

OMAR CRASHED THROUGH THE FRONT DOOR OF his apartment, bloodied and battered. He had been held and interrogated by the police for five days, with little food or water. Salim rushed to pick his friend up off the ground. Omar was using every morsel of pride to hold back tears, but the sunken bags, the concavities beneath the eyes, belied his strength and showed he had been weeping for days. Omar's stomach growled while Salim tried to hoist him into a kitchen chair, but Omar was too heavy and fell onto the floor. Salim had no recollection of how he ended up back in his apartment after the protest, but their mutual friend Mohamed had been sleeping on the sofa when he woke up from his blackout.

Mohamed had told Salim that they dragged him from the crowd before any officers could get a hold of him and that it had been too late to go after Omar. The General had unleashed the armored police on the crowd, and rumors had spread that snipers were on rooftops shooting at fleeing protestors like target practice. Four were dead and nine were still missing—all of them students at the university. Classes had been canceled indefinitely.

Immediately following the protests, Hannachi had spoken to "the world" on international broadcasts, claiming militants had seeped into the demonstrations and began assaulting officers, who reacted in self-defense. He promised he would not allow his country to succumb to terrorists and cracked down on all forms of opposition. New curfews and congregational limits were implemented—from now on, women could not cover their faces, and anyone could be subject to "random" searches on the streets, in cafés, and in their homes at any and all hours of the day. *La Peste* roamed the streets in plain clothes, questioning anyone who engaged in "suspicious" activity. Overnight, Algeria had become a police state lubricated with fear.

Police and the few military defectors had gone missing or were in hiding. Many believed they had been killed, executed under the auspices of the General. The more optimistic believed they were hiding deep in the Sahara or in Morocco and would return to the city to fight for them, for their families.

Omar scarfed down the first pieces of fruit and bread he could knock off from the table and let the crumbs and pits rest on his convulsing chest and stomach. Salim poured him a cup of tea and wrapped ice in a washcloth, hesitating before asking the haunting question, "What did they do to you?" as he helped his friend into clean clothes. In between gnarled breaths, Omar told Salim how they'd handcuffed him to a chair and questioned if he had ties to *al-Saif*, a growing Islamist militant group that had been behind raids on oil fields in Mali and had a growing presence in Saharan towns like Bordj Mokhtar and In Guezzam. Omar said that every time he swore he didn't know any members of *al-Saif*, the interrogators hit him with a large strap across his bare chest and stomach. They threw him in a cell with two other students, similarly dressed in white *thawbs* and *taqiyahs*, bloodstained and filthy. The police would randomly pull one of the three out, ask him the same questions, and beat him more fervently with each line of questioning. Omar never saw the General, but there was a large mirror that filled up the entire wall on one side of the room, and the entire time he was being strapped across the stomach or choke-slammed against the ground, he could feel eyes beaming through the glass and watching the entire escapade unfold, relaying instructions to his commanding officers, enjoying every shivering second.

"They have this apartment marked now," he told Salim. "If they suspect *anything*, they will come back for me, and you too."

Salim, who was spilling tea all over the table, his knees beginning to buckle as he listened to his friend's heart-wrenching experience, nervously added sugar to the cups to the point the tea became undrinkable. Mohamed finally woke up from his drooling slumber on the couch and listened as Omar replayed his experience. This time, Salim grew angry and pounded the table with a closed fist, rattling the teapot and cups. Mohamed turned on the small television in the living room and flipped to a French channel that showed President LaGrange speaking from a podium.

"At this point, we see no dire circumstances that would call for French military intervention against the Hannachi government. What we ask is for President Hannachi to open up talks with European and African nations, and not block the Algerian people from the outside world."

Omar, who was hovering over his plate of food, scrounging crumbs with his licked finger, said, "We don't need the French. We don't need Europe." Salim grabbed him another piece of naan and apricot jam.

"Then what do we do? Hide? Silence ourselves? Get killed?" asked Mohamed.

"They'll kill us anyway. You did not see it, Mohamed. I did. This country is doomed unless we fight back."

Mohamed was well known at university for being an excellent singer and songwriter—many knew him simply as the "Oud Player." It didn't hurt either that Mohamed had a pointed face with high cheekbones and a heart-melting smile.

"We hold a vigil. Then another and another," said Salim. "From now on, we record every moment out there. We put it on YouTube and Facebook. We show the world that we're being fed to the dogs."

"*La Peste* will find us," said Mohamed.

"I don't see any other solutions. We don't have weapons," said Salim.

"We will," said Omar. "When I was there, the guards would talk in between beatings. They would argue over the 'scum' defectors who were leaving for Morocco. More and more, they would say. Soldiers too." Omar lay on the couch, chest exposed for his friends to witness the intense bruising in purples and reds. Salim tended to his wounds as best he could. "They're forming an army," Omar added.

"What about wea—"

"Foreign investment. The Gulf is funding militias."

"Then we just need to hold out until then. Until they come back for us."

Conversation halted as each of the three young men imagined his own version of a triumphant army returning, riding through the Algerian sands, armed to the teeth, glistening green-and-white flags mounted on their Humvees and tanks.

"We need to get him to *La Petite Mère*'s house," said Salim. "I don't have the proper supplies here."

As Salim and Mohamed gathered their things, Omar lay motionless, staring up past the ceiling into the hidden stars stuck in the gooey pudding of space. "We go back to the Square." Salim and Mohamed shot each other concerned looks. "We go back, we take it over. We camp, we cook…"

"We hand out food to the poorest of the city," added Salim. "We make it all visible to the world."

Algiers was bleak and reeked of indigence. The Square had yet to be cleaned; forgotten shoes and sandals and scarves were strewn across dirt-covered cement. Bloodstains that speckled the white walls of the El Jedid Mosque were prohibited from being cleaned—their presence served as a caveat against further rallying against the regime. Shops and stores attempted to go about their business, but with each customer came glances of suspicion. *La Peste* usually took the form of middle-aged men, but the General was not above recruiting young boys and girls or the elderly as paid informants: "A service to your nation," he would say. The night after the protest, raids of an internet café, a kebab shop, and an antique store were carried out. The interiors were decimated; handcrafted statuettes from West Africa and intricately painted tiles from Istanbul were smashed to smithereens, and the old man who operated the antique store since the mid-1970s was taken in for "questioning"—he had yet to be seen. His wife stood at the gate of the police headquarters weeping for three days. Friends brought her meals.

It was easy for the regime to make the dissidents fear the government—guns and batons can do that—but with *La Peste* roaming the neighborhoods, the regime had incorporated a new spine-tingling element into its strategy: making the dissidents fear each other. You see, the regime had bigger problems to address—the Islamists, who were being funded by Gulf State donors, were gaining momentum in the South, and the regime anticipated attacks on major coastal cities soon. The protestors were peanuts compared to the firepower of Gulf-funded jihadists who condemned the actions of Hannachi and state officials on YouTube, Twitter, and Facebook.

Salim and Mohamed helped Omar down crumbling flights of steps that were missing stones and rocks at their edges. *La Petite Mère* lived only a short walk through the Casbah and was surely preparing tea, always expecting youthful company.

"How did you get home?" asked Salim.

"A black van dropped me off. They blindfolded me, even though I knew where I had been the entire time. For effect, I guess," said Omar.

Farah, a classmate and close friend of Salim's, who always thought Mohamed was so handsome and Omar so repulsive, was at *La Petite Mère's* house sipping tea and having a conversation with the old woman, but was more talking to herself out loud while *La Petite Mère* tended to yellow and white flowers lining her windowsill. Farah was short and stocky and had been her entire life. Her hair was curly and fell right around the middle of her neck, and her round-frame glasses did not much help her already round face. She was lucky enough to study for an entire year in London, where she became fluent in English, and would teach Salim popular phrases she had picked up from her English classmates; everything was hyperbolically "brilliant" or "dreadful." Her dreams of becoming a movie star faded as she hit puberty, coming to the quick realization that her "look" left much to be desired, and because of her curly hair and short stature, she wouldn't even be able to fill the spot as "Middle-Eastern/Arab Girl Number Three." Nevertheless, Farah only continued to fall more in love with cinema and would stay up watching films into the darkest hour of the night, studying the mannerisms of the best actors in the UK and US, the dialogue between lovers and enemies, plot twists, character development, lighting, and the history of period pieces—she especially enjoyed the show *Punic,* which she streamed online, and despite the proper British accents, she took a sort of pride in the story and its focus on the power of the North African empire that once was (plus, Damien Rogers put a warming sensation in the pit of her stomach).

At university, Farah was a student of medicine like Salim, but in her free time she worked on creating films, most of which were centered around her native city—her most recent work, *La ville blanche sur la côte* (*The White City on the Coast*), had started out as a documentary about the exorbitant levels of poverty and lack of opportunity for the youth of Algiers. But because of the turmoil, it had morphed into a recording of the protests against, and the corruption of, the Hannachi regime. Farah always carried her camera, and people lined up just to get a few seconds of ranting on film. At the most recent violent protests, she shot from ground level and from the rooftops, and was lucky to be at the latter when the General unleashed the scourge of the police force on the demonstrators—she didn't see any snipers.

When the three stumbling friends arrived at *La Petite Mère's* home, the little woman took one look at Omar and immediately rushed to his aid. Farah threw on her camera and began asking questions. For a third time, Omar had to retell the brutality he suffered.

"Did you actually *see* the General?"

"No. But he was there. Trust me, the entire time we were beaten, he was there."

Salim turned on his laptop and opened *La Liberté's* Facebook page—a couple of years ago they set up a WiFi network in *La Petite Mère's* home, which they paid for themselves. The group had fourteen new members, which put them at forty-five, all from Algeria and Morocco, except for a few from France. He opened their Twitter page; fifty-six followers, thirteen new. The picture for both their Facebook and Twitter pages was a clenched fist in the colors of a melting Algerian flag, with *La liberté ne meurt jamais* tattooed on the wrist—a design Salim had created himself.

"A human rights group from Belgium wants to come here and meet with me," said Farah. "They saw my video of the last protest on YouTube. They want to meet you too, Salim."

"Anything. We need to show the world… Oh no…" he said, jumping up from his seat. He read from his laptop screen, "Nineteen Tunisian students are 'missing' after police cracked down on protests in Tunis yesterday."

"An epidemic," said Omar, who was lying on the couch with his chest exposed as *La Petite M*ère applied an herbal rub to his bruising. "But the world doesn't care, my friend. This is the fight for Algeria, and therefore it must be fought by Algerians, not Belgians."

"Don't be so dense," snapped Farah, who eased her tone when she glanced at the bruising on Omar's chest. "The world wants to help. When I was in London…"

"Yes, yes, we all know. They will march in the streets in London; they will march in the streets in Paris. 'Free Palestine! Free Palestine!' they will shout, but they will never cross the Mediterranean and walk the streets of Algiers or Tunis or Ramallah. Like I have always said, this is a war for Muslims. Muslim blood for Muslim freedom."

"Well… we'll try anyway," said Salim over the sound of buttons clacking on his keyboard.

Mohamed tuned the oud he kept at *La Petite M*ère*'s* home at all times, while Salim pursued more recruits to join *La Liberté* on Facebook. Farah rewatched her most recent video on YouTube, reading the comments that trailed down the screen. Omar replayed the torment he suffered and sipped tea whenever he felt the pulling sensation of tears in his eye sockets as *La Petite M*ère watered her flowers and periodically checked on Omar to apply more herbs and freshen his tea. And for spells of several minutes, no one spoke. The silence was only broken by the call to prayer.

BINGE UNTIL TRAGEDY

She ran her hands over the mauve four hundred thread count Egyptian cotton sheets to ease her trembles. She'd never felt anything like it before. Only hours earlier she was taking care of her younger brothers, serving them breakfast and making sure they were dressed appropriately for school. Her father was paid enough, enough for food and rent for the next six months, enough to take the edge off, and enough to numb the pain of selling his daughter for three nights. That was the deal, three nights, no marks on the face or wrists, and she would be returned to their doorstep the morning after the final night.

The man who proposed the deal to her father approached him when he was leaving the market with a bag of figs and fresh milk. He had spotted the girl, who was on the cusp of womanhood and fit the description perfectly. He was an "appropriator," a job that entailed finding girls who met specified qualifications in Algiers, in Oran, in Marrakesh, and even in Marseille. When he made his final offer, he would pull his sunglasses down the bridge of his nose and comb back his jet-black hair. He was irresistible.

He approached her father, who was taken by surprise when this slick young man flashed 100,000 DZD (Algerian Dinar—about $1,050) behind the breast of his suit jacket. And since that kind of money is just not flashed in that part of Algiers, the man had both the father's attention and interest, and they stopped to talk business.

Her body was changing and she felt sick, like an aching something in her stomach and a sharp pain below that, and it was all new and scary. Her mom hadn't been around since she was an infant, which put even more pressure on her father, who now had three kids to raise alone. So that 100,000 DZD would let him breathe again.

They came and took her before she left for school. She didn't put up a fight because she didn't have any idea what was happening to her. Her father stood in the doorway to her room crying, pleading, "Never mind, never mind. I don't want the money anymore. Don't take my daughter." But the men were robotic in their procedure and told her if she didn't struggle, she wouldn't get hurt. So she walked out with them scared but brave and sat in the back of a black van as the pain thrusted inside her pelvis. And as they careened through the city and approached the Presidential Palace, her suspicions were quelled, for she knew then what would become of her.

That night, when the sun had set on Algiers and the only light came from the orange glow of candles, she stood trembling at the foot of President Hannachi's bed, spreading her hands on the mauve four hundred thread count Egyptian cotton sheets, which felt so nice on her calluses, and she wondered as she looked out the window, if she jumped, would it kill her? But she suppressed these thoughts because of her brothers, the two little ones who gave her a reason not to jump out of the window and instead to do exactly what the president wanted, because it was only three nights. And she had heard but didn't believe it until then that they would feed you well and bathe you in perfumed soaps if you went along with it and didn't scream or make a fuss.

So when he entered the room, she gave a rudimentary curtsy and said, "I am here to please you, Your Excellency." This was what she was briefed to say by a kind woman who sat her down only thirty minutes before and explained to her the nuances of her "appointment" as she got her dressed in her outfit. The president took off his jacket and laid it on the back of a chair that had been pulled out from an anachronous desk with gold flowers chiseled up the legs and a ruby-red top. It appeared to serve no function except for the chair, the back of which the president liked to drape his jacket over.

The president was shorter than she had imagined, and when he approached her, he did nothing to hide the erection screaming in his pants. She was dressed in lacy mauve underwear that hugged her budding pubescent body, and only then did she realize it matched perfectly with the four hundred thread count Egyptian cotton sheets that were smooth on the skin not gripped by lingerie. She leaned back onto the bed, and the president's erection jabbed her in the midsection, adding a new element to the pain she had already been experiencing all day.

BINGE UNTIL TRAGEDY

"Yasmina," he whispered as he licked behind her earlobe. She was expecting this, the name Yasmina. The woman who sat her down only thirty-one minutes before told her that for the next three nights, she was Yasmina. The woman, whose voice was soft like her schoolteacher's, told her the best thing she could do was to pretend it was all make-believe, that if she had any sort of imagination at all, to go and summon it, and that for the next three days and nights she was the Moorish princess Yasmina, who adored her king and wanted to please him, and no matter what, she warned, no matter what, "DO NOT tell your king your real name."

The president told the girl to undo his pants, starting with his belt, but when she was too slow and clumsy, he grabbed her by the back of the head and threw her on the bed. Those four hundred thread count Egyptian cotton sheets felt like a bed of four hundred serrated daggers and nails. She held back tears because the kind woman, her mortal angel who cleaned her and tended to her after each "appointment," told her tears would only make him more aggressive. He left her on the bed and walked to the corner of the room and opened a chest she hadn't noticed until now.

"This is my treasure chest," he said. He pulled out a long, thin rope, letting it dangle in the air like a zookeeper might do with a docile snake as he turned back to the bed. The girl didn't bother to ask how the rope would be used. She stared up at the ceiling, whose blue hues mimicked the sky, and in it were engraved dotted stars that represented a world free from pleasure and pain. The walls were purposely repainted turquoise over the original green (his favorite color), because the president had read that staring at something blue during an orgasm increased the ecstasy, and so far, either from placebo effect or genuine psychological changes, the president's orgasms had been unprecedentedly crippling.

And as she stared at the stars and cursed her father, she heard the president shout profanities and throw the rope across the room. You see, in his rush of excitement, the president had not checked the marks on the girl's arm—one red and one yellow. These marks signified that the girl was prohibited from being struck in the face (red) or tied up by her wrists (yellow)—these were in the contract signed by her father. He fought hard for these two stipulations, and even in the business of tween sex trafficking, one could find silver linings. The advisors to the president's "task force" highly recommended that in order for these escapades to continue without rebellion, he must follow the stipulations in the contracts, no matter how much he yearned to tie up the adolescents.

The "appropriator" made it seem like the girls were treated fairly well, like his clients (he never used the president or any other official's name) just wanted the attention of young beautiful girls, painting pictures from late antiquity, from Moorish or Roman times, when the concubines were a normal part of everyday life, dressed in beautiful clothes and jewels, and were treated more like walking eye candy, like child actors, instead of farm-animal sex holes—this narrative usually eased the tension on the approach and gave the "appropriator" the opportunity to complete his pitch.

The president caught his pant leg on the back of his cream white shoe and hopped around the bedroom, knocking into the armoires and tables and suits of armor that lined the walls. She sat up on her elbows and smiled—he reminded her of a flamingo she saw at the zoo. She fell back onto the bed and looked up once again at the stars, which seemed brighter and more full of life than ever, even though she had learned that the stars you see are probably already dead. And for a young girl of barely thirteen, she made the connection between her situation and that of a bright, glimmering star, and then and there, she decided that she would glimmer and shine and that is what the world would see, and in their admiration the world would be too distracted by her shine to see that she was already dead.

The hopping and banging stopped and she listened to the rough, regal panting. The president approached the bed, and she closed her eyes and prayed for a life after death, even if was modest. And she felt his hands on the fleshy part of her thigh and realized he was dead too, and she took solace in this realization, which numbed the emotions, if only for a cooing moment. And then he took her.

BINGE UNTIL TRAGEDY

Abu Bakr al-Maghribi sipped from a crinkling bottle of water. It was dry and hot and he had to wipe the dusting of sand off his brow every few minutes. They had successfully raided the small office attached to the oil field in northern Mali. Five hundred sixty-seven workers were lined up in rows and moved to groups depending on their citizenship—North Americans and Europeans were put together, Africans were separated between black African and North African—and then by religion (Muslim and non-Muslim). The few Japanese and Korean were eventually thrown in with the first group.

Al-Maghribi was considered the deadliest man in North Africa. He was the leader and face of the *al-Saif* group, which was designated a terrorist organization by every government on the planet. A one-time private in the Algerian army, al-Maghribi defected and became a leader in the violent Islamist uprisings that subverted the Olive Protests of the 1990s that called for reforms from the Hannachi regime.

Born Abdel Hamidou, al-Maghribi changed his name after his first successful capture of a small town on the Malian-Algerian border, taking the "Abu Bakr" from the name of the prophet Muhammad's companion in the seventh century, and "al-Maghribi" because it meant "from the Maghreb" or "from the West" in Arabic. The young Abdel had a thirst for glory and enjoyed learning about the Muslim generals who conquered much of Asia, North Africa, and the Middle East. He was obsessed with their wealth, their education, but most of all, their power. When he was old enough to join the Algerian military, he woke up early and signed all the necessary paperwork with his mother standing behind him as a witness. But military life left little to be desired, and cleaning bathrooms and marching in lines for hours and hours fell too short of the idealism created by his caliph forefathers.

In the middle of the night, al-Maghribi and forty-six other soldiers looted the barracks for weapons, ammunition, and trucks, and headed for designated checkpoints where more civilian soldiers waited for their instructions. From these checkpoints, al-Maghribi launched assaults on government buildings and personnel, oftentimes killing more civilians than government officials. These attacks became known as the "Black Wave."

Eventually, al-Maghribi and his comrades were beaten out of Algiers and escaped to the Sahara, where they lived a life of banditry. Their minor conquests gained them recognition from Middle Eastern Islamist groups, which provided them with funding. Over the course of five years, al-Maghribi banded together fractious groups roaming the Sahara and held successful internet campaigns to recruit young men from the cities of the Maghreb. He now commanded an army of over two thousand soldiers from ten different countries, and after every successful capture, he pointed his oversized scimitar toward Algiers and vowed to use it on "the soft neck of the Apostate."

After the groups were formed, 121 were in the group of North Americans/Europeans/Asians, 88 made up the group of black African non-Muslims, 240 were in the group of black African Muslims, and the rest were North African Muslims, almost all of whom were Algerian citizens—all the soldiers were men.

Al-Saif took the oil field after a brief firefight with the modest security force left to defend the workers. Ten of the soldiers had been killed in the shoot-out; the rest surrendered. Those who laid down their guns were thrown into the group with the Frenchmen.

Al-Maghribi paced along the platform and commanded that the three groups be separated into three different buildings and guarded. "Don't let them touch the outside world," he said. A soldier not a day over sixteen affixed a camera to a tripod, setting up a shot with the machinery and towers of the oil field in the background, giving the impression of an industrialist steel city in the middle of the desert. Al-Maghribi ordered his second-in-command, a Malian named Youssouf, to bring him the field bosses.

The soldiers were all covered in black headscarves that had *al-Saif* written in white Arabic script across the forehead. They pulled the oil field bosses from the office buildings and dropped them, trembling, at the feet of al-Maghribi. They were all French and only spoke French. Al-Maghribi refused to use the language of the colonizers, even though he could speak it quite well, retaining much of what he learned in school.

He demanded that Youssouf have them stripped down to their underwear and placed on their knees in front of the camera. As they were prepared, the commander went over in his head what he would say; he had prepared a whole speech in the hopes of victory and it was so damn hot out that he wanted to get it right on the first take. Masked so only his eyes were showing, al-Maghribi was only distinguishable from the rest of the soldiers because he wore a red headband, and for his obnoxiously large scimitar, of course.

He stood behind the six kneeling men with his hands resting on the butt of the scimitar, which swayed on its point in the golden sand. Right as Youssouf gave the "action" signal to the teen soldier working the camera to begin filming, the man farthest to stage right jumped from his knees and sprinted toward the desert. Youssouf yelled, "Stop," which was directed at the teen soldier and not at the stumbling Frenchman who was shot in the back by a soldier from Oran.

Al-Maghribi stood behind the *five* kneeling men and gave the go-ahead to Youssouf, who signaled to the camera boy. The leader pointed his finger to the sky and made a declaration to the world that would shock and appall and, certainly, go viral.

AMSTERDAM

THE TRAIN FROM PARIS TO AMSTERDAM TOOK A

little over three hours and the ride was damn flat.

"It says here that Holland is different from the Netherlands?" said Riley with the travel guide in front of her face so you could only see the top of her head. "I always thought they were synonymous, but it says here that Holland is two provinces, North and South, and that's where Amsterdam is and lots of other stuff, so people just assume it's all Holland. Huh…"

"Interesting," I said.

"You know that?"

"Can't say I did."

"Kev, you know that?"

Kev pulled off headphones that were blaring something techno-tribal, which sent me back to the mid-2000s. "Know what?" he asked.

"That Holland and the Netherlands are NOT the same."

"They the ones who wear orange?"

"Huh?"

"Their soccer team, they wear orange jerseys?"

"Oh, yes, the Oranje. It says here they hold the most appearances in World Cup Finals without winning one. They came in second in 1974, 1978, and 2010, losing to West Germany, Argentina, and Spain, respectively."

"Basic Dutch: *Ja*. Yes. *Nee* or *Neen*. No. *Alstubl… alstublie… alstublieft*. Please."

"Don't worry, everyone speaks English there."

"Really? Oh wait, you've been there before."

At least she was talking directly *to* me again and not through a liaison (Kev) like she had been the last few days in Paris.

"Yeah, it's…"

"You smoke a lot of pot?"

"Well, yeah, but the novelty…"

"I bet you had sex with one of those girls. You did, didn't you?!"

"No. I don't need to pay for sex, thank you very much."

Okay, I lied. I did have sex with one of those girls, and it was stupid and kind of a waste of money, but I was drunk and stumbling through the Red Light District at like, the darkest hour of the night, and she was standing in her window in a black lingerie garter belt, suspenders with matching little black ribbons and a bra that couldn't've been less than a 34C—it was as if she took the idea for the outfit from my diary. She was tan and tight and from Naples, which reminded me of my dad and his college girlfriend/exchange student sexual companion. This made me throw up a little in my mouth, thinking about my dad during sex, but it was okay, because there is a strict NO KISSING policy, and what you have to understand is that these girls aren't like the "ladies of the night" perusing the streets of Philadelphia for a wealthy john. These girls are young and fit and medically checked regularly, and taxed—even in the anonymous sex business there are taxes—gotta love Europe. So yeah, I paid for sex, but when you come back from Amsterdam, everyone asks you if you legally smoked pot and legally paid for sex. And I couldn't be known as the guy who pays for sex because it would've ruined any chances I had with any other girls on the trip, let alone Fantine, so I didn't go around telling those U of Iowa guys, whom I seldom keep in contact with anymore. I had to deny it—deny, deny, deny. So when Riley said, "I bet you had sex with one of those girls…" I had my response, locked and loaded.

Riley and Kev slept for most of the train ride, which I envied. I couldn't sleep in public, not a wink, not even on airplanes—a seven-hour flight equaled seven hours of movies I wouldn't watch otherwise. Ironically, I finished *On the Road* right when I was getting a taste of what the road meant, and as we beat through the flatlands of the Low Countries, I pictured myself as Sal Paradise crossing the flyover states en route to San Francisco.

We arrived in Amsterdam at the train station, which is a landmark itself that sits at the base of the aquatically divided city. We had waited too long to book our hostel and the Flying Pig Downtown, the most popular hostel in the city due to its proximity to the heart of the shenanigans, was booked solid. I managed to find three beds in an eight-bed mixed dorm with a still-excellent location and decent reviews. It was only a few minutes from the train station, and when we exited the mammoth building, Kev asked, "Where are the whores?"

"Jesus, dude."

"Come on, Kev."

"What? Isn't that why we're here?"

"They hate that, ya know, how people just come here to get laid and get high," I said.

"Well sorrrrrry for wanting to have a good time."

"Wow, it's like, really beautiful, actually," said Riley as we passed a group of yellow-jacketed people handing out JESUS SAVES flyers, asking us "to embark on the path of righteousness."

"Not today, brother," said Kev.

Our hostel was connected to a row of buildings that looked like one slab of brick painted different colors to differentiate between businesses. Hostel Meeting Point was written across the white trim of a burgundy section of the brick building, and despite the clearly printed sign in the window that said "No Bikes Please," a Technicolor assortment of bikes rested outside the front door. The inside lobby was cramped. A group of Australians was waiting in a stagnant line because no one was at the front desk. We dropped our bags at our feet and silently agreed that we'd look out for each other, for this was the first *real* city we'd have to break in without the help of a local.

BINGE UNTIL TRAGEDY

When the front desk worker finally returned, he was lethargic, and I know it's cliché, but it's what I saw: high, stoned, baked, scorched, torched. His eyes looked like he'd opened them in the Dead Sea.

"Let's ask him where he gets his *ish*," said Kev (ish = shit, stuff, supply, etc.). While Riley and I were in charge of the regular map, Kev stretched out his own personal map that had green highlighter marks over the coffee shops that were supposedly top-notch. "I bet it's from one of these."

"It's Amsterdam, everywhere is going to have similar options," I said.

"I'm salivating."

We got our room and passed through the bar and hangout area that had a designated "smoking room" situated in the back left corner, which was fogged up like a sauna. The stairs creaked as they cut and spiraled up floors with narrow hallways that seemed to be haphazardly arranged. Thumbtacked to the walls were flyers with promotions for bar crawls, bike tours, and coffee shop meetups. Our room had eight bunk beds with a path running down the middle to a window that offered a gorgeous view of the Centraal railway station and the canal that sat right below. The building was built into the water. The dark stuff slapped against the burgundy brick walls when motorboats pulled out of their spots and sped down the canal.

"Holy shit, look at that view," said Riley, which caused a curly-haired guy sleeping in a bottom bunk to cough and catch us by surprise. He wiped his nose with his bare hand and went back to sleep—you could hear the phlegm caught in his throat as he snored. His shirt was unbuttoned, and he had something illegible written in red marker across his chest and stomach. He wore a wool knit tie that was wrapped around his neck, completely ignoring the collar of his shirt, and he had a shoe on one foot without a sock, and a sock on the other foot without a shoe.

"Gross," said Riley.

"Oh, what the shit?!" said Kev. "That's my bed. Yo man, whatcha doin'?"

His eyes shot open and he jumped from the bed like he was a Minuteman and the warning bugle was sounding. He tripped over a shoe, I would assume his missing one, and got his foot caught in a backpack that was resting at the bottom of a group of blue lockers. His jeans had holes in the knees and his hair was at that neglected unwashed stage where it was beginning to dreadlock. He walked to the door and didn't take anything with him. We didn't say a thing, we were speechless, and right before leaving he turned to us and said, "But who are we, really?" And we never saw him again.

"Fuck that. I'm getting a new bed," said Kev as he left the room to make his demands. Riley and I skirted eye contact and I realized that everything was *not* in its right place.

"Hey Riles."

"Yeah?"

I had the opportunity right there to just man up and apologize. I was wrong; I was a dick. Sure, we ripped on each other often—I loved that about us. A lot of her friends thought it was weird how close we were, and they'd always say, "Why don't you two just get married already." I had the chance to put everything in its right place, and I blew it.

"Wanna go to the Anne Frank House?"

"Yeah… sure. I'll go check on Kev, make sure he hasn't offended anybody."

The WiFi was basically incapacitated on our floor, and as I was leaving to go back downstairs to find a better signal, I bumped into a tall, muscular kid. He was built like a swimmer with wide shoulders and back, and his calves looked like they had genetically modified onions lodged in the meat. He was wearing a sleeveless t-shirt that wasn't created sleeveless but had the sleeves cut off by hand, because I could see the unevenness of the cut on the seams. It was white and said *Follow Me Through the Valley of Color*.

"My bad," he said, and before I could say anything, he stretched out his hairy arm and introduced himself. "Layne, like Layne Staley of Alice in Chains. I changed my name from 'Spencer' because it's a disgusting name named after a disgusting person… Listen to me go on here. And you are? Please don't say Spencer."

I was impressed with his life alteration and I suppose a little bit jealous, because I never liked my name either, even though I didn't hold the resentment that he did.

BINGE UNTIL TRAGEDY

But I was in a new city and decided to reinvent myself, so I said, "Jackson. Jackson Belaire. A pleasure to make your acquaintance."

"Wow, you sound like a movie star. Hey, you here alone or with friends?"

"With friends. So wait, you just changed your name? Why Layne, in particular?"

"Well, I figure since Mr. Staley left us in 2002 and a proper mourning period has been realized, I wouldn't feel as bad about taking it. Like I'm paying homage, I guess. Plus, how often do you meet someone named Layne?"

"Can't say I ever have."

"Till now."

"Till now."

Downstairs, Riley and Kev sat the bar, laughing uncontrollably. Riley's laugh attracted the attention of a plethora of horny stoners. Next to them sat a white cat on a stool with a little glass of Heineken in front of him on the bar. "Look at him!" she shouted, trying to get her laughter under control. "He comes every day for his little beer so he can feel like one of us." She spoke in that voice that we reserve for babies and animals. "Hello, little guy. You have your own beer just like I have my own beer. Oh my god, so adorable." Without hesitation, Layne introduced himself.

"Hey guys, I'm Layne, like Layne Sta…"

"Have you *seen* this cat, Blaine? He's the cutest thing…"

"Actually it's Layne."

"… I've ever seen. Look, he thinks he's one of us with his little beer."

Kev finished eating the rest of what looked like a yellowy spongy pound cake, and washed it down with his second glass of Heineken. "Space cakes are delicious, man," he said, wiping the corners of his mouth with the back of his hand.

"Yeah it's fitting for a space cadet," I said. "I'm starving. I remember this burger place that was fucking incredible." The bartender shot me a look and I realized I was on a whole different level from the majority of the hangout room and needed to leave until I smoked or ate something with some THC.

The compact streets were a lively raucousness of tourists and music blaring from bars where cute young girls would stand at the entrance and call out offers like, "Hey guys, come in here. Drink beer, smoke weed." Motorbikes would weave in and out of clusters of Australians who didn't follow the organic street-walking etiquette of tight European neighborhoods.

"What's, like, typical Dutch food?" Riley asked Layne.

"I've been here for a few days already and can never really get a straight answer. Most people just say, like, Indonesian food and those fries with mayo…"

"I could eat the shit outta that right now," said Kev.

"No, we're going to the Burger Bar, I remembered the name. It's… Burger Bar, and it'll be worth it."

We nabbed the last unoccupied table, but quickly realized you had to wait in line to order your food. Layne was on a tight budget and carried with him a Patagonia backpack filled with energy bars, sacks of granola clusters, and other impromptu sandwiches made from whatever was available and cheap (today it was a sack of sriracha and hummus on whole grain) and therefore he saved us the table by the window, hidden in plain sight.

Starting with the patty choices and toppings, there were just too many options to siphon through. The line was closing in on me and Amsterdam was hungry and the entire city came in right after us, so I just ordered quickly, practically shouting at the young man in the baseball cap working the register. I ended up with a black Angus beef burger with goat cheese, avocado, grilled onions, and jalapenos and a side of fries with "samurai" sauce.

Kev and Riley also struggled with the menu because, as Kev put it, "it just all looked too goddamn good. But I always get grilled onions on my burger, so why change now?" And this is what I like to call the "American Paradox of Selection." We need our choices or else we feel cheated, but equally love our comfort and refuse to exit our bubble, especially when it comes to food, so we order the exact same thing every time anyway but gloss over the monstrous, ever-growing menus of our Cheesecake Factories and IHOPs that have morphed into something out of *Akira*, so as to give off the effect of deep contemplation, despite the fact that I'm ordering the twelve-ounce center-cut filet medium-rare with a side of garlic mashed potatoes and in no way ever really considered the monkfish special—but it made me warm and fuzzy inside to know it existed.

BINGE UNTIL TRAGEDY

We knocked into each other weaving our way through the restaurant and back to our table. Riley sliced her burger down the middle, releasing the essential juices, a criminal act in the Lupo household. When asked by the waiter if he could cut into the center of his burger so as to ensure the burger was cooked to his liking, my father responded, "If I did that I'd have to repent this Sunday, but I'm going to the Giants game and won't be making it to mass."

My burger was succulent; the avocado melted into the goat cheese and the black Angus beef, and each mouthful was a savory explosion. Kev and I made guttural animal noises of pleasure that drew looks and stares from a group of Dutch yuppies eating their burgers with a knife and fork.

Because Layne was the only one whose face wasn't crammed into a mound of beef, he told us his story while we gorged ourselves. He had been biking from Paris and planned to meet friends in Copenhagen in about a month, and "just didn't feel like flying there." Layne was born and raised in Florida, in that part that "has a self-identity crisis and cannot seem to decide whether or not it's 'Southern.'" He told us his hometown has this unusual problem with three-legged stray dogs that weren't born that way, but were just "too slow to evade the gators." His mother had devoted her life to finding these "tri-pedaled" friends decent homes, and his father had a patent out on a doggy-leg wheelchair that has a contraption that cools down the dogs and keeps them from overheating in the muggy, unbearable Sunshine State summers. Layne's father and brother were aspiring inventors, hoping to strike gold with the next Magic Bullet or Cleansa.

Besides the doggie wheelchair, his father had mild success when he created a magazine holder/armrest for when someone was on the toilet. He got the idea when he became fed up with the red marks on his thighs and the pins-and-needles feeling he got in his legs when he spent too long slumped over a *Soldier of Fortune* magazine while sitting on the john. His contraption rested on your thighs and the magazine or book was placed in something that looked like a stand for sheet music; the occupier could turn the page without holding the reading material. It sold well in the Deep South and the United Arab Emirates and for some reason sounded quite familiar.

He also told us how his brother created a jar for dips that would raise from the bottom as more dip was consumed so the dipper's fingers wouldn't succumb to that irritating thing when your knuckles are covered in nacho cheese or ranch. The "dip pusher" suffered a malfunction, however, and in beta testing, the walls and ceiling were getting pounded with French onion dip that got shot out of the jar like a trebuchet.

Layne, on the other hand, did not share his family's aspirations, and instead wanted to go to college far away from Florida. His near-perfect grades and exquisite college essay (written about his aspiring inventive family) landed him at Bowdoin College in Maine on a full scholarship. At Bowdoin, he majored in psychology and titled his senior thesis "The Secrets of Scandinavian Happiness and the Escape into Artificial Light" after witnessing how many of the Nordic peoples defy the onset of depression despite the lack of sunlight, during his semester spent in Gothenburg, Sweden. He was headed back to Scandinavia to visit friends he made during his semester abroad.

The three of us finished every damn bite of our burgers. I even wiped my thumb across the plate and shoved it in my mouth to savor any remaining juices.

"Okay, time to get high and see some boobs?" asked Kev.

"Is it bad that I'm, like, excited for the Red Light District?" asked Riley.

"I mean, considering you're a wannabe feminist with the bark of a Rottweiler but the bite of a gummed elderly man, nope, not at all," I said.

"Dick…" she said under her breath.

We first found our way to a coffee shop called The Purple Parrot that had a spiral staircase leading up to smoke-filled lounges with psychedelically colored wallpaper and trippy pictures of fantasy lands with nymphs and gnomes and Jimi Hendrix. It shared that universal smell that all these places have: pungent incense and a blend of smokes marred by shitty reggae music. Ever want to know what a coffee shop in Amsterdam smells like? Go to your nearest "smoke shop" run by aging hippies, covered in peace signs and all things neon—it smells exactly like that.

BINGE UNTIL TRAGEDY

We followed the proper weed-buying etiquette, which was posted on a board on the wall behind the "distributor." We split a gram of something sticky that had that dead green base color with hints of pretty indigo. Kev bought a bowl, which we were all welcome to share so long as he got to keep it after. It was probably a bad idea to share the bowl, because I had been feeling that pre-sick scratch in my throat and my immune system had been depleted from copious amounts of alcohol and lack of sleep. Layne had his own stash that he kept in his backpack and had been rationing since he first arrived in the city. He rolled a fat joint that was bursting at the seams and cared for it like a worker from Chipotle does to a burrito with extra guacamole and pinto beans. He asked us how we all met between rolling and licking the paper.

"You need to get it moist," he said.

"Ew," said Riley.

"But not too moist or it won't light."

"I hate that word."

"Moist?" asked Kev.

"Yes. Stop."

"So is like, 'moist coitus' like nails on a chalkboard to you?" I asked.

Riley covered her ears and let out that laugh that would make a blind man fall in love. Unfortunately, it attracted a batch of sandal-wearing, tank-topped, sunglasses inside to hide the "high eyes" but it's pointless because everyone *knows* you're high while in a coffee shop in Amsterdam, group of guys.

"Alright then, how are ya? Mind if we join ya 'ere?"

"Sure!" said Riley.

"Where ya from, love?"

"Oh, we're Americans."

"That's lovely now, isn't it? Let me guess, you're a California girl. I'm usually quite good at guessing these things."

"Nope, nope. Pennsylvania."

"Where in Australia are you from?" asked Kev.

And with a stone-cold glare like you just smacked his mother on the ass, he said, "We're from New Zealand."

"Kev, don't say it," I said under my breath.

"Well, that's like the same thing."

He said it.

It didn't matter how good Riley was looking that day, the three Kiwis marched out of the lounge and down the spiral staircase into the lower lair of the smoky den. I lit up the bowl and watched as the dead green marijuana with bits of pretty indigo began its descent into charred black. I coughed and coughed as I passed the multicolored smoking device to Kev, who called me a pussy for all the coughing, to which I replied that coughing gets you higher—something Sal taught me. The four of us burned through our stash like it was going to grow legs and get up and leave, and we sat in the loft and discussed the issues of the world that needed to be discussed.

"So… like… what flavor is Juicy Fruit anyway?" asked Kev.

"Like the gum?" said Riley.

"Yeah, like, it just says 'fruit flavors,' but doesn't specify. I'd like some specificity, man."

"Hey Joel, this pic of you I put on Facebook already has twenty-one likes," said Riley.

"Wait, you have WiFi? What pic? What the shit, Riley?" The photo was of me smoking the bowl with the caption: **When in Amsterdam, do as the Amsterdamians do.** "That's not cool. But I'm too high to be angry. Remind me again later."

"You know…" said Layne, "I started learning Bulgarian so I could understand the voices in my head."

"What the fuck, man?"

"… At least, I think that's what they're speaking."

"I think we need to get the fuck outta this room," I suggested, and we left the Purple Parrot and explored what else the city had to offer.

BINGE UNTIL TRAGEDY

We wandered into the infamous Red Light District and came upon the landmark brick church. The street that curved around the church was where the first red-illuminated windows began, and Kev, in his excitement, ran and jumped in front of the first one he saw, but the curtain was closed, so he ran and jumped in front of the next one. He lost his footing and fell to the ground and pointed at the window and said, "Oh my god, no!" In the window was a large black woman in lingerie that fought gravity to push and pull her body in unnatural ways.

"Don't be a dick, Kev," said Riley. "You're beautiful just the way you are," she said into the glass. The woman shrugged her shoulders and waved us aside, as if to say, "Your loss. Now move, you're blocking the view."

Kev ran to each window shouting, "No. No. No, no, no," as each girl was larger and blacker than the last. "Is this it? No way. I don't believe it. Is this it, guys? Guys?"

"Kev, relax, man. It's just this street. This isn't even close to it. And say what you want about these girls, they get good business. Just watch and see."

We hit the main canal, effulgent in fluorescent red, both sides filled with British stag parties and groups of horny Eastern Europeans. Signs with explicit pictures for sex shows that looked like they hadn't been changed since the early eighties filled the gaps between standard red-light rooms, where girls of all shapes, sizes, and colors posed in their windows, flashing enticing smiles and winks. I always liked when I saw a girl in her window sitting on her stool, scrolling through her smartphone, like she hit her quota for the day but her hours weren't finished yet. And then there was the girl in her window reading *Melymbrosia* by Virginia Woolf. That was my favorite moment in Amsterdam the last time around. This time I actively searched for that girl to ask her which came first, the book or the gig? But she was nowhere to be found, and I like to believe that she left this city of invasive sin and moved on to better things, like a tell-all book about the biz of her youth, spilling every juicy detail, or perhaps that she became a family woman and found a nice man—progressive, of course, who could overlook her loose past and treat her for the person she really is, living in Utrecht, packing lunches in little knapsacks, sending two peach-cheeked boys off to grammar school. Or maybe it was just her night off.

Riley took the neighborhood all in stride, and was relieved when the British and Slavic men were too fixated on the lingeried girls to pester her with nonsensical inquiries. Kev recovered from his traumatizing experience behind the church and wandered the streets separated by black canal waters like a seven-year-old wanders an Apple store for the first time, getting to pick out their first iPhone—speechless when one of the Geniuses acknowledges their existence.

Layne didn't talk much then, and he just nodded in compliance to the observations we made. He appeared to be deep in thought and was unnerved by the stimulants that encircled him as he peered ahead with glossy steel eyes. Kev and I played a game called "her or her," which was exactly what it sounds like, and we realized we each actually had a "type"—mine were those with character, a pretty face with a body that fit it. Emphasis wasn't placed on one particular aspect, and even if I was going to pay her for sex and sex only, I wanted to believe we'd have invigorating pillow talk nonetheless. Kev's type was "tits," as he so eloquently put it. He didn't like going into detail about the girls. After a couple of laps around the craziness it was midnight, so we headed back toward the hostel and stopped for a drink or five at an Irish pub that sat behind the brick church. We found a table outside and watched drunk young men stumble up to windows—men who lied to their friends and clandestinely found their way back to this row of midnight pleasures to quench an insatiable thirst. The young men wore caps or hoods pulled up past their peripheries and some even wore sunglasses. Kev and Riley were astonished at the amount of business this particular row of ladies received, and as we ordered another round of Heineken and made our way deeper into the darkest hour of the night, their customers only increased; I hypothesized that given their location, for the most part secluded from the main strip of girls, potential customers were more willing to take the plunge since they wouldn't have an entire street watching as they knocked and stepped inside the glass door.

"It makes sense," said Riley. "Maybe these girls chose to be put here. No, they aren't the most lavish ladies, but it's about the money, right? I think they're smarter than you think."

"No, no, no, it's because they're fucking enormous," said Kev.

"What do you think, Joel?"

"Who's Joe?" said Layne.

"What?" I said.

"What do you mean, Layne?" said Riley.

"I thought that was Jackson?"

My jig was up.

"Who the fuck is Jackson?" said Kev.

"He is," said Layne, pointing to me.

"Oh my god," said Riley. "He does this thing we're he'll go into Starbucks and give a fake name and he thinks it's, like, hilarious, but it really isn't."

"It's pretty funny," I said.

"So you're not Jackson? You're… Joe?"

"Joel," I said.

"I don't even know who you are anymore," said Layne.

"Guys, guys, look, look, look," said Kev.

And we watched as a slumped-over old man in a hoodless sweatshirt, khakis, and cap with the strap for adjusting size in the back waddled his way to the row of girls and waved at them like animals at the zoo. Two large men in tan suits stood a few steps behind him at all times.

"That could be any of our grandfathers," I said.

"That is so gnarly," said Kev as he sucked down his pint of Heineken.

"You think he actually buys one?" asked Riley. "I don't think I can watch this."

"He's like that old guy who shows up at every high school softball game," I said.

"Hey man, I hope I have that kind of sex drive when I'm his age," said Kev. "Oh my god, he's going in."

The old man pushed the door forward and watched his step as his lady closed the curtain to her chamber. The two tan-suited men stood outside the door smoking cigarettes.

"I can't believe that just happened. I love this city," said Kev.

"How long you think it lasts?" asked Riley.

"Fifteen minutes," I accidently said with confidence, hoping Riley wouldn't notice.

"Not a chance that guy lasts fifteen minutes. He'll fucking die in there," said Kev.

I had to piss like a racehorse, but when I got to the toilet it turned into a shit—I hated when that happened—and without thinking I sat down and felt warm liquid coat my butt and hamstrings and a queasy feeling of disgust came over me. *There is a spot reserved in Hell for those who piss on the seat and don't clean it up.* The more Heineken I sloshed down my gullet, the more I wanted to knock on one of those red-lit windows myself. I wanted to shop. I wanted to be wanted. I wanted to text Fantine something like: **Well you can't have me either**. Which was stupid and sophomoric, but I didn't care if she didn't paint anymore; there was something beautifully anachronous to her demeanor and that is something I'll always love. I don't think I ever told her that I love her, not in those exact words: "Fantine, I love you," I suppose. We would use "love" all the time, like "I *love* being with you" and "I *love* the way you make me feel." But that three-word psychological grenade never made it out, not in English nor French.

I didn't have any WiFi, so I couldn't use my phone—a luxury I didn't realize I'd sorely miss. So I read the graffiti on the stall to take my mind off Fantine, the Riviera Bitch. There were phone numbers if you wanted "to have a good time." There was a pattern of skulls and crossbones that took up most of the inside door. On my left, someone had quoted lines from a Mad-Mannix song: "I'm a motherfuckin' god, son. I'm the lost one, came back to save ya ass, I'm Jeeeesus, son"—he rhymes "son" with "son," and people pay a grand for his sneakers. On my right, a stanza from a poem I couldn't place began: "Out of the Night that Covers Me, Black as the Pit from Pole to Pole." And as I sat there shitting and thinking, a stag party crashed into the bathroom and started throwing wet paper towels at each other.

When I got back to the table, everyone was at the edge of their seats. Riley had her hand over her mouth and Kev was laughing. Apparently the old man was not just an old man, but a creepy old man who did something bad enough to get hit in the face by his lady. Kev said there was a scream and the man went stumbling out onto the cobblestone street with blood pouring down his nose. His glasses were bent and his pants were unzipped and falling. They got caught at his knees, exposing sagging white underwear where a butt once was. The tan-suited men exchanged words with the dark temptress as they lifted up the old man and pulled him away from the row of lights. Despite the blood and embarrassment, the old man was smiling and didn't bother to cover his face.

"I have a theory," said Layne, grabbing all of our attention since he hadn't spoken for an hour. "Well, maybe more of a social experiment, a scenario. Okay, so I call this the 'Spider Web Question.' Listen. So there is a spider web in a window, right? And trapped in it is a mosquito. The mosquito is trapped to the point of no escape, and barring outside intervention, the mosquito will die at the hands of the spider…"

Usually I despised when people got high and became all philosophical, but Layne had a way about him—the way he talked actually made you feel smarter, breathing the same air he breathed—even if it was peppered with Super Lemon Haze.

"… Now the spider is the type that cannot hurt a human being. Its teeth are too small to puncture human skin. This type of spider is very beneficial to the environment, but they are considered repulsive to many because of their gangling legs and irregular movements. So what do you do? Here are the scenarios. Option one: you don't do anything. You allow the natural order of things to occur, despite the spider taking up residence in your room and the known suffering of the mosquito trapped in the web awaiting its impending doom. Option two: you set the mosquito free. You cannot stand the thought of sitting idly by as a creature is tortured and then killed. However, the mosquito can harm you, and mosquitoes are known for being carriers of disease and therefore can harm others—you risk this anyway. Are you following? Okay, listen. Option three: you kill the mosquito. You put it out of its misery and do not risk any harm to yourself or others; however, you have killed. You allow the spider to live because the spider is beneficial to society. Option four: complete annihilation. You have no concern for the natural order of things nor the betterment of the environment by allowing the spider to live. You don't want to risk any harm to yourself and therefore wipe out the mosquito. You have made the world a worse place, but your well-being is totally secured. What do you do?"

"I hate spiders," said Kev. "Kill them all. 'The only good bug is a dead bug.' *Starship Troopers*? Anyone?"

"No," said Riley. "Do you know how important they are for the environment? Like bees are so important because…"

"Yeah, but we aren't talking about bees," said Kev.

"But still, insects in general, they do more than you think. You can't just kill them because you have this unchecked aggression toward them."

"So what do you pick?" asked Layne.

"Free the mosquito, let the spider live—even if I move it, I let it live. Live and let live. Love and let love."

"You're nauseating," said Kev.

"What about you, Joel? Or whatever your name really is?"

"… Option three, I suppose."

I found Riley and Kev downstairs with a group of people hovering over their shoulders, watching something on Kev's laptop. Each one of them had a petrified look on their face; some were covering their mouths, and one girl had a tear running down her cheek. I approached the table expecting to find one of those videos of the neglected dogs with an angelic song in the background or something like that, but as I got closer, I could hear the throaty cuts of Arabic. I situated myself right behind my friends and nestled my chin on Kev's shoulder.

"This is brutal, man," he said. He started the video from the beginning.

"I can't watch this again," said Riley, walking away from the laptop.

The video had been posted on every news outlet in the world, and the "You might also like" section of the page was already filled with videos of debates and explanations of what the video meant. The clip started with five men sitting on their knees in front of a masked man, the speaker, who held a comically large sword between his feet with his hands resting on the handle. The video was subtitled in English and the speaker prated on about "Western imperialists" who were sucking money from Africa, the "crusaders" who ran missions in West Africa and were bleeding the continent of money and of Islam.

The speaker, whose voice was deep and slow, moved behind the kneeling men with carefully planned-out mannerisms like a politician. He threatened the governments of Algeria, Mali, and Morocco, and pointed his sword to the capital, Algiers, and said one day he would use it on the soft neck of President Hamza Hannachi, the Apostate. He threatened Europe and the United States, but specifically addressed "the godless government of President LaGrange," and when he did this, he switched to French and pointed his sword to the camera and said the five men in front of him were French citizens, and that their fate would be the same as any European who attempted to fight *al-Saif*. Lastly, he declared a caliphate in "the Maghreb." He said, "I am Abu Bakr al-Maghribi of *al-Saif*, and I will restore the glory of Islam to Africa and then to the world." Then it happened.

The masked man lifted up his giant sword and plunged it into one of the kneeling captives, whose face winced in unexpected pain. Masked men entered the shot wielding large daggers and serrated the heads off the remaining Frenchmen, whose screams were high-pitched and daunting. I felt a sting in the back of my neck. The severed heads were placed on top of their bodies near the small of the back. Crimson meat and innards oozed out of the neck holes onto the sandy concrete. After a few close-up shots of the victims, there was one final shot of that giant sword, still impaled in the back of the first Frenchman. Then it cut to black.

"What… the fuck… just happened?" I said.

Kev read the information given with the video briskly, as if he'd already read it before and was focusing on the important stuff: "Okay, so *al-Saif*, meaning 'the sword,' is a terrorist group that has origins in the Western Sahara region of southern Algeria, but has gained ground in overtaking towns, oil fields, and even smaller cities in Algeria and Mali… one time just small-scale jihadists who were against the Algerian and Malian regimes… yada yada yada… they have surprisingly and rapidly grown in the past year or so, collecting not only Saharan recruits from small towns, but recruits from the bigger cities of Algeria, Mali, Tunisia, Libya… There are even reports of them having Saudi and Pakistani fighters sympathetic to their cause. Their aim… to create a caliphate in Africa and overthrow the governments of nearby countries. Needless to say, they believe in a strict, barbaric interpretation of the Quran and have been known to severely punish women, children, and even their own men if they break the Sharia code… Their leader, who you just met, al-Maghribi, is a grade A certified douche bag and psychopath… Real name and identity is still uncertain… but… given the light skin on his hands and around the eyes… his knowledge of French, and his disdain for President Hannachi, it is believed he is an Algerian citizen."

"We should smoke something," said Layne, who was watching the video behind us the entire time without us knowing.

"Jesus, man!" I yelled, practically jumping out of my shoes. "Sorry, didn't know you were there."

"Wake and bake?" said Kev.

We found another generic coffee shop and sat around and smoked and floated amongst the invisible daytime stars. Riley wanted to go to the Anne Frank House and I refused to go while I was high, because I'm a shitty person but not *that* shitty, so I told her we'd do it later and we went to the Van Gogh Museum instead.

We spent the next couple of days in Amsterdam visiting the main attractions and taking breaks to get stoned and eat. We took a group picture at the "I amsterdam" sign, which I made my cover photo on Facebook. I guess Riley and I had our arms around each other in an affectionate sort of way, which made one of her stupid friends from high school comment: **are you guys dating?**

Marcel had been texting Riley, asking about us, her and I, and if we were sleeping together, which she found to be so ludicrous she showed me the messages. She was worried about him. She said that every night he was out with Mehdi, and he would get fired up and start sending multiple-page text messages about the revolutions in the "Muslim world," specifically Algeria, and he would end every message with **I'm going to kill Hamza Hannachi** just like Mehdi had said that night at the bar. When I reminded her that he would always get drunk in college and get political (Marcel X), she said he gave up drinking, and when I really thought about it, he didn't drink a sip of alcohol our last few nights in Paris.

"So are you guys, like… together?" I asked as we walked past another British stag party, where drunk fat guys were getting dangerously close to the canals.

"I mean… like, no."

"Do you want to be with him?"

"I don't know."

"Are you going to get with other guys when you're here, in Europe?"

"I don't know, Joel!"

Splash! One of the Brits had fallen in the canal and his whole troupe was laughing, but the Dutch who walked by just shook their heads in disgust because they knew how polluted those waters were. When the fat Brit resurfaced, black inky water rolled down his hairy shoulders and got caught in the fat flabs of his back.

"I bet there are male prostitutes here. Let's find you a nice young boy from Bosnia or Belarus or something," I said.

"They have guy prostitutes?" asked Kev.

"You're disgusting."

"You're not saying no."

"You finish *On the Road*?" she asked, intending to change the subject.

"Yeah, on the train ride here."

"Let's get you a new book!" She pulled out her guide. "Here's a list of bookstores."

"I don't need to see 'em. Just pick one out. The closest."

We found the closest store, which was only a canal bridge and a turn away. It was slotted in a row-house-style building with small round tables lining the outside, where twenty-somethings dressed in black smoked cigarettes and "read"—most were on their phones with the book getting more use as a coaster. A man who appeared to be the owner, manager, and sole employee greeted us in perfect English.

"Well, what haven't you read?" he asked, and before I could give a smartass answer to the question, Riley interjected: "I've been trying to get him to read *Slaughterhouse 5* for like a year, but he still hasn't."

"Ah yes, Vonnegut. You're an American and you have not read *Slaughterhouse 5*? I find this surprising."

"I've read Vonnegut, just not that one."

"Well, I have it here for you," he grabbed the small book from a pile of best-Sellers. "You should listen to your girlfriend."

"She's not my girlfriend."

"Oh come on, honey! Joel, light of my life, fire of my loins."

"Stop it."

"My sin, my soul." She laughed as she grabbed my hand. "Do I embarrass you, sweetheart?" and she kissed me on the cheek.

I lied. I hadn't read Vonnegut, and for the longest time Riley had begged me to read him, saying, "He reminds me so much of you, the way he writes, his *snarkiness*." It was one of those things where she wanted the gratification of introducing me to something I'd love and looked toward receiving my infinite gratitude. I needed to change the subject, get off Vonnegut. I pointed to the first book title on a chalkboard of weekly recommendations list that hung behind the counter and said, "I've actually been wanting to read that," and pointed to *Homage to Catalonia* by George Orwell.

"A great selection. I made that list myself. This book will change the way you view war," said the employee.

We met with Kev and Layne back at the hostel. They spent the early afternoon sitting in the smoking room, making friends they would never remember.

"Have you ever... just stopped and thought about... how much you blink?" said Kev as we entered the room.

"You're torched," I said, pulling up a stool next to them.

"Guys, Layne was telling me about doing truffles. Sounds dope."

"Like mushrooms?" asked Riley.

"Yeah, but different. They come in different types and… and like, have different strengths and shit. I think we should try 'em. Totally legal too."

"Dude, last time you did mushrooms you barricaded our apartment and wouldn't let me in because you said I was KGB working directly with the Chinese to take over our country."

"I don't recall that."

"You were naked and wearing a football helmet. You hit me with an egg."

"I don't recall that."

"It was like you were having a flashback to a war you never fought in. I still don't know where you got the football helmet!"

"I don't recall that. Anyway, we can buy them right down the street. Layne says you can like… feel your skin…"

"Sounds terrifying," said Riley. "I'm out, but I'll watch over you weirdos if you want."

"Awesome, he suggested having a spotter. Dude?"

"Alright, fine. You know my saying, 'Try everything twice.'"

"There he is!"

"But if I get hit with an egg, you're buying my drinks for a week."

"Deal."

Kev and I bought different truffles with different stupid names and fantastical pictures on the packaging, like Valkyrie, Gryphon, Unicorn, and Hydra. Layne didn't partake because he said, "I already fought that beast one too many times" and was on too tight a budget to spend cash on "entertainment." He vowed to spot with Riley. We described what we were looking for in a trip to an overweight South Asian lady you'd picture working in a 7-Eleven instead of a drug distributor. She recommended a particular truffle for each of us. Kev got Hydra, I got Grand Voyage. Each package had category ratings for: Self-Reflection, One with Nature, Astrophysical, and Cartoon.

I was skeptical. In my experiences with hallucinogens, I had always been disappointed with the effects, which left me with a lighter wallet and an upset stomach. This is why I stuck to drugs with a guarantee, like molly and cocaine. We bought an overpriced bottle of orange juice to chase the fungus and gnawed at them on a bench facing a mucky watered canal.

"It's like eating dirt," said Kev. "I'll never get used to that taste."

"It's fucking disgusting. I hate you already."

"You guys feel anything?" asked Riley.

"It isn't instant," said Kev.

"Well, I'm starving. Burger Bar? Layne, that okay with you?" said Riley.

"Sriracha and hummus for me, but I'll join."

We moseyed to Burger Bar and sat at the same table as last time, in the exact same seats. I already felt like I ate something rotten and my body wanted to purge it out of me, whichever way was quickest.

"Dude, this is killin' me. I feel sick. I might just go pull the trigger and chalk it up to a loss," I said.

"No, you said you'd do this with me… Brothers in arms?" He held out his arm to give that full-armed medieval handshake where you grasped at the elbow.

"Brothers in arms," I repeated.

A gorgeous girl behind the bar was dumping cheese crumbles onto sizzling burger patties. I was immediately enamored. You just don't see girls like that working in burger joints in the States. Before I could point her out to Kev, he said, "She could cook my meat…"

"Don't say it," said Riley.

"… if ya know what I mean."

"Look at that *dexterity*," I said.

"What's with the ten-dollar word?" asked Kev.

"It was my word of the day. I try and use it in a sentence. I get an email…"

"Lame."

"Just because you're content with being *gauche* doesn't mean that I have to be."

"Fuck off."

"What was your word? *Gauche*?" asked Riley.

"No, today was *dexterity*. A few days ago was *gauche*, but I hadn't had the opportunity to use it."

"I'm going to *gauche* in my pants when I eat this burger."

"…"

"Did I use that right?"

"Not even close."

The three of us got the *exact* same burgers as last time, because they were, as Riley put it, "orgasmic." And as we were standing in line, drooling on the glass and admiring the burger gods, the lettuce and tomatoes, the sizzling meats began to shine and shimmer, and that beautiful burger goddess glowed and her eyelashes grew longer and longer and her eyes bulged out of her head like a praying mantis. Riley asked, "You guys feeling anything yet?"

"I don't think so, but your eyes are red," I said.

"Oh, that's probably just allergies."

"No, no, I mean your eye, the iris is red instead of that breathtaking auburn."

She was taken aback by my compliment and said, "Oh… thanks, I mean, then you're probably feeling something. Kev?" Kev didn't answer. "Why don't you guys sit down. Here, give me your money. I'll bring your food."

We sat down with Layne, who took one look at us and said, "Enjoy the ride, my friends. Fight back against the darkness."

When Riley put the burger in front of me, I was overwhelmed with color. I looked around the restaurant and everyone was a perfectly drawn cartoon, everyone was perfect. The first man in my line of sight was glowing. His cheeks were molded from rosy clay and his eyes were bulging and smooth, like stones beaten by a river's current. The walls moved like lungs trying to catch their breath, the chest rising and falling. My soda formed a slick foam over my teeth, the sugars building a colony in my enamel. A table of four next to us: Their eyelashes grew too, long, longer than the burger goddess's, so long they almost fluttered into each other. They'd catch me staring, so I'd look down at my burger, which I hadn't touched, I couldn't touch, because it was so beautiful.

"This burger is overwhelming," I said.

"Why don't you cut it?" said Riley.

I picked up my knife and thought of my father. *A sin! A sin! What a sin it would be to cut this beautiful concoction of savory flavor.*

"Kev, you cut yours?" Kev didn't answer. I gripped the knife hard at the wood handle and dug the serrated blade into the center and it slid through the meat and condiments like jelly. The juices that slid off the knife were like bloody fireworks illuminating a dull sky. I wanted to see it again, so I cut it into quarters and then eighths and then sixteenths, the entire time being serenaded by twittering birds. *Poo-tee-weet. Poo-tee-weet.*

"What do you see?" asked Riley, as if I was experiencing a different dimension entirely.

"It's as if life is a Van Gogh," I said.

"He got the good stuff," said Layne.

We left the restaurant without me taking a bite of my burger. The sun was high, higher than usual, practically out of reach. We walked the canals lined with whores; I admired the cobblestone streets. A zebra-haired man let the fish and the whales, the dolphins and sharks, swim freely on his arms without concern. The clouds raced across the oceanic sky and I felt closer to the sun. I started to sweat. I put on my sunglasses to hide from the world, but the world found me, it wouldn't let me go. The whores called my name even though we were never formally introduced. When I got close, I could see every bristle of hair on their heads down to the root, but Riley pulled me away; she wouldn't let me go. Layne rode his bike beside us. The ground coughed, but he rode over the bumps. He said he wasn't going to leave us.

"But how will we find you?" asked Riley.

"Don't worry, I'll find you," he said.

I was afraid I'd never see my winged friend again. When I thought I'd lost him, he would come back, riding across the canals like a skate park.

"Kev is starting to scare me," said Riley.

"He's fine. Let him be. It's a voyage, he'll come back," said Layne.

I took out a napkin I had in my back pocket and wrote in blue ink: *Things to do in life: 1. Run away. 2. Come back.*

We left the red-glowing streets, and Riley guided us to an art exhibit that was free to enter. We watched young artists go about their work. Riley kneeled next to an orange-bearded man with a t-shirt covered in white paint. I watched as descending faces formed in a jet-black canvas, some screaming while others smiled. I could see under the paint; I could see the veins of the wall. I said to Kev, "This one is upset." Kev didn't answer.

"I call this one *Circumstance*," said a painter with a boyish face and mustache. "You see, all we have in life…"

I tried to escape the painter but he followed me. His arms and legs lacked bones and he chased me around the room. The earth's crust crumbled below my feet like a coffee cake. He fell to the ground and slithered like a serpent, repeating, "You see, all we have in life is *Circumstance*. The name of my painting is *Circumstance*. All we have in life is *Circumstance*. But who are we, really?"

"Ah… ahhh… ahhhh… ahhhhhhhh…"

Riley grabbed me by the wrist and I dropped to my knees, holding her around the waist, saying, "Never let me go. Never let me go," into her stomach. She bloomed and blossomed and shot into the air like a great oak. Her fingers were twigs and her arms were contoured branches, and the harder I squeezed the faster she grew, up, up, up. "I'm sorry. I'm sorry. I'm sorry," I said. I latched onto her roots and I was pulled into the street. I called for Kev, but Kev didn't answer. The faces changed as yawns turned to screams and eyes were filled with the damning darkness.

Layne's bike screeched to a halt and he shook me and put his fingers on the back of my head, and I could feel the ice of spearmint gum coat my face, and he said, "Fight back against the darkness. I am here for you."

"Kev isn't talking," said Riley. "I'm worried."

"He's fine. We're going back to the hostel. Hold Kev's hand. Don't let him go. Joel, walk with me."

I crashed into the hostel, ran past the smoking room and the cat sitting with his beer at the bar, and locked myself in a tiny bathroom. The pipes dripped, the walls melted, and in the mirror I saw a pointy-faced demon staring back at me. *Knock,*

knock, knock, knock. Layne banged on the door. "Don't be afraid. It's you, it's only you in there. No matter what you see, face it, and you will overcome the darkness."

I stared back into the mirror and my mouth dropped to the floor, exposing fangs dripping with saliva. Thick blue veins burst from my skin. My sleeves were rolled up tight past the muscles in my forearms and my blue veins were bursting there, too. I called for Kev, but Kev didn't answer. *Who are we, really?* I sat on the ground and tucked my knees into my chest and rocked back and forth.

Knock, knock, knock, knock. "You can do this. It's a voyage. God didn't bring you this far to leave you."

The demon was still in the mirror. Large black wings sprung from its shoulder blades. *My shoulder blades. This is me, my demon, I suppose.*

"You are your own worst enemy here, remember that." Layne sounded muffled, like his cheek was pressed against the door.

I stepped closer to the mirror and scraped my claws against the porcelain sink.

"Repeat after me," he said. "Out of the night that covers me, black as the pit from pole to pole…"

My eyebrows pointed at the corners; snakes slid down the melting walls.

"… I thank whatever gods may be, for my unconquerable soul…"

Spiders dropped from strings and burst into flames.

"… Under the fell clutch of circumstance, I have not winced…"

I blinked, a long blink, and when I opened my eyes, Adam was standing behind me.

"… nor cried aloud. Joel? I can't hear you. Joel? Under the bludgeonings of chance…"

I closed my eyes again.

"… My head is bloodied but unbowed…"

I opened my eyes.

"… Beyond this place of wrath and tears, looms but the horror of the shade…"

Adam was inches from my cheek.

"… And yet the menace of the years finds, and shall find me unafraid…"

The veins in the black wings pulsated.

"… It matters not how strait the gate…"

I pulled at the tufts of my hair. The harder I stared, the more grotesque I became.

"… How charged with punishments the scroll…"

I listened to the blood dripping from Adam's open wrists. *Bloink. Bloink.*

"… I am the master of my fate…"

Adam whispered in my ear, "I am the captain of my soul."

"… I am the captain of my soul."

When I came to, I was facedown on the bathroom floor. A blood-stained, fist-sized crack was crumbling from the center of the mirror. The demon was gone and so was Adam. I could see Layne's shadow clogging the light from the other side of the door, humming gently. I wrapped my bloody knuckles in toilet paper. "I'm proud of you," he said. I didn't say anything back. I sat up, leaned against the toilet, unbuttoned my sweat-drenched shirt, and listened to the twittering birds. *Poo-tee-weet. Poo-tee-weet.*

Layne was gone the next morning. He left a note on my bag:

I'm off to Copenhagen. I've decided to get an early start. It was great spending time in Amsterdam with the three of you. I checked on Kev. He's fine, just went on a different sort of voyage. Maybe the three of us can meet up again soon. Way to battle back against the darkness, Jackson. Invictus.

Riley and Kev were already awake, sucking down cups of coffee in the bar area. They called me over and Riley hugged me around my neck. "You really went on a trip yesterday, huh? You've been asleep for like, fourteen hours."

"I can't even begin to describe to you what I saw," said Kev. "I was afraid you guys were going to get mad at me for acting so crazy."

"Listen to this, Joel. Kev thinks he was going nuts. Kev, you like, weren't speaking."

"I saw things…" he said.

"How's your hand?" asked Riley.

It was wrapped and felt fine. I could feel goo underneath the bandages that was probably Neosporin.

"It's fine, thanks," I said. "Who wrapped it?"

"I did," said Riley. "I was a first responder at school, remember?"

"I remember you getting kicked out because you showed up drunk—twice."

"What a thank you."

"Sorry. Thanks, Riles, I appreciate it."

We only had one more night in Amsterdam before we left for Berlin, and the three of us decided to take it easy. "No hard drugs" was the day's motto. Riley made us repeat it: "No hard drugs…"

We visited another free art exhibit where a young Dutchman greeted us at the door and walked us through a most peculiar exhibition. He wore a gray turtleneck and shorts that hugged his thighs tight. The theme: "Killing Jesus." In refined English, he said, "You see, crucifixion was a common form of execution during the Roman Empire and was not reserved for Jesus. For many years, prisoners of war, traitors, and slaves were crucified. So, what we pose to you is, what if Jesus lived during a different time? Hmm? Yes? Let's see here."

There was a chair with makeshift cables plugged into the wall and a headpiece that looked like something that belonged in a salon. A dummy with the beard and long hair commonly used to portray Jesus was strapped into the chair, wearing nothing but a loincloth covering nonexistent nethers. Actually, this same dummy was used in ten different exhibits in the studio: Jesus strapped to a table with a syringe is his arm, Jesus locked in a guillotine staring down at the floor, Jesus hanging by a noose with his hair flowing from underneath the burlap sack that had INRI written across the front, sloppily, as if it had been thought of moments before doors opened.

"Historically, Jesus was tried by his peers and sentenced to death…"

"So are you guys, like, anti-Christian or some shit?" asked Kev.

"No, it is not that. Not at all. You see… Let me grab the artist himself."

"No way," said Riley. "Miloš Lhota is here, right now?"

"Yes, yes, of course he is. I will get him for you."

"Guys, Miloš Lhota is here! I knew this was his work, but I wouldn't think he'd *actually* attend."

"Who the fuck is Miloš Lhota?" asked Kev.

We were both surprised when a young guy in a white t-shirt covered in what appeared to be stains from Indonesian food approached us and introduced himself. "Hello, friends. I am Miloš Lhota."

Riley had become one of those girls from footage of the Beatles getting off a plane in London, smitten to the point of tears. His assortment of rings and bracelets on his wrists rattled when he ran his hands through his silvery onyx hair, which does not come naturally to human beings.

"I studied your work in my Intro to Contemporary Neo-Expressionism of Central Europe class. You're like… amazing," she gushed.

"Thank you, thank you. And your name is?" Miloš took her by the hand and personally guided her around his exhibition. Kev and I waited outside, smoking cigarettes by a dirty canal, counting the number of girls who were taller than us. Riley came out after her private tour and prated on about "what an artistic genius he is. Ugh… and get this. He's *only* twenty-two. Like, can you imagine how much he'll accomplish by the time he's in his forties? Oh! And he invited us all to Prague!"

"Prague?" said Kev.

"Yes, that's where he lives. You haven't seen pictures? Here." She took out her phone and started scrolling through what seemed to be the same four or five pictures of Prague. "Doesn't it look beautiful? We *have* to go."

"What about Berlin?" asked Kev.

"We'll go after Berlin. It's in, like, the same direction. Here, look at a map." She loaded a map on her phone and shoved it in Kev's face.

"Okay, okay. I mean, we didn't really plan anything for after Berlin anyway."

"Miloš said we can stay with him. He will be back in Prague in a few days," she added.

"I don't see why not," I said. "It is, like, the porn capital of Europe."

"Joel is in," she said.

"I watch homegrown American porn because I'm a patriot, goddammit," said Kev.

We headed to a bar, where we sat upstairs in a wooden booth and drank Heineken and I smoked my first Marlboro Red—that stick of Americana—right there in socialist Europe. I avoided all conversation about the truffle voyage. Riley and I were finally really okay, and that's all I wanted. I didn't care what it took to get there. It started to rain and we talked about Layne. We thought about him pedaling his bike somewhere in the countryside, soaking wet, wearing that same damn t-shirt: *Follow me through the valley of color.*

None of us got his number or friend requested him on Facebook or even knew his last name. We toasted to Layne, and I stood up from the booth and addressed the entire bar and said, "A great man left us today, and he will always be remembered. I'd follow you, buddy. We'll always have Amsterdam." Because Sal taught me that toasting to a man, even if he isn't present, is one of greatest things you can do. So we clanked our beers and burned our lungs and I realized everyone in the bar thought Layne was dead.

We walked Riley back to the hostel—meeting one of her favorite artists proved to be quite exhausting—then told her we were going to have a few more drinks. She didn't ask any questions. Kev and I walked to the Red Light District in silence.

Toward the end of our street under draped rainbow flags was a slice of gay prostitution windows illuminated in blue instead of red. Beneath a closed curtain, I could see the hands and knees of a prostrate man.

"How much do you think they make?" asked Kev.

"Why, you lookin' for a side job?"

We reached the canal illuminated in red. We grabbed a couple of beers from a convenience store and made a mutual agreement to never speak about the night, not to Riley, not to siblings, not to anyone—I would probably tell Sal anyway. We finished the beers, shook hands, and then departed in opposite directions. I went further down the canal; Kev went back the way we came.

BINGE UNTIL TRAGEDY

I was hungry. I was weak. When you rid yourself of shame, when you've screamed like a child in an art gallery because you did too many drugs, when you've sat on a bathroom floor in the fetal position, rocking back and forth, paying for sex doesn't feel so taboo, I suppose.

The crowds of drunken cacophony hadn't subsided despite the rain. I walked past the famous sex stores and infamous bars, and as I passed the Bulldog, a bar known for its unrivaled rambunctiousness, a poorly dressed guy with studded earrings and a shaved head told me to "piss off" and added that I was a "knob jockey" and a "tosser"—it's a myth that everyone sounds smarter with an English accent. He was missing his top right incisor and had tattoos wrapped around his knuckles. I didn't say anything back. He was with a group of at least eight, but I remembered his face, and as I continued on my way, passing ambivalent prostitutes in lingerie, I fantasized about killing him—with knives and bats and all sorts of other toys.

My concentration was broken when I saw her. No, it wasn't the one from my last tryst in Amsterdam, but she was intriguing in a demonic sort of way, and that night, after all that had occurred the day before, I felt like quite the demon slayer. I approached her window and she posed for me, hands on her butt, chest out. Her hair was jet-black and up in a style you'd find on the Jersey shore. The protocol is you give a couple of taps or some type of signal to be let in. But there were too many spirits haunting the canal, so I tapped the window and poked my head in and asked her how much longer she would be working. She told me she'd get off soon: "In one hour, baby."

I didn't want to settle right then and continued to search the main rows and a couple of side streets—I learned not to overlook the side streets, you could find a gem. But how the first song I listen to by a new band is always my favorite, she retained her spot at the top of my chart, beating out the one in the sky-blue lingerie *and* the one in the Catholic school-girl getup—a personal favorite. I hurried back to her door just in case she was having a slow night and had decided to get off early. She wasn't posing and her curtain was closed, so I rapped on the window and waited for a few seconds. She whipped the curtain across and smiled and said, "You come in?" And in I went.

"First you pay."

"How much?"

"Fifty euro." Price hadn't changed. I handed her the amber-colored bill. She put it in a lockbox on top of a dresser. She hit a timer: fifteen minutes. "Okay, baby, clothes off now."

She checked her phone, which illuminated her face, revealing the caked-on makeup in her pores. I unbuttoned my shirt and pulled my guinea tee over my head, flexing my abs and arm muscles and flashing her what I had perfected as the perfect pre-sex smile—she didn't notice any of it. I untied my shoes and as I was taking off my socks, I asked, "So… where are you from?"

"I am from Romania," she said without looking up from her phone.

"Oh, cool. Bucharest is supposed to be a nice city."

"No near Bucharest."

I became more aware of the timer, which had already dropped to 13:42. So there I stood, completely naked and unsure of what to do with myself, especially with my hands. Last time the Neapolitan pushed me onto the bed and undid my belt for me, and slipped my jeans off with a *swoosh!*

But my date hadn't looked up from her phone, and I was discouraged when I moved my clothing with my foot and saw a gold watch under the bed. I inspected the band and face. It was a knockoff Rolex—my father wore all things gold and taught me at a young age how to spot a fake. He used to take Sal and me to Canal Street in the City where men whispered, "Rolex, Rolex, Rolex," while you walked by, and he'd show me the minute differences—the weight, the fluid motion of the ticking second hand, the etched crown near the six, etc. And this one was light as a feather, with a jagged second hand motion and no etched crown.

When she was finished scheduling another appointment or finishing up a round on Robot Farm, she said, "Okay, baby, lie down." The bed had soft black sheets stretched tight at the corners. I grabbed a matching soft black pillow and put it in the curve of my neck. She ripped a purple condom out of its packaging, slid it down my dick, and began to blow me. In all honesty, it was *okay*—you'd think she'd have perfected the art by now, but if I'm paying for sex she doesn't have any competition, and quality can afford to decline, I suppose. The room was very impersonal, and I figured if the girls were spending so much time here they'd want to spruce it up a bit, like have a cactus on the dresser or a poster of their favorite band. The room glowed like a photographer's darkroom. A mirror that cut off right at my neck ran alongside the bed. It gave me a view of the top of her head and my bare thighs. There was a sliver of light seeping through the curtain, enough space for someone to peek through, like that tiny anxiety-inducing opening in the bathroom stall that terrified me when I had to poop in elementary school. I moved my hand to touch her, something sensual, nothing malicious—if anything it was more of a habit—and she snapped, "No touching." The buzz from the lights started to get to me. I remembered there being music last time. I asked her if we could stop. If we could… ya know… get on with it already.

There was a tapping on the glass, which made me snap my head to the window, but it didn't faze her at all.

"Always the Americans with the fucking. Fifty more euro," she said.

"Wait, what? No, no, no," I said.

"But *baaaaby*. Come on. You pay me for blowjob. No sex."

"No, I know what I paid you for. You're trying to screw me. I could be some fat, hairy Armenian guy. In your line of work, I'd like to believe I'm a blessing of a customer. How many guys try and make small talk with you? Hmm?"

"Oh, baby. You are *soooo* American. But… you are cute. Okay. Let's go. Come on, come on."

She got up from her knees and let her wavy hair down, which bounced on top of her fake breasts. She lay down on her back, legs spread apart, resembling an overturned turtle. She was a pretty girl with a phenomenal body. Her teeth weren't perfectly straight, but it wasn't anything that couldn't easily be fixed. I would say a couple inches taller, a straighter set of teeth, and a birth in Western Europe and she'd be modeling high fashion in Milan or lingerie for Victoria's Secret. "Come on, baby. Let's go." I must've been staring. In my rush to start, I—well, my aim was off and I hit a little lower than the destined target.

"No, baby, not in butt. Fifty euro extra."

"Sorry! That was an accident."

"Okay, baby, you finish soon?"

"I just started."

"You finish soon."

I looked up to watch myself thrusting in the mirror. I looked awkward, clumsy—oh my god, I looked *gauche*, like a horny Cocker Spaniel. It was unsettling; I could feel myself going soft inside of her.

"I need to switch. Turn over. Please."

"No, baby, you finish."

The red digits of the clock were counting down: 4:37 left.

"Fuck," I said.

"Americans with the fuck."

"Bahhh! Okay." I needed to think quick. 3:32. "Okay, here." I pulled out and pulled up the watch I found and had tossed into my crumbled pants. "Here. If you let me… do this with you from behind, I will give you this watch. It's expensive, but I got a good deal. You can get at least fifty euro."

She sat up on her elbows, still spread out on the bed. "No cash?"

"I don't have any more cash."

2:37.

The tapping on the door returned, this time longer and more profound. There was ranting in a language I couldn't place.

"But I want fifteen *more* minutes from behind, doggie style, facedown…"

"Baby, I know what this means. Give me the watch."

I handed over the watch and she locked it in the safe on top of the dresser. She set the time to 15:00. She lay prostrate on the bed, her puckered dark star staring back at me. "Come on, baby. Let's go." I took my fifteen minutes.

0:00. She flipped around and took off the condom, tying it quickly so it wouldn't spill. As she walked to the shower, she said, "Go home, American."

I said goodbye over the sound of water splattering on tile. She didn't respond.

When I left the room and slid the glass and put my hood over my head, a fat, hairy Armenian was sitting on a bench directly in front of her window.

"Hey you!" he yelled. "You find a watch in there?"

"Sorry buddy. Already have one." And I flashed him the Fossil on my left wrist.

"That bitch stole it," he said. And I began walking back to the hostel to the sound of incessant tapping on glass. I would've just called it a night, made sure Kev was back, and gone to bed. But I heard the guttural, unrefined English accent that cursed me off before.

He was standing on the edge of the canal, smoking a cigarette with another prick left over from the *Oi!* movement. I stared at him but he didn't see me. He was wobbling, and although he *was* speaking English, I couldn't make out a word except "fuck" and "cunt." The night had died down drastically. Pockets of noise came from the bars, but besides that, the Red Light District, the oldest neighborhood in Amsterdam, was serene. A flock of swans floated down the canal, which made the girls in the windows point and smile. The bald-headed Englishman was alone now. His friend had finished his cigarette and was walking inside. He picked up a pebble and threw it at the birds, missing, but scaring them nonetheless. I'd had it. He was going in. I bent down to lace up my shoes; I wasn't going to allow a loose knot to be my demise. He was swearing at the birds, which picked up their pace down the watery path. I tightened my belt. He pulled out a pack of cigarettes and dropped them. That was my chance. I walked, quickly. I gave a small trot and looked at The Bulldog. No one was watching. He fumbled with the pack, still bent over. The girls in their windows across the canal saw me, and I sprinted and kicked. He wasn't even halfway down before I turned to sprint. *Splash!* I never looked back. I heard him, though; he surfaced mid-swear-word: "You fuck! You fuckin' wank!" It was like music to my fears. I composed myself; I don't run as fast when I smile.

FARAH'S VISION

SALIM SWALLOWED HIS SPIT TO LUBRICATE HIS DRY mouth. It was another scorching Algerian summer day.

Farah had a vision: to make Salim the face of the revolution. The student's unthreatening boyish looks and intelligence were bound to appeal to a global audience. Since Farah had had this vision, Salim was sent around the Square conducting interviews with citizens of all ages—Farah followed behind the camera. She had already uploaded five videos to YouTube with the help of a Canadian "hacktivist" group that breached the regime's rudimentary firewall.

In this same vision, she imagined Mohamed as "the voice" of the revolution. Farah had told him he reminded her of an Arab John Mayer. She got him an acoustic guitar to play in the Square and worked with him on songs about "Freedom and rights and all those things the American cowboys sing about." Students set up a makeshift stage under a wrought iron gazebo. They brought speakers and tied a gigantic Algerian flag to the back of the structure that waved in front of the Mediterranean Sea. For three days, the protests went uninterrupted by the government, and not a word from the General nor the president was addressed to the demonstrators. Police in riot gear lined the Square, but miraculously, not a baton was swung for those three days. Due to the period of uninterrupted peace, more people from beyond the city limits made it to the protests, which took on the feel of a carnival more than a demonstration. Mohamed strummed his new acoustic guitar and played his first original song, what would become the theme song of the revolution: "Hey Algeria, Hey People." He wrote and performed it in both Arabic and French.

Omar had not been seen during the first two days of the demonstrations, which was fine with Farah. She omitted him from as many videos as possible, believing his incendiary commentary on the West and liberalism would be counterproductive to their goal. Unfortunately, the new waves of protestors brought groups of the ultraconservative, who believed supporting *any* government, tyrannical or liberal, was anti-Muslim and against the will of God. Many students and residents of Algiers argued with the new religious protestors, who were viewed as subversive and contradictory to the original message of the revolution. Those who participated in the Olive Protests of the nineties condemned the "support" from those who wanted Algeria run under Islamic Law. An elderly man with weathered skin grabbed on to the iron of the gazebo, interrupting Mohamed, who was strumming vigorously at his guitar, and called the young men in the crowd holding Qurans above their heads "a scourge on what we have built!"

When Salim asked a skinny young man in a white *thawb* what he thought about the killings of the French oil field workers, the man replied, "The killing of crusaders is just in the eyes of God." Horrified by this response, Salim tapped the shoulder of the next man in the group, and Omar turned to answer.

He unfastened the leather straps from around her ankles, which had already begun to bruise and swell at the bone. He was shown the video of *al-Saif* only minutes earlier and demanded, "Send in another Yasmina immediately." He sent a message to the General ordering him to use all necessary force to crush the Islamists, even if that meant the protests in the capital would grow. The curtains were closed, and he conducted himself strictly by candlelight, passing barely legible notes underneath the gigantic door to his bedroom with instructions on food and concubines.

Next girl. More tea, he scribbled.

For three days, President Hannachi ate imported French cuisine and mounted fifteen young girls—at one point, he had six standing beside the bed, forcing them to watch as they waited their turn.

In the lavish nightstand that stood next to the bed sat an ornate dagger, unsheathed and forgotten. It had been a gift from the president of Tunisia, who had it made to replicate that of a Carthaginian general—"For Our Hannibal" was etched in Arabic on the steel. It was a large blade, but nothing one of the girls couldn't handle, for it would take one thrust, only one jab to the back of the neck as he licked the cheek of another "Yasmina," one swift cut across the throat, deep enough to slice the carotid artery, deep and swift, sending the tyrant gasping for air, spilling blood onto the Egyptian cotton sheets, stumbling to the floor, crawling, slipping on the slick, blood-covered marble, grabbing for the doorknob to get the attention of an armed guard only feet away but being stopped and smothered with a pillow until he died from asphyxiation or—God willing—blood loss. But the girls were unaware of the dagger stashed in the drawer, so they stood orderly and waited their turn as the president slid his tongue across hostile lips and pulled at tethers.

Al-Maghribi sat with his sword between his legs and poured water over the shimmering blade, like a Second Samurai moments before decapitating his disgraced comrade during the act of *seppuku*. He didn't bother to look up as Youssouf detailed the strategy he devised for taking Tamanrasset, a significant Algerian city in the Sahara. He told Youssouf that Algerian forces would shortly be on the attack. They needed to reinforce their strongholds and weave themselves like yarn throughout the people of their captured cities. Al-Maghribi, being a former soldier, knew the government's military was large in number and very equipped, but poorly trained and undisciplined. Two hundred Algerian soldiers had already defected to *al-Saif* and more were expected to join. So instead of discussing military strategy, al-Maghribi told Youssouf to set up the camera.

"Another execution?" asked the Malian. The group was still holding thirty prisoners.

"No, not tonight. A burning," al-Maghribi responded.

Youssouf was puzzled but didn't dare question his leader, who had still not looked up from wicking water from the scimitar blade.

After dinner, a group of men circled a meek bonfire that seemed more fitting for roasting marshmallows than for making a profound international statement. *Al-Saif's* numbers had grown drastically since the release of the beheading video online. Fighters from all over the world were attracted to the organization's Islamic idealism—Libyans, Saudis, Tunisians, Somalis, and Nigerians made up the largest groups of fighters besides Algerians and Malians. Although gracious toward the courage of these young ideologues (ninety percent of the fighters were between the ages of sixteen and twenty-four), it was a handful of new recruits that excited the self-appointed Caliph the most—these were the Westerners.

Within days of the video's release, sixteen "Westerners" traveled from their home countries to the Caliphate in the Sahara: four from England, three from Denmark, two from Canada, five from France, one from Australia, and one from the United States of America—this last one appealed to al-Maghribi the most. Out of those sixteen Westerners, fifteen were second- or third-generation Muslims with ancestry in Africa or the Middle East. But the American was something different, something unique.

Simon Turner, a nineteen-year-old rising junior at the University of California, Santa-Berkley from Flagstaff, Arizona, was a dusty-haired, blue-eyed poster child for all things American. He had high cheekbones and a tummy-tingling smile and looked more like a minor-league baseball player than a newly molded jihadist. His family was "blue-blooded American. Pioneers of this great country and founders of its Southwest."

In the fall semester of his sophomore year, he picked up a Quran at the campus bookstore for Islamic Studies 222 (it would count as his global studies requirement for graduation—he also started Arabic 101 in the spring) and never put it down. He made it to the Caliphate by way of Dakar, Senegal, which had become a growing city for tourism—the "Edge of Africa." He told his parents he was spending the summer studying abroad in Cape Town, South Africa, and that he would be receiving enough credits to graduate early—they didn't know Cape Town from Casablanca, and he was on scholarship, so they wouldn't be paying a dime.

In a journal entry written minutes after viewing the video for the first time, Simon wrote:

My whole life I've been looking for purpose. I've been searching for it from great men, but always, always have been let down, until now. President Meyer, unable to keep his promises, all politicians for that matter. Weak! My father, the "art exhibitionist," the furthest thing from a man. Weak! Jesus? WEAK! Son of God and he couldn't even get down from a wooden plank.

Al-Maghribi. Here is a man, and here, on this paper, I declare my allegiance to him and to the al-Saif Caliphate.

There is no God but Allah and Muhammad is his messenger.

Al-Maghribi gathered the Western recruits and aligned them in a cluster behind the crackling fire. He stood in the center, towering over the young men who all donned the same black headband with الســيف (*al-Saif*) in white script written across the forehead and had their faces covered in black—they appeared like a pack of ninjas. Al-Maghribi kept his face uncovered this time. He wanted the world to see him, to recognize him, to dream about him and pull their wet blankets over their dripping noses in fear.

The same young jihadist who filmed the oil field beheadings had so impressed al-Maghribi with his shots that he became the de facto cameraman for all *al-Saif* videos. Because the cameraman was short, his filming angles gave the fighters a naturally imposing appearance. The leader held his oversized scimitar in one hand, over his shoulder, the blade coming inches from bonking one of the Danes in the head. He clenched his free hand and punched at the air, resembling a comic book supervillain or Mussolini.

He spoke in French as he pointed into the rolling camera: "Western kingdoms bear witness, for we have your children. Before me stand new soldiers for God. They have abandoned you. They have left you to succumb to your ways and crumble to the wrath of God. These children have chosen to join the new order of righteousness and leave the lands of consumption and sin. Now they will prove their allegiance."

As previously instructed, all sixteen of the young men held up their passports and one by one, cursed their respective home countries and leaders (some were more explicit than others) and dropped them onto the fire. However, before Simon Turner could give his declamation, al-Maghribi stopped him, which caught him off-guard and made him fear he might have messed up.

In rehearsed English, al-Maghribi said, "Americans, here is one of your own. Once a child of the thieves, he has grown to be a child of the Caliphate. When we raise the *al-Saif* banner over the White House, he will take the honor for killing you, President Meyer." Then he nodded to Simon to continue.

Simon, who now felt the pressure to give more showmanship than his peers, given his regal introduction, threw down his passport into the flames and stomped on it with a jovial brio, as if he were crushing a cockroach. The embers shot up like a fiery dust and a flame burned through the picture and melted the face with the heart-fluttering smile.

BERLIN

BERLIN IS A SPRAWLING BLOCK CITY THAT REMINDED me of something found more in the Midwestern United States than on the threshold of Western and Eastern Europe. The wide boulevards and long city blocks had plazas surrounded by every type of cuisine imaginable, and like Amsterdam, Berlin was damn flat.

Riley cracked the fresh spine of a traveler's guide to Berlin—"For travelers, not tourists," was the brand's motto, imprinted in bubble letters in the top right corner. "The stereotypes typically associated with Germany," she read from the first page, "the lederhosen, giant stein glasses, and feathered hats, are NOT found in Berlin. That would be Bavaria in the South."

"Where are we stayin' again?" asked Kev, who chose to have no part in the hostel selection process.

"At this awesome-looking place in Kreuzberg," she said.

"…"

"Kreuzberg is like, the coolest part of Berlin. It's ethnically diverse and like, super trendy, according to this book."

Our train ride was smooth and efficient. I had started *Homage to Catalonia* and honestly was bored. Orwell was in a fucking war and all he talked about was the infighting between the communists and the anarchists and how dysfunctional it all was. I mean, the Spanish *are* insane, I'm convinced of it. I don't think anywhere else in Europe, shit could've hit the fan quite like it did in Spain. These guys, women too, picked up arms and went to war with each other, all because some megalomaniacal military man wanted to run his own nation. It was a miniature WWII, the Spanish Civil War, that is, *the* proxy war of all proxy wars—and I thought the Democrats and Republicans were bad.

"Kreuzberg is home to the largest Turkish population in Berlin and is renowned for its musical scene… first punk rock, then hip-hop. Kreuzberg is vehemently anti-commercial. When the chain Subway opened a shop, it barely lasted two weeks before being pelted with rocks and smashed by masked protestors—it has since closed."

"So don't ask them for the nearest McDonald's?" I said.

"… No. Instead, residents of Kreuzberg prefer local, independent shops, cafés, and restaurants, and the city has no shortage of exquisite dining options. Kreuzberg epitomizes the famous quote made by Mayor Klaus Wowereit: 'Berlin is poor, but sexy.'"

Because we had decided to continue our trip east into the Czech Republic, we cut our stay in Berlin to only a few nights. Our hostel was carved out of an old warehouse and in parts of it, you could still see the exposed brick of the industrial skeleton. Riley had indulged in two espressos on the train and was eager to take the first tour available that day: "Zat vould be ze… let me see… ze Counterculture Street Art Tour," said a tall, blond, thick-rimmed-glasses-wearing desk worker.

"Sounds perfect!" said Riley. "Let's go let's go let's go."

"But I haven't even connected to WiFi yet," Kev whined.

"No time. It starts in twenty minutes and we have to get to the Berlin wall."

"I thought they tore that down?" said Kev.

"… Are you serious?" said Riley.

"Um… no?"

We rushed to the tour's meeting point, which was in front of the mural "of two dudes making out." Our guide, a tan Australian with blond dreadlocks pouring out from under a dirty gray hat, greeted us and assured us this was the best tour in the city: "You'll see the *real* Berlin." He asked each group of traveling companions where they were from, and unsurprisingly, the total makeup for the group was the standard: mostly Australians, followed by Canadians and Americans, New Zealanders, a few from countries of the UK, a speckling of South Africans, Italians, and Spaniards, and if we were lucky, something fun, like a pinch of Brazilians or dab of Taiwanese.

"Alright, mates, this is a street art tour, and yes, we are standing in front of the infamous Berlin Wall, but what I am going to show you is Friedrichshain-Kreuzberg, two rival neighborhoods straddling the river, and what they have to offer, or what I like to say: a world... of infinite inspiration." When he said that, he pushed out his arms and spread them to his sides, as if rehearsed and repeated for the umpteenth time.

He took us to a mural of a long-legged girl with stringy teal hair, oversized glasses, a beanie, and a slender nose. This was the first of many works by an Italian artist named Josephina Castellino. Artists like Castellino are hired by property owners in various neighborhoods throughout sprawling Berlin to add life to blank façades. Josephina was our guide's personal favorite, and he took pride in the fact that he had a drink with her only a few months ago as she was doing work in Germany on her way to Prague.

Next he brought us to the Oberbaum Bridge, a cherry-brick creation that, during the city's split, separated the rival neighborhoods Kreuzberg (West Berlin) from Friedrichshain (East Berlin) and was a passageway for immigrants. Now the bridge stands as more of a symbol than a jurisdictional marker—a recurring theme throughout Europe, I suppose.

The piece he took us to see on the bridge was of two young people kissing. Its pastel color scheme and manga-cartoonish features resembled something found on a CD cover for an emo band that hit it big in the mid-2000s. The bridge had two facing "rock-paper-scissors" hands in neon lights that would randomly change in perpetual combat.

"This represents the arbitrariness of which immigrants were allowed passage," he recited. "Also, everyone listen, this is cool. Also, once a year, the two neighborhoods go to *war* with each other. I'm serious. They fling tomatoes and vegetables and eggs and use water cannons and attack each other from either side of the river. I fought last year for Kreuzberg to take East Kreuzberg back from the rebels." When no one understood what he was saying, he elaborated. "We call Friedrichshain 'East Kreuzberg' and they call us 'Lower Friedrichshain.' It's all in good fun… Who won? The East Kreuzberg rebels have outside investment… better water cannons… they did."

Kev was beginning to lose interest and was only summoned back from the depths of whatever matter makes up that noggin of his when the guide told us we were going to take a refreshment break, and reminded us that in Germany it's "totally cool to drink on the street." He recommended a tall bottle of Augustiner: "The undisputed best beer in Deutschland." The beer *was* delicious and it cleansed my dried-out mouth. I was going to ask Riley for a swig of her water, but she had been flirting with a guy from Auckland since the beginning of the tour and I didn't want to intrude on the *magic*—it was lust at first sight.

"Seems like Riley is getting over Marcel, huh?" Kev said, leaning into my ear.

"Love is easy when it only lasts a few nights at a time."

We continued with the tour, and our guide asked us to grab one of the empty wooden crates piled on the side of the road and take it with us: "It's light enough to carry in one arm. You can still have your beers." Mine had originally carried Brazilian limes and Kev's held dates from Algeria. On every space imaginable, Berliners found a canvas to create art or graffiti. When asked the difference between the two, our guide gave a vague political answer, like, "Art is in the eye of the beholder." To which Kev scoffed, "What crap. A lotta this shit is ugly as shit."

While I never liked tagging—the shit that covered the NYC subway throughout the seventies and eighties—I disagreed with Kev and found most of the art if not charming, provocative. My personal favorite: Superman on one knee, riddled with bullet holes, his head in his hands.

"Okay, everyone, we're going to my home," the guide said nonchalantly. "This is where the crates will begin to make sense."

We entered a park that was full of tents and makeshift homes of scrap metal, tarps, and wood.

"No pictures. I'm serious," he said. He tried to maintain our attention by pointing out the art on the large brick building that formed one of the borders for what can only be described as a shantytown. But no one was interested in the murals of bulbous yellow creatures making political statements, or the shackled man in a suit and tie, representing a slave to capitalism. We were surrounded by destitution, and by the looks on the faces of my fellow tourists, they had never witnessed such a thing—never actually been *in* the shit, I suppose. Now, I'm not saying I've had any serious experience with poverty. I mean, we'd go to Newark every once in a while to visit my dad's old neighborhood and pick up zeppoles from a holdout Italian bakery (the rest of the neighborhood had moved out to Bloomfield or Belleville). "Don't ever forget where you come from," he would say as we cruised down Bloomfield Ave. But this place made 7th Avenue Newark look like the Champs-Élysées.

As we walked through the camp, a man with missing teeth and multiple coats jumped in front of the group and asked, "What's the password?" Everyone froze. The guide simply rolled his eyes. Our gatekeeper pointed to his hat and said, "Swordfish, duh!" And on his hat was a swordfish.

Shoeless children ran around aimlessly and when Kev dropped a Dorito on the dirty ground, one of the children rushed to pick it up and shoved it in his mouth.

"I feel sick to my stomach," I said.

"I thought we were in Berlin, not India," said Kev, rolling up his bag of Doritos.

"Shut up, dude," I said.

"You can toss those in a pile right here," said the guide, pointing at the ground near remains of burnt wood. "It gets cold here at night, even in the summer."

"Did we just carry a bunch of firewood?" said Kev.

We followed the guide to the river, where we met a few of the locals who called the encampment home. The guide explained that soon the government would kick them all out, back to the streets. Initially, the lot had been empty and undesirable and was slowly inhabited by Berlin's homeless. Because they were crime-free and kept to themselves, the authorities didn't bother them. But there had been a recent investment surge in Berlin, which was slowly becoming the Silicon Valley of Germany. Its friendly business taxes and cheap real estate had turned Berlin into a startup city, and with it came the foreigners, from both inside and outside of Germany.

"We're right on the river here," said the guide. "See that?" He pointed to the building next door with new-age architecture and glass walls. "That will probably become new luxury apartments or a yoga studio or some crap like that." He brought us to a more secluded area of the camp and stood in front of a scrap metal home and said, "This is where I live." The roof was a mixture of scraps and tarp and there was a couch, chairs, and makeshift kitchen with dirty pots and pans. He was about to give us the grand tour until he yelled, "Motherfuckers! Those motherfuckers! I hate those fucking Gypsies! Always shitting wherever they want!"

The guide grabbed a shovel and dug a hole off to the side in a sort of no-man's land, picked up the turds, and buried them, swearing and sweating the entire time. Apparently the Gypsies didn't follow camp protocol and allowed their kids to just shit wherever they wanted.

"Sounds like the dream," said Kev.

"It's fucking disgusting," said the guide, who leaned the shovel up against the scrap metal wall so it was easily accessible. He then pitched different ways we could all help the homeless of Berlin and gave us some flyers and asked us to sign a petition to keep the Gypsy-plagued shantytown intact, but all I could hear was Kev lean in and whisper, "See, even the homeless hate Gypsies."

After our guide brought us back to the Wall, Kev and I grabbed a currywurst, a Berlin staple, from a nearby vendor. Riley came back with the Kiwi and his two friends, so we all examined the Wall together, and Riley demanded pictures in front of her favorite works so she could upload them to Facebook and "the Gram."

We sauntered down the Eastside Gallery and I tried to keep the sauerkraut and mustard off my shirt. I dodged in and out of people posing for pictures and came to a halt when I saw a mural that struck me deep in the pit. It was partially hidden behind an overgrown tree, but I got closer to see it more vividly and dropped the currywurst onto the sidewalk.

A blanched white boy was on his knees, grasping the legs of a girl. I could only see the back of the boy's head and he was shirtless. He was wrapped around the legs of an equally blanched girl whose head and arms and fingers were literally branching out as she entered a tree-inducing metamorphosis, and from her branches exploded leaves of oranges, yellows, and reds. Her head was tilted to the side; her eyes were closed. Vines wrapped around her waist and encircled her breasts and neck. I looked at Riley and pointed to the mural, but she was too busy taking a picture with the Kiwi and clandestinely giving him bunny ears. She wouldn't've understood anyway.

"It's like I'm reliving it," I said loud enough for Kev to hear.

"Reliving what? Dude, your wurst!"

"Oh… nothing… Look at this shit," I said, pointing to the transforming girl. "How come people have to do that shit?"

In the girl's midsection, *Julie and Becca were here!! U of Indiana 2016!!* had been scribbled in purple Sharpie.

"Like, here we have a priceless, literally priceless, piece of history…"

"Oh, God."

"… and these girls, these two sorority bitches take it upon themselves…"

"What's Joel saying?"

"You'll catch on."

"… to defecate on it. It's the same bullshit…"

"Got it."

"… millennial entitlement. We can't just admire something. No. We have to leave our stamp on it, our opinion, our little comment, like the Berlin Wall is a fuckin' Facebook post."

"You have a pen?"

"Fuck *Julie and Becca U of Indiana 2016*… fuck them."

"Take 'er easy there, Buck. Let's get a drink."

BINGE UNTIL TRAGEDY

Because we were sick of walking and my shirt was sticking to the crevice of my spine, we hailed a cab and hit a different part of the city, and the Kiwis joined us. Riley picked one of the recommended bars from her travel guide that had a communism theme, and from the outside tables we could see the Berlin TV Tower—a remnant of communist Berlin that looks like something from a futuristic science-fiction comic.

"You know that's the tallest structure in Germany," she said.

"It's weird…" said Kev, doing that thing where the person hopes you entertain the thought and say, *What's weird, Kevin?*

"What's weird, Kev?" said Riley.

Damn it.

"It's weird that a country that was so divided by something, in this case communism, goes on to celebrate it, with guys selling those Russian hats with the Soviet symbol in the middle… and like… places like… like this, where they have communist memorabilia from Che Guevara t-shirts to Marx's manifesto being sold behind the bar."

"That's ironic," I said.

"Like, communism tore this country and city in two. What the fuck are they doing?"

"People have short memories," said one of the Kiwis.

"I guess that's true," said Kev. "I don't even remember your name."

Kev and I went into the bar to order another round. I kept an eye on Riley, who was entertaining the Kiwis, smitten by their unarranged competition and feats of bravado. One didn't shut up about how many mountains he'd climbed; the other had swum with sharks in "two different bodies of water."

"Do you have WiFi?" Kev asked the bartender. "What's this shit?"

Inside the bar, a mounted flat-screen television that usually played Soviet propaganda videos and stock footage of tanks rolling down Red Square was instead showing the news—the scrolling caption read: *Junge Westler schließen sich Terroristen in Nordafrika an.* German commentators spoke over the soundless video as one by one, guys who looked about my age stomped down their passports into a small, simmering fire. It seemed like the guys were from all over the world: England, Australia, Denmark, Canada.

"It's the future," said a hoarse voice from a few seats down the bar.

"Thanks, buddy, but what do you… wait a minute… Joel…"

"You're Lucky Star!" I yelled, almost knocking my beer off the bar with my elbow.

"In the flesh," he responded.

"No. Fucking. Way," said Kev.

Lucky Star was one of the biggest childhood actors of the nineties. In terms of volume alone, he starred in more movies, television shows, and commercials than any other celebrity for a decade. Born Saul Tereshchenko in Brighton Beach, Brooklyn, he starred in his first commercial—for Whacky Blocks—when he was only four years old (he was the kid who destroyed the other kid's meticulously arranged castle set). By six he was doing voiceovers for Disney movies, and by eight he was the star child on the family sitcom *The Smiths and Company:* an altruistic family who could never seem to say no to a needy child—tumult ensued. In *Buck and Larry Get Stuff Done,* Lucky was neither Buck nor Larry, but a conniving smart-ass teen named Leo who stole the show. Every teenage boy wanted to be Leo whether they admitted it or not. But it was his dramatic role in the 1996 film *Window Washer,* about window washers at a children's hospital who dress as superheroes as they rappel down the side of the glass building, that shot Lucky into true stardom.

Lucky had played the ringleader, a chronically ill, seasoned patient who understood the ins and outs of the hospital and acted as the big brother to the younger, newer kids. It was this film that won him an Oscar, inflated his ego, and led him to legally change his name to Lucky Star. Despite Lucky only being in his thirties, his face was wrinkled and cracked like an old baseball glove. His two gold loop earrings dangled in each earlobe and the pewter strands of hair sprouted out and mixed into his famous black-as-night coif—I remember wanting to dye my hair the same color when I was a kid. A mélange of rings and bracelets jingled when he spoke and gesticulated—in true Brooklynite fashion—as he spilled

Augustiner on his t-shirt, which said *Jugosalvija* (Yugoslavia) with the flag of the old soviet puppet racing across his chest.

"Mr. Star…" Kev gushed.

"Please, call me Lucky."

"Lucky… my friend and I here, man, we're big fans. Like, *big* fans."

"Welp… I'm honored to hear it, boys."

"We quote your movies all the time. Take 'er easy…"

"Please don't," he said.

"… Sorry."

"What brings you two to Berlin?"

"Just graduated college, traveling Europe."

"Spectacular idea. Don't ever grow up." He fixed himself in the chair and leaned forward, as if to tell us a secret. "Boys, I'm going to tell you a secret: don't ever grow up."

"Yeah, well, that's kind of…"

"Here's another secret. Lean in close. It's *all* bullcrap."

"It's all bullcrap?" we repeated.

"All of it. Where did you boys go to school? What university?"

"This liberal arts college near…"

"Ahh, yes, the *liberal arts*! And how much did you pay for this education?"

"Um… a lot," I said.

"Yes, of course you did. It's all bullcrap. Here in Germany there are *no* tuition fees. That goes for international students too. *And* you can even learn in English."

"…"

"Think of growing up in school. They teach mathematics that 99.9 percent of you will never use in your life. Trigonometry—when was the last time you even used long division? Instead of how to pay a mortgage or file your taxes, hmm? Because one person, or 0.1 percent of you will use the mathematics and be really fucking good at it, and, look at me, those people will work for profitable corporations that pay taxes to the government or work for the government themselves, making weapons or oil drills or whatever they need at that time to beat China and

Russia or the Arab states. So think of your childhood education as less of a learning experience and more of a weeding-out process, determining not 'what will you be when you grow up,' but what it is you won't be."

"…"

"Listen to me. It's all bullcrap. It's a mirage, you see. Los Angeles? It's a mirage. It's a dumping ground of consumerist filth." He took a long swig of his beer. "Look at me. They threw me out. I haven't done a movie in that shithole in ten years, and I won an Oscar, for Christ's sake! Listen to me: go stand for something. Don't become a slave to loans, to the media. I moved here three years ago, to Kreuzberg that is. That neighborhood saved me. It stood for something, we stood for something. They tried to put in a Subway and we smashed it. We smashed it to fuckin' smithereens, boys!"

"That was you?" said Kev.

"Listen to me. The world is run by money, it always has been. Look at me. But that doesn't mean you can't stand for something else, something important. I don't mean to be the harbinger of depression here, boys. God knows I'm depressed, but that doesn't mean you can't still *make* something outta all of this shit. Sure, we have 'social media,' but did you know people now are lonelier than ever? Lean in here, boys, I'm not going to bite. In New York, that giant concrete wasteland, a dead guy sat on the subway for five hours before anyone did anything? FIVE HOURS! Holy cannoli, boys, it's all bullcrap. We're addicted to screens and the fear of missing out—FOMO, that's what you call it, right? You, brother. What's your name?"

"Kevin."

"Kevin, look at me, what was the first thing you did when you walked in here?"

"… asked for Wi…"

"Asked for WiFi! You're in a new bar in a new city in a new damn country and the first thing you have to do is scroll a feed of updates and nothingness just to feel complete. And, listen to me, I'm not blaming you. You boys didn't stand a chance. I know that I'm on the cusp, but you millennials didn't stand a chance. Look at how they market to you: *I*pod, *You*Tube, *My*Space, *I*phone, me, me, me. Look at the television. *I* don't want to, but I will. Look at television—*reality* TV that is—there is no more talent, but everyone wants to be famous even though they don't deserve it. Everyone *needs* that sense of meaning, of purpose, but the truth is, there is no meaning. You have no purpose. And destiny? Destiny is only for the blessed. Try explaining 'destiny' to the parents of a child with cancer."

Lucky took a finishing slug of his beer and signaled to the bartender for another one. "Look at this idiot, for instance." He pointed at the television where a kid that looked about our age was holding an American passport to the camera. "Since this kid is void of any social substance, he's latched on to these religious leeches and will now become an enemy of the world. The media will destroy this kid, just like they destroy everybody. You guys aren't media, right? Look right here in Berlin! When MJ held his baby over the balcony at the Hotel Adlon. They ruined him, the media. He was a close friend of mine. Did you know that? Yep, I've been to Neverland quite a few times, and Michael never touched any child inappropriately, not around me at least. Listen to me, the media ruined one of the greatest stars in human history. They tore him apart in the tabloids. And after he passed, they lauded him like some type of beautiful creation of free expression and talent? It's all bullcrap, boys. Look at the television, again, it's combative in nature, look at the shows: *Cake Wars, Whale Wars, Cupcake Wars, Storage Wars…*"

"Hey guys. Holy shit, is that Lucky Star?!" Riley screamed as she approached us.

"… *Parking Wars, Garage Wars, Shipping Wars…*"

"Yup."

"I want to ask him to take a pic with me for the album."

"Don't!"

"… *Whisker Wars, Border Wars, Fan Wars, Design Wars…* did I miss any?"

"Oh… I… I don't think so," I said.

Riley stood next to us with her hand on my shoulder, digging her nails into my shirt and bouncing on the balls of her feet.

"Hey there, I'm Lucky Star. I've been giving your boyfriend some life advice."

"He isn't my…"

"Sit down and listen to me."

Lucky prated on about the meaning of life (or lack thereof) for another hour, and the more we drank, the more it started to make sense, and not in the artificial way that will wear off with the alcohol, but in the pit, like the planets in my brain started to align and I could see the meaning of life (or lack thereof) coming to fruition.

"Look at this shit," he said, pointing to the TV, which was showing grainy footage of the police state that was once known as Algeria. "Bomb Los Angeles, save Algiers!" he shouted, leaning over the bar and falling into the well.

By June, the tinderbox known as North Africa and the Middle East had conflagrated past the point of repair. What didn't help was that we, the West, had put "the tyrants" in power, in one way or another, however you'd like to spin it. So after two or five Augustiners and Lucky's rant still rattling around my skull, I had this frisson of excitement tickling its way up my spine that mimicked the effects of cocaine.

Riley got her picture with the former movie star, "skinny arm" and all, and uploaded it to Facebook and smiled as the likes came piling in. Lucky had a meeting with "some Turkish fellas" back in Kreuzberg, but gave Riley his number and told us we should all meet up again for a drink.

We headed back to the hostel for a nap and much-needed sobering up, but I was grinding, the cogs were churning, and I was even surprised with myself at how much Lucky's ranting had me thinking. Back home he'd been cast off as the washed-up child actor who couldn't keep up with the fame, but the guy had a moxie about him. I couldn't wait to see him again. Was I falling… in love with this guy? They say love and cocaine have similar effects on the brain, which is why we spend our lives chasing love and our Saturdays chasing lines.

The hostel hangout room was furnished with white and black leather couches, chairs, and loveseats. Flags were draped from exposed piping left over from when the warehouse packed meat instead of horny young travelers. Nobody spoke to anybody else; each and every person, even those traveling in groups, had a screen in front of their dilated eyeballs. Phones, tablets, laptops, phones the size of tablets, and laptops the size of phones, and all you could hear was the faint muffled music bouncing off eardrums from earbuds and whimpering in the air and the giggles from YouTube videos of pets or the results from quizzes telling you "which character from Harry Potter is *actually* your spirit animal." I squirmed and squeaked in the uncomfortable leather couches that were not yet broken in. I stared at people for uncomfortable lengths of time—not a single person noticed. I read the stickers from the tops of their laptops, little snippets of inspiration like, "The problem with traveling is that you only get a lifetime to do it" and "Live life to the fullest, then let it *overflow*." There must've been various nationalities represented in that room, a plethora of languages and insight and different ways to get drunk, but the taste of the internet, the sweet nectar of a good WiFi connection, had thwarted any chances of cultural cross-pollination. The sole moment anyone focused on anything together was when an unexpected crack of thunder bolted us wayfarers from our squeaky seats and the rain began to fall.

    I wanted to wake up Kev, for he so loved the rain that he didn't even own an umbrella, so I went to our twelve-bed room to find him. He was lying in bed, headphones blaring, deep in a trance. Riley was asleep, passed out without ever making it under the covers. I left the hostel to wander Berlin alone, because every new city should be experienced in the rain. I went back to the area where we took our tour earlier that day and I found him, my bullet-holed Superman. I put my hand on his chest and watched as rain slid down my fingernails and got caught in my arm hair.

    I went into a becoming little coffee shop where I sat to dry off and warm my insides. I ordered an espresso, a bitter son of a bitch, and closed my eyes, sat back in my padded wooden chair, and listened to the scratching and screeching of the coffeemaker and the metal slicing of the milk frother. I didn't ask for the WiFi password; I just let it be.

BEN D'ALESSIO

In a bar illuminated only by the buzzing glow of neon in the depths of Kreuzberg, we met Lucky Star and a few of his friends for a drink. Typically, I wouldn't entertain the blatant ulterior motive that the guys had when inviting Riley & Co. out with them, but I wasn't finished with what the former child actor had to offer, so I buttoned my shirt and brushed my teeth and swabbed the golden wax from my ear canal.

Lucky was visibly upset, and before we could exchange pleasantries, he said, "Look at this shit," brazenly pointing to a group of twenty-somethings. "One fuckin' blurb in some travel guide and this place is crawling with punks. Australians. Invasive fuckin' species."

I suspected Lucky hadn't stopped drinking since the afternoon. But man could Lucky and his Turkish triad drink, like really put 'em back. Each one of them was wearing a tracksuit jacket with dark jeans and crispy white sneakers. Lucky was in a CCCP jacket, and the other three guys wore Rhodesia, Siam, and Catalonia, respectively. The Turk in Siam watched as I analyzed their jackets and said, "It's a comment on society."

"He means it's a commentary," said Lucky.

"Yes, yes, that's what I said."

"None of these countries exist anymore. I'm sure you've realized that."

"I don't get it," said Kev.

"We wear clothing depicting nonexistent countries to remind the world that nations aren't invincible, they are not omnipotent entities, they, like human beings, can die."

"Whoa."

"Now sit down and drink. We're having *raki*, it's a Turkish drink."

In the middle of the table stood a slender bottle surrounded by tall glasses and empty beer bottles. The tallest Turk poured out three glasses of the *raki* and added chilled water, which made the drink turn a cloudy white.

"Lion's milk," he said, smiling.

"This drink reminds us of our home country," said the third Turk, who had a profound beard that didn't fit his boyish face.

"Your home country?" said the Turk pouring the drink. "This is your home country, Deutschland."

The three Turks squabbled in a mixture of German and Turkish that escalated to the point of them jumping from their seats and jabbing fingers in chests. And just as quickly as it escalated, it dissipated, and they sat shaking hands and pouring more *raki*. Apparently, only one of the three Turks was actually born *in* Turkey—the one who made the provocative comment. This topic of identity had been one of those sore subjects that always came up when they got together to drink, which had led to tussles and tiffs on more than one occasion. The native Turk spoke with an enviable confidence, and explained how an American in Istanbul taught him English, his fourth language, and because of that he was always grateful to Americans: "You are not all bad," he joked. He was born and raised in Istanbul to an ethnic Turk father and a Kurdish mother, and that identity was what forced him to learn how to fight at a young age.

"Where are you guys from? New York City, like Lucky?"

"Sorta," I said.

"No, we aren't," said Kev. "Jersey."

"Jersey? *Jersey Shore*? Tony Soprano?"

"… Yeah," said Kev.

"Ahh, don't be ashamed of where you come from. Have you been to Istanbul? Wonderful city. It's magic. I recommend it there."

"I don't want to have to cover myself," said Riley, sitting back in her seat as if to say, *here we go again*.

"No, no, you don't have to there. Or in Turkey at all. My mother and my sister, they don't wear that shit. Not all Muslims wear that shit or follow those rules. They are… Lucky, what word did you use?"

"Archaic," he said.

"Yes, *archaic*," he said, mimicking Lucky's distinct accent. "Look at us, we are Muslim and we are drinking and having a good time with Americans, and we *don't* want to kill you."

The three of them laughed. And it must've been that high-pitched mesmerizing Riley cackle that attracted the pod of Australians. They surrounded our table and asked if we'd like to join them for a "schooner of lager."

"I think we're good here," said Lucky.

The Australians pulled up chairs anyway, either ignoring Lucky's blatant denial or not catching his tone. They were all wearing short-sleeve button-down shirts with ridiculous patterns like red lobsters or multicolored pineapples. When Riley inquired about the shirts, they resolutely responded: "Party Shirts." They explained that a Party Shirt was designated as a shirt strictly worn to party and was never washed, ever: "Not even if, like, some pissed bogan spoons right onto it."

We hadn't touched our *raki,* and the young Turks and Lucky seemed less than amused that the Aussies had invited themselves to our lovely soirée.

"That looks like spoont in a glass," said one of the Aussies, pointing at the *raki*.

An Aussie in a powder-blue Party Shirt with little ships all over it poured himself a glass of the *raki* without asking, sucked it down, and slammed the glass on the table.

"*Uhhkk* this is fucking putrid, mate."

Lucky and the young Turks muttered something to each other in German. The *raki* absolutely *was* putrid, but I wouldn't dare say it, and instead asked Kev and Riley if they wanted beer, on me. I asked Lucky and the young Turks too, but they were glaring at the Aussies and didn't seem to hear me. When I got back to the table, three Augustiners in hand, there was yelling and swearing and the Aussies were mocking the Turks' accents.

"How many languages can *you* speak?" said the Turk from Istanbul. "Because I can speak four."

The Aussies bragged how they had been drinking all day. Clearly their filters had been breached.

BINGE UNTIL TRAGEDY

"I thought Arabs couldn't drink?" said an Aussie before throwing his arm around one of his buddies and sucking down his beer.

One Aussie got in the prostrate prayer position carried out by Muslims, and began to bob up and down, waving his arms in the air, while another made guttural noises in a mocking imitation of the Arabic language.

"We aren't Arabs and we don't speak Arabic! You imbeciles!"

The Turk in the Catalonia jacket, who had been more or less silent the entire conversation, rose from his seat undetected by the pack of drunk Australian hyenas, walked behind the seated group, and unleashed a kick into the jaw of the "praying" Aussie, whose teeth flew across the bar and hit the bathroom door.

Lucky tackled the hyena nearest him, who had been laughing directly in his ear, and the Turk from Istanbul jumped over the table, taking out two more. I grabbed Riley, who was seated directly in the middle of it all, and pulled her out of the fray. Kev had his arms pulled behind his back and was about to receive an open shot directly in the mouth, so I charged across the floor to tackle the revved-up Aussie before he landed his haymaker, but slipped on the puddle of mouth blood from the one who was hunched over on all fours and ironically panting, "Oh my god, oh my god, oh my god," and I fell short of the target. Luckily for Kev, the third Turk had timed his roundhouse kick to connect with the chest of impending doom perfectly, and Kev wrestled himself free. Like most bar fights, the whole thing lasted only a few moments, but felt so, so much longer. Lucky told us to "get the fuck outta here. Use the back door." I pulled Riley by the hand and smashed through the door and cut through a back alley and hoped Kev was following.

"Jesus Christ!"

He was.

"What the fuck just happened?!" shouted Riley.

"Joel was gonna leave me for dead! That's what happened! Thanks, fuckwad!"

"What are you talking about? I grabbed Riley and was coming back for you but slipped."

"Yeah, sure. Fuckin' almost got my face removed."

"What was I supposed to do? *Not* protect Riley?"

"Whatever, dude."

And we argued like that as we walked back to the hostel, and we could hear the piercing sound of sirens begin to grow from a distance.

PRAGUE

ONCE THE ALCOHOL HAD WORN OFF AND WE WERE on the road again, I had figured Kev and I would be back to normal, but that didn't happen. I had underestimated how angry he was, and even those few inside jokes that always pulled out a laugh didn't land. Riley was giddy to go and stay with Miloš Lhota. She had been texting with him since Amsterdam and was smitten. I could see it on her face. I would catch her smiling, peering out the train window as we shifted from Western Europe to East.

"You know he's going to expect to get it in," I said.

"Joelie, you think this is the first time I've entertained a guy interested in me solely for my body? Come on."

"You gonna fuck him?" blurted Kev.

"Jeez, I don't know. I mean, it's *Miloš Lhota*. This isn't just some guy from Sigma Chi."

"How's Marcel?" Kev continued to prod.

"Shut up, Kevin. You know, this is sooo typical. Since I'm a woman I get shit for maybe, *maybe*, sleeping with more than one guy when I'm traveling Europe, but you guys have a competition about banging a different girl in every country."

"It's called planting the flag," I said. "One of the Australians explained it last night."

"I don't care what it's called."

"The one that almost knocked me the fuck out?"

"Relax, dude. You're fine."

"Whatever, guys. My point is that I had a slutty reputation at school because I kept condoms in a drawer next to my bed, *just* to be safe, and you guys high-five and buy each other beers when you sleep with more than one girl in a weekend. Kev, you bought Joel a shot of Hayman's because he had sex with Meghan McSorley on Thursday night and then Nikki Fontaina on Saturday."

"…"

"It's a double standard."

"Don't go all pussy power on us," said Kev.

"I'm trying really hard not to hit you in the face right now."

"Oh, well, by all means, don't expect Joel to stop you."

"I fuckin' slipped!"

From the train station, we took a taxi to the Žižkov neighborhood east of the Old Town. Miloš's giant apartment was in a lime-green building that sat at the corner of two busy streets where the quintessential European songs of humming motorbikes serenaded us all night. Long windows offered romantic views of the endless sea of red roofs speckled with Gothic spires, and of course, like many previous Soviet possessions, a gigantic TV tower. Miloš greeted us with huge pork sandwiches and a fridge stocked with Pilsner-style beer—all those piss-yellow mass-produced beers in the US are cheap imitations of the style that originated in Pilsen, Czech Republic.

"This is some pad you got yourself here," said Kev as he scanned the open-plan apartment.

"Thank you. This is my home, but I also have apartment in London and Dubrovnik."

"I've always wanted to go to Croatia," said Riley. "It looks, like… so amazeballs."

Kev and I rolled our eyes and cracked a beer. Miloš's apartment was well furnished with interesting art, but it was much less… bohemian than I had expected. There were no works of modern art, nor any dead Jesuses hanging from the rafters. In fact, I don't think he had a single piece of his own work on display. I was pleasantly surprised by the lack of pretentiousness.

BINGE UNTIL TRAGEDY

On a long white wall that served as the backdrop for the living room, a horizontal portrait of a distraught girl lying in a field of teals, blues, and greens was holding a mythical-style sword whose blade was shimmering and covered in bright red blood. In the background a little castle sat on a hill, with a turquoise sun shining above it.

"Is this… Josephina Castellino?" I asked.

"Well done… what was your name again?"

"Ozymandius," I said.

"Ozy…"

"It's Joel," said Riley.

"Okay. Well done. Are you familiar with her work?"

"That I am," I said, crossing my arms and stroking my chin.

"Well, Josephina is a good friend of mine and this she did for me, at no expense. I gave her full freedom to do it as she pleased. It is a self-portrait."

"It's fantastic," I said.

"Ehh, it's okay," said Riley. "A little vain to put a self-portrait on someone *else's* wall. Don't ya think?"

"No, I do not," said Miloš, as if taking offense.

"You must be close friends," said Kev.

"Well, we were also lovers."

I had to cover my mouth from doing a spit-take all over Josephina's sword, and Kev started to laugh.

"Or how do you Americans say it, 'friends with advantages'?"

"*Benefits*," laughed Kev.

Riley looked like she wanted to puke. She stormed into the bathroom, where she fervently texted Marcel, who had been unresponsive for the past few days. While she was gone, Kev and I chose the L-shaped couches we'd be crashing on—I made sure I would wake up to that stunning view of the skyline each morning.

We had just arrived in a new city and needed a pick-me-up, so there was no time for a nap. Miloš brought us to a café famous for being the de facto choice for the caffeine-seeking Czech intelligentsia. The walls were adorned with black-and-white photos of writers, musicians, and artists, and I recognized *none* of them—for all I knew they could have been photos of random passersby. But Riley seemed to know all of them, adding a little insight as she stood next to each photo.

We sat at a circular table in wooden chairs that probably had not been replaced in the past thirty years. Next to us, a rotund man with stringy black hair and a gray beard smoked a cigarette while reading a paperback book whose cover was crumbling into pieces. At the bar, a black man in suit pants with suspenders and a crisp white shirt sipped a neat brown liquor. Next to him sat a girl with red hair, rose-colored lipstick, and white skin that was barely a shade darker than her friend's crisp shirt. She wore pearl earrings and smoked a cigarette in what I can only describe as "a French sort of way." She wore a white sundress with white shoes and when she laughed, she would kick back her head and hold her glowing cigarette out to the side. She kept a sweating glass of white wine in front of her that would get refilled without asking. The whole place seemed to be stuck in a time period I couldn't articulate. I suppose I was staring at her, because Miloš asked, "Do you like her? She is a very popular poet. She is not of this world. I like her very much."

Maybe it was the coffee or the milky poet sitting at the bar, but I felt a tingling sensation on my skin and a random burst of mirth, and it was then I felt that Prague would be a special kind of place.

Riley overcame the jealously she felt—every day having to see a portrait of another women who had slept with her newest tryst—and was once again enamored with the young artist. But when Riley liked a new guy, she ceased to be Riley as we know her; instead she transformed into a sex-crazed, dim-witted airhead whose brain seemed to empty out her entire education on the pavement like a freshman who'd drunk too many skippies. If she wasn't using faux portmanteaus like "amazeballs" or "listicle," she was shortening every word, like "totes" or "cray" or "adorbs." Kev and I let her have her space with Miloš because we found this intolerable, and went to an underground bar in the Old Town that was dark and windowless and full of exhaled smoke.

We sat at a tiny square wooden table under a domed roof and sipped Pilsner fresh from the tap. He and I still weren't cool, but neither one of us wanted to man up and address the situation. I passed the time by slicking the condensation from my beer glass; Kev fiddled with the WiFi.

"You aren't going to get a signal. We're in a fucking basement."

"Fuck off." And he went back to the bartender to see if he had the correct password.

I hadn't spoken to my family in a while and wondered about Carlo and Sal. Sal was going to be a father. The same guy who taught me how to puncture a beer can with a car key properly so I could "shotgun" it, the same guy who threw me in his Jeep at fifteen and had me driving around a downtown parking lot while I was on the verge of shitting my pants *and* puking, and the same guy who received a citation at Stanford for running through a men's basketball practice with his dick tucked between his legs, yelling, "I'm the goddess of fertility! Call me Nuanda! Call me Nuanda!" was going to be a father. (When questioned by the university, he told them it was a moment of poor judgment instead of telling them the real reason—he was pledging his fraternity. His loyalty to the organization earned him his letters and his was the first ass to appear in the *Stanford Daily,* probably.)

In the middle of my daydream, picturing Sal's drunk bare-ass sprint past the head coach, two girls appeared in front of me, breaking my stare. The blond stuck her hands in the back pockets of her jeans while the brunette put hers on the table, pushing her tits out of her shirt. They were real—the girls I mean, I wasn't sure about the tits. I caught myself staring and realized I had to speak.

"Would… you two like to sit down?"

"Yes, of course," said the brunette with a distinctly Slavic accent. They were danger with four legs.

"Would you like a drink?"

"No. We want to ask you something. And we do not have so much time. So listen to me."

I was all ears.

"You are American, no?"

"What gave it away?" I said, leaning in in an attempt to be suave.

"Your shoes."

"… Oh." I was wearing classic black-and-white Chuck Taylors.

"But that's not all we want to know. We are actresses and we want to work with you."

"Work with me?"

"Yes. We search Prague for foreigners and select to work with them. We have a special right now about Americans. You are perfect."

"Oh, like an interview? You want to interview me? We could probably do it right…"

"No. Not like interview."

"I'm sorry. There must be something lost in translation here."

"We are *adult* actresses."

I was stunned. They giggled and said something to each other in Czech.

"Porn," said the blond one, speaking English for the first time.

"Listen, Mr. American. There is not pressure. But we like you, we saw you from over there," said the brunette as she pointed to a dark corner of the bar. "If you are interested, here is the telephone number and address." She placed a thin white card on the table and slid it across the wood. "You will be com-pen-sated for your time. You will work with Inka and myself, and maybe some of our… friends." They giggled again and stood up from the table. "We hope you will join us. We will work tomorrow, if you are interested." And as they started to leave, she turned back and said, "And your friend can come watch, but only if he does not have erection." And they were gone.

Kev came back to the table and said, "What did they want?"

I put the card in my pocket and didn't say a word. The smoke made my eyes itch, which soon became unbearable. We left the bar and emerged on the surface, and I threw my arms in front of my face like Dracula; my eyes needed to adjust to the sunlight. We walked through the beautiful Old Town, which was packed with tourists and souvenir shops selling t-shirts that said "Czech Drinking Team." Eventually, we hit the Charles Bridge, which was packed with the city's tourists, artisans, and indigents. A man with a python wrapped around his neck caused me to jump out of my American shoes and screech like a little girl.

"Everyone just saw you," said Kev.

"I wasn't expecting that."

The bridge was lined with black statues of saints and kings and other significant men of history and led to the other side of the city, across the river, where a cathedral sat perched on top of a hill. And it seemed that underneath each saint or king, a prostrate beggar lay with his hands or a baseball cap out to collect change. I dropped a few coins into the cupped hands of a man with long, disheveled hair. "God bless you," he said in English, never looking up.

"Why do you do that?" asked Kev. "They're just going to blow it on like, drugs or alcohol or some shit."

"What have you spent money on this whole trip?" I snapped back.

"Yeah, but I'm not homeless. You know, they found a guy in the City who was begging for money every day, and the whole time he had, like, a hundred thousand dollars taped to his body. These people…"

"These people are just people, man. So what if they want to spend my change on a beer? If it gets them through the day, it doesn't matter to me. Once the money is out of my hands it's their decision to do whatever they want with it. Just like how that change was in the hands of someone else before me and someone else before them and so on. You don't get to be *more righteous than thou* because one time you dropped a dollar into some guy's cup in front of Penn Station and he used it to buy a Budweiser tallboy."

"Whoa, okay, dude. Relax."

"No, man, why are you on my ass so much? Cause you were stupid enough to get your arms wrapped around your back in a bar fight and I couldn't save you in time?!" I was yelling, and the vendors began to take notice and tourists made space as they passed.

"Ya know what? Fuck you, Joel."

"Fuck you, man. Your dad didn't teach you how to fight? He's former IRA, for Christ's sake!" A collective gasp rose up behind me and I turned to see people gathered around a large crucifix attached to the bridge that had something in Hebrew forming a semicircle around Jesus, which was very peculiar, but I didn't think much of it at the time. "Sorry," I said to the group.

"Yeah, well, at least my dad isn't in the fuckin' mafia."

"What are you talking about? My dad's a contractor."

"Oh please. And why do you think he *always* gets the premium state contracts?"

"I'm about to knock you the fuck out."

"You're fuckin' blind, idiot. I'm outta here." And he headed back down the bridge the way we came.

I continued across the river and found a French food festival. I ordered a ham-and-cheese crepe and a cup of wine. I didn't know how to get back to the apartment and Kev had the map in his back pocket. I snatched a cup of water from a table without asking if it was free and lay down on a bench. I poured the water on my face and felt the warming, drying sensation of the sun's rays. I put my empty cups on the ground and closed my eyes and listened to the different languages bounce around the festival. I realized we hadn't decided where we would go next. *Perhaps farther east. I heard Krakow is a good time. Or maybe we'll head south into Bavaria or the Balkans. I could please my father and go to Venice or Florence or Milan. 'Mafia,' what a gas. The man who gets light-headed trying to get out of his La-Z-Boy is a regular Sammy the Bull.* And as I was on the cusp of dozing off, I was startled by the clanking sound of loose change hitting the base of my cup.

BINGE UNTIL TRAGEDY

Luckily, when I finally got up off the bench, I found Riley and Miloš at the John Lennon Wall, not far from the French food festival. We stopped for a drink in the John Lennon Pub and Riley rapid-fired her ideas for upcoming plans.

"Miloš wants to take us to Kutná Hora, this small town not far from here, and get this, it has a BONE CHURCH!"

"Like, actual bones?"

"Yes, Joe, they are from…"

"It's Joe*L*."

"Excuse me. But yes, they are from real people. During the Middle Ages, people believed they would reach heaven more quick if they are buried near this one church. The problem is that so many people come to the church, they had no more space. Eventually, many years later, they begin to put the bones in interesting designs and *voilà*! Bone church."

"There is even a gigantic chandelier all made from skulls and femurs and shit." Riley showed me a picture on her phone.

"Looks terrifying," I said.

"Wait… where's Kev?"

"We had a tiff and he stormed off."

"About what?"

"Our fathers…"

"You guys are pathetic."

"I know."

We found Kev back at the apartment, sitting outside the building like a lost puppy. Riley told us to "have a beer and make up. You guys are best friends, don't be idiots." And she was right. Miloš recommended a local bar just around the corner and was thrilled to have us out of the apartment so he and Riley could fornicate like beasts—the sexual tension was palpable. We got so drunk, in fact, that before midnight, we were shouting how much we loved each other and made a bunch of Czech friends that we'd never see again; we told them we loved them, too. And that was something I found beautifully romantic about traveling: sharing stories, drinks, and genitals with people you'd never see again.

The night turned into a rolling blackout, and after the first bar (we went to three more) I don't remember much. I did have one memory of a searing pain shooting through my arm, and when I came to, I was looking into the shiny scalp of a giant bearded man puncturing my skin with a needle.

In our drunken stupor, Kev and I had decided to get tattoos. Being the self-destructive creature I am, I decided to have mine put on the fleshy soft inner bicep area, which is one of the most painful places to get ink.

"What does it say?!" I shouted.

Kev had his shirt off and a girl with purple hair down to the roots and multiple nose rings was etching a clover into his right shoulder blade. He turned his head and said, "I think it says: *Spring Forever.* Or something. You insisted it had something to do with you and your friend from back home! The one who…"

"Yeah, Adam."

"Are you boys too drunk?" asked my new friend who was jamming ink into the layers of my skin.

"No, sir!" said Kev, shouting over the vibrating buzz of the needle. "We don't even drink!"

I was woken by the jab of Riley's pointy foot. I was on my back on the floor next to the giant window that presented the fabulous view of the city. Riley stood by my head and held a piece of paper with both hands—I couldn't read what it said. I swallowed some spit to speak and ran my tongue over my dry, beer-coated teeth.

"What is that?"

"Tickets to see the Cavalry tonight."

BINGE UNTIL TRAGEDY

I had completely forgotten about the concert. Not a chance there were still tickets available this close to the show.

"How'd you get those?"

"Miloš grew up with the manager who runs the MeetFactory, and he got four tickets."

I tweeted: @TheCavalry Yo Jersey boy going to see you guys tonight in Prague! I didn't expect a response. But ten minutes later, I received a direct message from the band: **Great to know Jersey will be represented tonight. Meet us after the show brother. Have this code written down: 973908732 and proper identification.**

The venue was more intimate than I had expected, located in the southwest part of the city across the river; it was once an industrial building located next to the train tracks. The base was painted white and the top half was a sea-foam green. Red-painted cars hung from spikes gashing through their hoods, giving the cars an effect like they were melting in the sun.

We arrived by taxi and crammed our way through the socialites spilling out the front door, forming a human shield beside the train tracks. Miloš must have been stopped four or five times before we reached the front door, and one girl even asked for his autograph—Riley grabbed him by the arm while he was signing the napkin and plopped a kiss on his cheek. I was in a Cavalry t-shirt I had bought at a show down in Asbury Park at the Stone Pony, back before the band hit it big, before they were invading Europe and Asia. The shirt hugged my fresh tattoo, which was tender and glistening from the A&D ointment.

Kev and I were cool again, I suppose. We didn't address it or anything, but clanked our first beer and put our arms around each other and waited for the opening band to start. A band called A Murder of Crows from Asheville, North Carolina, was touring with the Cavalry throughout Europe and would be the only opener. I'd listened to a few of their songs before the show and thought they were indie and cool with an unrefined garage sound that kept knees bending and feet thumping. Their bassist was a girl who also sang backup vocals, which added a beautiful harmony when blended with the lead singer's raspy resonance.

BEN D'ALESSIO

We found a spot with a good view in the back where we weren't squished like sardines. We met another group of Americans who were touring Eastern Europe and had just come from Krakow. I had become bored of having to explain our situation every time we met a new group of travelers, so I just started making shit up, and this time I fabricated more than just my name. To them, I was a Rhodes Scholar studying the reintegration of Eastern Europe into the capitalist world and the effects of Westernization, especially from the United States, on a fragmented one-time Soviet bloc—that is why I was at this American band's concert in Prague. I threw in some Lucky quotes and spurts of rants and could tell I was garnering the attention of a cute girl from Alaska. Oh, and my name was Ryan this time.

"Plant the flag," Kev leaned in and whispered in my ear.

I had never met someone from Alaska (I saw an Alaska license plate once when we were driving down the shore), let alone slept with one, and her flannel shirt and nose ring bordered on lesbianic, but she stood by me throughout the show and seemed genuinely interested in my life, even though that life she knew was complete fiction. Kev, who was never great at speaking to girls, was making inroads with a college girl from the University of Colorado, Boulder, and I couldn't have been more proud of him.

The Cavalry came on and revved their guitars, and Jack Janowitz, the best damn drummer on the planet, started off the show with a freakin' drum solo—gotta love that Jersey gall. The three of us each had our prospects for the night (Riley's was obviously a lock) and we did our own thing, barely speaking to each other during the show. The band rocked the walls and splintered the stage with shredded guitar and anthem-style heart-wrenching lyrics. They played all my favorites: "Wings of Mercury," "Drown," "The Ballad of Earl," "Electric Soul," and even "Spring Forever"—it wasn't until the opening chords of this last song that I looked at my tattoo and realized why I had gotten it.

"Spring Forever" was a long-lost song on the band's first album. Adam and I loved it at first listen, and each spring before our baseball catch in early April, we'd throw on the song as we broke in our mitts with our fists. Its mellow dark beginning erupted into a rock-and-roll flamethrower of vocals by Tommy Devine, *the* new face of rock. Devine would mosey onto the stage in jeans and a guinea tee (a term my father despises) and a trilby or Yankees hat. The guy was covered neck to wrist in ink, like a white Yakuza. He'd put his lips so close to the microphone you could hear him exhale at the end of a song: Riley once described his voice as "pure sex." And it was the chorus, that addictive hook that always could get even the most ignorant of drunken partiers singing along:

And I'm gonna live like it's SPRING FOREVER!

But between the *it's* and *SPRING*, Janowitz would thump the kick pedal twice and the crowd would scat *bump bump*. So it went something like:

And I'm gonna live like it's (bump bump) SPRING FOREVER!

Like it's (bump bump) SPRING FOREVER!

Because it's (bump bump) NOW OR NEVER!

After the show, I pulled everyone backstage and had my napkin in hand with the code I was told to write down and handed it to the first security guard I saw. The guard held the flopping napkin in his palm and said, "What dis?" in a Slavic accent. Before I could respond, a girl in glasses and a high-and-tight ponytail came out of the dressing room, pointed at us with her clipboard, and said, "You must be **@VisigothJoel**. The guys are just… freshening up now. Give 'em a few minutes and Tommy or one of 'em will come get you. They know you're here."

At fifteen minutes, the same girl, who I figured was the manager, cracked open the door and reassured us they'd be with us soon. While we waited, I more or less ignored the Alaskan. I was too excited, like a child in line for Santa at the mall, and I sat there air-drumming the solos to "Spring Forever" and "The Ballad of Earl." When life came to the door, it was none other than Tommy Devine. I jumped up from the floor and introduced myself. I heard the Alaskan say, "I thought his name was Ryan?"

Tommy shook my hand but didn't even look at me. He was shorter than I imagined, and he sort of looked around me like I was missing something. I could see into the dressing room and there were empty bottles of Hayman's whiskey and King's Natural beer strewn across the tables and floors. A girl quickly walked by holding a towel to her chest with an exposed butt. Janowitz stumbled into the room shirtless and holding a rolled-up gold euro bill, knocked the beer cans off the table with one swipe of his forearm, dumped a little mound of cocaine on the glass, and began to chop it up with a credit card. He looked up and we made eye contact and he said, "Shut the fucking door!"

Tommy, still not even acknowledging my existence, said, "You and you"—pointing to the University of Colorado girl and the Alaskan—"and you," pointing to Riley. "You guys can come in."

"Hey Tommy. I'm the guy who tweeted at you. I'm from Jersey also. You said we…"

"Oh, you're from that shit stain too? Man, come on, I don't handle the Twitter. That's Kelly's job. The mousy chick who's running around with the clipboard who said we'd have Jack Daniels and not that shit." He pointed to the bottle of Hayman's. "Now how about introducing me to your friends?"

"Eww," said Riley.

I couldn't believe it; Tommy Devine was a total prick. It was all fake, a façade, the blue jeans and white t-shirt, working-class Jersey-pride heroes was all bullcrap. He was a phony! When none of the girls were interested in joining the band in post-show festivities, Tommy didn't say another word and just slammed the door. It came inches from smacking me in the face. I stood there for a few seconds, speechless. Riley would later describe the scene as "watching a child lose his balloon."

To get my mind off the traumatic experience, Miloš insisted we walk the Charles Bridge at night. We took two taxis to the western side of the bridge so as we crossed we had the East Tower and the rest of the Old Town beaming back at us. The city appeared as if covered in a black blanket, with pockets of gold piercing through the veil like lighthouses bursting along the coast. It was our group of four plus their group of four: the Alaskan, the girl who was studying abroad from Boulder (she was from the Bay Area), and two guys from Vermont who just graduated from University of Vermont and were working with a nonprofit here in Prague that brings awareness and aid to the Roma (Gypsy) population. And "awareness" they brought. I couldn't finish a conversation with the Alaskan before either of them chimed in with a statistic about inhuman poverty levels or lack of educational opportunities for Gypsy children. They were exact replicas of each other—the liberal-douche crunchy version of Tweedledee and Tweedledum. They were drunk and loquacious and couldn't take a hint.

"Did you know the Roma people have a presence in every country in Europe?"

"That's nice," I said.

"They make up one-third of the population of Bulgaria." (There's no way that is true.)

"Mhmm, that's interesting."

And if one couldn't get the factoid out in time, the other would jump in: "They originated in… in…"

"In India. Did you know that? That they originated in India and came *all* the way over here. It isn't fair…"

"… Cool." I just nodded and bobbed my head. The Alaskan had gotten even cuter by the end of the night, and in the back of my head, I replayed Kev's voice saying, "Plant the flag."

"The Roma are the most misunderstood people in the world," said Tweedledee.

"That's a fact," reassured Tweedledum.

"Yeah, yeah, that *is* a fact," said Tweedledee, reassuring me even more.

Kev was making headway with his squeeze, already having wrapped his arm around her waist. The Vermonters split up, using a divide-and-conquer strategy for spreading their awareness.

"The Roma people *choose* to live in isolated communities."

"Okay," I said.

"Why should they have to assimilate? They are preserving their culture."

"Mhmm."

The Alaskan appreciated my patience. She gripped my hand and we looked out into the Vltava River next to the statue of St. John of Nepomuk. Riley and Miloš joined us, and when bombarded with Gypsy inquiries, Miloš pretended he had difficulty with English, and the Vermonter didn't speak a lick of Czech. This caused the remaining Vermonter—Tweedledum—to focus his attention on me (the Alaskan had already listened to his spiel).

"They are persecuted just like any other minority."

"Worse!" yelled Tweedledee, attached to Kev down the bridge.

"Yes! Worse!" he yelled back, as if correcting an error.

But in the midst of a senseless statistic-laden rabble, he stopped himself and said, "Hey, is that a new tattoo?"

I was taken aback by his change of subject and said, "Oh, yeah, it is. Got it last night."

"What's it mean?"

"Well, it's for this friend of mine who… you know that song the Cavalry played at the end? He and I loved it. He actually took his own life a few months ago…"

The Vermonter had taken out his phone and was scrolling through his Facebook newsfeed. The artificial glow from the phone pierced the beauty of the bridge with the Old Town in the background. I was irate. I clenched my teeth so tight it pained my jaw. My lips went numb. I ripped my hand from the Alaskan's grip and made fists.

"Are you fucking kidding me?"

"Hold on, look here. The Roma culture has actually…"

"Are you FUCKING KIDDING ME?!"

He held his phone so it beamed in my face, causing me to squint.

"If you read this, it will show…"

"I listen to you blather on all night and you can't… can't even… Gimme that!" I snatched the phone from his hand and launched it into the Vltava River.

"Hey!" he said, leaning over the side.

I stormed down the bridge and into the Old Town without saying goodbye to the Alaskan or anyone else.

"Joel! Where are you going?!" Riley yelled after me.

There were screams and swearing and the last thing I could make out from the cacophony was Kev yelling, "Yeah, well, I don't fucking like Gypsies either!"

BINGE UNTIL TRAGEDY

"They have AKs and sniper rifles and shotguns and I think you can even shoot a damn bazooka!" said Kev, hovering over me with that "just been laid" grin.

I was lying on a couch that was too small for my body, my feet poking out from under the blanket. The sky was spotless; I felt guilty about it, but all I wanted to do was melt into that couch, become one with that couch, but Kev wanted to shoot things.

"Dude, that shit last night was hilarious. Those two jabronis wouldn't shut the fuck up. You just snatched his phone from right out of his hand and *phewm!* Like you were El Angelito throwing someone out at first."

"..."

"I got with that girl last night, the one from Colorado."

"Good for you, Kev," said Riley, peeking out from the master bedroom.

"Thanks. She was kinda weird, though."

"Oh? How so?" He had my attention. I yearned for deranged sexcapades.

"Ever heard of *Yaoi*?"

"Sounds Japanese."

"It *is* Japanese. She's like, obsessed with these comics filled with bug-eyed boys being all deep and shit. Like, questioning their existence. They never wear shirts."

"Oh?" said Riley.

"Apparently she lived in Japan for a few years because of her dad's job. She gave me one of the mags. She said I reminded her of one of the characters." He started flipping through the magazine and turned back a few pages and said, "This one." He showed us the picture with his finger tapping the ruffled paper. It was a doe-eyed boy with reddish-brown wheat-field hair, a small mouth, and a button-down shirt slipping off his lean shoulder.

"This guy, huh?"

"Yup," he said, snapping imaginary suspenders. "She kept calling me *seme*—*'seme* find your *uke.'* All bubbly and shit. Like she had completely changed into some cosplay fiend."

I skimmed through the comic and could feel the smile grow on my face, "Kev… have you actually *read* this comic?"

"No… it's in *Japanese.*"

"I mean, have you followed the pictures, the story, at all?"

"Why would I?"

"Dude… this shit is *gay.*"

"I know it's childish, but you watch *South Park* and *Archer* and those are cartoons too."

"No, I mean *gay*. Homoerotic. Teenage boys rubbing their hands over rock-hard nipples. Look!" I flashed a scene where Kev's "doppelganger" was caressing a sorrowing companion's wet naked body.

"Oh shit," he said.

I flipped through a few more pages "Dude! They're making out! Look! Wait, did you *actually* have sex with this girl?"

"Oh shit," he said, again. He stumbled over his words. His face went red. "Well… no… I mean…"

"Was there insertion? Penis in vagina?"

"Wait. No. But…"

"When I left last night, where did you go?"

"Her and I… and those two douchers went to a bar and had some more drinks. They were really pissed at you. We had absinthe."

"I told you no absinthe!" said Riley.

"Where were *you*, Riles?"

"Miloš and I came back here. You were already asleep."

Kev started to leave the room.

"Hey mister! Get back here!"

"Dude... It's all starting to come back to me... We went to their hostel, it's this mammoth of a place across the river. The four of us. We were all *really* drunk. We took our clothes off..."

"Who did?" I asked.

"All of us."

"Kevin!" yelled Riley.

"No. Fucking. Way."

"No, dude, fuck this. I don't want to talk about it."

"What happened...? What happened? What happened? What happened?"

"No. I don't want to talk about it anymore."

"Oh my god," said Riley, putting her hands over her mouth.

"She tricked me! She said she was going to join... but... but... she never joined."

"You... you fuck them?" I asked.

"No!" He snatched the comic from my hands and frustratingly started tearing out the pages and turning them into shreds.

"That was a first edition!" I laughed.

"Fuck you, Joel!"

Riley stood with her hands over her mouth.

"I think I'm going to be sick," he said, stumbling into the bathroom.

"It's Europe! Everyone's a *little* gay!" I called after him.

Miloš came out from his room and Riley stuck to his hip like a magnet. He had work to do at a friend's studio and invited Riley along with him, but I knew he didn't want us there, and honestly, I didn't want to be there either. I didn't see the "genius" in his work. He was good, better than a lot of the modern art garbage that was put in the Guggenheims and MOMAs of the world, but it wasn't my style. For instance, in his upcoming project, he would be traveling to London and LA to photograph the used plates of celebrities' meals—I don't give a fuck if Michael Fassbender doesn't finish his soufflé.

I told him we were going to one of those gun ranges where we can shoot assault weapons for cheap. He rolled his eyes and said, "Of course, Americans come to Europe to shoot weapons."

"For cheap," I said. "For *cheap*."

I thought it might cheer up Kev. The kid needed it after discovering he might be suppressing something in his id.

I'd never shot a gun before. Hunting never appealed to me; the concept of killing for sport seemed barbaric. When I told this to Miloš, he didn't believe me: "You are born with guns in your hands." He was putting us up gratis, so I didn't respond.

When Kev returned from the bathroom, no one commented on his puffy, bloodshot eyes. Riley asked if he had ever shot guns before and he got defensive: "No shit I have. What? You don't think I can shoot? I could outshoot any of you!"

He wasn't lying. Kev had grown up shooting guns, and he was one helluva shot. In the summers, to escape the incessant crowds pouring into his shore hometown, Kev and his family would cut against the grain and go to Pennsylvania for a couple of weeks—"summers in the country," they would call it. There, he and his brothers would go shooting every day at a local gun range. They became so well known (mostly because of his father's reputation) that the owners would let them go after-hours to fire unmodified fully automatic rifles left over from Desert Storm.

We selected a range that was on the outskirts of the city in an industrial-looking complex of rusted metal. We were picked up in a van that would pass for an SUV in the States and made it to the range in twenty minutes. There, we met five Australian teenagers, four Japanese "salarymen," three Ukrainian women, two Scottish stag parties, and a partridge in a pear tree. Our package was: fifty rounds 9mm, fifty rounds AK-47 (semi-automatic), ten rounds from a Dragunov SVD (sniper rifle), and five 12-gauge shotgun shells. But when we got there, one of the "salarymen" told us to "buy automatic," so we upgraded, and for the small price of 500Kč (about $20) we could unload the magazine of a fully automatic AK-47 into an unsuspecting paper target.

The targets were perched on mounds of dirt unevenly piled throughout the complex. If you were standing in the firing room, you had to wear goggles and headphones to alleviate the thumping noise. That was the first thing I realized when I entered the huge warehouse room: how fucking loud the guns really were. The targets were divided up into three different sections, which meant three different shooters could be firing at once. Although we had to stand behind a faded white painted line about twenty feet behind the shooters, you could still hear their barbaric yawps through the noise-canceling headphones when they finished their rounds.

Kev was practically jumping up and down in place, shaking out his hands like he was easing oncoming carpal tunnel. He turned to me and said, "No matter how many times I go shooting, I still get a raging anticiperection."

I never really understood it, the infatuation with firearms that my country has. Killing people, like psychopaths? That I could see quenching some carnal desire—not that I condone it at all, but I *get* it. But just shooting a gun at a target? Never really appealed to me—that was, until I released that first bullet from the 9mm pistol.

"Sweet mother of God," I said out loud, turning and observing the gun in my hand like it was some alien object dropped down from outer fuckin' space.

"Pretty great, right?!" yelled Kev over the intoxicating bursts.

I unloaded my fifty rounds in about fifty seconds. Before I knew it, I was on to the AK.

"Breathe. Fire! Breathe. Fire!" Shouted one of the Czech instructors covered in military fatigues. He paced behind us as if he were training soldiers, reliving glory days of a Soviet past. The butt of the rifle smashed against my shoulder with each shot. "Keep it tight!" he yelled. I didn't feel the pain, though, not until after I emptied my magazine in neither an accurate nor precise fashion. I didn't care; I didn't even keep track of every shot. I liked it in my hands, I liked how heavy it was, so much heavier than I had imagined. I liked that I needed to use strength to hold it up—I could feel my biceps and forearms cramping.

When we lined up for the sniper rifle I felt like I knew what I was doing, and approached the weapon as if I were a member of SEAL Team Six. Kev had shot well, really well. Even our pacing commando commented on his ability to hit kill shots. He challenged me to a sniper shoot-off. I knew I wouldn't win, but I couldn't back down from a challenge, especially not from Kev. Most of the others had finished their shooting, either taking vans back into the city or moseying around behind the faded white line, gloating over who had the best aim. The target was numbered from ten to seven, starting with a small circle directly in the middle worth ten points and decreasing as it expanded outward. We were instructed to aim for the middle. "Do not go for headshots. You will miss." But just for this round, Kev and I decided a headshot was worth an even twenty, and that's all he went for.

He went first and nailed it, between the eyes—twenty points. I walked up to the rifle, which was perched on a wooden table with a bipod. I crouched below the gun and aimed for the skull of the target. I imagined it was that limey fuck from Amsterdam, the one I super-kicked into the canal. I exhaled and pulled the trigger. *Pop!* The round sight recoiled and smacked me right in the eye socket, a perfect ring around the bone. "Fuck! Fuck. Fuck. Fuck. FUCK!"

Kev, the stag parties, and the Ukrainian women were all laughing at me. Kev was pointing. It was emasculating. Our general asked if I was okay and I tried to laugh it off, but man, did it fuckin' hurt. "Keep your eye *tight* to that sight," he said, as if he'd given that instruction to one hundred noobs before me. Oh, and my shot went wide by like a mile.

"Good shootin', Tex," said Kev in an awful attempt at a Southern twang.

His next eight rounds went: 20, 0, 20, 0, 0, 0, 0, 0—he had a sixty score with one round to go. He got cocky with the headshots. He was visibly frustrated and there was snickering going on behind the faded white line over how it was maybe too soon to have given him the nickname "Whiz Kid." "If I just got to take two shots in a row, I'd hit the second one *every* time. Like a free throw," he said.

"Yes, okay, but this sniper rifle, not basketball. You miss shot, target drop behind wall," said our instructor.

After my first try, I realized I probably couldn't hit a headshot if my life depended on it, so I aimed for that big midsection in an attempt to salvage some points, and respect. My next eight rounds went: 7, 7, 8, 0, 10, 10, 0, 9—I had a score of fifty-one with one round to go. At this point, everyone at the range was watching our shoot-off and keeping score; a salaryman had even made a bet with one of the Scots and gave me a fifteen-point spread. Before Kev got situated behind his rifle for the final shot, I called out to him: "Hey! If you have any more questions, you can ask one of these Japanese businessmen about *Yaoi*!"

He was so infuriated he couldn't say anything, and immediately after I said it I felt bad, I suppose. Also, bringing up a friend's recent questionable sexual exploits while he's aiming a rifle probably wasn't the smartest thing I'd ever done, but he laughed at me when I hurt my eye, so we were even.

Kev lined up his shot, but I could see his leg shaking; it was his nervous tick. He was going to miss. He fired. He missed. The expletives were so colorful that even our general needed to calm him down. When I approached the Dragunov, I realized I could win this thing. All I needed was to hit the center. But I felt remorse for my comment and decided to lose on purpose. I didn't want to make it obvious, so I aimed for the seven, but before I could pull the trigger, I heard Kev say, "At least I didn't run away from my problems, you little bitch."

I didn't turn around. I readjusted my aim, for the center. I pulled the trigger. *Pop!* Ten—61-60, I won. We didn't speak the entire ride back.

We had been in Prague for over a week and didn't want to overstay our welcome. Prague is a lovely city, but for me it had been a series of disappointments and arguments. I craved somewhere new.

"Let's fly somewhere," said Riley as we were all sitting around the living room sipping our morning coffee.

Kev and I hadn't spoken since the gun range and Riley knew it. And despite all her best efforts, acting as a sort of mediator for a divorcing couple, she could barely get us to look at each other. "How about Istanbul?" she said. "Those guys from Germany really seemed to love Istanbul."

"Eww, no way," said Kev.

"Oookay... oh! What about... what about like, Stockholm? Or, or Copenhagen? Isn't that where Layne is?"

I went onto one of those price comparison sites and searched "leaving Prague." The least expensive flights were to Germany, Italy, the UK, and Portugal. It would've really made my dad happy to see me go to Italy, but I had already been there and wanted to try something new. Kev scoffed at the idea of going to the UK, and we had already been to Germany—although it was only Berlin and this flight was to Cologne.

"How about Portugal, then?" asked Riley. "Our cleaning lady, Rosa, is from Portugal and she's so sweet. Where is it to, Lisbon?"

"Lisbon," I said.

"We met that guitarist from Lisbon, remember? The one in Paris? Kevin, are you okay with going to Lisbon?"

"Yeah, fine, whatever," he said.

I booked the flight with one of the European budget airlines for the day after tomorrow. Riley was texting away and when I got up to get a refill of coffee, I glanced at her screen and saw that she was talking with Marcel.

"Really? Right when he's in the other room?" I said.

"Will you *shut* up. Mind your own business. And besides, I've seen you fuck two different girls at the same party."

I shut up. "Is he going to meet us there?"

"Shhhh." She looked toward the door. "Yes, yes he is. But just don't talk about it anymore. Okay?"

"You got it."

We spent the day wandering the Old Town, drinking beer and eating delicious food. Czech food is severely underrated, and the cost alone should attract any gastronomist. Kev didn't speak to me—he barely spoke in general. Looking back, I wish I had made more of an effort to make things right with him.

As we strolled through the Old Town, I counted how many people took pictures with iPads covering their entire faces: twenty-seven. I said, "I think if someone takes a picture with an iPad you should be allowed to give it a little tap, nothing malicious, but just a little tap with your hand, knocking it back in their face." Riley and Miloš found this funny; Kev didn't even acknowledge my existence. As we stood craning our necks to view the *orloj*—the medieval astronomical clock that attracts lemmings in droves—I put my hands into the pockets of my jeans and pulled out the card that had the contact information for the porno girls. And when we got back to the apartment, I locked myself in the bathroom and called the number.

A girl answered and spoke in Czech. I replied in slow English and she gave the phone to someone else, the little brunette from the bar—I recognized her accent.

"Hello, Mr. American. We did not think you are call us."

"I am interested," I said, not really knowing how to continue.

"That is good, Mr. American. You have address, no?"

"I do."

"Good. You are in the luck, we just have American cancel. Meet us there tonight. I don't know how to say time in English. Be there three hours. We have pleasure to meet you." And she hung up the phone.

I had so many questions but didn't want to call back, didn't want to seem high-maintenance. *What do I wear? How do I get paid?* (Even though I was hardly doing this for the money.) F*uck, do I shave… down there?* I decided to trust my instincts: dress nice but casual, and don't wear the Chuck Taylors. *Or wait: They specifically picked me because I was American. Definitely wear the Chuck Taylors.* I opened my toiletry bag and pulled out my five-blade razor. The stubble on my face was at a quality George Clooney length, because I had maintained it with my electric razor since Paris. The manual razor was a different story. I hadn't used that thing on my balls in years!

In high school, my first girlfriend would only fuck me if I was clean-shaven down there. A single hair and she was turned off, and I'd be back in the bathroom, sitting reverse on the toilet, paying more attention to detail than a heart surgeon working on a fat president—my neck hurt just thinking about it. But in college, I'd let my manliness bloom, but not to the point where it took away from the aesthetics. Every porno I'd ever seen after 1979, the guys are clean-shaven (don't act like you don't notice, I don't care how hetero you are). I couldn't go there, drop trou, and be kicked out because my snake was poking out from the brush. I commandeered a handful of shave gel from Miloš and put the five-blade razor under the tap with hot water, and then got to work. After forty-five minutes of arduous attention to detail, I was as smooth as a newborn, and looked bigger, too.

I couldn't sit still for the next two hours, so I looked up the directions on Google Maps and made up some story about how I was going to meet the Alaskan from the other night for a drink, and nobody questioned me. The building was actually only a fifteen-minute walk from Miloš's apartment, so I hoofed it up the avenue, waving and smiling at people as they passed by.

The building was a leftover from the Soviet occupation. It was a concrete giant without a hint of color. Its sole distinction was the four statues of four different types of workers on a platform above the front entrance—my favorite was the shirtless hunk in a hardhat holding a hammer, eyes raised to the sky, looking back to Mother Russia. I rang for apartment 973, and when they heard me say, "Hello," they buzzed me right up.

Inside, the building was dull and unwelcoming. I found a rickety elevator and took it to the ninth floor. I got out and walked down a hallway that had gray carpet and white walls and was dark with light peeking in through the window at the end, which gave it the feeling of a tunnel, like I was dying and should follow the light. But unit 973 was well before the window, and I could hear voices inside. I knocked on the door and a guy answered: he had a deep voice but the face of an eighteen-year-old.

"Ah! You must be the American. Hello. Welcome, welcome. You trouble finding us?" He had to turn sideways to allow me through the narrow hallway that led to the living room. White sheets were draped from the ceiling, covering the windows and disabling sight into the kitchen.

"Uh… no," I said.

There must have been five or six girls sitting around in their underwear, smoking cigarettes, cooking on a little stove, or checking their makeup in cracked mirrors. It smelled like flesh and spices and rice, and my eyes itched from the smoke. The little brunette greeted me and asked if I was excited. I was, I really was, but I couldn't form sentences, because I felt like I was in a movie and at some point, men with large guns were going to bust through the door, demanding back their drug money—but there weren't any drugs, at least none that I could see. I heard a sonorous voice coming down the hallway, and when I turned, all I could see was a flaccid meat stick smacking itself from one thigh to the other.

"Oh, fuck." I averted my eyes. "Is that registered? Jesus. You could club a seal with that thing."

The joke went over their heads, but the guy who greeted me at the door, the only other person wearing clothes, who I realized was the director, said, "Do not worry, no one in Czech Republic is as big. Trust me, I check. Oleg is from Russia. I import him from streets of Moscow."

The tiny brunette took me by the hand, and she and the Director explained to me how I would get paid: cash. Worked for me. They showed me the money in an envelope, but since the conversion rate from dollars to Kč (Czech koruna) is so drastic, I didn't really know how much I was getting paid until after I had finished. I held the envelope in my hand, pretended to count the money and do some mental math, and said, "Okay. Looks good."

"Okay?" said the Director with a smile. "Okay. Let us work!"

He told me I would be working with the tiny brunette I had met in the bar, whose name was Katerina, and a girl named Eliska. "Eliska, very sexy. You will like her. Still new, but she is quick learner," assured the Director.

Eliska entered the room while Katerina and the Director were sharing their vision for the scene. She had unnatural blond hair that was very dark at the roots. Her big green eyes were double in size because of her eyelash extensions. She was in a robin's egg–blue pushup bra that accentuated her 34C breasts. Her butt was high and tight and sat snug in her matching robin's egg–blue underwear with the seam hugging her curves. Her teeth were adorably tiny and crooked and even with her in heels, I was significantly taller than her. She didn't speak any English, and when I introduced myself, she giggled and looked at Katerina.

I hadn't realized it until I went to stand, but I was already hard—erect, I mean. The apartment was full of beautiful Eastern European women moseying around in their underwear—I didn't stand a chance. One was topless, over by the stove, stirring something that smelled like curry.

They told me to undress, so I did. It didn't bother me. My freshman year of college, when I was riding the whole "independent from my family can do whatever I want" phase, I posed nude for an art class throughout the spring semester. I had also gotten naked at many parties, for one reason or another, and never really had a problem with it. It runs in the family, I suppose.

The Director and Katerina inspected me like an extraterrestrial and spoke back and forth in Czech. They liked what they saw, I could tell from the inflections in their voices. Luckily, I had just been hard and was sporting a half chub that was flattering, but not offensive or unbecoming. And now I know what you're thinking: how big is he?

I wouldn't say I should be famous for my penis, but I kinda considered myself above average. But so do most guys; sorta like how most Americans believe they're "middle class." I hadn't actually measured my penis since middle school, but I was endowed enough for them to continue with the shoot. Their conversation was loud enough to grab the attention of the people in the other room, and before I knew it, six more girls and Oleg were examining me like I was a piece of art. They asked about the cuts on my hand—I told them it was from weeks ago and I'd taken care of them. They asked about the tattoo—I told them it was recent, but I'd been applying the proper ointments and there's nothing to worry about. They asked about the ring around my eye—I told them I got in a fight with some neo-Nazis.

"Yes, I like very much. Good selection, Katerina," said the Director. I had never been so happy that another man approved of my penis. "We shoot in a soon minutes. Here are your lines, Mr. American."

I read over the few lines and skeleton of the script. It was bad, like truly awful stuff, but my negativity passed when I read over: *Katerina mount American and Inka join sex*. Which reminded me, where was Inka? The tall blond from the bar who I had thought would be the third member. They asked me if I needed to use the bathroom, and when was the last time I had sex or masturbated. I didn't get specific and just said "the other day." The Director assured me that if I needed to come then to just come—"But do not waste it. Yes? Make sure a girl is receive it in mouth or face." They went over some of the rules with me: no choking or smacking in the face, only smack on the ass. If I'm going to pull hair, do it deep in the back of the head, no yanking. Basically, don't go atavistic on these girls: "If you want hardcore shit, go to Germany, okay?"

"You eat pussy?"

"Yes."

"You do anal?"

"I suppose."

"You eat anal?" This one took me by surprise.

"Huh? Like eating ass?"

"Yes," said the Director, blankly staring back at me.

"Yikes." I ran my fingers through my hair. Never done it. Never wanted to do it.

"I mean, if I *have* to," I said, hoping it wouldn't even come up.

"Okay, American, very good. What is your name?"

"Joel," I said without thinking. *Fuck. The one time I give my real name it's to a porn director.* "But I want to go by Dante Knollwood." They stared at me. I had always heard that your "porn" name was your middle name and the name of the street on which you grew up. And I always liked the way mine sounded, and was eager to actually use it. "It's my middle name and the name of the street..." I knew I was losing them, so I just stopped.

"You can call yourself anything you want, American. Okay? Okay. Let's go."

He had me put my clothes back on. He said my jeans were good and he loved the Chuck Taylors. But he didn't like the shirt, so he gave me an extra-tight plain white t-shirt that stuck to my vascular arms like a greaser's. I was to start with Katerina. Eliska would join later, *discovering her roommate having sex with a boy.*

The Director had Katerina take some solo time for the camera, posing in maroon lingerie that outlined her boobs but didn't cover them, and from the bra, matching tassels hung and fluttered with every step. Her bottoms were two thin straps that left a line of exposed skin in between them at the waist, and hugged her butt halfway through each cheek. She lay spread-eagle and blew kisses. She bent over and threw back her hair and blew kisses. She crawled on the cream-colored carpeted floor with a look that could melt ice, and blew kisses. Then I entered stage right.

It was weird, if I'm being honest. The Director and Oleg (who was talent *and* worked a camera—a regular Renaissance man), were capturing different angles of Katerina's body. But this was it. Were all those times I watched porn and said "Shit, I could do that" a big fat lie? I harnessed my inner thespian and delivered my lines.

"Hey, someone called about an English lesson." I pretended to be taken aback by the lingeried nymph who greeted me. "Whoa, am I in the right place?"

"Oh, yes. You are the American I order, no?" she said, purposely making her English worse than it really was and thickening her accent.

"Okay… then let's start with basic grammar," I said, sitting on the couch.

"I don't want to work today." She dropped to her knees in between my legs. The Director was hovering over my shoulder with his camera. Oleg was getting the shot of her ass. She rubbed her hands down my thighs.

"Whoa." I pretended to be uncomfortable. "But… I'm your tutor?"

"And I want to pay you again."

"Back," I corrected. I went off script. *Shit.* I hoped it wouldn't get me in trouble.

"Huh?"

The Director didn't say anything; we kept rolling. She undid my belt, unbuttoned my top button, zipped down my fly, and pulled it out—my penis became immortal.

It was blood-hard like a mini redwood. I'd never been so proud of an erection. Starting at the head, she licked and sucked her way down to my balls, which popped out one after the other from my boxer briefs. She stood me up and slid down my jeans, which rested at my ankles above the Chuck Ts. I put my hand on the back of her head and guided her along. I tried to ignore Oleg, who was getting a close-up of crimson lips on American sheath. I took off my shirt by grabbing around the collar and pulling it over the front of my head. I tossed it aside, skimming the top of Oleg's melon. My tattoo was shining from the A&D ointment. I had thought we'd cut, to change positions. My shoes were still on and I was immobile with my jeans around my ankles, but she sat me back down and hopped on top and I slid right in, as snug as a glove. I felt her warmth and realized I wasn't wearing a condom. I started to sweat and could feel an itch under my armpits. Her hands rested on my shoulders, then interlocked at the back of my head. I gripped her ass tight and spread her cheeks—Oleg took notice and captured the shot.

She went in for a kiss; I saw it coming. All of the cocks she'd sucked went flashing before my eyes in a phallic montage. I evaded but made it look passionate instead of in disgust. I bit her earlobe and gnawed at her neck. She rolled her hips, front to back, and pulled her nails down my spine. As a reaction, I smacked her butt in an upward motion. She moaned. For a few moments, I forgot about the cameras. I forgot about the Czech guy hovering over my head and the Russian with the gigantic dick crouched on the floor. I could've been back with Chloe or Trisha or, fuck it, Fantine. I was enjoying myself, but snapped back to reality when Oleg sneezed, and the Director yelled, "Cut! Okay, very good, American. Take off the shoes."

Katerina hopped off me and checked her makeup. Oleg and the Director discussed their shots in Russian. When I bent over and untied the Chuck Ts, my ass was sweaty and stuck to the pleather. I took off my shoes and kicked them to the side. I took off my jeans with the naturally occurring rips, not that shredded denim bullshit you could buy at the mall. And I sat naked on the couch and felt a wave of uncertainty fall over me, and I felt real loneliness for the first time in my life.

Katerina threw back the cotton sheet divider and asked me how I was doing. I told her everything was fine and asked if I had hurt her when I smacked her. She laughed as if to say, "Please, that was nothing. You have no idea what I can handle."

"Okay, okay, let's go," said the Director, marching back into the room. He wanted to get Eliska involved soon, so he set us up in the same position and yelled, "Action!"

So I grabbed Katerina's ass again and pulled her cheeks apart and she ran her nails down my spine and in came Eliska, dressed absurdly in cropped jean shorts and a shirt cut to expose her under-boob that I was surprised didn't have "Kiss

My Rebel Ass" plastered across the chest. She gave a melodramatic gasp and said something in Czech. Katerina turned around and said something back in Czech. Whatever Katerina said was the single easiest convincing of a threesome in world history, and Eliska took off her shirt. She pushed me down and shot me a smile and started to kiss my neck. Katerina hopped back on top and played with Eliska's butt as it rested on my stomach. Her boobs would smack my chin as she bit the arch of my ear. I wanted to come but didn't—I held it in. She turned around and plopped herself on my face, almost giving me a concussion. She tasted tangy and clean, as if she had washed herself only moments before. Usually I'd keep my eyes closed, but the Director was hovering directly over me, making the pleather couch squeak. I could see one of his eyes; the other was in the camera. I knew not to look into the camera. Her butthole was centimeters from my nose. I could hear them making out, the fake moans of kissing. Katerina reached behind her and started pawing my balls. I wanted to come but didn't—I held it in. *Don't come. Don't cough. Don't fart*, I'd tell myself, over and over. *Don't come. Don't cough. Don't fart. Don't come. Don't cough. Don't fart.* But I could feel it building up, the thought alone that I was having sex with two girls made me want to come, but I didn't want to finish, I wanted to keep going. I never wanted to leave this apartment, and like a Sisyphus in sexual slavery, I wanted to spend every day approaching the threshold of orgasm, only to have Oleg sneeze and start the whole process over. *Where was that giant-cocked ogre when I needed him!* I got lucky.

"Cut! Very good. Okay, good." The Director hopped down and instructed the girls to get on their knees on the couch, facing the back with their asses pointed up in the air. He was sweating and dilated, and looking back, he probably was snorting blow between shoots. "Okay, you pick one to suck from behind, okay?" I went with Katerina; I felt like I owed her something. I dropped to my knees and went at it, and tasted the unpleasantness of salty sweat. Again, my nose was only centimeters from a butthole. And as I was licking and sucking Katerina, I used my fingers to play with Eliska. The Director loved it. I could hear him saying "good, good" to himself. The girls kissed. And finally, when I was tired of having my nose so close to a danger zone, I rose to my feet and stuck it in Katerina, who was taken by surprise and gave an authentic moan. And like a senior citizen searching for the right slot machine in Atlantic City, I switched to Eliska, smacking my hips against her ass.

"Stroke me, big boy," said Katerina, whose face was half buried in the pleather. That was it: doggy style was my kryptonite, and as I watched myself thrust against the tight Czech, I could see my dick pulling out part of her pink, stuck to it like rubber. I pulled out and tapped Katerina on the butt. Like trained canines, they dropped to their knees and opened their mouths. I pushed their heads together, took a half step back, and fired a rope, catching them both in the side of the mouth. The second burst hit Eliska between the eyes. The third nicked Katerina in the chin. I felt Oleg breathing heavily by my knees. The Director smiled.

The girls got cleaned up; I got dressed. The Director offered me a beer. I accepted, and we all sat in the kitchen at a comically small round table. He told me I was great. He offered me to shoot again this week, but I told him I was leaving. He handed me the envelope of cash and shook my hand. He asked if I wanted to watch any of the video. I declined. I figured it would be on the internet soon, and if I really needed to watch it, it'd find me. *There goes my chance of running for president.*

I left the kitchen. Katerina passed me in the hallway. "Well done, American," she said, giving me a wink and going on her way. I wanted to get one last look at the room, and when I pulled back the cotton curtain, I saw Eliska sitting on the couch, texting on her phone. I sat down next to her and she smiled. I told her she was very pretty. She smiled and said, "Thank you"—the first English I heard her speak. I asked her if she was from Prague; she nodded her head yes. I asked her how old she was. She paused and flashed up two hands, and then a third single hand. I figured maybe they used a different numbering system, which didn't make any sense, or she forgot a fourth and fifth hand and was twenty-five, which was older than me and surprising, because she didn't look it. But when I went to correct her, she flashed the same three hands, slower, five fingers each. Five times three is fifteen. I did the math again: 5+5+5=15. She looked down at the ground. The blood drained from my face. I felt nauseous, like I had walked through a spider web. The saliva coated my coffee-stained teeth. I got up to leave. She looked up and said, "Sorry." I should've said the same.

 The walk back to the apartment was solemn. I barely looked up from the sidewalk and made two wrong turns from inattention. I carried the envelope of Czech Korunas and handed it to the first homeless person I saw. I didn't want the dirty, easy money. I could smell the apartment on the paper. The homeless man shuffled through the envelope and rushed to thank me. I just nodded and said, "You're welcome." I got to the green apartment and went to sleep and wished it had all been a wet dream.

BENEATH THE ASH

OMAR DEFENDED HIMSELF LIKE A FOX BACKED INTO a corner, gritting his teeth. Salim and Farah ridiculed him for his association with the Islamists. *La Petite M*ère was accustomed to arguments occurring in her apartment, but asked them to keep it down for their own safety. When Omar spoke, he did so in Arabic. Farah and Salim used French but would oftentimes repeat themselves in Arabic, just so Omar would acknowledge them.

"What about those men who had their heads chopped off? You agree with that? Hmm, hmm?" said Farah.

"No. I wouldn't do that, but…"

"But what?!" screamed Salim.

*La Petite M*ère asked him to keep it down.

"Excuse me," he said. And in hushed tones, he continued, "Omar, you are brainwashed, my friend. That is *not* Islam."

"It's that imam you see, isn't it?" said Farah. "He is awful. He should be put in jail."

"He is a good man. A man of God!"

*La Petite M*ère looked up from watering her plants on the windowsill and glared. Salim frantically stirred his tea. Mohamed tuned his oud and hummed quietly to himself. Farah sat shaking her head, trying to get Omar to watch the interviews of the Islamists from the Square to show him how destructive they truly were.

Violence in the city had been minimal during the last couple of weeks. The military was sent to the south of the country to meet *al-Saif* before they came to the coast. *Al-Saif* was only gaining more soldiers as they took over towns that were ill-equipped to defend themselves. But when Islamists supportive of *al-Saif* began to outnumber the other groups of protestors, the police shut down all demonstrations. The General warned that military personnel still remained in Algiers and would deploy troops on anyone who was "publically insulting the president."

The Square was quiet. Those photos of students locked arm in arm, waving banners for *La Liberté,* shouting with strained vocal chords and wrapped in the national flag, were a thing of the past. Classes at the universities never resumed. The General issued a curfew: nine p.m. Everyone had to carry identification, and if you were caught out past the curfew, you were taken in for "questioning." The prison was cramped and overcrowded. Cells meant for four were now housing twenty. *La Peste* broke in to apartments and stores and took whatever they could find: food, goods, people. They no longer operated surreptitiously; they flaunted their stranglehold. They wore suits tailored to their specifics at gunpoint. They wore stolen high-end sunglasses and drove in loud convertibles and SUVs instead of black vans with tinted windows. And they were always drunk. The smell of whiskey became associated with the roving federal gang, and spilt Hayman's on the street meant *La Peste* was not far.

Fortunately, the internet had not been shut down. Instead, it was heavily monitored by specialists hired by the government. Some of them were students themselves, rewarded handsomely for their work.

Salim continued to operate the Facebook page for *La Liberté*. He spoke to his mother often, who begged him to come home, back to Tebessa where there was little government activity. He said he still had classes and told her not to believe what she heard about the happenings in Algiers. He told her it wasn't that bad; he lied to her, something he had never done before.

Omar was rarely at their apartment anymore. He spent most of his time at a small mosque, listening to a fiery imam with a pack of other young men. When *La Peste* shut down the mosque, the imam moved his preaching to his home, where they sat on carpets and drank tea and cursed Hannachi and his regime in secret. Eventually the imam was taken in for "questioning," and Omar never saw him again.

Mohamed had basically moved in with Salim, taking over Omar's spot. He played his oud during the day, but it was forbidden to play past curfew. One day he was playing outside of the apartment when three members of *La Peste* stumbled down the steep steps of the Casbah and demanded he play them a song. So he did. He began to play an old elegiac song of Algeria, and before he could reach the humming chorus, one of the thugs pulled out a pistol and demanded he play something else. So he did that, too. He played an upbeat song that he learned watching the master guitarists of Jajouka on YouTube, and after only a few chords, a different thug screamed and hollered, "Don't play that filth from Morocco! They're traitors harboring the enemy!" Mohamed was confused and tepid and played the first thing he could think of: "Hey Algeria, Hey People," the song of the revolution. He wasn't thinking, he was nervous, and before he could realize his mistake, the pistol-wielding thug shot a bullet straight into the air above his head. Mohamed ducked for cover behind his instrument. The thug squatted down so he was eye level with the cowering young musician and said, "If I ever hear that song again, I will break your instrument, and then I will kill you." He took out a knife and cut the strings to the oud, then pulled out a flask and took a swig, the whiskey dribbling down his chin. They continued on their drunken raid of the Casbah, leaving Mohamed shaking on the ground—he never played outside again.

Farah continued to upload videos to YouTube, but from various aliases, and she stopped showing her interviewees' faces. They all had the same message: "The Revolution is NOT over." They were praised in the comments section—in French, in Arabic, in English, and in German—but nothing came of them. No one was entering Algeria, and no one was allowed to leave. The Belgian human rights group that was monitoring the revolution was sent back to Brussels under threats of incarceration. Farah made pleading videos to the defectors of the army, begging them to return to Algeria and fight for their families and friends—there were few responses.

BEN D'ALESSIO

The city wasn't dead, but it was paralyzed and parched. It hadn't rained since April and the ground was always hot. And if you listened closely, you could hear the faint changes in the seagulls' caws, crying out for a thirsty Algiers.

The guard who stood watch maintained his solemn demeanor and looked straight ahead as the General knocked on the president's ornate bedroom door. *Knock, knock, knock… knock, knock, knock*—nothing. There was a scramble of bare feet pitter-pattering on cold marble. *Knock, knock, knock… knock, knock, knock, knock.* "Your Excellency?" He put his ear to the door. "Your Excellency? We request your seasoned insight on matters of domestic security. If you are busy at the moment, it would be most helpful if I was given authority for this particular meeting." This was all a formality. The president was not much of a strategist and never made an important decision without approval from his administrators. If anything, the General wanted the president as isolated and contained as possible. His current grotesque sex bender had kept him occupied for two weeks. Workers, soldiers, and administrators around the Presidential Palace had only seen him once, when he drunkenly stormed out of his bedroom with an Egyptian cotton cape, blabbering about how he was going to rid Algeria of "backwater pests" and then take over France. "I am the modern-day Hannibal!" he shouted five times before being returned to his room.

The General started to leave when a note was slipped under the door. The guard picked it up and handed it to his superior.

"*Kill them all. More wine.*"

BINGE UNTIL TRAGEDY

Simon Turner was accustomed to the pounding rays of the sun. He found his new Saharan home not much different from Arizona. His Arabic was improving and he impressed al-Maghribi with his ability to perfectly recite passages of the Quran.

Al-Saif created a stronghold in Tamanrasset, and for the time being, declared the Saharan city as the capital of the Caliphate. Al-Maghribi nominated a commander in each city or town that was captured, and within a month of releasing the oil field beheading video, *al-Saif* controlled huge chunks of southern Algeria and was creeping closer to the coast. Al-Maghribi directed his commanders up through the eastern side of country, recruiting young soldiers from small towns, from desert cities, and spillovers from Niger, Libya, and Tunisia to join their cause. They were promised glory in the name of God and a chance to battle their repressors. Many youths throughout the Islamic world viewed *al-Saif*'s meteoric rise as a sign of righteous power, and on the internet, they were compared to the Omayyads who first swept across the Maghreb, spreading the Quran as far north as the Pyrenees during the eighth century A.D.

However, despite online propaganda videos showcasing the group's military might, *al-Saif* was far from the powerful conventional army they portrayed. Al-Maghribi was blessed with a perfect shit-storm of military blunders from Algiers, where rumor had it that drunken thugs were terrorizing the city's inhabitants and the president was sick or vacationing in Monaco or the Maldives on another one of his opulent holidays.

The Tunisian and Libyan borders were poorly monitored, which allowed easy access through an already difficult–to-guard Saharan divide. Giving in to the rumors, Hannachi sent an overwhelming amount of troops to the western border with Morocco, fearing a surge of returning defectors armed with Western-backed weapons. He pulled soldiers stationed in the South and East, which gave *al-Saif* free range to set up checkpoints in the desert and gain control of the geographic majority of the country undisturbed. Day by day, *al-Saif's* numbers grew, while those of the National Army dwindled, creating a zombie effect.

By the end of June, al-Maghribi had the most diverse army in the world, controlling territories that spanned over three sovereign nations (Algeria, Mali, and Libya). He recorded weekly videos brandishing his scimitar, which had become such a recognizable symbol that it was found spray-painted on city walls from Calgary to Jakarta. He moved quickly and efficiently throughout his Caliphate, never successfully being tracked by the French or the US Special Forces. When French airstrikes hit Reggane, a small town in the Algerian Sahara, the blasts incinerated twenty-seven people, eleven of which were children—not a single casualty was a member of *al-Saif*. Al-Maghribi quickly sent men to videotape the wreckage after the French had left, and uploaded the carnage to the internet. The videos and images left much of the Western world in despair, and protestors in Europe and North America deplored any further activity in the region. President LaGrange made a statement assuring the world that unless French lives were in danger, French forces would not be intervening in the "rise of the black tide in the Sahara." He demanded that President Hannachi, with the second largest military in Africa, allocate his forces to fight the Islamists instead of his own citizens—the Green Eagle never issued a response.

Al-Maghribi had been leading his forces up the eastern edge of Algeria, eyeing Biskra, one city closer to the gems near the coast. If he captured Constantine, the third-largest city in the country, he would make it the new capital of the Caliphate, planning his assault on Algiers from there. But the tenacious leader was headed back down south, back to Tamanrasset, to halt a Tuareg uprising.

The Tuareg are a seminomadic people renowned for being gracious hosts, treating their guests as kings. When *al-Saif* entered the city for the first time, they were greeted with fruit and sweets and tea. And in the beginning, the Tuareg viewed the rebel leader and his soldiers as freedom fighters against the tyrannical Hannachi regime. But quickly enough, their ideologies clashed, and Tuareg women who not only had freedom but power unprecedented in North Africa were forced to succumb to the desires of the *al-Saif* soldiers. A fourteen-year-old who refused to have sex with one of al-Maghribi's henchmen was being put on trial for assaulting her aggressor—she mocked him when he pulled down his pants and smacked him in the face when he advanced on her.

Al-Maghribi's armored caravan tore through the desert. He sat in the back of a monster SUV, trusty Youssouf on his right and Simon Turner on his left. The young American hadn't left the leader's side since he joined *al-Saif*. He was given a pistol, a classic AK-47, and a brand-new dagger with a serrated blade. Youssouf had a sword: He was the only other person besides al-Maghribi who carried one. Al-Maghribi would tell him that when the Caliphate was fully established, he would be assigned a city of his choosing to lead: "You Americans like Europe. How about Paris or Madrid, or perhaps Rome?" He said Algiers would become the new Damascus, and eventually the war would be taken to the Israelis, where they would liberate Jerusalem from the Zionists.

Simon would fantasize about the New World Order as his eyes tirelessly followed the swaths of desert that flew by. He pictured himself marching down the Champs-Élysées in front of giant *al-Saif* flags, columns of soldiers following him, waiting for his orders, foaming at the mouth to realize their leader's bidding. Simon Turner would be a hero. He would be the most loyal leader to the Caliph, following orders from Algiers. He would broadcast shows on the internet to be seen by millions of young boys. He would speak to them in Arabic, he would forget English—he wouldn't need it anymore. Arabic would be the new international language, required learning in all schools—start them young. President Meyer would fear him, no more Middle Eastern oil would make its way to North America. Their jets and ships and tanks wouldn't even be able to start! President LaGrange would be dead—a public execution, hanged from the arched curve of the Eiffel Tower. The Eiffel Tower would serve as a minaret, the tallest in the world, bellowing the call to prayer across Western Europe. The Pope would be exiled to South America or the Philippines, constantly on the run as *al-Saif* conquered Asia, Africa, and the "New World."

Youssouf asked why he was smiling as their caravan neared dusty Tamanrasset. But Simon didn't say anything. He didn't even hear him. He just thought, *I'll need a new name, a title. Oh! And I'll need a sword, definitely need a sword.*

LISBON

IT WAS ONE OF THOSE BUDGET AIRLINES WHERE you aren't assigned a seat—first come, first served—which *never* made flying more aggravating than it already was. This particular airline wasn't just budget, it was cut-rate. Charging forty bucks to print out a boarding pass; five bucks for a pack of crackers. The plane was shaking and rocking and I couldn't sleep. I was almost finished with *Homage to Catalonia*. I hadn't known Orwell took a bullet to the jugular and lived to write about it. He probably just had to roll down his turtleneck and he'd bag any chick he wanted.

Riley sat next to me. Kev sat a few rows behind, which was fine with me. I didn't want to listen to the thumping beats emitting from his oversized headphones anyway. I never told them about my acting stint—that's what I was calling it, an "acting stint." I didn't know she was only… you know… that she was the age that she was. I didn't know that. It wasn't my fault. How was I to know, anyway? It's not as if girls walked around with their age drawn on their forehead in crayon. What about twenty-five-year-old beauties who have sex with, like, eighty-year-old businessmen? Hmm? Those guys aren't psychologically castrated, they're given their own reality television shows.

We took a bus to the main square of the city, which had these dark-gray, almost blue stones in a wave-like design washing up and down the square. From there, we walked to our hostel. It was hot and muggy and I thought there would be more bustling activity in a Western European capital, but it was nice and old, and

I didn't see her nor hear her, but I knew that somewhere in this sloping city, an old woman was singing a painful song about better times past.

The hostel was located on the top floor of the train station, which itself was a gorgeous Gothic-style building with two inter-looping ornate horseshoe arches and a clock tower with jagged spires. We took a steep escalator to the top floor and pushed through the two glass doors to enter the hostel. At the front desk sat a tan guy with long chestnut hair that winged out from his ears. He was one of those naturally handsome guys who could wear whatever he wanted, even the ridiculous shit they tried to sell us in men's magazines. He even had a moustache and *still* looked good. The hangout area was filled with beanbag chairs and little tables with wooden stools. There was a green turf that served as the carpet extending all the way back to the kitchen, which had long dining-hall-style wooden tables that looked like something from the Middle Ages. The ceilings were extremely high and windowed and poured in natural light. Our room was on the first floor—an eight-bed mixed dorm. Tonight it would be the three of us and five others, but tomorrow Marcel was flying in from Paris and would try and stay in our room.

Apparently, Riley had been texting him since we left Paris. She said that for a while he was acting weird, curt with his responses, and when she was about to sever communication, he came around and was acting almost overly affectionate, saying he needed to see her again. Lisbon worked well for Marcel because he was planning to visit his sister in Fez, Morocco. She would be arriving there from Istanbul in a few days to begin the last leg of her three-city thesis trip on women's studies in the Islamic world. He would make his way south through Spain and take the ferry to Tangier.

Riley was her usual ebullient self and wanted to take the first tour offered that day. Kev didn't care to join. He didn't even take off his headphones when we got to the hostel and immediately went to take a nap. Riley and I asked the handsome devil manning the front desk which tours were still available for the day, and he told us that he himself would be giving a general city tour in an hour. We waited at one of those small tables with stumpy stools.

"Kev isn't doing so well," she said, broaching a subject I really didn't want to broach.

"He has to get over it," I said. "He doesn't even know *exactly* what he did."

"Joel… do you think Kev is gay?"

"What?!"

"Honestly, I've actually thought about it. He might be gay. Like, he *never* hooks up with girls, doesn't even talk to them."

"He had a bad breakup. A succubus ripped his heart out."

"And there was a time last year… I never told you this… Remember when he was like, MIA for a few weeks?"

"Not really."

"Oh, yeah, you were seeing that goth chick who liked to get beat up. What was her name again?"

"…"

"Oh my god, you're the *worst*. Anyway, while you were off doing god knows what with her, Kev was hanging around with this kid from my Death, Grief, and Dying class…"

"Wait, what?"

"This kid…"

"No, what class?"

"Death, Grief, and Dying. Psychology like… 304 or something. Dr. Kestenbaum teaches it."

"What's it about?"

"Death… grief… and…"

"I got it."

"So he was hanging with this kid Robin, who is definitely gay. He moved into the 'Queer House' on Main Street the next semester."

"I thought you wanted to hook up with Robin? Isn't that the kid I told to get lost in the dining hall?"

"Different Robin."

"There were two Robins at school?"

"Yup."

"Of course there were."

"I heard a rumor that they did shit together, but I didn't make much of it, because it was from this bitch on the softball team who spread that rumor that Jason Burcham had a tiny penis, and trust me, he didn't."

"Nice."

"So what do you think? He always just wants to get high or drunk. Perhaps trying to numb his true feelings?"

"I suppose."

"Possibly trying to call for help, but no one has answered."

"I suppose."

"How come you're being so trivial about this? He's like, your best friend."

"Good word."

"…"

"I don't know. It's like, cool to be gay now. Everyone is gay."

"*Everyone* is gay?"

"You know what I mean. It's accepted, at least where we live."

"If it's so 'cool,' then why doesn't he just come out?"

"Because the Caligans are Irish Catholic, and that entails a certain level of debilitating guilt that you WASPs just don't understand."

Before Riley could respond, a sun-battered baby-faced guy with spiked blond hair sat next to us. His stubble was a shade darker than his hair, and his eyes a shade darker than that. He was also handsome, which annoyed me at first, but I'd actually come to like Pete—the first Australian whose accent didn't make me want to punch something. He didn't sit down with us to hit on Riley, shockingly enough. He told us the guy at the desk just told him to sit "over there" because we'd be gathering shortly to go on the walking tour.

Apparently, it's very common for Aussies and Kiwis to just quit their jobs and travel for a year or so. He said it's because they're all the way "down there," so if they're going to travel to other continents, they might as well do it big. Pete was just beginning the European section of his hiatus, and Lisbon was his first stop. He had flown from Melbourne to Mexico City, hitting thirteen countries going south, ending in Brazil. He told us how cocaine was easier to obtain than clean water, and that being a *gringo* had its benefits. "I was in line to get on a bus in Colombia. And there was a guy with a machine gun patting down people before they took their seat. So when it came my turn, naturally, I followed the rest of the group—I put my arms up and looked straight ahead. The guy took one look at me and high-fived my raised hand. '¡*Pasa, amigo!*' he said, laughing. Good thing, because I had forgotten about the ounce of cocaine sitting in my bag."

"So do you speak Spanish now?" I asked.

"Not really, but when I drink I think I can."

Pete was more interesting than me. He was well spoken and well traveled. Every story he told started in a fascinating way, like, "When I bought this crap motorcycle and took it through Nepal..." or "When I stayed with this hashish king in the Moroccan desert somewhere outside of Marrakesh..." He rarely visited the typical places and never took the most direct way to get somewhere: "Sometimes the travel itself is the trip, mate."

"Oh! Did you know drugs are decriminalized in Portugal?" he said.

Riley and I looked at each other, looked back at Pete.

"Oh, yeah, they did it in 2001. It's called the 'Portuguese Experiment' and it works. You know what they found? Drug addicts dropped by fifty percent and drug-related diseases reduced by more than fifty percent. Like STDs and overdoses. And Portugal was *bad* with drugs. All parts of society. One in a hundred people were addicted to heroin! Can you fucking believe that? Now it's one of the lowest drug-using countries in the EU. Heroin addicts halved. They took the opposite approach to you Americans and the 'War on Drugs.' It's all about treatment, not punishment."

And as if the word "drugs" had a magnetic pull, Kev moseyed out of the room and dropped onto the bench, headphones wrapped around his neck.

"Kevin, would you like to join the walking tour?" asked Riley.

Kev said no in a brusque way that made it seem like Riley had inquired about his mother's bra size. When it came time to leave for the tour, Kev fell into one of the beanbag chairs under a map of the world where the continents were outlined in rope, and put his headphones on to escape from the world.

The tour was exhausting. Lisbon is built into hills with streets like waves, rising at seventy-degree angles before crashing into café-riddled plazas. And although my calves were screaming, I indulged in the city's beauty, which could only be described as the epitome of Old-World romantic. There was this persistent smell of crackling fried fish and freshly poured beer from the tap that made me want to sit with one of these old Portuguese and listen to their life story from start to finish.

These two guys on our tour, one American and one English, thought they were funny—funnier than they actually were. The American kept answering all of the Handsome Guide's questions, and at one point even explained why tiles were so prevalent in Lisbon's medieval neighborhoods. He had that douchey European haircut where the sides were buzzed and the longer hair on top was parted—like a greaser. His stubble was starting to form a beard from neglect. He wore mirror-lensed Aviators that sat crooked on his Roman nose, and jeans and a button-down shirt even though it was like one hundred degrees that day. When I heard him speak for the first time, I knew he was from Jersey too, which sorta pissed me off. And of course Riley liked him. When he introduced himself, he said, "I'm Benjamin, but you can call me Ben."

His friend John spoke with a neutral English accent through big lips. He said he was English going back generations and hasn't a clue how he got the curly hair or dark complexion or those big lips. He gave an anecdote about how racist some people are in Birmingham, telling him to "Get the fuck out of England!" So he did. After graduating from "uni," he left England with the intention of living abroad, and after two years away, he thought he might never go back. He and Ben were English teachers in this southern Spanish city I'd never heard of called Jaén.

"Olive oil capital of the world," they would say. "If they could use that stuff as currency they would," said John.

"*Oro líquido*," said Ben.

"Ya know what? I give that place a lot of crap when I'm there, but when I'm away, I always catch myself defending it," said John.

"It's our adoptive home. If I could compare it to an American city, it would be somewhere conservative in the Midwest, like Topeka or Omaha."

"Or Texas!" said John.

"Texas isn't a city, dumbass."

"He gets so mad when I do that. You Americans take it so personally when we don't know things about you. You get so offended, but I bet most Americans couldn't even name the prime minister!"

"I thought you guys had a king?" I said.

"Ha! Good on ya, lad! I love an American with a dry sense of humor, reminds me that we aren't so different after all."

"Did you know that in Norway they say 'Texas' as slang for 'crazy'?" said Ben.

We marched up and down the Bairro Alto like ships on the sea. Clotheslines held parched underwear vacillating in the sparse breeze. Old men drank a red spirit called *Ginjinha*, a liquor made from sour cherries.

"If you go on the bar crawl tonight, you will come back to the Bairro Alto. Most fun part of the city," said the Handsome Guide, who was being followed closely by a group of girls who all of a sudden found Lisbon's history invigorating.

"Doesn't he look like Johnny Depp?" said Riley.

"Yeah, like *Secret Window* Johnny Depp? I could see that," said Ben.

We ended the tour in a shady corner of the *Praça do Comércio*, which opened facing the Tagus River. The tour was free, but the guide made it clear that he *only* made money off tips, and stressed how much Portugal was struggling economically. Of course, there had to be one American who refused to tip.

"It was advertised as free. So it's free. If it isn't than it's false advertising."

"Just tip the guy," said Ben.

"Are you really that stingy?" said John. "You can't toss him a few euros?"

"It said free," she said before walking away.

"Are you serious?" said Ben.

"It said 'free'!" she yelled, hoofing it back toward the hostel.

"What a cunt," said John.

I was standing next to Riley and could feel her shudder at the word.

"Did you see that?" said John. "The cunt wouldn't even tip."

"Could you stop with the…" She couldn't finish.

"What? Cunt? Oh, right, Americans don't like that word. Why is that?"

"Because it's gross," said Riley.

"He's got me sayin' it now," Ben added. "I just know better than to say it in front of a girl." And he lowered his Aviators and winked.

"What a gentleman…" I murmured.

Instead of heading back to the hostel, the five of us sat at a rustic café and indulged in Brazilian coffee. Ben and John also sipped shots of *Ginjinha*, while Pete and I drank flat, skunked Portuguese beer. "You should try Super Bock," said Ben. "It's much better than that one."

I replayed my acting stint in my head. I couldn't forget her: Eliska. *I had to be selfish. I had to fuck two of them. Well, it wasn't really my choice. I could've walked away, I suppose. They didn't know anything about me.* I thought about the girls I was with when I was fifteen and how pissed off I'd get when they'd date the older guys. Then they'd come back around when we were juniors or seniors, but we didn't want them. We wanted something young, fresh, untainted by varsity hands. Carlo's girlfriend was tiny and Dad hated it. "They won't breed ballplayers," he'd say to my mother in the kitchen after a glass or three of wine, like my younger brother was a racehorse.

Dad had Carlo on a hobbit diet, and if it were up to him, Carlo would be "breeding" with a track star from Barringer or Shabazz.

How could I not see it? She wasn't a virgin, either, sick fucks. How long did they have her doing that? Since she was thirteen? Eleven? I'd punch that director square in the nose if I saw him again.

"You only have yourself to blame," said Pete.

"What? What the fuck?"

"If this guy is going to play games with you, you only have yourself to blame," he said to Riley.

"Oh."

"I like… don't even *really* want him to come."

"What are you saying, Riles? You're in love with the guy."

"I most certainly am not!"

"Mhmm."

"His sister is in Morocco, so it's like, on his way. It's ironic, I guess."

"It's not ironic, it's a coincidence."

"Ugh, he's so annoying with that shit."

"Don't talk about me like I'm not even here."

"You're from Jersey, aren't you?" Ben asked me in an attempt to diffuse the situation.

"Yup."

"North or south?"

"North."

"Oh yeah? Me too. I'm from Millburn, it's like forty-five minutes from…"

"Millburn Deli, Millburn?"

"Yeah! You know it?"

"Of course, it's phenomenal."

"I know. It honestly might be the single food place I miss the most living here. In Spain, I mean."

"How long you been in Spain?"

"Since September. Incredible country. I fell in love."

"Oh, you have a girlfriend?" asked Riley.

"I meant I fell in love with Spain. But I *had* a girlfriend."

"Lad just broke up with her," said John, sipping his dark red liquor. "Regular heartbreaker, this one is."

"Oh, I'm sorry," said Riley, scooting her seat a little closer to Ben's.

"Don't be," said John, speaking for Ben. "He's been swimming in clunge."

Ben gave a laugh of embarrassment.

"I don't even want to know what *clunge* is," said Riley.

"It's like you're speaking a different language," I said.

"The Queen's tongue. Proper English."

The five of us decided we would do the bar crawl that night. Riley, Pete, and I went back to the hostel to check on Kev, who was curled up in the same beanbag chair, asleep. The Handsome Guide was sitting at one of the tables with a skinny black guy who was wearing tight track clothes and no shoes. He had a shaved head but a Mohawk of slightly not-as-shaved hair coursing down the center.

"Friends, this is Black João. He will help me direct the bar crawl tonight. You did sign up for it, no?" asked the Handsome Guide.

"Yeah, we did. Nice to meet you," I said. The Handsome Guide was drinking a Super Bock beer, and Black João had a bottle of water.

"Black João doesn't speak English. Only Portuguese. He is from Cape Verde."

"Okay."

"He is the happiest person in the world."

"Mhmm, okay."

"Yes he is. He doesn't smoke weed or drink alcohol. He is high on life. He enjoys everything."

He said something to Black João in Portuguese and Black João laughed, and confirmed whatever it was he said.

"Sometimes he even sniffs the water, because he does not believe that something which gives life has not a scent. I call him the 'Cloud Walker.'"

"What about blow?"

"Huh?"

"Never mind."

Riley woke Kev up from his marathon slumber and asked him to eat with us. I found Pete in the bathroom and asked him to join us, too. And as we were leaving through the double glass doors, Ben and John were ascending the escalator and Riley called to them, insisting they join.

The six of us wandered the sloping neighborhood of meandering streets that sat behind the hostel until we found a suitable spot.

"This place is great," said Ben, pointing to a homey-looking restaurant with a lavender door and green façade. "We ate here yesterday and loved it. It's cheap. Like, under-ten-euros-for-wine-and-a-three-course-meal cheap."

"Sold," said Kev, which took us all by surprise, because he hadn't spoken a word until now.

The six of us crammed into a corner table and each received our own jugs of wine, which Riley called "adorable."

"I know, right?" said Ben.

"This queer wrote a poem about it!" said John, grabbing Ben by the shoulders and shaking him.

"What?" said Riley.

"Huh?" said Pete.

"Yeah, he carries around this little blue notebook and writes down observations and things. I caught him writing a poem about the wine yesterday. This wine!"

"Thanks, dick," said Ben.

"Come on, mate, read it for us, yeah?"

"No way. I don't have it on me anyway."

"Bollocks. I saw you bring it. It's in your back pocket."

Ben glared at John, who stared back at him blankly, flashing a shit-eating grin.

"Come on, I'd love to hear it!" said Riley, flashing that smile that turned even the most frigid men gooey.

Ben begrudgingly stood up from the table, having to push it forward enough so he wouldn't bang his knees, reached into his back pocket, and dropped a little notebook with a blue cover and white spiral spine onto the table. It had a crease in the cover and was weathered from absorbing ass sweat. Then he sat down.

"No. No. *Stand* and read it," said Riley. "Like a beatnik!"

God, was she a manipulative little minx. Ben stood back up, playing with the rosewood bracelet of saints and holy figures that was suctioned onto his right wrist, cleared his throat, scanned the tiny restaurant, and began to read aloud, shouting over the crackling of fryers and smacking of pot lids and boiling water.

"Little plump jug…" He paused to check our faces. John was smiling wide and Riley was enraptured in mirth. "A rounded eggplant purple…" I tried to hold in my smile, but squeaks slipped out of my mouth. I mean, come on, the guy was such a douche. Who writes poetry? "… Why do you represent everything that I love?"

John started to giggle. Pete was respectful. "The Old World. The Latin World. Or, perhaps, the Greek? You ease my angst on sight." Riley cupped her chin in her hands, her butt pushed back in the seat of her chair. I don't think she blinked. Kev looked bored. John was laughing. "Why are you so divine?" John was pounding the table. "My plump little jug of wine."

The guy's face was crimson, but I had to respect that he actually finished the poem. I would've punched John in the teeth.

"I *loved* it!" shouted Riley.

"Well done, mate," said Pete, raising his cup of wine.

"Good on ya, mate!" shouted John. "How about a round of applause?" And he clapped, getting a few of the other patrons to clap along with him.

"… Don't patronize me," said Ben.

"Come on, you know I just like taking the piss outta ya!"

I looked at Riley, who was undressing Ben with her eyes. She needed to have him that night, because Marcel would arrive the next day. She never looked that way at me. I said, "That was kinda gay. No offense, Kev." Riley smacked me on the arm and Kev shot up from his seat.

"Fuck you, Joel. Fuck this. I'm out." On his way to the door he knocked into a table of old Portuguese and spilled their olive oil onto the floor and clipped a waiter, who acrobatically maintained his footing on the spilt olive oil and held on to the plate of sardines. John and I clapped for him.

"Why do you have to be *such* an asshole, Joel?" said Riley as she left the table to go after him.

"Your mate is gay?" asked Pete.

"Why do you give him shit?" said Ben. "You aren't cool with him being gay?"

"No, it's not that. I'm not cool with *him* not being cool with being gay. I couldn't give less of a fuck what he puts in his mouth."

"Well, he seems pretty hurt, amigo." I hated that shit. Ben said stuff like "groovy" and "gnarly" and "comrade" and "*amigo*" like some old geezer who was stuck using seventies argot, thinking it was cool.

We ordered without Riley and Kev. I got the *alheira* chicken sausage, which came with a fried egg, French fries, and Ben needing to tell me the provenance of the dish—"That's a really interesting dish. You know why it's significant?"

"… No. I don't."

"Well, during the Inquisition, the Portuguese Jews were forced to convert and abandon their practices, like abstaining from pork, and if you didn't have sausages dangling from the windows, they'd be like 'Hey, you guys are totally still Jews,' because everyone ate sausage, so they would make *this* sausage with chicken or game meat to deceive their oppressors while still being kosher. Brilliant stuff, right?"

"Totally."

"Fuck. You Americans and your food. I swear every conversation is about steak or burgers or sandwiches," said John.

"You'd talk about food more too if England produced anything edible," I said.

"Valid point," said Ben.

"Ehh, the grub isn't that bad. And at least we have good beer!"

"You're telling me…" But before I could finish, John stood up from his seat and with his glass of wine in his left hand and his right hand over his heart, began to sing, "God save our gracious queen! Long live our noble queen! God save the queen!"

We were asked to leave before dessert.

Everyone attending the bar crawl met in a small room in front of the two sets of glass doors that separated the hostel from the train station. Groups of three to five or more assembled, checking out other groups of three to five or more, who, after a few rounds of liquid courage, would be the objects of international ice-breakers—some landing, others being repelled by the cruel language barrier. I sat on an uncomfortable couch with Pete, Ben, and John, the four of us doing our best to not let our knees touch. Riley pierced through the crowd. Her tight jean shorts with prepurchased rips around the pockets complemented her tight butt. Her shirt with three buttons, the top one undone, allowed a teasing amount of cleavage that was tasteful, and when she walked, the heels of her boots knocked on the floor because she refused to tie the laces tight. She was a head-turner, and both the guys and girls followed her with their eyes—one guy even licked his lips, the pig.

"He isn't coming," she said, but with her tone it sounded more like, "This is your fault, Joel. Do something about it."

Kev hadn't left his bed since dinner.

"That sucks," I said.

"This is really shitty of you, Joel."

"Why? So I would have to take care of him while you gallivant around Lisbon? I stood up and approached her. "So you didn't feel guilty and could get in that guy's pants while I dealt with the kid consumed in an existential crisis?"

"What are you *talking* about?"

"Never mind. Forget it."

Black João and the Handsome Guide, who had tied his hair back in a bun, gathered the thirsty travelers and departed for the Bairro Alto. At our first stop, we were given a "free" shot of something neon-sweet that I doubt had any significant percentage of real alcohol in it. I started talking to a gaggle of Catalans, but only one had any grasp of English, and despite the linguistic similarities between Catalan and French, my French fell on deaf ears and blank stares. Instead, Ben and John swooped in with their Spanish and quickly won them over.

"Were you just speaking French?" said an electric-white-haired girl with milky skin and cleavage that was accentuated by both of her hands in her back pockets, pushing her chest forward.

"Why yes, I was. Parlez-vous français? Je crois qu'il est la plus belle langue et apprécie de belles personnes, comme vous, qui peuvent parler aussi."

"I don't speak French."

"… Oh."

"But I'm sort of a Francophile. I follow all of the French designers on Instagram and was Fantine in *Les Misérables* in high school. I'm going to Biarritz next week!"

"You're a Francophile?"

"Yes."

"But not a Francophone?"

"Well, no. I mean, I took French in junior high, but it got too hard."

"…"

"You're American, right?" she asked.

"Yup."

"Where from?"

"The City."

"…*which* city?" she giggled.

"New York City."

Riley decided to join us at that exact moment. "He's from New Jersey."

"… Thanks, Riles."

"Oh! Like the Jersey Shore? You ever see them? The guys with the abs?"

"No. What about you?"

"I'm from Louisville," but she said it like *Lou-ville*—one congested word.

"Louisville? Like, Kentucky?"

"Yeah! *Lou-ville*," she said, this time accentuating the accent even more.

Riley patted me on the shoulder and said, "Enjoy." I told the girl I was going outside to have a smoke, even though I didn't have any cigarettes. She followed me. The lamps, the neighborhood of robust gas lamps illuminated the pulsating iridescent imbibers spilling out onto the stone streets. I was enervated from having the same conversations with people I would never see again. Like the girl from Kentucky; I knew I was going to fuck her, so long as she didn't cross the Andrea Santoro too-drunk threshold where things get scary and weird (also known as the "Karen Grajewski bubble" in the greater Wilmington, Delaware area.)

"My ex-boyfriend is a Marine."

"Is he a good swimmer?" I said, taking a drag of a commandeered cigarette.

"What? He's in Japan right now."

"Is he a fan of *Yaoi*?"

"What's *Yaoi*?"

"I bet he's a tentacle porn guy. Does he like tentacle porn?"

"Huh?"

"So in Japan they can't show insertion."

"I hate that word. *Insertion*. Yuck!"

"What about moist coitus?"

"That's fine."

"Oh… okay. Anyway, so in Japan this animator really started the modern concept of tentacle porn, which circumvents the country's strict censorship regulations in regards to… insertion. It's pretty cool. Like a slimy middle finger to the government."

"Evan definitely does not watch *that*."

"Ya never know. The Orient changes people."

"Wait. I think I get WiFi out here. I'll show him to you." She almost dropped her brick of a phone pulling it from her skin-tight jeans. I watched as she opened up Facebook, signed out of her profile, and signed into a different one with a different name and picture. She typed "Evan Alberts" into the search bar and clicked on his profile pic and began to scroll. After ten pictures was a string of him and her: on the beach, on the couch, at a Louisville basketball game. "Isn't he hot?" she said, not looking up from the phone.

"This whole time I was picturing a Dutchman. Not sure why. *Is* he a Dutchman?"

"You're kind of an asshole."

"You're just not used to the Jersey sarcasm. Where I'm from, everyone talks like this."

"Oh. I like your tattoo. Is it new? It still looks glossy."

"Yup. Just got it. In Prague. My friend and I got drunk and got tattoos. Don't even remember it happening. Gotta love your twenties, right?"

"That girl you came here with?" Her body shifted, her hand fixated on her hip.

"No, no. My friend Kev."

"Is he still in Prague?"

"No, he's in the hostel."

"Why didn't he come out?"

"He's busy reading *Yaoi*."

"What is *Yaoi*?!"

"How about another round?"

Riley had Ben pinned to the bar (I knew those Catalans didn't stand a chance), while Pete and John decided which type of shot to take. I recommended Hayman's whiskey. John called it "shite."

"Who is your friend?" asked Pete. I honestly didn't know. I saw her name on her Facebook, but couldn't remember. It was something with an R. Ryan or Rachel—was it Riley, also? I was past the point of asking, so I pretended not to hear him. She introduced herself. "Nice to meet you, *Rose*," he said, stressing her name and looking at me. I gave him a nod. I liked Pete. The beer smelled like throw-up, but I sucked it down anyway. I lost count after ten because I ran out of fingers and couldn't see my toes.

Rose insisted we dance together. I couldn't believe she didn't want to punch me in the face, let alone fuck me, because that's how I felt; I sorta wanted to punch her in the face, but I sorta wanted to fuck her. I hated dancing but I did it anyway. I danced in the overcrowded bar, and I danced on a thread of wavering sexual and violent ambivalence. That is, if you can call it dancing. The guys were suctioned to the girls' behinds, swinging side to side. That's all we had. There was no tango or salsa or mamba or polka, no limbo, swing, jig, jive, or zamba. We, as humanity's youth in the twenty-first century, have spent all choreographed forms of dance (besides those that only belonged to one song, like the Macarena, the Soulja Boy, the Dougie, etc.) and have resorted back to what can only be described as dancing in atavistic form—grinding. Man's first dance, I suppose.

"You're a much better dancer than Evan!" Rose shouted over the skull-splitting music.

"He didn't learn to dance at Parris Island?"

"What? Evan has never been to France."

I pulled her out onto the street and we took a taxi back to the hostel. I had an irrational fear of my shoelace getting caught in the escalator, so I high-stepped it up and waited for her at the top. She called me "weird." She said we couldn't go to her room because it was "girls only" and she could get kicked out of the hostel for breaking the rule. At least Kev would be in my room, and he didn't appreciate it in college when I brought girls back and he was asleep or watching Netflix. We both walked with our heads down while passing the front desk. The nightshift worker was watching something on his phone. I pulled Rose into the spacious sexual sanctuary that was the handicapped bathroom, swung around, and locked the door.

The fluorescent lighting didn't do us any favors. I had dark bags under my eyes and my skin looked greasy. My throat was dry and I had a very unbecoming cough that scratched my throat. I could see the roots of her hair, which were unnoticeable at the bar, and her cheeks were pudgy, which dwarfed her already small mouth. She was thicker than I realized, and I was so exhausted I considered leaving her for my bed, but she started to say something about the Marine, so I pushed her down on her knees and she took care of the rest. God bless Rose, she didn't have a gag reflex. She took me until my pubic stubble scraped the bridge of her nose. She didn't complain once—that Southern hospitality, I suppose. I pointed at myself in the mirror and admired the back of her head bobbing to and fro. I suppose I was so caught up in the moment that I ignored the knocking on the door, and Rose's finger creeping toward my virgin asshole. I felt the first inch of her finger pop inside of me and I leaped from the ground like a rocket. I could've put a hole in the ceiling, and I barely missed her chin with my knee. I fell with my pants wrapped around my ankles; the sound of my belt buckle hitting the tile reverberated off the walls. I felt a second jolt as my sweaty bare ass hit and sucked to the floor. I fumbled to get my pants up.

"What the fuck was that?!"

"I thought guys liked that. With Evan I usually get up to here." She held up her index finger and portioned off a two-inch chunk like she was a football referee giving the "short by inches" sign to the crowd. The knocking continued on the door.

"Are you crazy?"

BINGE UNTIL TRAGEDY

"DON'T CALL ME CRAZY!"

I left Rose on her knees with dribble on her chin. I didn't even feel bad about it—she represented all things broken. I opened the door to find Riley drunk and crying, holding a blue note card with a short message written on it.

Dear Riley,

I left. I'm going to Ireland to stay with my cousin for a little. I have some soul-searching to do. Have a great rest of your trip and safe travels. Tell Marcel I said thanks for letting us stay with him in Paris.

Kev

"Did he leave a note for me?"

"No… You fucked with him too much. He was hurting, Joel, and you just kept ripping on him. Giving him shit." I walked past her and she followed me to the door of our room. "He's your best friend and now he's gone."

"He definitely didn't leave a note for me?"

"No!"

The front desk worker looked up and said, "Sshh."

"Yeah, well, then fuck 'im."

"What the hell is wrong with you?"

I opened the bedroom door and went to bed.

My stomach turned upside down at the darkest hour of the night. I rushed to the first stall in the men's bathroom, but missed my target and spewed green vomit on the crisp porcelain. It came from deep, deep down and it was painful. I started to cry. I had thrown up from drinking on a semi-regular basis in college, but this wasn't a clear-your-stomach beer-vomit; it felt like a creature clawing its way up my throat, dragging a tail of thorns behind it. I had to get out of there and not get caught. There were signs in the hallways and on the bathroom doors stating a 50€ vomiting fee. There wasn't a chance they would believe I was sick when they found out I was on the bar crawl. I peeked through the sliver of space in the stall—the coast was clear. I thought about cleaning it up with toilet paper, but it was four a.m., the darkest hour of the night, and my eyes were closing, and all I wanted was to drown under blankets and pillows. I snuck back into my room. Riley was gone. I felt better and slept, until the same sensation came bubbling back, this time in the form of diarrhea. My asshole couldn't catch a break.

Between the hours of seven and ten in the morning, I must've shit and/or puked five times. Riley had placed glasses of water next to my bed, along with a few ibuprofen—she figured I was just hung over. I made it to the front desk and told them I had food poisoning and needed to get medicine. One of the workers walked with me to the nearest pharmacy and translated my symptoms. I promised I'd give him a rave review on Hostelworld and TripAdvisor.

When we arrived back at the hostel, I could hear Marcel the moment I opened those glass doors. He was angry, speaking in his bombastic voice he used when accusing a professor of being racist or a lacrosse player of being Islamaphobic. He was standing at a circular table where Riley, Pete, John, Ben, Black João, and the Handsome Guide were seated. He looked different. He had a budding beard without the mustache. The *taqiyah* he wore on his head seemed out of place, juxtaposed against the rest of his Western clothing. I had never seen Marcel dress that way. Riley appeared upset and scared.

"So is there a *White* João?" Marcel asked the Handsome Guide.

"No. There is not."

"So why can he not just be João? Hmm?"

The Handsome Guide asked Black João if there was a problem with identifying him as "*Black* João." He told him if he preferred it, they would just call him João, and that they never meant to be racist. Black João smiled and said something back to the Handsome Guide in Portuguese. Then he looked up at Marcel, whose shoulders were brooding, and spoke in slow, reserved English: "I like my name. My friends give me my name. I am happy. You have hate. If you no like my name, you not use my name. Okay?"

Riley got up from the table to talk to me. She said Marcel had barely been there ten minutes before he started arguing. "It's awful," she said. "It's so awful. I don't want him here. It's so awful. He isn't the same."

"I have food poisoning. I have no idea from what. I don't remember eating anything weird last night. But I don't want to hear about this right now. I'm getting back in bed."

When Marcel saw the state I was in, he rushed to my side and gave me a big hello. He asked if I needed anything. I must've looked like shit. I sat at the table, slumped over like a sickly orphan. "You look like shite, mate," said John, affirming my insecurity. They had another walking tour planned for today, this time to the Alfama, the oldest neighborhood in Lisbon.

"The name *Alfama* comes from Arabic," said Marcel.

"Are you a Muslim?" asked John, sarcastically.

"Yes, I am."

"I couldn't tell…"

Riley and Ben were exchanging looks from across the table. I figured they fooled around last night, perhaps after I left Rose in the handicapped bathroom. In front of Ben was a thick book with a purple cover. "I call it his doorstop," said John.

"It's the craziest book I've ever read," said Ben. "It's emotionally exhausting. In a good way. Brilliant writing. I finished it this morning."

"What is it?"

"*Infinite Jest* by David Foster Wallace."

"Didn't he off himself?" asked Pete.

"All the best writers do," said John.

"It's really the only thing we have control of in our lives," said Ben. "When to end it." Riley shot him a look like he did something wrong. It didn't bother me, it didn't even register at first, but it was nice to know she cared.

"Hey man, I actually need a new book. I'm going to be in bed all day, can I borrow it?"

"Yeah, here." He tossed the brick, which landed on the table with a *thud*. "But I'll need it back when we head to Spain in a couple of days. You won't be able to finish it by then."

"I read pretty fast."

"It's difficult to read quickly when you're on the floor rocking back and forth in the fetal position."

I took the book with me and lay in my bed and only stopped reading to vomit, or have diarrhea. I would fall asleep for five, ten minutes at a time, waking up when another young wayfarer would laugh while Skyping. I hadn't Skyped with my family since Paris and had a couple of unread emails in my inbox from Mom. It took a fourth trip to the toilet in three hours to set up a Skype date with her. You begin to question things when your face is staring into a toilet bowl every hour, like: Is there a God? And if there is, am I being punished for something? I started to apologize in my mind: to Mom, for not responding to her emails; to Kev, for not being more understanding of his sexual revelation. I started to tear up again. Okay, I was full-on crying.

I apologized to Riley for being a dick. *Breathe. One, two, breathe, four, one, two, breathe, breathe.* I apologized to Chloe for being a dick. I apologized to Rose for being a dick. I apologized to the kid whose phone I launched off the Charles Bridge in Prague. I apologized to Sal for not being more supportive of his future child. I apologized to Carlo for not speaking to him, ever. I apologized to the stripper on whose back I had puked. I apologized to the prostitute I deceived in Amsterdam. I apologized to the fifteen-year-old... It didn't matter, they'd never know.

I hated the bathroom. I never wanted to see it again. Constipation would be a blessing. I listened to the other guys come in, their shower sandals making that irritating snapping noise against the tile. I hated when they laughed. I was miserable. You can die from that shit, ya know. They wouldn't be laughing if they knew the trauma I was experiencing. I still had that pit. My mouth was coated with acidic fluid. *What will I do with my life? It could be worse. I could be in a hut in Ethiopia or Bangladesh. I could be a slave. Slavery still exists. I could be getting tortured in Syria.*

BINGE UNTIL TRAGEDY

I crawled out of the stall with glossy, bloodshot eyes. Someone asked me if I was okay. I didn't respond to him. I wanted my mother. Whenever I wasn't feeling well, Mom would tell me to take a shower—it was her panacea.

I crawled into an empty slick white booth, curled up in the corner, and turned on the water. The steam made it difficult to breathe. I imagined her on the other side of the curtain: "Joelie, how are you doing in there? Joelie? Okay, I'll make you some soup, my love."

This time I just let the diarrhea go, let the drain take care of it. It was mostly water at this point anyway. If one of the flip-flopped threw back the curtain, I would've been mortified, but that was a risk I was willing to take.

I sucked down more of my medicine and dropped onto my bed and escaped into *Infinite Jest*. I tried my best to avoid getting lost in the prose, but he used such damn big words, words I had never heard, that were never amongst my "Words of the Day." I could tell he was brilliant—too brilliant, I suppose.

Riley woke me up with a sandwich and drink. "You have to eat something," she said. "And check your emails. I think your mom is blowing up your phone."

"She treats emails like text messages."

"Just write her back."

"I'm nothing but a collection of memories from years gone rotten."

"Shut up and eat." She sat on her bed across from me and scrolled through her phone.

"How was the Alfama?"

"Magical."

"You said the same thing about red velvet cake fro-yo."

"I think I want to sleep with Ben."

"Of course…"

"We were going to do it last night, but *someone* was hogging the handicapped bathroom."

"Oh, that was you the whole time?"

"Yeah. Ben wanted to wash his hands and I was going to pounce on him in there. He actually washes his hands a lot. He carries Wet-Naps in his pocket."

"I really don't see the appeal, Riles."

"What? You don't? He's sexy. Like, his eyelashes go on for miles. Have you seen 'em?"

"Who the fuck looks at eyelashes?"

"*Moi.*"

"Well, what about Marcel?"

"You know he doesn't drink now? This is the guy who explained the intricacies of Bordeaux blends to me on our first date. He would pour himself a glass of pastis in the dining hall before lunch. He's not the same guy I loved junior year. He's not even the same guy I loved in Paris. It's that stupid friend of his. *Mehdi.*" She spat his name like it put a bad taste in her mouth. "Like, why wouldn't God be okay with wine? It's just fermented grape juice. Didn't Jesus turn water into wine or something?

"…Yeah, I'm pretty sure Marcel isn't reading the New Testament."

"Whatever! You know he got in an argument with Ben and John while we were on our tour? About, like, *Algiersia* or something."

"Well, it's either Algiers or Algeria. Algiers is the capital and…"

"I really don't care. Like, I hope no one else gets hurt, but that isn't our problem."

I was going to apologize then, tell her how much I appreciated her looking out for me, but Marcel flung the door open and stomped to his bed, a top bunk at the end of the room. He lifted himself up, demonstrating the rippling muscles in his forearms, and swung his legs around all in one motion. Riley rolled her eyes and left. For those few minutes she spent with me, I had forgotten about the vomit.

"She's changed," said Marcel, not looking away from his laptop.

"I suppose," I said, and left it at that.

By breakfast the next day, I had recovered my appetite and was producing solid bowel movements. Riley, Marcel, Ben, John, and Pete signed up for a day trip to the ancient city of Sintra, a world heritage site. They had one spot remaining in the van, so I decided to sign up at the last minute—I needed a break from *Infinite Jest* anyway. Black João and the Handsome Guide, who drove the van, took us to the basin of the Sintra Mountains, where we trekked upward at calf-splitting inclines. Riley purposely sat next to me in the second row of the van, making sure Marcel didn't sit immediately next to her. Ben was unaware of their sexual past, and a couple times when he spoke to her, he would put his hand on the small of her back or touch her arm or just look at her admiringly, the way she deserved, the way Marcel used to look at her back in college when we lived uninterrupted. But Marcel hadn't noticed a thing; instead of admiring Riley, he was enamored with the Moorish architecture of Sintra, remnants of the Arab occupation, a time when Portugal and Spain were distinct from the rest of Europe.

"Look at that!" he exalted, pointing across the street to a sky-blue tiled Moorish façade with arches that trickled like symmetrical icicles. Inside, a bubbling fountain sat in the center of two benches. "You don't see art like that anymore. Not in Europe, and surely not in the States!"

"You're from Paris," said Riley. "The art capital of the *world*."

"Yes, yes, but we don't have *anything* like this," he said, boxing the façade with his hands. "Although the Islamic exhibit in the Louvre is nice."

We were given a couple of different options for how we would spend our time in Sintra. There is a plethora of sites in the city and surrounding area; we couldn't see them all because we had to make it to Cabo da Roca by sunset. Marcel was adamant about seeing the Moorish castle—"The one taken from us by the Crusaders," he said, like he had been holed up there himself. The rest of us chose *Quinta da Regaleira,* an early twentieth-century palace with stunning gardens and subterranean passages. Riley had brought up pictures of the palace on her phone and the place looked, well, "magical." The grounds were a forested labyrinth of tunnels and caves and although Sintra was crawling with tourists, we still managed to get delightfully lost, finding remote shire-like nooks of cascading gardens. We stood on a bridge overlooking a moss-covered pond where brave tourists hopped along a string of arranged stepping stones.

"I hope that fat one falls in." John said what we were all thinking.

Because Marcel had left for the castle, Riley was openly flirting with Ben. As usual, he seemed to know everything about the place, even though it was his first time visiting.

"These stepping stones were an initiation path for the Knights Templar," said Ben.

"I never have to pay for tour guides when I travel with him," said John.

"I have a hard case of *werifesteria* right now," said Ben, doing that thing where you use a big word, expecting no one else to know what it means, but acting surprised *when* no one else knows what it means and then taking pleasure in explaining it.

"Ooh, what's that?" asked Riley.

Ben looked out into the greenery and with maudlin stoicism explained, "It's a verb from Old English meaning 'to wander longingly through the forest in search of mystery.'"

"How beautiful," she swooned.

"Alright, Thoreau," I said. "How do we get outta here?"

"Well, you don't really 'get out' of 'here,' per se."

"Holy shit, dude! Okay, I'm going this way, whoever wants to join me."

I walked along a slightly declining path that lacked any sign of human intervention in the past two hundred years. I was alone and continued on my own until I couldn't hear Ben lecture or Riley swoon. I stumbled upon a tiny chapel overgrown with emerald ivy. The glass-stained windows were covered with a film of filth, and when I peeked through the pebble-sized hole, I could only see dusty pews and a hanging crucifix. There was this light pulling sensation in my chest. I touched the stone wall of the chapel: It was cold. It was a dead building plopped down in the vivacious forest. I was going to leave and be on my way, but I pulled on the iron ring door and it opened. I stuck my head in and was overcome by the acrid odor of Nonna's closet—my favorite hiding spot when I wanted not to play with my cousins and just be alone. I stepped into the chapel and stood slightly crouched. My head skimmed the ceiling and I ducked down to avoid getting a cobweb stuck in my hair. If I sat in one of the pews I felt like I wouldn't be able to get out, so I turned to leave, but caught something move in my periphery.

I flung my head around before my body could catch up, like a possessed child, and I froze. I suppose he was completely covered in that dark-green blanket and that I had overlooked him because he was motionless, but from under the blanket appeared a little creature of some kind.

He was a small fellow with white skin that glowed. Although his face appeared childlike, he had a graying beard and gray hair only on the rim of his head, and the rest was a glowing bald. Under the blanket, it didn't seem like he was wearing any clothes, but from the way he held it up to his neck, I could only see his soot-covered bare feet, like he had been walking on coals. I didn't feel threatened by him, but I was still paralyzed. I was about to tell him I don't speak Portuguese, but before I could get it out, he said, "Hello there, won't you have a seat?" in perfect English. He didn't even try Portuguese—did I look *that* American? "If I was expecting company, I would have shined my shoes."

I wasn't sure what to say, so I asked, "Are you a priest?"

"Oh no, no, no," he said, waving his hand like he was telling a waiter to stop grating the Parmesan.

I was still only steps from the door and remained standing. "What brings you to Sintra?" I asked like a game show host.

"It's this forest, it's unearthly. I quite like unearthly places."

I stayed put. There was an odor of something burning. I became uncomfortably aware of what I should do with my hands. Sal said never to talk to someone with your hands in your pockets, but I couldn't possibly lean on anything. Everything was filthy. That's why my family all talked with their hands—the "Calabrian way"—so they wouldn't have to worry about putting 'em in their pockets, I suppose.

He fidgeted in his spot, avoiding the sunlight beaming in through cracks and splits in the stained-glass windows.

"So how long have you been in Sintra?" I asked.

"Oh, I just arrived," he said, keeping the blanket up around his chin. "But I quite like it. I think I'll stay." He said this last part as if making the decision right then and there.

"So do you want some food or something?" I said, surprising myself with my sporadic burst of altruism.

"Oh, no. I'm quite alright, Joel, thank you."

"Did… did I introduce…"

"May I ask you something?" he continued. "And just know that I'm not going to hurt you, so you can unclench those fists. Your hand seems to be healing properly." Clearly I was hallucinating, probably having a lucid acid flashback from a concert with Kev. It was odd, but I wasn't afraid, so I stayed. *Everything is in its right place.*

"I bet the WiFi signal is garbage here, huh?" I said.

"Pardon?"

His hair started to change color. It became darker, healthier, fuller. His venous legs and shoulders smoothed. His skin became a honey amber, glowing and juvenescent.

"How are you doing that?" I asked.

"Naturally," he said.

"You aren't of this world, are you?" I don't know why I phrased it that way. It was more dramatic, I suppose.

He looked at me confused—confused that I wasn't more confused.

"Do I not scare you, Joel?"

"No. I mean, I'd like to know how you know my name. But besides that, no."

He let the blanket fall from around his chin. He now had a thick head of effulgent blond hair. His eyes turned red. I didn't like that—okay, *that* scared me—but I didn't want him to know I was scared, petrified really. He stood up but remained cramped in that back corner of the chapel. He was taller than I had thought, or perhaps he grew. He was inches from the ceiling and staring at me.

"Have you been to the farthest edge of Europe?" he asked me.

"I don't believe so," I said.

"I have to go there."

"Right now?"

"After I shine my shoes." I looked down at his feet. They were still bare, but clean.

"What is the meaning of my existence?" I asked.

"I'm not here for you," he said.

"What's the meaning of life, then?"

BINGE UNTIL TRAGEDY

"I'm not God, Joel."

So I left. I continued my descent through the gardens until I found the mouth of a cave emitting the laughter of children. I was trembling and constantly looking back over my shoulder. I followed the voices and I followed the laughter and found a spiral staircase. At the bottom was a marble floor with four brick-red triangles in a circle of tawny yellow. A stone cone wall shot up, with windowless arches so stair-climbers could poke their heads down and see how far they'd ascended. I stood in the center and looked up at the golden sky, at the children's heads smiling and giggling. I felt the funnel of laughter upon my face, and I realized that everything was in its right place. The sun warmed my nose. I felt a buoyancy in my gut, something guileless, like the rush from the commencement of summer. I stood in the middle of those triangles and began to spin with my arms stretched out, my palms facing the sky. I'm not sure why I did that, I had done so very little right. I had alienated myself, had been a poor brother, lover, and friend. But there I was, twirling like a Gypsy, laughing like some sort of free spirit, ignoring the jeers from teens in languages I couldn't understand. That was pure joy, I suppose, knowing they are insulting you only feet away but not understanding enough to care.

When it started to rain, I was surprised, but I spun on, eyes closed and face rident. I thought about Kev. He was probably happy in wet Ireland. I pictured him somewhere lush, riding a horse, already speaking with a brogue. At some point I would text him and things would be mended, I suppose. I thought about Sal and his new baby. I knew he wanted a boy. I hoped he would get one. It was after this thought that a mucus glob plopped on my forehead, and I realized it wasn't raining: they were spitting on me.

Marcel was late getting back to the meeting point from the Moorish castle; he didn't care. When he saw Ben, John, and Pete sipping a *Ginjinha*, he scoffed. "There is nothing of substance in alcohol. You will crumble due to your *ithm*!" They held their little glasses of red liquid and stared. "Did you know the word alcohol comes from Arabic?" he added.

"Yeah, well, I'd rather have empty calories than empty memories, comrade," said Ben.

We crammed back into the van and cruised to Cabo da Roca.

"What is Cabo da Roca?" I asked.

"It's a cliff," said Ben.

"You never listen," said Riley. "I told you we were going there back at the hostel. You're like, in your own world these days."

"I thought we were going to the beach. What is so important about this cliff, anyway?"

"It's the 'Edge of Europe,'" said Ben.

"Wait…"

"Well, of mainland Europe, that is," he added. "It's really incredible how much power this small country had at one point."

He prated on about the former power of Spain and Portugal. He used the term "split the world in half" one too many times, so I blocked him out and stared out the window or down at my hands, and listened to Marcel's lips gently smack each other as he mouthed verses from a pocket Quran.

We arrived at the base of a sloping hill with a gravel road surrounded by lush, tall green grass speckled with white flowers that swayed to the rhythm of the wind. While I approached the cliff, I ran my hands through the grass and plucked a flower. It seemed like the right thing to do. Standing tall was a stone column with a stone cross on top, and behind that was blue ocean and blue sky separated by the electric-white horizon.

"Look. At. This!" said Ben, overly enthusiastic at seeing water. "There was a time when this was considered the end of the world. The Romans called this *Promontorium Magnum.*"

"I have an *erectus magnum*," said John.

Black João walked to the rocky edge, farther than any of the other tourists, and sat on a large slab of rock in a meditating pose.

"He does this every time," said the Handsome Guide, whose long hair kept getting stuck on his face from the wind.

"He's at peace," said Pete.

We stood there staring out into the sea. Black João hadn't moved a fiber. It was as if the wind didn't affect him. Marcel wasn't with us. He was a few feet away, back turned to the ocean.

"Don't you find any of this beautiful?" Riley asked Marcel, turning her back to the ocean, too.

He didn't turn back to look at Riley.

"Did you know that Portugal enslaved more Africans than any other country? Then they forced their religion on them and raped their women. Islamic kingdoms in West Africa flourished before the barbarians pillaged the cradle of civilization!"

"Oh, forget it," she said, defeated.

"I will not celebrate their tyranny." He pointed at the Handsome Guide. "I will not celebrate what your people have done any longer!"

"But I am Brazilian," said the Handsome Guide.

"I never should have come here."

"Ya know…" Ben started.

"Don't even bother," she said, turning back.

"… Arab Muslims were also very much involved in the African slave trade. They looked at the black Africans as inferior too. There was the trans-Saharan slave trade and the Swahili coast. Look at Zanzibar."

"Nonsense!" he shouted and stormed down the hill.

"Screw him," said Riley. "Hey! This would make a great cover photo. Let's get someone to take our pic. Ask one of those Chinese tourists."

"I'll just do it," I said. I wasn't in the mood to be in a picture.

And in the serene cerulean sky, which only moments before was unblemished, a cloud cluster formed and expanded, blocking the sun. I held Riley's obnoxiously large brick of a phone and flipped the camera horizontal. The six of them—Riley, Ben, Pete, John, Black João, and the Handsome Guide—put their arms around each other's shoulders, holding cheesy smiles, their backs to the ocean.

"It's too dark," I said, lowering the phone.

"Just take it!" yelled Riley over the whistling *whoosh* of the wind.

I snapped a few, but each time a group of tourists was awkwardly right behind them, or a teenager photobombed them with a stupid face. There was also a couple sitting near the edge of the cliff, who must have taken ten selfies already and wouldn't move.

"Ugh, these suck," she said. "Here, let's get one in front of the marker. Joel, you mind taking another?"

We switched spots and they lined up, facing the ocean, in front of the marker that explained the meaning of the cape, the one with the stone cross on top. The wind had picked up, putting Riley's and the Handsome Guide's hair in disarray. This time there weren't any packs of tourists behind them, just one guy standing alone, his head covered by a hood. I waited for a few moments, but he wouldn't move. It got darker still. I snapped a few pics.

"Don't move," Riley said to the group as she looked over the pictures so they were to her liking. "Okay, one more. But I want to be next to Ben." The group rearranged themselves. I went to take the picture, but stopped and lowered the phone.

"Did you take it?!" yelled Riley.

"Get on with it already!" yelled John.

It was him. From the chapel. I wasn't hallucinating anymore. *Was I ever hallucinating?* He pulled back his hood, letting his long auburn hair fall. His nose was pointed to the ground, but he looked at me and grimaced. It was poignant. It was something sinister.

"Come on, amigo!" yelled Ben. "Let's go!"

I snapped one, and then another, and as I was lining up a third, Riley let out a blood-curdling scream and pointed to the water.

"OH MY GOD!"

"JESUS CHRIST!"

"AHHHH, OH NO!"

I swung myself around but didn't see anything. When I turned back, Riley's face was buried in Ben's chest. John had his hand over his mouth.

"What? What happened?"

No one answered me. People timidly began to gather near the edge, but not getting close enough to take a good look down below.

"What the fuck happened?!" I yelled, feeling uncomfortably left out.

"They fucking fell!" yelled Riley, wet and snotty.

"Who fell?"

"That couple. They were taking a selfie and then they fell and now they're dead."

Ben pulled her head back into him, making a comforting cooing sound. The Handsome Guide called the emergency number for Portugal and explained what had happened. Black João looked spooked, probably thinking that he had, only moments earlier, been sitting near that edge, no farther than the now-dead couple.

The sun came back out and the strong wind eased to a pleasant breeze. I looked for him, the... the *thing* from the chapel, but he was gone. I figured maybe he would be in the background of one of the pictures, the last one. I opened the camera and it immediately popped up—the moment they witnessed death. All six of them had looks of horror on their faces. It was frightening in the purest sort of way. I wanted to send it to myself before Riley deleted it. And in the background where he would have been standing was a fuzz, a black mass, like a smudge. I zoomed in on it, but that revealed nothing.

"Maybe they're still alive. They could still be alive, right?" Riley said.

"You know how high up that is?" I asked, rhetorically. "They're definitely dead. Dead as disco. Dead as..." I saw two little children, a boy and a girl, looking at me. I stopped myself, but it was too late. They fell down in the tall grass and began to cry.

For our last night in Lisbon, we went to the magical Alfama neighborhood, the oldest of the city. Riley and the other guys had already been there, back when I was curled up around the toilet, and insisted I must visit before leaving the city. Iago, the dexterous Portuguese guitarist we met back in Paris, was going to be playing the harrowing style of music cultivated in that infamous neighborhood, called fado. Riley had kept in touch with him since Paris, and with Enrique the Spaniard. The bar was an intimate establishment tucked away in some forgotten corner of the neighborhood where the same guy that seated you also acted as MC.

Everyone was depressed. I was already depressed and therefore the least affected by the fall. "The Selfie Spill," one tasteless London-based tabloid labeled the incident. They were Polish, or Hungarian, or Slovakian or something like that, and those *were* their children. That gave me the chills. That made me uneasy. But we bought absurdly cheap bottles of bold red wine and sucked the stuff down as different singers took turns serenading us with poignant Portuguese ballads of lovers lost or lovers left behind while Iago strummed the guitar.

When one singer finished, another, someone who appeared to just be a patron sipping a beer or *Ginjinha* in the corner, would take their turn belting their song of woe. I didn't understand a word of it, but honestly, I didn't have to. Portuguese is a pretty language in its own way, and even though it is Latin-based, the constant *sh* sound makes it sound like something from Eastern Europe. And toward the end of every song, the singer, on the verge of tears, would build up to a climax where your heart was in your throat. I think I saw Ben cry a little. He was kind of a pussy.

"My goodness, it's as if every person in this city is a singer," he whispered, leaning in on the candlelit table and wiping a tear from the concavity beneath his left eye.

"I know, right?" Riley agreed.

"It's fascinating," he said.

Iago was focused and barely looked up. He was dressed entirely in black—jeans, t-shirt, boots, the leather on his wrists, top hat—all black. He was ghost-pale, and his stunning blue eyes emitted their own light like a cat in an empty house.

Ben and Riley held hands beneath the table as Marcel sat right across from them. He didn't notice, or didn't care, but she considered it a game, something fun that added an element to her newest tryst. That kind of shit would catch up with her eventually and she would ruin something good, I suppose.

After each singer performed their song or two of woe, Iago put his guitar away and joined us for a drink. His English was polished and proper. He told us the

Portuguese speak English well compared to their Spanish counterparts, because they watch their American and British television in English instead of dubbed in their own language. Also, it's in the Portuguese's blood to travel the vast expanses of the globe, and because of that, English is a necessity.

"Native English speakers do not understand how good they have it. They expect everyone to speak their language, even when they are not in an English-speaking country," Iago said, taking a delicate sip of bloody red wine.

"The British are especially guilty," said John. "There are enclaves of Englishmen all over Europe who just refuse to learn the native language. It's a sin, really."

"Like in Torremolinos?" said Ben.

"Exactly! *Guiri* capital of Spain!"

"That place is a gem. I read about it in *The Drifters*. Have you read it, Joel?" Ben asked.

"What? No. Why? Never even heard of it."

"It's my favorite book, by James A. Michener. I mean, it's my favorite book in *general*, not just my favorite by James A. Michener. Any person who likes to travel *has* to read it."

"Sounds great! I'll have to check it out too," said Riley.

"Yeah, yeah, alright, I'll get to it. I have a lot already on my list," I said.

"Oh yeah? I'd like to see your list. I always like seeing what other people…"

"Okay, okay, well, I don't have it on me right now. Maybe later, okay?"

"Sure, comrade… no worries," he said, regressing into his seat.

"You tell your parents about tomorrow?" she asked me.

"What?"

"Tomorrow? Spain? We're going to *Sevilla* tomorrow."

Nothing registered. I hadn't realized what we were doing tomorrow, taking "living in the moment" to a new meaning, I suppose.

"Ugh, you never listen to me. Okay, pay attention. Tomorrow we are waking up early and taking a BlaBlaCar to *Sevilla* and staying with Enrique. Remember him?" she said, condescendingly.

"Yes, I remember him, and what the shit is a BlaBlaCar?"

"Don't worry about it, Joelie. Just be up and ready to go by nine."

I hated when she spoke to me like a child. "Why are you saying *Sevilla*? Why not Seville?"

"Because that's how *they* say it…?"

"Well, that seems stupid. You don't say Paris like the French, without the 's.' *Paris*." I pronounced it in a think French accent. "Or Rome like *Roma*. Or Lisbon like *Lisboa*. You have to stick to one or the other. Can't be picking and choosing to sound cultured."

"… Okay, Joel."

"Have another glass of wine, amigo," said Ben.

Fuck him.

"Hey man, you finish my book yet?" he asked.

"No! I haven't. You see the size of that thing? I'm not going to steal it, okay? I'll finish it in Spain."

"Okay, well, I'll need it before I go back to Jaén."

"Jesus! You will, man. Fuck…"

I got up to leave. I could hear Ben ask Riley, "What the fuck is wrong with that guy?" I left with Marcel; he didn't want to be there either. He was headed to Tarifa tomorrow, at the southern tip of the Iberian Peninsula. I considered going with him, but I didn't. As much as I couldn't stand Ben, I did end up going to Seville and am thankful for it, because that was where I met her.

THE GIFT AND THE SAFE

PRESIDENT HANNACHI SCRIBBLED MADDENINGLY on crumpled pieces of paper in the eye-straining glow of candlelight. Sweat dripped from his forehead and down his chin and onto the moist parchment. A "Yasmina" stood by his side with a pitcher of water, another with a carafe of blood-red wine. He made guttural noises of satisfaction as he dotted his final period and added the title to his masterpiece: *The Gift*.

He pushed back his lavish desk throne and declared, "I have done it! I have written that which will unite Algeria and all of the Arabs!" He scuffled from his seat, slipping on the marble, wet from the condensation of the sweating water pitcher, and slid his handful of papers underneath the door. Attached was a note for the soldier standing guard.

Give this to the General IMMEDIATELY! The future of this great nation is at stake! Make haste, my son!

The startled guard scanned the note, mouthing the words to himself, and sprinted through the ornate hallways of the massive Presidential Palace, calling for the General, waving the papers frantically.

BEN D'ALESSIO

Al-Maghribi made sure to lock the door to his chambers in his self-appointed palace—an abandoned military barracks in Tamanrasset. *Al-Saif* banners were draped over the walls and a giant horizontal banner with a sword and فـيسلا (*al-Saif*) sitting in the pocket of the sword's curve stretched from one lookout tower to the other. Soldiers patrolled the high walls with machine guns and RPGs—the RPGs were more for show than for practical use, but al-Maghribi believed that if morale was high, if it appeared enjoyable to be a soldier in his Caliphate, more young men would come to the desert and add to his army. And it worked: they flocked in droves. Brigades of Algerians, Nigerians, Libyans, Somalis, Malians, and Tunisians had already formed, and they continued to grow by the day.

The barracks were gray and bleak, but the inside of al-Maghribi's chambers was furnished with Moorish opulence. Intricately designed carpets of turquoise and violet and tangerine covered every inch of the banal original flooring. Crimson blankets and pillows with gold stitching were stacked on top of each other at the head of the bed. He had a fountain installed in the center of the room. He preferred to sleep to the trickling sound of water—it relaxed him. Being a jihadi caliph was a strenuous job, and although it had its inherent perks, al-Maghribi was constantly being asked to advise on a Quranic interpretation or preside over a trial or perform an execution—these kids didn't know how to properly swing a sword!

Finally he had some time to relax, so he hopped onto his high-rise bed, opened his Macbook, and typed **www.pornacopia.com** into the search bar, misspelling the site on his first try.

Big-Boned Blond Deep Throats Mandingo—skip.

Asian Teen Takes on Football Team (College Girls Special)—skip.

Voluptuous Latina Double Penetration—skip.

Adorable Arab Bombshell (no pun intended) Jasmin Guzzlawi Makes American Pay Jizzya Tax—he was irate.

BINGE UNTIL TRAGEDY

The montage of preview pictures had Jasmin Guzzlawi, who was actually one of the most-searched porn stars at that time, on all fours, creamy brown ass in the air in nothing but a hijab—**click**. The male talent was a hackneyed American redneck in sand-colored combat boots, a green camouflage tank top, and an American flag bandana covering his crew cut. He would drop trite lines like, "Those twenty-seven virgins might be in heaven"—flipping the numbers and incorrectly citing the "virgins hadith" of the Quran, which states that seventy-two virgins will accompany the martyrs in paradise—"but I've got myself a big butt browney. I'm about to go jihad on her ass!" and "I've got yer jizzya right here!" as he howled like a wolf and lowered his penis into Jasmin's spread asshole.

"I'll cut his head off!" al-Maghribi shouted, stopping himself from launching the laptop across the room. Bangs came on the door as he held the laptop above his head.

"Are you okay, sir?" said his guard, one of the new soldiers from Kuwait.

"Yes, yes! Leave me, Bharath, I'm fine!" It was only after a few moments he remembered that Bharath had been sent to Ouargla, and was from Qatar. "Eh, I always mix up those Gulf States," he said to himself. The new guard was Fahad. "Fahad. Fahad. Fahad. Fahad," he repeated so he would remember.

He clicked on the **Categories** section and scrolled. He checked his history: He forgot to erase it last time. He couldn't forget again. He got out of bed and went to the door and placed his ear on the cold metal. "Bhara—" he started to say "*Yela'an!*... Fahad... Fahad?" He corrected himself—nothing. He was alone. He hopped back into his gigantic bed and tossed around a few of the superfluous pillows. He scrolled the **Categories** section and clicked on **Gay**.

Al-Maghribi had only recently discovered pornacopia.com, and had previously been using slow pornography sites that offered vanilla videos with stock storylines. He scanned the options of homosexual porn with dilated pupils: **Twinks, Bears, Twinks and Bears, Interracial, Military, Studs**. He checked the clock: forty-five minutes until he had to make a ruling on whether or not a Tuareg slave girl would be found guilty of "withholding" and "assaulting her master." He clicked on **Twinks** and found a video with two blond boys—the skinny one with budding muscles reminded him of Simon.

They lay together in a small bed in a tiny apartment that overlooked a gloomy port; it definitely *wasn't* America. Al-Maghribi didn't like that. One of the boys, the one who looked like Simon, began to kiss his partner's bare chest. He said something that wasn't in English and al-Maghribi started to panic. He hit the **Back** button, which brought him to the **Gay** options again, and then hit the **Back** button again. On the **Categories** menu he clicked on the first thing that appeared: New Uploads. There was a knock on the door. He clicked on the first **New Upload** to blend the gay pornography into the canon of regular pornography, make it look like a mistake if someone checked. He kept his Macbook in a safe in the back corner of his room and changed the lock combination regularly. He went to clear his browser history. He had forgotten how to do it. There was another knock on the door. "Sir, there is a problem with the Tuareg girl. Sir? Are you okay?" He clicked on a random video: **Czech Beauties Suck and Fuck American Tutor**: tags: **Face-Sitting, Doggy Style, Teen, Cumshot.**

"I am coming!" he said, scrambling out of bed, knocking the laptop onto the floor. He threw on his black robes and grabbed his scimitar, which was leaning against the wall in the corner in an umbrella holder he had requested from a recruit from East London.

The laptop lay on its side as the video played. The American was standing with his jeans around his ankles as one of the Czech girls sucked his dick. He picked up his laptop and plopped it on his bed, but before he exited the website, he stopped to admire the American's tan pole and pictured himself in the girl's submissive position. The boy looked like he could be Arab, or perhaps Turkish. He reminded al-Maghribi of a soldier he met while in the army—a beautiful young man. He pictured Simon standing with his American designer label jeans around his ankles, his blond hair in a messy coif. Al-Maghribi ran his hands along the crimson silk sheets, rubbing off the clammy sweat, imagining it was Simon's milky skin.

Knock, knock, knock. "Sir?"

BINGE UNTIL TRAGEDY

Click. Exit tab. Click. Exit page. He swung the scimitar over his shoulder, which rattled as it hit the door on his way out.

Salim and Mohamed heard a thud on the door of their apartment at 6:30 in the morning. When they opened it, they found a little book with a green cover and a note attached to the front that said:

MANDATORY:

Dear my sweet children, brothers and sisters of Algeria,

It is with great pleasure that I extend to you this gift: a guide for life. Please read it at your leisure and carry it with you always, in your mind and in your hearts.

I love you all,

Your President,

Hamza Hannachi

At the bottom was a disclaimer, a less flowery note:

It is MANDATORY that all persons of Algeria carry with them AT ALL TIMES the Great Leader's GIFT. It is MANDATORY that all persons of Algeria MEMORIZE and be able to RECITE The GIFT at all times.

Salim's cell phone rang. Farah started ranting before he could say a word: "Can you believe this? Is he serious? Is that despot serious?"

"Farah, quiet down," he said, covering the receiver of the phone. "You don't know who could be listening."

"Okay, okay. Let's meet at *La Petite Mère*'s house. Did you eat breakfast?"

Salim and Mohamed careened through the Casbah, avoiding streets where they could hear rambunctious noise—only *La Peste* was rambunctious anymore. Children rarely played soccer in the streets now, after the incident.

A couple of weeks ago a group of children, eight and nine years old, was playing in a nook of the Casbah known for being a soccer hangout. When they were approached by *La Peste*, they were "disrespectful." Understand that it didn't take much to be "disrespectful" to *La Peste*; it was a wildly arbitrary charge. As an "extension of the president himself," the group of regal marauders demanded the same treatment any of the president's closest advisors would receive. So when one of the kids, wearing a Lionel Messi Barcelona jersey, told a drunk "officer" that his tie was "stupid," which provoked uproarious laughter from his peers, he was smacked on the side of the head. The blow was so hard and unexpected that he didn't break his fall and landed directly on a poorly maintained flight of jagged-edged steps. The men sauntered away without checking on the boy. The child's friends tried to wake him up. He made a few noises but couldn't form words. One ran to get the boy's mother, and the rest dispersed, frightened. The child was dead before his mother could cradle him in her arms one last time. There were minor protests in the Casbah, in Martyr's Square, but nothing came of it, and even some of the more raucous protestors were taken in for "questioning."

Farah was already at *La Petite Mère*'s house, arguing with Omar in whispers, when Salim and Mohamed arrived.

"This is an insult to Islam. To God," said Omar, waving the little green book in front of his face. "Right here. Read here." He put the book on the table and followed the words with his index finger. "'God is always and forever in our hearts, but during our time here on Earth, the Algerian people will keep their beloved president in their hearts, always with God and forever, and shall submit to their beloved president before submitting to God.'"

At the bottom of the page was a note, which Omar read in harsh, cutting whispers: "'When the call to prayer wakes Algeria and puts Algeria to sleep, the people of this nation will give thanks to their beloved president before submitting to God. Officers are permitted random and frequent inspections on the matter.'"

"He has stripped *us* of our rights too," said Farah, flipping through the little green book to a dog-eared page with the title: "The Role of Women in Society." When she began to read, Omar rolled his eyes and reread the section on religion to himself. Salim and Mohamed sat quietly sipping tea and listening to Farah.

"'In order for our beautiful nation to prosper, our women must be protected. Our women must be kept in a safe environment in order to populate our nation.

Women will no longer need to be educated nor maintain a job. Women will be compensated in relation to how many children they produce for this great nation.' He wants to make us baby-making machines," she said, slamming the book on the table.

Hannachi believed the war with *al-Saif* would last the rest of his life. He wanted to give incentive to women to churn out children who would, in turn, become soldiers for the regime. As the group read the little green book in *La Petite Mère's* home, Hannachi's advisors were ratifying a conscription amendment to the constitution—it would be enacted immediately.

La Petite Mère poured the group more tea before their cups went dry. Sunlight seeped in through the cracks of the eroding walls. When Salim offered to do some work on the wall, as a thank you for the copious cups of free tea, she declined. She said the extra sunlight tickled her flowers in a different way that they very much enjoyed. She had also received a little green book at her front door, but didn't think much of it. If it hadn't been for Farah coming over early that morning, it would still be sitting there in a puddle of semi-translucent mucky water.

Farah powered on her camera and placed it on the table facing a large pot of heather. She never appeared in any of the shots, and instead would speak from behind the camera as it taped a beautiful building or a plant or the Mediterranean. She gave an introduction, dated the shot, and briefed local current events.

"*La Peste* has killed a child. That's right, you heard me correctly. They killed a child with their bare hands. And NONE of them will be held accountable. This is the Algiers in which we live now. This is the sad truth. The revolution is not over. In the South, *les fous*"—she used this word, meaning "the crazies"—"are recklessly killing and enslaving Algeria's women and children…"

"They will liberate us from these scoundrels!" yelled Omar, interrupting Farah, causing her to violently snatch and turn off her camera.

"How could you…"

But before she could finish her sentence, Salim interjected, "Oh, shut up already, Omar!" They were stunned. Although Salim and Omar disagreed on many issues, rarely had Salim spoken to Omar in such a way. "Will you shut up! Are you insane? How could you speak a single word of praise for those berserkers?!"

"Salim, they are fighting…"

Salim switched from French to Arabic. "They are killing! Innocent people, Omar. They are killing and enslaving and distorting our religion. They are a parasite!"

"Al-Maghribi…"

"Al-Maghribi is a wretched, horrible man. Algeria will be no better under a man like him than under Hannachi."

"But with al-Maghribi, we will be led by God."

Salim launched himself from his seat, and leaning across the table, said, "Do you really believe that, Omar?! Do you really believe that *God* is on your side?" He sat down. He caught his breath. He started to type on his laptop.

Mohamed began to say something, but Farah stopped him, quickly shaking her head. "Why don't you leave, Omar?" said Salim. Go to Tamanrasset. Go to Biskra or El Oued or any of those poor places enveloped by the tide of filth." Omar didn't say anything. "Did you see the video?" (Omar had viewed the video numerous times.) "How they cut off the heads of those workers? Is that what you want? 'Exterminate the Crusaders'?" he said, mockingly. Omar remained silent. *La Petite Mère's* humming filled the silent gaps. Salim knew the taking of Tebessa, where his mother still lived, was inevitable. Even though the president of Tunisia, a close friend to Hannachi, had sent troops to the border cities including Tebessa, and even as far into Algeria as Constantine, their efforts against *al-Saif* would be fruitless. He had told his mom this. He told her *al-Saif* would eventually invade Tebessa, and that she would have to be careful.

"Please, Mother, remember to cover yourself when you leave home."

"Yes, Salim, don't worry about me," she would say, as if not fully understanding the situation. "I lived during the Olive Protests, remember? Oh, how could you remember? You were only a child."

"I think I'm going to come home."

BINGE UNTIL TRAGEDY

"Oh no, Salim. Stay in the city. The army will take care of those crazy men. I'm sure your classes will begin again soon." This is what she would say. She didn't have a clue.

Salim sat silent, typing away at his laptop. But he actually wasn't typing anything legible. He had opened an empty document and just started to tap away, nonsense really. Some words, some lines of **nfdsfqiffjfjifj** or **jpidjhwfjfpijf**. He needed a release but didn't want to yell. Mohamed peered out the window. He wanted a cigarette but couldn't handle another imbroglio with *La Peste*. Omar was going to ridicule Mohamed for the smoking, but stopped himself. Instead he got up to leave. He said goodbye. Salim didn't say anything back. You could see the dust particles floating in the seeping rays of sunlight that danced along the room. They never saw each other again.

SPAIN: SEVILLE AND THE GEMS OF ANDALUSIA

WE CRAMMED INTO A FADED BLUE VAN THAT WAS comically square and set off across the vast expanse of emptiness that blends the fringes of Portugal with its peninsular neighbor, Spain. Riley set us up on a website called BlaBlaCar.com, which is an ingenious way for people who are driving to a certain destination to make some extra money. You make a profile and select your pickup and drop-off cities, and it shows you who is making those trips, and when. The drivers have profiles and ratings and everything to help you feel secure enough that you won't get ax-murdered. It's cheaper and more direct than trains and buses. Our driver was a Spaniard named Antonio who commuted to Lisbon every few weeks.

Riley, Iago, and I planned to stay with Enrique and his mother in the Triana neighborhood of the city. Riley had purchased an Andalusia guidebook in Lisbon and shared what it said about the fabled neighborhood: "Triana, being detached from Seville proper in its own 'island' in the Guadalquivir River, has created a unique and celebrated culture that has helped form the *Sevillano* identity, which has become synonymous with all things Andalusia." She scanned some more, reading out tidbits of information. "Juan Belmonte… that matador that Hemingway was obsessed with, he was from Triana… It's also known for having a sizable Romani population AND controversially considers itself the birthplace of flamenco."

"Wait… Romani as in Gypsies?" I asked.

"Oh… yeah, I guess so," said Riley.

Ben, who was sitting in the back of the van with John, popped his head forward and said, "They believe the name is taken from Trajan, the Roman Emperor born in Italica, which was the first Roman settlement on the Iberian Peninsula."

"Yeah, it says that here!"

"I love Seville. It might be my favorite city in Spain. Maybe in all of Europe. I stayed here for three weeks for orientation before teaching, with a young mom and her one-year-old. That was in the Casco Antiguo, not Triana." He said the Spanish words with a Spanish accent.

"She's so fit!" yelled John. "I remember when you first got to Jaén and showed me pictures of 'er. I can't believe you weren't on the pull."

"She was my host mom!" yelled Ben. "Her… ya know, I don't know what he was. Baby daddy I guess… He would come like, every day after work and take them to the park."

"Still, should've copped off with 'er," said John, who then started speaking to Antonio in Spanish, filling him in on what Ben didn't do with his host mother, I suppose.

"Do you still keep in touch with her?" asked Riley, ostensibly acting curious but actually becoming defensive.

"Oh yeah," said Ben. "I talk to her on WhatsApp. It's what everyone uses in Spain. I'm getting lunch with her tomorrow."

"Are you?" she said with a piercing inflection.

"… Yeah. You're welcome to join. She doesn't really speak English, but…"

"No, no, it's fine. Trust me, I'll find someone—I mean *something* to do." She vigorously began flipping through the pages of the guidebook and then started to text. She texted Pete, who had decided to head in the opposite direction, to Porto, and then to visit his extended family who still resided in England.

Marcel didn't travel with us, although he could've easily made his way to Tarifa from Seville. But when I connected to the WiFi at Enrique's apartment on Calle Betis, a popular street that faces the river and Seville proper, my phone erupted with texts from Marcel. This was strange, because they weren't texts about Riley, and because even though Marcel and I *were* friends, we weren't in the way we would plan anything without Riley being involved, I suppose.

Text from Marcel X: 2:56 p.m.: Joel you should join us in Tarifa and then to Maroc. We want to do some real exploring.

Text from Marcel X: 2:56 p.m.: Maroc is a beautiful country. I think you would really enjoy it.

Text from Marcel X: 2:56 p.m.: Nous allons laisser en quatre jours.

I also received a lone text from Sal.

Text from Sal: 2:56 p.m.: Hey buddy! Hope Europe is treating you well. Hey, give mom a call when you get a chance. Enjoy, well, wherever the heck you are! Love you.

Enrique had lived with his mother and a cat named César (that's THésar) in the apartment on Calle Betis his entire life. It was painted the typical cream white found throughout southern Spain as a mechanism to repel the assaulting rays of the sun. It had red trim and green shutters. The top row of windows had new-age Moorish arches and a terra-cotta roof. Outside, two orange trees stood watch over the building, their fruits not used for juice, but for that marmalade so adored by the pasty English. I'd learn the Andalusians oftentimes catered to the English—for sherry, for beaches, for marmalade. Enrique's younger sister, Isabel, attended the University of Seville, but was studying for the year in Cologne, Germany, on a work/study program.

"Yes, I studied in Bristol, *Inglaterra*. Spanish people try and go to UK or Germany for the jobs. People of the UK and the Germans come to *Andalucía* for the sun. It is a transaction, no?" Enrique explained in a thick Andalusian accent. "I do not speak *castellano*. ¡Hablo andaluz!" he shouted, pounding his chest. "¡*Viva Betis!*"

Ben explained the intricacies of the dialect to me against my will.

"A distinct aspect of the Southern Spanish accent compared to the rest of Spain is the lack of final consonants. No words are ever finished. *Gracias = gracia. Los pescados = Lo pescao.* And then there is the whole 'lisp' thing, 'which isn't a lisp at all!' It is just part of the peninsular Spanish. So everywhere in Spain—well, almost everywhere—they pronounce words like *gracias* as *graTHias* or *azul* as *aTHul* or, the one every obnoxious person who doesn't speak a lick of Spanish but uses it to sound cultured, *Barcelona* as *BarTHelona. BarTHelona. BarTHelona!*" He was losing it; I enjoyed that.

"Tell us how you really feel," I said.

Ben and John were staying in a hostel across the river in the *barrio* Santa Cruz. You could see the Giralda from their balcony—Riley showed me pics. They made the twenty-minute walk across the bridge to our tapas bar meeting point. Scrunched-up tissue-paper napkins were strewn across the floor. A weathered green- and white-striped banner with a crowned "double B" in the center hitched to a wood post waved above us.

"That is *Betis Balompié*," said Enrique. "They are my"—he looked around the bar—"*Our* football club. ¡*Viva Betis!*" The bar echoed his call.

"*Betis* is like, Andalusia's team," explained Ben, taking over for Enrique. "So everyone in this country likes like three fucking teams, *Real Madrid, Atlético Madrid*, or *Barcelona*. But *Betis*, who share the colors of the Andalusian flag, are like the loveable..." He looked at Enrique and realized where he was. "They're like the Cubs. You can't *not* root for 'em."

I ordered a beer called Cruzcampo. It was *the* beer here in Seville. "The beer of the South," said Ben.

"Yeah, it's shite, but cheap," said John.

"Good thing, I'm running low on monies. If I don't check my bank statement, it doesn't change, right?" said Riley, as if it really mattered. One text and her dad would direct deposit a four-digit amount into her account.

Iago and Enrique shot glances at each other from across the table. Enrique had a cute half-crescent smile that was impeded by cratered dimples.

I texted **Queen of Campus <3<3: 3:40 p.m.: Are Enrique and Iago gay?**

Text from Queen of Campus <3<3: 3:40 p.m.: Duhhhhh you couldn't tell?? We went over this in Paris.

Text to Queen of Campus <3<3: 3:41 p.m.: I thought the Portuguese and Spanish hate each other??

Text from Queen of Campus <3<3: 3:41 p.m. Love conquers all stupid!!!
Text to Queen of Campus <3<3: 3:41 p.m.: I told you, everyone IS gay.
Text from Queen of Campus <3<3: 3:41 p.m. bahaha shut upppp!!!

"What will you do after Spain?" Enrique asked Ben.

"I was supposed to go to law school right after college but decided against it. I needed a break from school for a little and wanted to learn a new language. Plus, I love traveling, I'm addicted to it. I'm actually… never mind."

"What?" asked Riley.

"I'm writing a book, but it's tacky to talk about your writing. So yeah, college was solid, but…"

"Where'd you go to college, again?" she asked.

"A small school in Pennsylvania… Ursinus College? You ever heard of it?"

"Yes! Of course. I don't live far from there at all! Our school wasn't far from there either. How have we *not* gone over this?"

"I don't know!"

"We've been there," she said, wrapping her arm around the back of my neck. "Remember, Joelie?"

"Yeah, I remember Ur-Anus."

"Never heard that one before…" he said, then took a slug of beer. "So what are you doing now that you've joined the real world, Joel?"

"Fuck, man, I don't know."

"Joel is really smart. He's just an asshat most of the time."

"Shut up."

A waiter dropped off little plates of succulent morsels of food, and gave Enrique a wink.

"Ah, yes, the best part of being Spanish," said Enrique. "In Portugal they charge money for this." He gave Iago a little push.

"Wait, this is free?" I said.

"Yes. Here in parts of Spain you get free tapas with your *copa*."

"Yeah, but not that many places still do this," said Ben. "Really the only three provinces are Granada, Almeria, and Jaén. I actually didn't think Seville did this," he directed toward Enrique.

"*Pues* … no, but I am *familia Betis*. For that, we get free *tapita*," he laughed.

The Sevillian sun was something merciless. I rearranged my bar stool every hour so as to avoid its brandishing rays. "But it's a dry heat," said Ben. "It's a dry heat. I'd rather have a dry heat than a sticky, wet heat, ya know? I prefer a dry heat."

"Me too," said Riley.

"Well, I need to get out of this dry heat," I said and sucked down the rest of my beer.

We crammed the remaining bits of *tapa* into our mouths and went back to Enrique's apartment. His mother made us coffee in a rattling moka pot with brown stains caked onto the chrome. Riley and I were advised to guzzle as much coffee as we needed to make it through the night—the Spanish start the party late. "When we were in Salamanca, we pregamed until three in the morning!" shouted Ben.

"Tonight we will start at Calle Alfalfa. There are many bars there," said Enrique.

"And many *guiris*," said John.

"You are *guiri* too!" said Enrique.

"¡*No, no, tío! Soy español. Hablo español perfectamente. ¡Pues ya ves tú!*" he responded in what could be considered a racist accent.

We trekked from Triana across the river, thwarted the overpriced trinkets and drink traps that charged a pretty penny for the waterfront view, and down Paseo de Cristóbal Colón, past the Torre del Oro. "A remnant of the Almohad Dynasty that ruled al-Andalus in Seville from the early twelfth to the late thirteenth century. The Almohads, who specialized in architecture…" Ben prated on.

"Back when Muslims, Jews, and Christians coexisted peacefully," I said sarcastically, which of course, Ben couldn't let go.

"Actually, no. The Almohads were *very* much the fundamentalists and actually carried out massacres of Jews and Christians."

"My Arabic professor said Islamic Spain was tolerant and progressive compared to Medieval Europe."

"He..."

"It was a woman."

"*She* was right AND wrong. You see, there was a Muslim presence in Spain for over eight hundred years. It wasn't, like, one group ruling the entire time. There was a ton of infighting and different dynasties and even different types of people ruling. There was even a time when al-Andalus was split into tiny kingdoms called *taifas*..." Riley reached for his hand, which he accepted and continued, "But it was really the Omayyad dynasty that epitomized the medieval tolerance and educational progression of al-Andalus, but that was like... two hundred years before the Almohads. And their capital was Córdoba."

"Where all the hot Spaniards are?" I said, sarcastically.

"Exactly!" yelled John.

"He is correct. How do you know this?" said Enrique. "It is correct, but do not say it so much loud—the *Sevillanas* get jealous." He laughed.

As we passed the Torre del Oro, Ben said, to no one in particular, "If I could go back to any point in time, it would probably be tenth century Córdoba."

"I'd go back to eighty-two," said John.

"Last time *Villa*..." Ben started.

"Last time *Villa* were the champions!" John finished.

We went through the heart of the city, passing the Alcázar and the cathedral. "The second-largest cathedral in Europe!" said Ben. "They say, you know, they say that when the architects were designing the structure, it is believed they said, 'Let's build a church so beautiful and so grand that those who see it will think we are mad!'"

"Don't have to convince anyone he's mad," I said, turning to Iago, who wasn't paying attention to me.

Riley craned her neck looking up at the Giralda. "That tower is like..." *If she says 'amazeballs,' I'm going to flip.* "... breathtaking." *Okay then.*

"The Giralda, first a Muslim minaret, now the bell tower for the church, was also a construction of Almohad origin..."

"Holy shit, dude." I walked away from the group to admire the intoxicating creation in peace.

The cider and jam-colored tower shot into the sky, lit up in honey-gold, high above the myriad of Gothic spires lining the top of the cathedral. Islamic arches and diamond-patterned designs covered the bottom two-thirds of the structure. The top third, the Christian third, featured slim, rectangular openings so the bell could be heard from all corners of the city. The highest tip of the tower was adorned by a statue of a little woman dressed in a tunic, carrying a shield and a palm branch; revered by the *Sevillanos* as *El Giraldillo*, she symbolized the victorious Christian faith.

"Isn't it beautiful?" said Ben, sneaking up on me and catching me by surprise.

"Yeah, yeah, yeah, it just surpassed the Eiffel Tower as my favorite phallic symbol."

Calle Alfalfa was humming. International imbibers buzzed from bar to bar like bees in a honeycomb, savoring their cheap Pilsner nectar. Ben pulled Riley through the crowd, and the rest of us followed them to a bar where they handed out giant plastic cups of beer from a *Para llevar* window. "It is how you Americans like it, no?" said Enrique. "Always 'on the go.' Coffee. Beer. Coffee. Beer. Go! Go! Go!" He laughed.

"Is that an old man?" said Ben, pointing with his chin toward an elderly man in a baseball cap holding one of the giant beers with both wrinkly hands. "I have to talk to this guy." Again we followed Ben, weaving our way through groups of five or ten until we reached the old man surrounded by tall guys with blond hair that mopped over their ears in… Party Shirts. Australians.

"Have you met Henry?" one said to us before saying anything else, his beer spilling over the edge of its cup and flopping onto the stone sidewalk.

"He's famous, ya know. The ninety-seven-yurr-old backpacka."

"He's been in magazines 'nd shit."

I put my hand over my mouth and whispered to Riley, "I don't think you want to witness another death."

She bit her bottom lip and said, "You're *such* a dick," trying not to laugh.

"Tell 'em about that time that thing happened, Henry, in Dresden."

"He's great with the ladies. Watch out," an Aussie directed at Ben. "He'll snatch that one right off ya shoulda," he said, as if Riley were a parrot.

Henry gently drank from his massive beer that left him with a foam moustache. When he started to talk, we all leaned in a little closer. "I first started doing this trip when I was eighty-nine years old. I go on it every two years. I fly from Sydney to Berlin and hop on the bus there." He was referring to one of those "hop on, hop off" bus trips that are run by English twenty-somethings and filled with Aussies.

"There was an age limit before Henry," said an Australian wearing a short-sleeve button-down shirt covered in blue pineapples.

"Yeah. It was like thirty-five or something but, wasn't it, Henry?"

"Yes, I believe that when I…"

"Now Henry does it every couple of years."

"Yeah, he said that," I snapped.

"He brews his own beer but. Don't ya, Henry?"

"I started brewing my own beer in 1973. To avoid the tax on…"

"He's a world trav'la but."

"Would you like a beer?" an Aussie wearing a Party Shirt with yellow stripes and a bluefin tuna directed at Riley, who was holding Ben's arm and already drinking a beer.

"Easy there, chief," said Ben.

"He's trying to nick your bird!" said John.

"What did you call me?" asked Riley.

Through a gap of Australian shoulders, I saw a group of girls standing in a circle. She was up against the wall, drinking a sweating gin and tonic from a straw: Our eyes met. I immediately felt self-conscious about my clothing. I had given up on dressing up. I never wore a t-shirt "out," ever, but I'd been on that trip for so damn long and it was so damn hot and all my nice shirts were dirty or wrinkled or both, that I threw on the first thing in my backpack. My jeans had a natural rip in the thigh. One pant leg was rolled to the top of my Chuck Ts while the other rested below the star. My t-shirt had a wine stain on the bottom, which I tucked into my belt—at least I was wearing a belt. She smiled at me while biting on the straw. I mouthed, "Hello."

"Aww man, she's fit," said John, hauling me down from the clouds. "You have to go chat her up, yeah? Before one of these knob-jockeys snatches her right out from under ya."

I was pulled through the Australians. I had no control over my feet. I didn't break my stare, nor did I care that my wine-stained t-shirt had come untucked. Her eyes were hypnotic. They were green, I suppose, but green is too simple for what they were. They weren't olive or emerald or fern or pear or shamrock or sage or even chartreuse. The human eye can see millions of colors (they weren't pine or lime either, by the way) and I am convinced evolution had peaked, at that moment, to allow me to appreciate those gigantic (yes, they were absolutely uncanny), effulgent eyes.

"Hi, you have the most gorgeous eyes I have ever seen in my entire life." She smiled. Her friends whispered to each other, making a *psspsspsspsspsspss* sound like they were trying to communicate with a kitten. "What color are they?" I asked, not rhetorically.

"Green," she answered.

"Just green? I don't believe it. They are so much *more* than green."

"I call them green because I am a princess, and princesses have green eyes."

She was a princess. Dark skin, dark hair. A descendant of a Moorish princess, I suppose.

"Are you Spanish?"

"Jyes."

"I am American."

"I know."

"What is your name?"

"Lucia." She pronounced it "LuCia."

"Is that L-U-C-I-A?"

"… Jyes?"

"So why don't you pronounce it 'LuTHia'?"

"I do not talk this way."

"But you are Spanish. As in *Spanish* Spanish. Like from Spain, right?"

"Yes, but I am from Córdoba. We do not speak this way."

I shot an angry look at Ben, who was yucking it up with Riley and John.

"What is your name?" she asked. I almost gave a fake name, but I caught myself.

"I'm Joel. Not Joe. It is like Joe, but with an 'L' at the end," I said, extending my arm for a handshake.

"So American. Look, we do this." And she kissed me on both cheeks—I melted. "The name is *dos besos*. You have not heard of this?"

Some of her friends were chuckling. I wanted to tell them to fuck off. I had enough drinks in me to do it, too, but I bit my tongue instead.

"Well, Lucia, I want to know everything about you, and don't spare a single detail. You are interesting—no—intoxicating. And I'm afraid if I don't know everything about you I will not be able to proceed with my night, and quite possibly, my life. So in the spirit of preservation, please join me in that cramped, narrow bar and let me buy you a drink."

I ditched my giant beer. I wasn't going to let some drunk idiot ruin my chances with Lucia because he bumped into me and I spilled the stuff all over her tight black dress—God's gift to mankind.

Lucia was living in Córdoba when I met her, but she was from Zuheros, a *pueblo blanco* in the mountains in the south of Córdoba Province. She was working in Córdoba as a pharmacist. In Europe, pharmacists recommend medicine and don't just count pills. She had specialized training from the University of Madrid and learned English studying for a year at the Imperial College in London.

I was loquacious, to my surprise, and she pulled me into a dark corner of that cramped bar and kissed me on the chin. I had thought it was an accident until she did it again. It was unusual, but I liked it. I tried to get her to leave with me. I wasn't sure where. Anywhere, really. Anywhere to keep her safe. That was unusual, to me also. I had never felt *that* before. Did I want to sleep with her? Yeah, sure, of course. But man, I just wanted her to be safe with me somewhere, alone. A group of Eastern Europeans—Serbs, I think, or Bosniaks—were checking her out, right there in front of me. I didn't need to know their useless fucking language to understand what they were saying. I was irate. But I held it in. *Long game*, that's what I told myself. *Long game, Joel. Don't be shortsighted. Don't fuck it up.*

Man, could she dance. She'd put her hands on the sides of her head and ruffle her hair and drop her butt down real slow. I only danced ironically, but that night I stayed against the wall and enjoyed the show. She made me feel special. Like *I* was the regal Moor and she was sent to me and only me. The torrents of love and lust swirled around me and I was a benevolent prisoner. She grabbed my hands and guided them through the muggy bar air, smiling and laughing at my dancing ineptness. I saw the gaggle of unamused friends trudging through the bar to rip her from me, so I asked for her number.

"*Tienes* WhatsApp?" she asked. And after seeing the dumbfounded look on my face, she said, "WhatsApp? The application for the mobile? Every person in Spain use this."

I hurriedly scrolled through the surviving apps on my phone (I had eliminated many of them back in Berlin after listening to one of Lucky Star's spiels) and remembered that Riley had added a couple when I had food poisoning so she could contact me and—*Yes! It's WhatsApp*.

"I have it!" I said overenthusiastically.

I took down her number and she whispered in my ear, "I would like to see you again, American Joel," and kissed me on the cheek before being whisked away by her jealous friends.

I texted her so quickly, she was probably still in the bar. I had never done that before either. "Always wait to call them," Sal would say. "Or text. You guys don't talk on the phone anymore." I regretted it immediately.

BEN D'ALESSIO

Text to Lucia <3: 12:02 a.m.: Hola Lucia! It was so very wonderful to have met you this evening. I hope that I have the pleasure of seeing you again. I believe there is much more for us to discuss. Ciao, Joel.

Discuss?! Is she a client? A coworker? Ciao?! I had heard Enrique say it and it sounded cool at the time, but when I reread the text, I sounded like a douche, like the kind of guy I made fun of, and Riley dated. All I did was think about Lucia—for the rest of the night, when I tried to sleep, on the toilet, in the shower, when Ben would play his annoying logic games and try to get me to participate as we were having our breakfast of tomato spread and olive oil on toast, with coffee.

"Joel. Hey, man, you want to play? If so, you should pay attention to the beginning."

"Huh?"

"Okay, this shit is actually pretty fun. A friend showed it to me. Okay. So this one is called 'Pelican Burger,'" he continued. Riley, Enrique, Iago, and John all sat in silence waiting for Ben's instructions. "So"—he sat upright in his seat and spoke with his hands—"a blind guy walks into a bar, orders a pelican burger, takes a bite, cries, goes home, and kills himself." Everyone stared. "What happened up to that point?"

"Mate, how the fuck are we supposed to tell you what happened with that little info?" said John.

"Ask questions. I didn't say that? Oh yeah, you get to ask me questions to help piece together what happened." Ben continued to eat his toast and licked his fingers after every bite. He had an armada of paper napkins circling his plate.

"*No me caigo*," said Enrique.

"Okay, okay, guys, listen, just start asking questions and I *promise* you'll catch on."

"Why is he blind?" said Riley.

"*¿Por qué él es ciego?*" Ben repeated for Enrique, who spoke English fine. "And they have to be yes or no questions."

"Was he blind last year?" asked Iago.

"Good!" shouted Ben, bits of toast crumbling from his lips. "And *no*, he was *not* blind last year. See?"

"Was it an accident?" asked Riley.

"Yes." Ben pointed to me. "Joel?"

"..."

"Johnny Boy?"

"Do we have to go in order?" asked Riley.

"No."

"Was it tragic?" asked Riley.

"Wouldn't any accident be *tragic* if the victim goes blind?" I interjected.

"... Yes, it was tragic," said Ben.

"Was it a plane crash?" asked John.

"Holy shit! Yes! Wait, have I done this one with you before?" Ben asked, all squinty-eyed.

"No, mate, neva."

"Okay, well, yes, it was a plane crash. *Accidente aéreo*."

"Was it in the ocean?" asked Riley.

"Yes!"

"Did he make it to an island?"

"Yes!"

"Was he alone?" asked John.

"No, he wasn't."

I wanted to get my hands tangled in her hair. I wanted our bodies intertwined like strands of DNA. I checked my phone—nothing. She hadn't responded from the night before.

Text to Lucia <3: 2:22 a.m.: It is me, your American boy!

Text to Lucia <3: 3:17 a.m.: Are you there Cordobesa?

Text to Lucia <3: 4:45 a.m.: ???

I didn't remember sending the last two. If I scared her away, I would never forgive myself.

"Did he get attacked?" asked John.

"No, and not important. Go the other way with it."

"Well, were there other people on the plane?" asked Iago.

"Yes!"

"And… and… They did not live the… No, wait… Survive the fall?" continued the Portuguese.

"Yes. Go, Iago, go!"

"And he did not have food. So the other survivors helped him…" Ben's eyes grew wide; he was loving this. "Wait… were the other survivors blind too?"

"No."

"So…"

"Wait, I got this!" yelled Riley. "So the other survivors had to feed the blind guy, right?"

"Yup."

"And since they were on an island, he could hear the birds. The… pelicans?"

"Keep going."

"So his friend would feed him hunted pelicans and the taste in the bar made him so upset that he killed himself?"

"No… Close, but no."

I decided to make my entrance. "The survivors fed the blind man the dead bodies of the plane crash and told him it was pelican to get him to eat it. Upon the revelation in the bar, when he realized pelican did *not*, in fact, taste at all like that to which he had grown accustomed, he went home and killed himself because he was a cannibal."

"Yeah… that's right."

"Boom," I said, throwing my hands behind my head.

"Yeah, after we did all the work!" yelled Riley.

My phone vibrated in my pocket. I felt a wave of solace flow over me. Finally, I had heard back from the woman who'd absconded with my heart. I checked my phone: **Text from Marcel X.**

"Son of a bitch!"

"*Hijo de puta*," Ben translated for Enrique.

"What? What happened?" asked Riley, genuinely concerned.

"Nothing. Nothing. Forget it."

He had sent me a link listing the heads of North African and Middle Eastern regimes. Number one was Hamza Hannachi of Algeria, followed by his peers in Libya, Syria, Tunisia, Iraq, Egypt, and Yemen. The article listed Hannachi's atrocities like statistics on the back of a baseball card:

HANNACHI: 25 years in power!

- Thousands of innocent citizens murdered!

- Hundreds of little girls raped!

- Thousands tortured!

- Hundreds of mosques closed!

- Universities closed!

- Freedom of speech quashed!

How much more can Algeria take?! We must cut down the "Green Eagle." Join the fight! End tyranny!

The only thing that was keeping me from scouring the streets of Seville for Lucia was that my texts were **sent** but not yet **read**. I could handle that. I begrudgingly went with the group to see the Alcázar and wander its gardens. I didn't want to leave WiFi. I had become an addict. I would check the windows of every café we passed for that symbol of connection like I was seeking clues to the Holy Grail. But we didn't stop at any shop and went straight through the gates of the Royal Palace.

Architectural beauty couldn't do it for me anymore. I didn't care about any of it. And if I heard Ben say the word *Mudéjar* one more time, I was going to take poison. I craved the fleshy beauty of Lucia—her perfect Spanish skin, her aura of serendipity, her eyes… Christ. Those eyes! (They weren't sea-foam or seaweed and definitely NOT just green. I don't care what she tells you.)

"Are you coming tonight, Joel?" asked Riley. I hadn't been paying attention at all.

"Where?"

"This *discoteca*," said Enrique. "Bilindo. It's *superguay!*"

"Supergay? Like a gay club?"

"No, no!" they laughed.

"*Guay*. It means 'cool,'" said Ben. "They don't say, like, *chulo* here. That's Latin American, amigo."

"Is there going to be a line?" I asked.

"Probably…" said Ben.

"Fuck that. Jesus Christ better be in there turning water into whiskey if I'm going to stand in line for a club."

"Great imagery, mate," said John. "Could you imagine that? Jesus lighting flaming Jell-O shots from his finger?"

"Hey Joel, you could invite that Spanish *mamacita*," said Riley, shaking her hips as she said it. "She looked like she enjoyed dancing."

I could, and I did. The second we returned to Enrique's apartment across the Guadalquivir, I sent her a text explaining every detail of our plans for the night. Within seconds, I received a response.

Text from Lucia <3: 2:31 p.m. Hello my American! I am sorry for not answering the messages you have sent me last night. My phone had no battery. However, I am in love with (my heart was in my throat) **the idea of going to Bilindo with you tonight** (it went back down). **Would you like to see flamenco? It is very typical of Sevilla. Tell me yes or no and I tell my friends. Besos xoxoxo**

"What'd she say?" asked Riley, who had been watching me mouth every word of the text.

"Oh, um, she's down. But she wants to see flamenco? Can we do both?"

"Ahh yes, of course!" said Enrique. "Flamenco! How can I forget to take you to the flamenco?! Of course we do both. In Spain we don't go to *discoteca* until very late in the night."

"And we are in the birthplace of flamenco, right, Enrique?" said Ben.

"Of course we are! Do not listen to what those *jerezanos* say to you."

"He's referring to Jerez de la Frontera, another city that claims to be the cradle of flamenco," said Ben.

BINGE UNTIL TRAGEDY

"Got it."

I was elated. I had a burst of exuberance and felt that everything was in its right place. I laughed with Riley, I exchanged American and British derogatories with John, I even humored Ben when he explained to us the complexities of the legend of El Cid—"Nothing is ever as simple as it seems," he said.

"You got *that* right, comrade," I responded.

"Hey, you finish *Infinite Jest* yet?" he asked, knowing damn well no mere mortal could've finished that tome of fiction in that short amount of time. I hadn't read a page since we arrived in Seville, actually.

"Not yet, man. Plugging away at it, you know how it is," I said, hoping he actually knew "how it was."

"Alright, well, we're leaving for Jaén in a couple of days, so I'm going to need it back by then."

"Yeah, yeah, yeah, okay... So you said Columbus *is* or *isn't* buried here in the cathedral?"

Everyone took a nap before going out, but I couldn't sleep, not a wink. *Infinite Jest*'s grinding prose couldn't quell the sensation I felt right down there in the pit. When I heard the clinking and clanking of the Spanish coffee maker, I jumped from the bed, scaring César (that's THésar) the cat, who had been sleeping on the floor, and I rushed into the kitchen for some human connection. I must have had a menacing look on my face, because Enrique, the culprit of all the noise, looked startled when I came crashing into the kitchen.

"*Hola, hola, hombre*," I said in an awful accent. "We *vamos* for flamenco soon?" I asked, making the motions of the castanets and imitating their clicking sound.

"Yes, we can go soon, *tío*," he said, warming milk on the stove in a pan.

"It's weird taking a nap and waking up at nine," said Riley, yawning while fixing herself a cup of coffee. Within minutes, all of us were in the kitchen drinking coffee, then a beer, then another beer, and then for Enrique, Iago, and Ben, another coffee, before I was waving them to the door and down the steps like a captain sending paratroopers out of a Blackhawk helicopter, yelling, "GO! GO! GO! GO!"

Lo Nuestro, the flamenco bar located just up the street on Calle Betis, was already exhaling the intoxicating rhythms of Spanish guitar and stomping heels on wood. Lucia was not there yet, so I held my glass of wine and tried not to appear too anxious.

Different young men would take turns strumming the guitar like opening acts. Enrique pleaded with Iago to go up and do his thing, but the timid Portuguese refused.

"I do not play Spanish guitar often, Enrique. This you must understand!"

"Fine then. Dance with me, handsome." And the Spaniard pulled Iago onto the dance floor, where they twisted and turned and fell into each other without anyone batting an eye.

"Ya know, that's something I find so fascinating about Spain," said Ben, leaning in so we would pay attention. "Spain is one of, if not the most, gay-friendly countries in Europe, and yet it also clings very tightly to its Catholic identity. It shows they can both not only coexist, but thrive."

"That's really interesting," said Riley, stroking his smooth and pointed ego.

"I really think the Religious Right in America needs to analyze Spain. One day will be gay pride, and then the next they'll literally be carrying a crucifix down the street to applause, song, and tears."

"That's so beautiful," said Riley. "Are you religious?"

"I mean, I don't know how to answer that," he said, sitting back in his chair. "I believe in God and Jesus, but I don't, like, follow the strict laws of the Good Book. What about you?"

"I'm not really sure. I haven't been to church in a while, but I definitely feel more spiritual here in Europe. It's really enlightening."

Oh brother. Yeah, one time when Riley and I had to visit a church in Philly for our What Role Will Religion Play on Urban Revival? (Is There an Urban Revival?) (What IS Religion?) class—yes, that was the whole title for the class—she asked the priest if it was divine intervention that gave Jesus those cut lower abs up on the cross…

"What about you, Joel?"

"Joel's family is like, *super* Italian. He's definitely religious."

"What?" I said, taken aback by Riley's presumption.

"Yeah, your dad wears a giant gold cross on his neck and your mom runs a church group."

"Don't answer for me."

"But…"

"I'm *not* religious," I snapped.

"Do you believe in God?" asked Ben, putting down his glass of bloody red wine.

"I don't know. No." I wanted to be firm. "No. No, I don't."

"That's okay," he said, looking past me and into the group of smiling, dancing Spaniards, "because He believes in you."

"… I suppose." I wasn't expecting that.

"Hey, isn't that your bird?" said John, pointing to the entrance.

It was her. She was more magnificent than I had remembered. I never really got nervous for girls. Fantine was an exception—she was special and I hated her for it—but for Lucia I was nervous, bats-beating-their-furry-wings-in-my-stomach nervous.

She was trailed by three friends who believed they were above the raucous dive. They were Habsburg ugly, with oversized noses and protruding chins: Lucia's ugly stepsisters, I suppose. "I'll snatch up one or two of 'em for ya, mate," said John. "Get 'em out ya 'air." I smiled and waved her down, and she shot a smile that beamed through the bar and smacked me in the chest. I swear it was hard to breathe looking at her that first night.

She sat down next to me and whispered, "Hello, Mr. American." I let it float in the air for a few moments, fully intoxicated by her eyes that weren't pistachio nor pickle nor scaly crocodile.

"Hello, *Cordobesa*. May I get you a drink? A gin and tonic, perhaps?" Ben told me it rains gin and tonic in Spain.

"Thank you, love."

My heart skipped a beat. When I got up from my seat, I had to tuck my burgeoning erection behind the meaty part of my thigh. When I got back to the table with two sweating gin and tonics, Ben was deep into sharing his passion for traveling, describing how badly he wanted to see South America.

"I'm thinking Colombia, Brazil, and Argentina," he said.

"The Argentines don't like us Brits," said John. "After we routed them in the Falklands."

"You mean *Las Malvinas*," said one of the ugly stepsisters, the one with a particularly pointy, unbecoming nose.

"Yes. The Falklands are sometimes called the Malvinas. But not by anyone who lives there."

"Typical *Inglaterra colonistas!*"

"Oh! Because *Spain* didn't conquer half of the world?!"

"Are you from Argentina?" said Ben, attempting to diffuse the situation.

"Yes. Well… no. My family live der for some years *anterior*."

"I would love to go to Buenos Aires. 'Paris of South America.'"

I wanted to say, "Are you high, man?! Buenos Aires can't shake a stick at Paris. Paris is Paris and can't be duplicated. You can't duplicate the greatest city in the world! I'm sick of this 'Paris of South America' bullshit. Or Bucharest, the Paris of Eastern Europe. Beirut! Paris of the Middle East. Just because a city plows its streets into boulevards doesn't make it Paris." But I didn't say that. Riley saw my pupils dilate and threw a ripped piece of napkin at my cheek.

"Lucia, you speak English so well. Where did you learn it?" she asked.

The show started and a spotlighted lone guitarist addressed the excited crowd in both Spanish and English. He welcomed a study abroad group from a high school in Kansas City, which is one of Seville's sister cities. "Oh, *that's* why they have a Calle de Kansas City here," Ben said, smiling at the revelation.

BINGE UNTIL TRAGEDY

After introductions, he focused, closing his eyes and gripping his guitar. The bar became darker and the curved arch above the stage made it seem like he was performing in a candlelit cave. He strummed the guitar with brio, biting his lip and occasionally exposing his tongue. He had wavy black hair that matched a thick, sweaty beard. The top three buttons of his black shirt were undone, exposing chest hair creeping through the button holes like black ivy. His sleeves were rolled up, albeit sloppily, to his elbow. His fingers were switching chords so quickly I pictured smoke rising from the guitar's neck. I was into it. Everyone was into it—the entire bar was drunk off gin and tonic and Spanish guitar magic.

I felt Lucia's fingers creep over my knuckles, where they interlocked with mine. My erection was in full throttle, testing the fiber elasticity of my tight tan jeans. Riley was encapsulated. Ben looked like he wanted to cry. John was texting. Enrique snuggled into the patch between Iago's shoulder and chest, pulling the Portuguese's arms around him like a WASP wears a sweater. Lucia watched the guitarist and would sometimes close her eyes.

"Why would you ever close those gorgeous eyes of yours?" I asked. "The world loses its eighth wonder every time you blink."

"I close them to fall in love with the guitar."

"It isn't *that* great..." I said under my breath.

The truth is, he *was* great, greater than great. If I'm being honest, it was fucking phenomenal, and I couldn't enjoy it because she was enjoying it so much. I was jealous of the guitarist. *Son of a bitch. Maybe I'll learn guitar. How hard could it be? Sal used to play a lot. He could teach me if his kid doesn't take up too much time. Or maybe I'll learn on YouTube. You can learn anything on YouTube, I suppose.*

It was getting hot in that cave. I grabbed the glass of gin and tonic, wet with condensation, and slugged it, the ice hitting my front teeth.

"Fuck!" The entire table turned to me. "Sorry..." I whispered.

"What happened, *cielo*?" she said.

She clutched my hand, gave me a kiss on the cheek, and turned back to the music. I didn't want to leave that stuffy cave. I never wanted her to let me go.

"Never let me go," I whispered in her ear.

"*Perdón?*"

The guitar burst with an Iberian atavism that I could feel in my fucking bones. The entire bar was on the edge of their seats and stools. An elderly man stood up, removed his cap, and placed it over his heart. The guitar picked up. My knee started to bop up and down, up and down. Riley looked at Ben, dramatically mouthing, "Wow." Sweat dripped from the guitarist's brow. I hated him, but I wanted to take a napkin and wipe the sweat nonetheless. The song felt immortal. *Has he been playing the same song the entire time?* Lucia surreptitiously stroked my knee; I swear I could've come.

"Are we spending the night together, *Cordobesa?*"

"I don't believe we can tonight, *Americano*. But we can soon. This I promise to you."

Riley bit down on her lower lip and made faces I had only pictured in daydreams. Iago shook his head in appreciation of the master. Enrique sat up and said, "I said to you that this place is authentic." John stopped texting, allured by the build-up. Even the ugly stepsisters wiped the scowls from their faces and returned their eyebrows to repose. The guitarist was in agony.

"Those calluses are going to pop!" Ben shouted across the table.

I pictured blood flinging off the guitar strings and speckling the audience, like Tilikum after an ordered belly-flop at Sea World, while Enrique screamed, "¡Auténtico! ¡Mira, mira! ¡Auténtico! ¡Olé!"

Lucia's hand moved up my thigh, but my erection was stuck on the other leg. *Why the fuck did I wear such tight jeans?* I began to sweat. Her friends took notice, whispering and pointing and glaring at me in disapproval, like *I* had put her hand there. She moved back down to my knee. *She must think I'm inadequate, minute, one of those poor souls stricken with a micro-penis. If only I could show her. I could go on pornacopia. Perhaps my video was up, but there wasn't any WiFi in that godforsaken cave!* I had to tell her. *What is "penis" in Spanish, anyway? In Italian it's "pisciali." Or is that just my father's Itanglish?*

I leaned in to tell her, but she was mesmerized by the strum. "My penis is…" I started. She looked at me but couldn't hear what I was saying.

"Just a moment, *cielo*."

Slow down, Joel. "I'm adequate," I said. She didn't hear me, but patted my hand in what I took as pity.

The music got louder. The guitarist was beating at the strings like they had offended his mother, but somehow it was still beautiful.

She didn't look at me. I was over, a goner, kicked to the curb and left for the buzzards. She would find a man who could satisfy her. A bullfighter, or even this fucking guitarist. God, I hated him. *Why am I so fucking average?! What am I saying? I'm endowed. Above average at least. I was in a porno!*

"I'm adequate!" And as the planets aligned and the gods laughed, the guitarist felt my hatred and ceased on a sharp chord.

"N'oh my god," squeaked Riley, her face turning a tomato-paste red.

John covered his mouth, attempting to suffocate his laughter while the rest of the bar clapped.

"Did you say something, *Americano*?"

I attempted to melt into my seat with Jedi-like intensity.

"No, *Cordobesa*. I didn't say anything."

"Okay. My friends and I, we must be leaving now."

"When will I see you again?"

"Tomorrow."

"Will you love me until then?"

"I promise this to you."

"I want to go to Córdoba."

"How nice does that sound?"

"Take me with you."

"Find me tomorrow, *Americano*."

"Amongst the moon and clouds and every fiery star."

She gave me a kiss on the cheek and left the bar. I stayed in my seat for as long as awkwardly possible. I was stone-hard. I kept replaying a moment in the seventh grade when I was instructed to go to the board to locate the Battle of Vicksburg on a map and just kept pointing and saying, "Down there, down there. Near stupid

Alabama." Taylor Yakavetta's bright-pink thong had been creeping up her lower back since Mr. DeSalvo took the role, and I had been watching it ascend like the Confederacy approaching Gettysburg.

"Joel, let's go," urged Riley. "Bilindo time!"

"What about the rest of the show? The dancers with the colorful dresses and stomping their feet and shit?" I said nervously.

"We're ready to party. We want to go now."

"But we came to get the Andalusian cultural experience and I won't miss out on it. I just won't do it!"

"What are you talking about?"

"We ready?" asked Ben.

"What's tha matta, bruv?" asked John.

I flexed my calves, a trick Sal taught me after I disclosed the Taylor Yakavetta thong debacle. "The blood will go to your flexed muscles. Do that and sing the 'Star-Spangled Banner.'"

"By the dawn's early light…"

"What was that, mate?"

"Nothing."

When my dick finally returned to its flaccid state, I quickly told Enrique I wasn't up for partying tonight and that I'd rather go back to the apartment, and left for the door. I was flying down Calle Betis, dodging spilled wine and ashed cigarettes. The inescapable sound of guitar blasted from the rows of bars, each one as beautiful and delicate as the last. I realized I was just about to run past Enrique's building, so I clutched on to one of the guardian orange trees and swung myself, with all of the momentum from my sprint, toward the door. I frantically buzzed his floor and his mother, who was watching a game show, let me in and asked me something in Spanish that I didn't understand. "*No, gracias,*" I said, catching my breath. Stupidly, I had forgotten his mother would even be there, so I went into the bedroom and attempted to compose myself.

But it didn't work: not my phone, not my music, not even *Infinite Jest*. My phone, which had automatically connected to the WiFi, vibrated uncontrollably to the rhythm of my panting. Five text messages, all from Marcel, shot across my front screen.

> **Text from Marcel X: 11:57 p.m.: Joel ça va?**
>
> **Text from Marcel X: 11:57 p.m.: Come with me to Maroc.**
>
> **Text from Marcel X: 11:57 p.m.: It will change your life!**
>
> **Text from Marcel X: 11:57 p.m.: Live the life only the bold can duplicate!**
>
> **Text from Marcel X: 11:57 p.m.: Revolution is in reach!**

There was no time for Marcel. My imagination was molding different forms of Lucia and spurting them out in front me like some kind of sick joke. I saw her blowing me a kiss. I saw her in newly purchased Victoria's Secret lingerie—red, no, some sort of green that would match her eyes that weren't green or basil, or parakeet. I wouldn't be able to match it anyway, so what was the point?

Then my imagination, that draconian fucker, started to play tricks. I saw her out with her friends, in a crowded bar, talking to some light-featured, clean-shaven Eastern European trash, probably from Bulgaria or Belarus. She smiled at him just like she smiled at me. She shot him those eyes and he was enamored, like a spell, an intoxicating hypnosis, which instantly makes the victim drool with love. I tried to claw back to normalcy. I fought my own percolating imagination with memories of lovers lost—*Trisha, Chloe, Fantine, Riley. No! Not Riley. I would never have her.* I heard Ben's irritating voice waft throughout the bedroom. "Don't think you can ever 'have' them. Comrade, when you stop viewing women as property, you'll appreciate that they're God's gift to this big blue earth of ours."

"Shut up!" I shouted. I threw open the door and hurried into the bathroom. Enrique's mother was too deep into some *telenovela* to notice. I undid my belt and dropped my pants and underwear to my ankles and started to tug away to invented images of Lucia. But first, I imagined murdering the Eastern European fucker from Romania, or was it Slovenia? After he was nice and good and dead, I had Lucia all to myself. I was dry and there wasn't any lotion. I went to grab a couple of squares of toilet paper, but there wasn't any of that either; so I beat on, back against the curtain, bare ass borne back ceaselessly into mental trash. I'd finish right into the toilet, the still water, no cleanup. My eyes raced behind my eyelids like I was in REM sleep.

Lucia grabbed a hold of my collar and pulled me onto the bed with her, laughing and kissing, letting out peeps of refined Castilian. I did my best to imagine her naked, rubbing my fingertips along her Moorish spine and down to her voluptuous behind.

I started to shake and could feel my knees fight back against buckling. I was dehydrated and my butt cheeks were tightening and dripping sweat. My eyes were still closed and I thought I was lined up properly to directly hit the back of the toilet with a violent rope, but I hadn't notice the deep-sea blue fish carpet slipping underneath my clammy feet, so when I fired, I gyrated forward and slipped onto the tile and missed the toilet entirely. Then I saw something move.

A curled-up furball let out a whiny cry from behind the toilet. It was César (that's THésar), Enrique's cat. I came on the cat. I grabbed for the feline, smacking my belt buckle against the porcelain of the toilet, which scared him, causing him to dart for the door. Realizing the door was closed, the cat backed itself into a corner, propping up its spine and throwing back its ears, resembling a pit viper ready to strike. I could see the glob of cum gnarled on the cat's hindquarters, becoming more entrenched in its fur with every passing second. I could hear a melodramatic actor from the *telenovela* crying ¡Vete! ¡Vete! ¡Cabrón!

I hated cats, never saw the appeal. Ungrateful fuckers, and this one knew it, he could sense it; and when I went to grab him, he swiped at my bare hand, opening up a recently healed cut I had received after punching that mirror in Amsterdam. He let out a hiss, showing teeth. I slowly pulled up my pants, keeping eye contact with him like he was a burglar pointing a gun. I scanned the bathroom, looking for a towel or anything to protect my precious skin from further abrasions. The place was bare, besides a vintage Seville travel poster that had a winking sun smoking a cigar in a traditional *feria* hat and some toiletries scattered around the sink. I realized I could use the mat I had slipped on. I flung the mat upward and snapped it back down, watching bathroom debris float in the humid air, and took one last lunge at the cat. But before I could wrangle the enraged beast, I noticed the *telenovela* voices had gone silent and footsteps were coming down the hallway. I dropped the mat and turned on the faucet, flinging water at César (that's THésar) in one last-ditch effort to clean my translucent jizz off him, but he dodged every water molecule like he was Neo dodging bullets, and slid back behind the toilet. That was when I panicked.

I flung open the door, missing Enrique's mother's nose by a cunt hair. "*Ay!*" she let out. I slammed the door behind me.

"Sorry, sorry," I said, shimmying past her.

"*¿Dónde está el gatito mío?*"

"Sorry, no Spanish!" I yelled back, turning the corner and sprinting into the bedroom.

Fuck. Fuck. Fuck. I looked at my shit scattered across the floor and began to pile whatever I could grab into my backpack: laptop, sneaker, guinea tee (a term my father despises), *Infinite Jest*—I wasn't finished with that beast yet. How could I explain this? Riley would think I was some kind of sick fuck who gets pleasure out of masturbating on animals when in reality César (that's THésar) was just an unforeseen casualty in a totally normal act. What? I'm human, I suppose.

I crept out of the bedroom and peeked around the corner, hugging the wall like an escaped jailbird. Enrique's mother was opening the door to the bathroom—it was now or never. I ran for the door, my poorly packed backpack pulling me from side to side as I leaned in the opposite direction of the weight so I wouldn't fall over.

"*¡Por Dios!*" I heard as I was thundering down the stairs.

I hit the street, my head on a swivel, looking for an escape route out of the Triana. I booked it to the bridge, following the glittering light emanating from the Torre del Oro. Enrique's mother was shouting from the window, "*¡Páralo! ¡Páralo! ¡Ay, mi gatito!*"

Dodging traffic across the bridge, I arrived at Seville proper. I cut through a few tiny streets away from the hum of tourists and Vespas. I desperately had to piss, because I had to skirmish with the cat after masturbating instead of relieving myself like I usually would. I hid in a corner and undid my fly. I watched as the amber urine slid down the creamy white wall like a frothy-headed snake. I sat on a slightly raised stoop to catch my breath and collect my thoughts. I hit my front and back pockets and felt a deep, depressing sickness—I had forgotten my wallet. I tore through my backpack, hoping that in my frantic rush I had tossed it into the wormhole of clothing, and that if I just dug deeper I would find it. I leaned back against the front door to someone's home in disgust, smacking the back of my head against the wrought-iron gate. My entire plan had been foiled: find WiFi, stay in a hostel, go with Lucia to Córdoba, live happily ever after. Spain was fine with me. I'd pick up Spanish quickly, I suppose, and I was only a short flight from Paris. I had my passport, but what good was that? "Here, I'm an American. We saved you during WWII, pay for my shit and we'll call it even." Is there a statute of limitations on playing that card? I didn't have a single euro on me. I could hear my mother's voice: "Remember to always keep a twenty in your sock in case of an emergency."

All those college nights where I pulled out that sweaty twenty-dollar bill from my sock at the darkest hour of the night to buy some sticky Bubba Kush or Sour Diesel. My irresponsibility made me sick.

I took out a couple of t-shirts and balled them up and put 'em behind my head. This was just as good a place as any to fall asleep, I suppose. I watched the stupid bugs bang against a hanging yellow lamp, some so hard they'd kill themselves and drop to the cobblestone.

THE WAVE OF THE FLA

THE RUMORS HAD BEEN TRUE, AND SALIM WAS enveloped in mirth. Last night, rebel fighters who had been gathering troops and supplies in the desert of eastern Morocco successfully breached the heavily fortified border and fought their way to the outskirts of Oran—the second-largest city in Algeria. The rebels, mostly composed of young Algerian citizens and defectors from the army, were trained by Moroccan forces and—as unverified rumors claimed—the French and American militaries. The creation of the FLA (*Force de libération algérienne*) turned the arid country into a suicidal Cerberus: three forces with their sights set on the jewel on the coast.

"I told you! I told you!" shouted Salim as he swung open the door to *La Petite Mère's* home. "Our brothers are returning to us to set Algiers free! Mohamed, we must join them in the fight for Oran."

"How do you expect to leave Algiers?" said Farah, who was fiddling with her camera.

"Immediately!" shouted Salim.

"Quiet down," snapped Farah.

"How is that possible? How can *you* be silent at our time of liberation?"

"A war must still be fought, Salim. We are not 'liberated' yet."

The realization of Farah's words hit Salim hard. He sat down at the table and switched to that tone of frightened whispers he had never wanted to use again. Mohamed held his oud, which had a fresh set of strings and a new red marker inscription lining the bottom curve of the wood: *Liberté ne meurt jamais* (liberty never dies).

"This will be my weapon," he said, fixing the oud into his shoulder and aiming it like a rifle.

Farah opened up her laptop and began to click away. "What are you typing?" asked Salim. But before she could answer, the roar of an engine followed by the screech of brakes broke through the cracks in the wall that permitted the light to tickle *La Petite Mère's* flowers ever so delicately.

"*La Peste*," said Farah. "Get out your booklets."

Mohamed dropped his oud, which made a vibrating *dummmmm* sound, and shot back his chair. He frantically checked all of his pockets and got down on his hands and knees to see if it had fallen onto the floor.

Farah splayed the green-covered booklet out on the table, her eyes scanning the words in an attempt to lap up any last-second answers to questions that *La Peste* might ask.

"They are going to test us?" shot Salim in harsh whispers.

"Yes," said Farah, her eyes sticking to the page.

"I didn't think they were serious."

"Why would you think that?!"

Salim looked at his booklet like it was written in a foreign language. "But none of this will matter when we are free."

"Shut up and read," said Farah.

"Found it," said Mohamed, his chin level with the table.

"But what about *La Petite Mère*?"

La Petite Mère had been out on her rooftop the entire morning. She never once opened her booklet. When Farah would tell her, politely, that she had to read it just in case she was tested, the old woman would respond, "When is there time for reading that thing when my flowers wait all night for me to sing?"

"She hasn't even opened it," said Salim. Farah and Mohamed didn't say anything; their noses were hovering over the open pages. Salim grabbed *La Petite Mère's* booklet, which had been sitting under a flower pot since it was brought inside the home, and began vigorously bending the spine and making it appear weathered. Then came the sound of shattering glass and pounding on the door.

"Open! Official government... business." The man's voice was slurred.

Salim opened the door. One man, clearly the leader of the three, was in a white-hot suit with a lime-green shirt and dangling gold chains. He leaned against the door frame, all of his weight on one arm. His sunglasses were falling off his nose and when he spoke, his breath reeked of American whiskey. "What is the"—he took deep breaths between his pauses, as if to hold back vomit—"the... fourth section of the... Recite the..."

"Gentlemen, can I offer you..."

"Don't interrupt!" shouted one of the two men standing behind the struggling leader, both in matching black suits and aviator sunglasses.

The leader stumbled into the apartment and leaned on the chair in which Mohamed was seated. Mohamed shot up and offered him the seat, visibly holding the green-covered booklet to his chest.

"Tell me the chapter to the fifth chapter..." said the leader, directed at no one in particular.

"..."

"Answer me! You." He pointed at Farah. "Answer me."

Farah, understanding that asking for further clarification wouldn't be good for anyone, began to rattle off verse after verse from the chapters she had fully memorized: "Since the economy of Algeria will be a benefit economy, that is to benefit the beloved Algerian people, the government, which loves the Algerian people, will provide all of the benefits and distribute money to the hardworking people of Algeria." She was perfectly reciting the text.

"Enough!" shouted the leader. "Good. You are a good... Algerian." His chin was to his chest, and at times he appeared to be falling asleep.

Mohamed noticed the oud with the new revolutionary inscription leaning against the wall, taunting the thugs. He inched toward it, trying not to grab their attention. Salim, who was witnessing Mohamed's move, walked to the other side of the table and ostensibly asked which was their favorite verse of the beautifully articulated booklet. The black-suited henchmen looked at each other, each waiting for the other one to answer. Salim, realizing that embarrassing their guests—who clearly had not read the booklet themselves—would have violent repercussions, opened the booklet and melodramatically read aloud the first verse he could find. "Mother Algeria's role in the world. Algeria was an integral part of the powerful Carthaginian Empire…" Salim read the words as if preaching from a podium. His rhapsody created a long enough diversion to allow Mohamed to tuck his oud behind a chair in the corner of the room.

"You," said the leader, pointing in Mohamed's direction, but still looking down into his lap. "Get me the whiskey."

Mohamed knew there wasn't a drop of alcohol in the apartment, let alone the cheap Hayman's whiskey the thugs were duped into believing was top-shelf booze. Not knowing how to handle the situation, Mohamed froze, stuck in a Gallic shrug.

One of the thugs stepped forward. "You must have whiskey! It says so in *The Gift*!" he shouted, calling the booklet by its official name. Farah and Salim flipped through the booklet until the last page. They looked at each other, perplexed.

"Sir… I cannot find anything in regard to whiskey…" said Salim, holding open the booklet for the thugs to see.

"Give me it." The thug stepped forward, whipping the machine gun draped across his neck behind him. He scanned the pages and turned to his associate. "There is nothing in here about whiskey."

"Did you drink it?!" snapped the henchman, who was silent up to that moment. He turned his gun on Salim, then Farah, then back to Salim in a paranoid frenzy.

"No, no!"

"No! We don't drink whiskey," said Salim, his hands above his head.

The leader burped and sniffled and came back to life. "Where is the old woman?" he asked. Salim and Farah looked at each other for someone to answer. Mohamed was pinned up against the wall. "The old woman! Where is she?"

La Petite Mère came in from her balcony. "Welcome, gentlemen. Would you like some tea?"

"Are you the woman who owns this apartment?"

"Why yes, of course. Can anyone else in Algiers grow flowers this beautiful?"

"Recite the ninth verse and deliver its meaning."

"I have a delicious assortment of teas right here." She pulled a large wooden box off the shelf.

"Don't ignore the order."

"I would recommend the Moroccan mint."

"Nothing from the Moroccan traitors!"

The leader pulled out a handgun and pointed it at *La Petite Mère*, his arm as stiff as a tree branch.

"Please don't!" yelled Farah.

"Shut up!" said one of the henchmen, who now pointed his machine gun at her as she began to cry.

"Gentlemen, please," said Salim, arms in the air, frozen. "She is an old woman who doesn't possess the capacity to understand the intricacies of our president's beautiful yet complex ideas." Salim knew *La Petite Mère* was sharp, but he needed to insult her intelligence to save her.

They stared at him for a few moments and then put down their guns. He looked at his watch.

"The call to prayer will sound shortly. Don't forget to thank the president."

"We will not forget."

"We will be back."

The leader went out the door, and one of the henchmen broke a potted plant with a roundhouse kick, not even pretending it was an accident. The door slammed and Farah burst into tears. Salim immediately went to console *La Petite Mère*, who was shaking but not crying. Mohamed sank to the ground, sitting with his face in his hands. After a few moments of silence, Mohamed asked, "What will we do now?"

Salim let go of the old woman and said, "You stay here. Protect the apartment and *La Petite Mère*. I'm going to Oran."

Simon Turner's shoulders bobbed up and down to the rhythm of his panting. The sand that clogged his nostrils made it difficult to breathe. He looked down upon the convulsing body of a Tunisian soldier, whose soul was oozing out of his slit throat, and smiled behind the light *keffiyeh* wrapped around his nose and neck. He held the soldier's knife, which he had obtained during hand-to-hand combat, and wicked the dripping blood onto the ground, which made a pretty spattering sound on the floor.

Al-Saif crept toward the third-largest city in Algeria, battling mostly Tunisian forces that had been sent to aid the Hannachi regime's war on two fronts. Constantine proved to be far and away the most difficult city to conquer. It is a city naturally adept at withstanding a siege and fending off enemies; built on top of a mountain, it can only be reached by a series of bridges and is fiercely adored by its inhabitants. Its nickname: the "City in the Sky."

Al-Maghribi was fully aware of the city's premier geographic location and desired to move his Caliphate's capital from Tamanrasset in the deep desert South to the mountain city barracks—that is, until he captured that gem of Algiers.

"Are you okay, sir?" asked a newly imported baby-faced Chechen recruit in brutal Arabic.

"Yes, fine. This one snuck up on me. Here, clean my knife."

"Yes, sir." The Chechen continued, "The Caliph, he will be here shortly and requests that you meet with him, al-Arizona," he said, using Simon's new Arabized moniker.

The pummeling sound of assault rifles and heavy artillery had been the background music of Simon's life since they had engaged the Tunisian Army in the east. He was constantly high—not on drugs, but on what the internet had dubbed "caliphating." The term caught on after Clayton Wright went on a tirade during a Republican National Debate: "These kids, gallivanting around the so-called 'Caliphate'! Caliphating around the desert! It… it makes me sick!"

BINGE UNTIL TRAGEDY

But Simon loved it, every waking second of it. Sometimes he didn't sleep, and instead stayed up through the night imagining row after row of fresh prisoners on their knees, awaiting their execution. At first, Simon had questioned how they could kill fellow Muslims, especially women and children, but al-Maghribi explained that those they killed weren't *real* Muslims, and the children would grow up to be soldiers of a false Muslim army, and those women would shoot out more false Muslim babies who would then grow up to be soldiers of that same false Muslim army, and it would threaten the stability of the Caliphate. So when he peered down at the fledgling Tunisian soldier, sucking in his last breaths of life, Simon lowered the black *keffiyeh* to his chin and shot that million-dollar smile that was better suited to be on the cover of GQ than behind a piece of cloth.

During the siege of Constantine, al-Maghribi held his meetings in a bunker that was carved into the side of a mountain, south of the city. The blasts of the mortar shells became fainter as Simon drew closer to the cave in a truck operated by a nineteen-year-old Saudi. Youssouf lounged in the front passenger seat, his boots hanging out the window, with his AK-47 nestled on his shoulder. The truck weaved along the ill-maintained streets that hugged the base of the mountain. Every mile or so, a small group of men brandishing the iconic weapon, usually dressed in black from head to foot, would wave at the passing truck—the young Saudi yelled, "*Allahu Akbar!*" at each group, which started to get on Youssouf's nerves.

When they arrived at the temporary headquarters, al-Maghribi was standing outside the cave, his eyes closed, breathing in the fresh mountain air.

"This is the cleanest air in Algeria," he said as Youssouf and Simon walked toward him.

"Sir, we need more antiaircraft to thwart the Tunisian airstrikes," said Youssouf.

"Tunisians," he said, his eyes still closed. He took deep, dramatic breaths as if the mountain air provided eternal life. "I have taken more than half of Algeria and I am battling the Tunisians. Where is that coward Hannachi?" he asked, rhetorically.

"He is cowering to your might, sir," said Youssouf.

"They are calling us a 'Black Wave,'" said Simon.

Al-Maghribi opened one eye and looked at the blond soldier. "And the tide will rise over the Presidential Palace, drowning it in a sea of black, God willing."

Simon smiled. Youssouf shot a few bullets up into the air.

"Come inside. I am expecting a brigade of Sudanese. Help me decide what to do with them."

Upon entering the cave, two bewildered girls, covered head to foot in black, immediately offered Simon and Youssouf tea and sweets.

"What kind of tea is it?" asked Simon in his improving Arabic.

"They don't speak Arabic," said al-Maghribi. "They are Tuaregs. I brought them with me from Tamanrasset."

The girls had never left the Sahara, but being taken to the alien mountainous edge of the country made the intimidating desert vastness of their home more of a comforting blanket than arid ocean.

"Can we have them?" asked Youssouf, which took Simon by surprise.

He had not touched a girl since the last week before finals of his sophomore year—Mary Wong, a physics major. They met at a party at the International House on campus. He had really gone to speak with a couple of students from Pakistan to discuss the Quran. Simon had stopped drinking at that point, and found the red-Solo-cup-beer-games-and-hallucinogens scene beneath him. But when he went to leave, Mary asked if he wanted to "study at her place."

After confirming the Pakistanis weren't watching him, he left with Mary and had his way with her inebriated body. He left early the next morning and he prayed until lunch.

"'Those whom thy right hand possesses out of the prisoners of war, whom Allah has assigned to thee,'" al-Maghribi said, responding to Youssouf's question. The Malian grabbed one who was holding a plate of figs by the arm. "But first, the tea."

BINGE UNTIL TRAGEDY

"Yasmina" stood at attention as she heard footsteps pounding down the hallway. Last week she was sent home from her school because of the Executive Decree, and instead spent the time working in her father's tobacco shop, filling orders for the regulars. The shop was founded by her great-grandfather in the 1920s during French rule. He was the first Algerian to run his own business on that block—an accomplishment her father was proud of. Her father had been devastated when a group of *La Peste* stormed into the shop after parking their truck on the sidewalk and demanding cartons of Carolina Filter cigarettes "on the house." When he told the men that he did not carry that particular brand, they used the butt end of their machine guns to smash a glass casing containing high-end cigarette holders, lighters, and cigar cutters. "Yasmina" stepped on a shard that afternoon, and her father had to tweeze it out of her pinky toe. The thugs took handfuls of cartons from the shelves and sped away, leaving a shop of fear behind them.

So when a tall dark man in a black suit and sunglasses entered the shop, her father pleaded that the man take what he wanted and leave without destroying anything. The man told him he wasn't there to steal cigarettes, and that he had an offer that could help pay for the damages done by this group of hooligans.

"It was *La*…" He stopped himself, for *La Peste* was the derogatory term for the president's secret "police force." "They were government men," he said, sulking.

"Sir, I am not a police officer. I am a businessman."

"Yasmina" was in the back examining "the books," looking over her father's work. She liked math, it was the subject she missed the most. She couldn't make out what they were saying until her father began to roar, "No! No! No! I will not stand for this!" The suited man remained calm, and after a couple of minutes, she could hear them approaching the back office.

"We need to talk in here. Please go to the register and help the customers." His forlorn appearance made "Yasmina" uneasy. But she had just looked over the books, and yes, the altercation with *La Peste* cost them some, but the business was doing well nonetheless.

The suited man left the tobacco shop, nodding to "Yasmina" on his way out in an awkward way that didn't seem genuine. She stayed at the register waiting for her father, but he remained in the back office for a couple of hours. She put her ear to the door and could hear him muttering to himself in between sniffles.

"Papa?"

"Go home and start supper," he said, remaining behind the door. "I'll be back soon."

They took her on her walk home.

She stood at the foot of the bed in lingerie that was too tight on her skin. Her arm had two marks on them: one red and one yellow. The footsteps had stopped at the door's threshold and there was a conversation taking place right outside in a mixture of Arabic and French. She scanned the candlelit room: There were five other girls standing around the bed—all of them had thin veils that matched the color of their respective lingerie. They had the same marks on their arms—one red, one yellow—except for the girl in the jade lingerie, who didn't have any marks at all.

There were piles of books everywhere, reaching the ceiling like paper pillars. "Yasmina" observed that they were all the same book: *Le Cadeau—The Gift*. One green booklet was open on an ornate desk with gold leaves wrapping around and running up the legs.

It was muggy in the room, and the air seemed to get stuck in her throat. The door opened. It *was* him. Until he walked through that door, she had considered all of it a dream.

He hurried to his desk, not even acknowledging the scantily clad group of girls waiting on his every wish, and began signing a pile of booklets. After each signature, he held the booklet up to his face, closed his eyes, and kissed the front cover. Once he'd signed at least twenty booklets, he rose from his throne. The little girl in jade lingerie offered him a glass of mint water, which he accepted and sucked down in three gulps. He took off his jacket and another girl approached him to take it, clearly prepped on the protocol. Slowly, he walked toward "Yasmina."

She knew she *had* to courtesy—that's what the kind woman had told her as she was getting fitted for the lingerie.

"Hello, Yasmina." His face was inches from hers, his breath reeking of onion and sour yogurt despite the mint water. She swallowed a cough.

"Good evening, my king."

He waited a moment and then rolled his eyes and led her hand down to his belt, as if she should have been prepped on the maneuver already. She froze. He lifted his hand to smack her but stopped, checking her wrist for the red mark—the prohibition of striking the girls in the face. The red mark stared back at him, and with an angry thrust, he tossed her onto the bed.

Intuitively, she looked around the room for one of the other girls to intervene, to end the suffering. But they had all suffered already—why should she get out of it? No one had helped them. Most of the girls looked down; one looked dead ahead, as if retreating to another compartment of her psyche.

Hannachi stripped until raw. The girl in jade lingerie hurriedly picked his crispy white clothes off the floor. His face was menacing, the cracks and wrinkles becoming more demonic with each girl he "took." He planned to populate his nation like Genghis Khan and form an army composed of his offspring—the largest in Africa. He crept toward the young girl, teasing her by swiping at her feet as she instinctively continued to retreat along the soft sheets of the endless bed.

She reached the edge, she couldn't retreat any further, so she gave up. She tried to get lost in the ceiling mosaic of twinkling stars as his hand ran up her thigh and took it all away.

EVERYTHING LUCIA

IF THEY HAD KNOWN HOW LOVELY A DREAM I WAS
having, they wouldn't have woken me up. Instead of the hot, unwelcoming side street in a little-known wedge of Seville, I was in a candlelit room tending to Lucia's every need—she was Cleopatra, Queen of the Nile, and I was the boy who fed her grapes.

They shook me lightly, with expressions of genuine concern on their faces. "¿*Oye, chaval, estás bien?*"

I threw my arms in front of me in a spastic defensive motion, my eyes humming and red. Once I realized I wasn't going to be ax-murdered or raped, I asked in my rudimentary Spanish, "¿*Tienes WiFi?*"

"*Venga, un tonto*," they said and left.

"I'm not homeless… I'm a bohemian!" I yelled after them. They didn't look back.

My stomach was eating itself and there wasn't a drip of WiFi to savor. I listened for the bustle of civilization, but seven in the morning in Andalusia is a destitute place. Eventually I heard the sounds of men unloading meat and fish and kegs of beer from trucks that barely fit in the narrow streets—their tires popped up onto the curb, leaving the mammoths tilted to the side. I found a Starbucks filled with pasty foreigners up and about their work before the Spaniards had brushed their teeth. I rushed to the register and pointed and said, "That one. What is the WiFi password? You have WiFi, right? ¿*Tienes WiFi?*"

BINGE UNTIL TRAGEDY

"Your name, sir?"

"… Hannibal."

I remembered that I had forgotten my wallet back at the apartment and began to sweat with embarrassment. I checked my pockets again, more thoroughly this time, and found a handful of coins that was just enough to pay for the coffee.

The cashier handed me a slip of paper with a ten-digit code of letters and numbers that I fumbled with when I entered them into my phone. When I finally got 'em in correctly, on the third try, I watched as the circle in the top left corner lethargically spun, over and over, mocking me like some sort of pathetic, drooling addict waiting for my fix. When it finally latched on to the weak WiFi signal, my phone burst with texts.

Text from Queen of Campus <3<3: 7:35 a.m.: WHERE THE FUCK ARE YOU???

Text from Queen of Campus <3<3: 7:35 a.m.: Did you seriously jizz on Enrique's cat?

Text from Queen of Campus <3<3: 7:35 a.m.: His mom wants to KILLLLL you. She is threatening to call the police! There's soooo much yelling.

Text from Queen of Campus <3<3: 7:35 a.m.: Btw, Ben wants his book back. He like won't shut up about it.

Text from Marcel X: 7:35 a.m.: Bonjour Joel. We have not left for Maroc yet but we probably will depart soon. We are still in Tarifa. I pray that you may join us.

Text from Lucia <3: 7:35 a.m.: Americano! I am going to leave Seville tomorrow for Cordoba. I wish to see you again. Please write me. <3<3<3 xoxoxo

"Wait!!!" I screamed into my glowing phone. A table of Germans glared at me. I frantically began to type: **Cordobesa wait for me. I must go with you. My body, my soul aches every moment I am without you. Please please please wait for me.**

There I waited. I stared at my phone and felt every painful moment that I didn't receive a text deep in the pit. I accidently ignored the calls for *"Aníbal... Aníbal!"* and continued to refresh the screen.

Across the street, a homeless man lay on the sidewalk, shoeless and filthy. I imagined walking over to him and handing him my money, all the money I had in my wallet, and not even thinking twice about it. And then that money would give him a fresh start. He could take a shower and then find a job, and rekindle the flames with his lost lover, I suppose. I caught myself sporting a doofy grin, daydreaming about how great of a person I was for *thinking* about helping the homeless man. And then I remembered I didn't have any money, I forgot my wallet in that den of screams in the Triana.

Even though indie rock serenaded the coffeehouse patrons, I could still hear the *click-clack, click-clack* of horse hooves on the cobblestone outside. The Starbucks sat along a main street across from a new-age Moorish-styled building with a green–and-white swirled dome on top that reminded me of something out of Czarist Russia. I checked my phone; my message had been **received** but not yet **read**. I pulled out *Infinite Jest*. I had made a dent in the book and really had no intention of returning it—I was hooked. I figured I'd never see pretentious Ben again, and I even signed my name right under his in the top right corner: Hannibal, King of Carthage. I sat in that Starbucks for two hours, checking my phone every thirty seconds, before I received a text from Lucia.

Text from Lucia <3: 9:23 a.m.: Cielo, I already departed for Cordoba this previous morning. :(I wish for you to visit me whenever you may receive the chance. There is a train from Seville to Cordoba direct. Did you know about this?? Find me soon amor. <3<3<3

I left for the train. I'd find the money, beg for it if I had to, whatever it took to get to her. *Perhaps that homeless guy could lend me the cash.*

CÓRDOBA

I HAD ALREADY PISSED OFF THE TRAIN CONDUCTOR
twice: once for being in the wrong seat (he didn't care for my explanation of no assigned seating on NJ transit), and once for putting my feet on the armrests. The third time he passed by, I gave him a goofy "*Buenos dias!*" He shook his head and continued down the aisle.

I was exhausted, but the moment I closed my eyes, I saw Lucia and burst with a frisson of mirth. *How am I to sleep when love awaits me at the end of this fucking train ride?* I fidgeted in my seat as we passed through olive groves and pastures that blended clay pastels into lush emeralds. Every so often we'd pass a little white town that looked like it was dropped from the sky and had decided to just make do right there in its spot. *Córdoba isn't like one of these towns, is it?* I knew it had historical significance, but that was like, a thousand years ago, before everyone in Spain below the age of thirty was booking it for Germany or the UK. For one second, for one tiny moment of weakness, I wished Ben were sitting next to me so I could ask him about the city.

I arrived at the station and sprinted to the nearest exit. Outside, an armada of white taxis waited for new arrivals. Three drivers asked me in broken English if I needed a ride: "This way to *La Mezquita*." I was already sweating and the belting sun made my temples swell. The thought of seeing Lucia was the only thing keeping me from napping on a bench—I had overcome my fear of sleeping in public, I suppose. I headed toward a draping palm tree for shade and sat in the sand. I smelled awful, like acrid shame. I shuffled through my dilapidated backpack in search of a rogue stick of deodorant—it was a lost cause. To stink was my destiny.

If I had any money, I would've accepted one of those cabbies' offers and said, "To Starbucks, *más rápido!*" Instead, I walked down a broad boulevard toward where I felt the tug of civilization. My stomach continued to eat itself. It felt like a trapped rat was trying to escape from my fleshy lining. The street was lined with orange trees. I stretched my arm and plucked a fat one from the branch. I peeled the orb. I was fucking drooling. My patience subsided and I took a bite out of it. Sour juices shot into the back of my throat, cheeks, and slid down my chin—it was gross. I swallowed the chunk and took another bite between breaths. I ate about half the thing before dropping it onto the ground, and when I looked up, a table of restaurant patrons across the street stared at me in abhorrence, like I had carved out the heart of a sacrificed child and needed an afternoon snack.

"*Je suis Canadien!*" I shouted across the street. I would say this when I was in Nice and the guys from U of Iowa were making asses out of themselves—the French sported a similar look of repugnance, but more refined, I suppose. I don't know how many times I said, "*Nous sommes Canadiens. Nous sommes Canadiens.*" But Americans already carried a stigma when traveling, and I wasn't going to add to it. It didn't hurt to throw the Canadians under the bus. Those bastards are planning something up there anyway, I suppose.

I continued on my way, picking bits of sour orange from my teeth and gums. I spotted a group of Chinese tourists cramming their way down a narrow street and decided to lag a few feet behind, figuring they would lead me closer to the heart of the city, and there, I would find a Starbucks.

This part of the city was painted white, and the only color came from buckets of flowers hanging from balconies; cascading reds and violets and blues hung in the heat from green vines. Elderly women watered the flowers, and the water trickled onto the cobblestone and seeped into the slanting gutter in the middle of the street.

I hated to admit it, but Ben and John were right—the Cordoban women *were* gorgeous. They gave Milan a run for its money. In Asia, I've been told, you've "made it" when you have an elite Japanese car, a Korean computer, and a Thai wife. In Spain, you want a Cordoban wife... and nothing else really matters, I suppose.

The Chinese led me down a broad street lined with designer stores, and onto a plaza cornered with cafés and a statue of a man mounted on a horse. His body and steed were a greenish-black; his head was white. I left the tour group, which took a hard right upon entering the plaza, and walked straight ahead toward the statue, scattering a flock of pigeons that was pecking at breadcrumbs. I felt the bludgeoning of defeat, like nothing was in its right place. I stunk so bad I could feel my lips curl, and for a brief moment, I considered taking the soonest flight I could find back to Newark. I thought I must've been hallucinating, because I could hear the faint cries of "*Americano! Amor!* Is that you?!"

I started to sway from side to side, picturing the beautiful Lucia finding me in that godforsaken plaza. I thought if I ever made it home, I would give Chloe a chance, but the odds were that I was going to die in this place, a sweaty, putrid American—they'd probably just let the pigeons pick at me because it was getting close to *siesta*. Then I felt the tug on my shoulder, which spun me around and held me straight.

"*Cielo?*" It was her. "*Mi amor,* you have come to me." I almost puked. *Tell Ben I believe in God.*

If she hadn't been holding me by the shoulders, I might have fallen over. I realized I was giving her a doofy grin instead of responding, and I pulled it together. I became aware of my stench and shot backward.

"*Cordobesa!* I've been looking for you."

"You have found me. Or... I believe I have found you." She giggled.

She smiled at me and rubbed my sweating, prickly face. Her breasts popped out of her Ramones t-shirt, right at the Y of "Tommy" and J of "Joey." I tried to think of a Ramones song, any song, but kept singing "London calling from those faraway towns" over and over in my head. I knew this wasn't the Ramones, it was the Clash. The Ramones weren't even fucking British, so I don't know why I kept replaying the lyrics, and I didn't have WiFi to check for any Ramones songs, so I didn't say anything.

"How long have you been waiting, my love?" she said.

"My entire life, I suppose."

"You are fun, *Americano*. I message you to meet me here." I checked my phone and never received that message. The only conclusion: destiny.

We got into her sleek silver manual BMW convertible. The constant rigid stops of the gears through the tight streets didn't do my stomach any favors, but I hid my discomfort so I didn't appear weak. Even though it was a scorcher, she kept the top up and seemed to be constantly checking for something when we turned tight corners and halted at stop signs. To park, she clicked a button that opened a giant red gate leading down to a tiny underground lot. The slope was a ninety-degree death trap and I clutched for the invisible railing in front of me like I was about to drop on Kingda Ka at Great Adventure.

The building had a stoic wooden door with a clutched fist for a knocker. I pulled it back and let it slam against the beaten metal stopper, which erupted with a *bang!*

"Shh!" she snapped, but then smiled. "*Americano,* you must be quiet. There are other people in this building." Inside, we walked along a cobbled path that led to a trickling fountain that sat under a canopy of palm trees, shielding the area from the excessive Spanish sun that plowed in through the open square in the ceiling. Winding wooden steps meandered around the fountain and took us past apartments 1, 2, 3, and 4—there wasn't an elevator. Her apartment, number 5, was spacious and looked unlike anything my friends had back in the City or in Hoboken. The furniture was sturdy and rustic, and there were old-timey photos of women in groups dressed completely in black and men holding rifles, displaying their critter victims.

"You live alone, right?"

"Yes. This was the *piso* of my *abuela*, but..." I felt sicker, thinking I had incidentally brought up a recent death. "... she went back to Zuheros, where my family is situated." I could breathe again.

"Oh... I would love to see Zuheros."

"Jyes? Perhaps, my love. We will see," she said, like it was out of the question. "Are you hungry?" she asked as I leaned against the wall, trying not to pass out.

"Famished."

"Huh?"

"Yes."

As if preprogrammed, she prepared and fed me a tomato-heavy meal of Spanish toast with drizzled olive oil and tomato puree and a bowl of *salmorejo*—a cold, thick, tomato-based soup, which she explained was very typical of Córdoba (and not to be confused with its lighter cousin, *gazpacho*). On a tiny plate next to the bowl, she placed a neat arrangement of cheeses ranging from hard to brittle to oozy, and next to that, paper-thin slices of *jamón* (with throaty emphasis on the *ja*) that shined a greasy translucence and melted in my mouth. She cut the slices of meat from a dried-out pig's leg displayed in a holding contraption, which placed the severed haunch parallel to the counter. She grabbed the knife and bent over, her nose inches from the indent where leg meat had been sliced away. Her white shorts rode up bronze legs—her ass was screaming to get out. She looked back at me and I quickly turned my head—a piece of *jamón* hanging from my lips—and pretended to be interested in a row of framed photographs on the wall.

"Would you like more?" she asked while meticulously carving the leg. I could've eaten everything in that apartment. I imagined taking the ham leg and sinking my teeth into like a barbarian, like a Visigoth, but I said no.

I bathed in a shower the width of a phone booth, where each time I dropped the soap, my ass smacked and slid against the slick wall. I assembled the best outfit I could muster out of the haphazard assortment of button-down shirts and beaten-up jeans I had in my backpack. I had eaten too much too quickly, and the steam made me sweat—I could feel the olive oil coming out of my pores. I hopped on the toilet and subconsciously checked behind the base for a cat. When I was finished,

I realized there wasn't any toilet paper—not that she didn't use toilet paper, but she was just out. The brown haggard tube of the roll mocked me. But next to the toilet was the infamous bidet—as European as extensive paid vacations and universal healthcare. The first thing Carlo asked me when I got to Nice was, "Did you try the thing that shoots water up your ass yet?" And although I did have access to a pristine bidet in my apartment, I never utilized the thing—not because I was afraid I wouldn't like it, but because I was afraid I'd like it *too* much. But she was out of toilet paper and going for a no-wiper was out of the question, because I planned to make love to her soon.

I hovered my ass over the spout and pulled a little gold lever that released the water, but I had miscalculated my positioning, missing my asshole and hitting my taint. I dropped the lever and gathered myself and said, "You can do this. It isn't gay, most of… many of the guys in Europe aren't gay." I readjusted myself and pulled the lever once more—bull's eye. A rush shot up my spine; I wouldn't have been surprised if my hair frizzled out like a mad scientist's. It wasn't so bad—it actually felt kinda *good*. I thought about how Riley used to stick her finger in my friends' butts (some requested it) and I felt like I had been missing out. I might have been too hard on that Rose, I suppose.

I left the bathroom and opened the bedroom door to find her reading in her underwear on the bed—I like to believe she was striking a sexy pose or something like it, but I had taken too long and she got bored. I felt bidet water trickle down my leg.

"You're out of toilet paper," I said.

"Oh? There is more under the sink."

"…"

She put down her book and motioned for me to join her on the bed. The comforter and sheets were white; the pillows were white, too. I hoped the bidet had worked. I started to take off my clothes until she stopped me: "Come here, *Americano*. Allow me to do it." Her kisses were delicate and deliberate, and any time I started to use my hands, she stopped me. "No, *Americano*. Please. Allow *me* to do it." I was afraid if I didn't keep active, I was going to pass out between her thighs. I ostensibly grabbed her ass like I couldn't help myself and shoved my face between her breasts.

"No patience with you!" she laughed.

Her phone set off a spree of rings and vibrations, and a list of texts piled onto her screen.

"You need to get that?" I asked.

She didn't answer and continued to kiss right beneath my jaw. I wasn't wearing any underwear because I didn't have any that wasn't putrid, so when she began to slide my jeans down, my dick popped out, genuinely startling her.

"Baby! You don't wear knickers?"

"What…? Oh. No! I mean, yes! I do. I just… am out."

She looked at me like I was a helpless animal, which I hated, and my erection started to whimper. It didn't help that my jeans were snug around my ankles—she left them there instead of taking them all the way off—and she sat right above my knees, rendering me immobile. I was so tired I could cry.

"How many tattoos do you have, baby?" she asked, running her fingers over *Spring Forever* on the inside of my bicep.

"That and this one," I said, turning over to show the *Survive* ink across my ribs.

"I don't like tattoos," she said with disappointment. "So many British boys have tattoos."

I considered running into the kitchen and slicing off the inked skin with that filleting knife, as if my bicep were a shining piece of *jamón*. Her phone continued to vibrate. I caught a glance of a text; it was in English:

Mensaje de texto de Harry: 14:21: Lucia please answer me. I miss you. I just want to talk.

My face started to burn. She was somewhere between my chest and belly button. I stared at the phone. Her hand reached up and stroked my chin. I played with the back of her head.

Mensaje de texto de Harry: 14:23: I can come there next weekend. I have to see you again.

Both of her hands were around my penis, and she lay between my legs and stuck her feet in my rolled-down jeans, causing her butt to arch and stick into the air. My head was on a swivel: ass to phone, ass to phone.

Mensaje de texto de Harry: 14:26: I will fly you here. It's quite pleasant in England at the moment. You can escape that bloody Spanish heat.

Her fingers began to wander. She grabbed at the lobes of my butt cheeks—I froze with a pounding heart. The phone vibrated. With each text **Harry** sent, the phone crept closer to the edge of the wooden nightstand. I splayed my arms at my sides, my fingers inches from the phone. I stared at the screen, waiting for the next text. She let out an exaggerated moan that shot my head back to her.

"*Americano*, are you… okay?" I had been going limp again, worrying about fucking **Harry** and his tattooed penis. "Does it feel good for you?"

"Oh, yeah! Yes, *Cordobesa*, it feels amazing." I shot a glance at the phone. I couldn't help it; I have no self-control.

"Why do you look at the phone?"

"Make love to me," I said, sliding my midsection up through her legs' vise grip. I threw her to the side, kicked off my shackling jeans, and dropped on top of her. Her neck hung over the same side of the bed as the nightstand. I started at her chin and kissed down her throat and through her parted breasts, down, down, down, until I reached her clitoris, which had popped out for the occasion. For me it was standard procedure—it was as if every other girl was just practice, I suppose.

She tasted apple-y, like sour Champagne. Her convulsions were so severe I began to wonder if she was mocking me, if they were pity convulsions. I dug my tongue into her lips and gnawed at her—she swooned. The phone vibrated. I thought about how many guys would be texting Chloe when we'd be sitting in my basement together. *She's probably with a guy right now. I could never date her.* I popped my head up, my mouth and chin soaking wet; hers was still hanging over the side of the bed. "*Amor?*"

Mensaje de texto de Harry: 14:37: You have my heart Lucia…

I dropped my face back down into the liquid mush between her thighs before she could lift her head up to check why I'd stopped.

"*¡Por Dios! ¡Por Dios!*" It was stereotypical but sounded legit.

"You like it, *Cordobesa*?"

"Jyes!"

"How about this?" I sucked and bit.

"*Sí*, baby!"

"Is it better than Harry?"

I froze, then slowly lifted my face up to see those eyes, that weren't juniper or moss but not quite green either, glaring back at me—they were still gorgeous.

"Why have you said this?" She sat up and put her knees to her chest. Her phone vibrated.

Mensaje de texto de Harry: 14:39: Cordobesa, my lips miss…

She swiped the phone from the nightstand.

"Have you read my messages?"

"What?! No! I mean, I just saw his name come up… I… I don't know why I said that. I'm really sorry."

"He is a stupid boy from London."

I wiped sweat and sour liquid from my chin. "Do you still talk to him?"

"No! I do not like him. I told him 'Harry, we are over' a long time ago. He is… very… how you say… always want to talk?"

"Persistent."

"Jyes. He is always *per-sis-tent*."

"Well, you don't have to say *always* persistent, because…"

"Are you scared about Harry, *Americano*?"

"What? Me? No."

"You have a much bigger *pene*, Joel." (She pronounced it "Ho-el.")

"No, 'Joel.' *Americano* is fine, I also like… wait! Pardon?"

She laughed and pulled me on top of her, and we kissed and made love until it was time to eat again.

The history of Córdoba is incredible. During those pockets of time between eating and love-making and drinking Spanish wine, I googled the city. It was a pretty big deal dating back to the Carthaginians, who provided its namesake—for a Numidian general named Juba. And when the rest of Europe was stumbling around the Dark Ages, Córdoba was a hub of culture and learning that blended Muslim, Christian, and Jewish people into what would become the largest city on the continent at that time.

Lucia took me to *La Mezquita* (the Mosque), *the* symbol of the city. Although the building had not served as a mosque in a thousand years, and the official name was *La Catedral de Córdoba*, when one asked for directions, locals referred to it, congenially, as "the Mosque."

The behemoth was the focal point of the city, with tiny meandering streets snaking out from its base. Its grandeur seemed out of place—the minaret-turned-bell tower soared high above any surrounding building. Lucia took me to the orange tree orchard that was inside the stoic walls but outside of the mosque itself. We perused the orchard to the sound of bubbling water. Because it was so hot, there were hardly any tourists and it felt like the gates had been opened just for us, I suppose. I tried to grab her hand on three separate occasions, and three times I was rejected; that morning I had her feet to her ears after she sat on my face, but she refused to hold my hand in public.

She distanced herself from me and stood beneath an orange tree, closing her eyes in the shade.

"You know not to eat this, *Americano*," she said, cupping one of the oranges like an overgrown testicle. "They are very bitter."

"I got notes of sour."

"Pardon?"

"I know, *amor*."

"Please, *Americano*…" She lowered her voice to a whisper. "No *amor* when we are in the public. I have told this to you."

She *had* told me that morning to just call her "Lucia" when we were out, that it was "for the most best."

I figured it was a crazy ex. I pictured him as the stalker type, not Spanish. Perhaps from Albania or Macedonia, Poland or Estonia—he was *definitely* Eastern European and was *definitely* lurking around every corner in a tricolored jumpsuit.

"Is it… an ex?" It hurt me to say it. It made me sick even thinking about her with another guy. I couldn't get the image out of my head. What the fuck was she thinking? Flashes of Oleg mounting her from behind made me double over and heave.

"What? No! Joel." (She still said it like "Ho-el.")

"No, 'Joel.'"

"*Americano*… it is *not* an *ex-novio*." Thanks be to God. "Let us go to lunch."

She took me to Bodega Guzmán, one of the most famous bars in the city, located on the Street of the Jews. No, not Wall Street—Calle de los Judíos—Street of the Jews or Jews' Street. Córdoba's old Sephardic Jewish neighborhood is ancient and intoxicating and you can still find expert craftsmen tinkering away in little shops selling leather, textiles, and jewelry. The bar had a homey feel, with beleaguered old men running the operation. Framed newspaper cutouts of *matadors*, or *toreros* as they call them in Spain, lined the arabesque-tiled walls. Huge black barrels sat behind the bar that shot out *fino* and *manzanilla* from the tap. This stuff wasn't your mother's Chardonnay sitting on two ice cubes: after a couple small glasses, you can feel it behind the eyes.

We sat in the corner of a room, off to the side of the bar. It was occupied by elderly men who erupted in muddled Castilian and violent gesticulations.

"What are they talking about?" I asked.

"The upcoming *corrido*."

"Bullfight?"

"Jyes. It is Sunday. Would you like to see it?"

"I suppose."

"I cannot go with you, however. I must work this Sunday."

"I'll go alone?"

"*Sí*. It is going to be funny."

"... You mean fun?"

"Jyes, *fun*. Pardon me, *Americano*. I must use the toilets."

She got up from the table and as she passed, her hand slid across my knuckles. I watched each ass cheek bounce up and down as she walked. One of the old men at the table saw me watching her and winked. I went to the bar to get our third round of tiny glasses of *fino*—I had texted Sal about my wallet; I told him it was stolen in Seville. He didn't ask any questions and wired me a bunch of cash that I picked up at a Santander bank.

I stumbled a bit and plopped down on a stool at the bar. I turned, glassy-eyed, to a girl with pasty white skin and rose-colored lipstick. I had seen her before, at a café in Prague, I was sure of it. She didn't seem of this time—more like Gatsby's time, I suppose. I imagined she'd kick her head back when she laughed and say things like "Ha, ha, darling! How dare you, you brute," the cigarette a permanent extension of her fingertips.

"I didn't think you could smoke in a bar in Spain," I said. She shot me a look and rolled her eyes. I ordered two glasses of *fino* that were filled to the brim and spilled onto the bar. "You're a poet, right?" She continued to stare at the giant black barrels sitting behind the bartenders, letting side stream smoke snake from the cigarette into the air. "I bet it's the bodies in the barrels that give the wine its unique taste," I said. "Like from "The Cask of Amontillado"? Not a fan of Poe, I presume." I didn't like being ignored. She left the bar, disgusted; I'd never see her again.

I finished my third glass of *fino* and ordered my fourth before Lucia returned from the restroom. She didn't like how much I drank. She called it "English." She said I reminded her of the boys in London who would "drink drink drink silly." I told her I could out-drink any of those limey Brits tomorrow—she didn't find it amusing. At the table, she kept averting her eyes from something behind me. Eventually I caught her and insisted she tell me what was so annoying.

"It is that picture, *Americano*." I turned around. All of the pictures looked more or less the same—cutouts of thin, dark-haired men in sparkling outfits of pinks, blues, and golds.

"Which one? That one?" I said, pointing to a handsome *torero* in a tight blue outfit, holding the bright red cape, the skinny sword tucked behind it.

"… Jyes."

"What is he… your cousin?" They looked similar enough to be related.

"No." Her head sunk and she lowered her voice. "He *is* an *ex-novio*."

I shot around in my seat, startling the old men, who must have been five or six *finos* deep that afternoon, and glared at the cutout.

"Are you serious? You dated fucking Juan Belmonte?"

"Joel! Quiet yourself. Calm down."

"Is that why you want me to see a bullfight? Huh? So I can see your tight-assed boyfriend slaughter something with a sword?"

"No! *Amo—Americano*… he does not fight anymore. He does not even live in Córdoba."

"I beat Kev in a shooting contest in Prague, ya know?"

"Huh?"

"I used a sniper rifle. That takes skill. Barbarians stab animals with a sword."

"*No seas tonto.*"

"What?"

"You are being a silly boy."

I swirled my half glass of *fino* rigorously, and it dripped from the edges and seeped onto the table. "I'm not a boy," I murmured into the wood. She took out her phone and aimlessly scrolled. I drank more wine.

Texts from friends and family woke me up from a much-needed *siesta*. The concept of the *siesta* is wrongly translated by North Americans as simply "a nap." What

I'd come to learn is that instead, the *siesta* is a block reserved every day for personal time. It comes after lunch, which is the largest and most family-oriented meal of the Spaniards' diets, unlike Americans', which is undoubtedly dinner. I equate this with the fact that despite the olive oil/mayonnaise/fried-everything-heavy diet of the Spanish, you rarely see overweight people, let alone obese. So after lunch, everyone retreats to their rooms or hangout areas and does what they please, so long as it is relatively quiet.

My phone vibrated again, inches from my nose. I wiped drool from my lips and looked down to see a dark puddle of slobber. Lucia was in bed next to me, sitting upright, reading the same book.

"Whatcha readin'?" I asked.

"*Cien años de soledad* by Gabriel Garcia Marquez. He is *colombiano*."

"What does that mean in English?"

"Um… one hundred years of… loneliness. Jyes?"

"I suppose."

"Do you like to read?"

"Yeah."

"Oh?"

"… Yes." I was surprised that she was surprised. "Why?"

"I do not believe that Americans enjoy to read."

"Wait… seriously?"

"Jyes. In the movies it is always drinking and killing and *follando*… 'fucking,' no? Always the fucking!" She laughed without taking her eyes off the page.

"…"

"No? Am I incorrect, *Americano*?"

"I like to read. I am reading a book now. It's in my bag."

"Oh? What is the name?"

"*Infinite Jest*."

"What is the story?"

"… I suppose I don't really know."

BINGE UNTIL TRAGEDY

Text from Marcel X: 3:45 p.m.: Joel! The bastards are killing women and children! But the rebels will take Oran. The assault on Algiers will begin shortly. Join us! Make history. I have already purchased you a ticket. salam alaikum

Text from Sal: 3:56 p.m.: Hey buddy! How's Spain? You excited to be an uncle? Would be cool if you brought something back from Europe for your new nephew. Yes I think it's going to be a boy. The Lupo gene is strong! Carlo made the North Jersey All-Stars, so he's pretty proud of that. Let me know if you need any more $$ Love ya. And yo, call Mom. She misses you.

Text from Queen of Campus <3<3: 4:01 p.m.: Joelie, where are you? Are you still in Spain? I left Seville. I'm in Jaen with Ben. He really doesn't like you haha.

Text from Queen of Campus <3<3: 4:02 p.m.: So if you're still in Spain let's meet up. You couldn't have gotten far. I'm assuming you're with Lucia? Ben wants to take me to Granada. Let's meet there. That is unless you're in like Iceland! Haha. <3 Miss you.

Text from Queen of Campus <3<3: 4:02 p.m.: P.S. I hope Lucia doesn't have a cat!! ☺ **<3<3<3**

Before I could respond to any of the texts, Lucia snatched the phone from my hand and rolled away from me.

"Who is this? Who is this?" she said, her eyeballs scanning every word with precision.

"Hey! Gimme that!" I knocked the phone onto the floor and flipped her on her stomach. I grabbed the waist of her pants and yanked. They were stuck on her hips. I undid the button and zipper and with my index finger, made a "come hither" movement between her underwear and skin. I rubbed the top of her slit until I felt like I was losing my fingerprint, and when I pulled my finger out, it was covered in a dark brownish-red—I looked like I had just voted in an election in the Middle East.

"*Cordobesa…*" She opened her eyes. "What is this?"

"¡*Dios mío!*"

"Are you okay?"

She shuffled from the bed, taking off her pants, and hopped on one leg to the bathroom.

"Yes! Yes! *Amor,* I am fine. But I am sorry, I believe that I have the menstruation."

"That's okay," I said. She didn't hear. I started to put my clothes back on. I had sex with Chloe when she was on her period once. She insisted. It was awful.

As I buttoned my jeans, Lucia pranced back into the room and hopped on the bed. "Baby, what are you doing?" she asked, surprised by the shirt and pants.

"You… you have your period?"

"Jyes. This is not a problem." She positioned herself on all fours. The tampon string dangled between her legs.

"You have a tampon in."

"You can… introduce it in the butt, no?"

"Wait… what?"

"Oh, you Americans," she said, as if I had made an innocent faux pas.

Don't get me wrong: I had done butt stuff before… with Chloe, too. But we were both piss-drunk in my basement, and I had watched a clip on pornacopia.com earlier that day that made the whole endeavor seem like a gas, but actually, *it* was awful, too, and it bothered me how much she enjoyed it, as if she did it regularly. And it was right around then I stopped talking to Chloe, and my mom would say, "I haven't seen Chloe in a while. Are you two okay? She's such a nice girl, so well-mannered. And always so happy to see you." To which I'd have to bite my tongue from saying, "Like a pig in shit."

But not Lucia. She was perfect; she had to be. Her coy smile and tan skin and stare with indescribable eyes when I slurped my *salmorejo*—perfect. Her cascading hair—perfect. Her eyelashes that bloomed from her eyelids like aster and tickled my cheek every time we kissed—perfect. Her scent, an amalgam of soaps and lotions that had been blended together for years and now nestled in the fibers of her skin—perfect. Her laugh, the only thing that wasn't foreign about her—perfect. Her breath, a perfect delicate hallelujah. Even that which wasn't perfect *was* perfect, like the thin layer of dark hair on her arms and down her back, and how she had a blemish or two, which reminded me that she was human, and *that* made her perfect, because gods are supposed to be perfect. It isn't so easy for the rest of us.

So while Lucia posed on all fours and pointed to the table next to the bed, jostling through her brain to come up with the word for "lube," I stopped her and said, "Not now, *Cordobesa*. Why don't we grab a drink and go for a walk on the Roman Bridge?"

She had to begin work at the pharmacy again, however sparingly. It *was* August, and the continent basically shuts down for the month. She didn't want me hanging out in the apartment all day because she would worry about me and didn't want me to be alone. She said a bullfight would be a "funny" way to spend the day—I stopped correcting her on this.

It wasn't common for bullfights to happen this late in the summer, undoubtedly the hottest time of the year. But it was some special occasion, and supposedly, a couple of really great fighters would be participating in the events.

Spaniards' opinions on bullfighting ranged from staunch advocates who believed it was *the* most Spanish of Spanish pastimes, to animal rights activists who sought its total demise. Most Spanish, especially the younger generation, had no desire to support the events, but they weren't going to demonstrate in the streets either.

Lucia dropped me off at the bullring before she went to work and told me to be back at the apartment by two for lunch, but not before then. She stressed not to go to the apartment *before* two, and gave me a list of sights and cafés I could enjoy to "kill time."

"I do not know this expression. Always Americans and the killing," she said. She rushed a kiss on my cheek, handed me a ticket, and told me to go wait in the line to the right. Then she left.

I had imagined the bullring being located far outside the city limits, having to cut through olive groves and orange tree orchards with windmills sticking up far out in the plains and anything else stereotypically Spanish, but it wasn't. The short and round stadium sat awkwardly between clusters of apartment buildings, close enough that bull's blood could spatter on the t-shirts and underwear drying on the clotheslines that hung from the balconies.

It was called *Plaza de Toros de los Califas* or Bullring of the Caliphs—the Moorish leaders who once ruled this part of Spain. I found it odd how much of Andalusia paid tribute to the Muslims who were eventually violently killed and banished from the continent, but then again, how many American sports teams and states of our country are named after Native Americans?

Like most of the time I was in Europe, I felt underdressed. My perceptions of the bullfight being a spectacle for the peasants, like a Shakespearian performance during Elizabethan England, were grossly miscalculated. If anything, the bullring pulled the most dapper of Cordobans from a city that already had a reputation for being wealthy and refined. High-school-aged boys stuck expensive sunglasses in moussed-up coifs. Their three-buttoned collared shirts were pastel teals, violets, and oranges. All of the women were in heels—some held children who couldn't have been older than three. They'd become numb to the violence, like children in warring states, I suppose. The same two *toreros* appeared on posters plastered on the outer walls of the ring: Eduardo Corrochio and Diego "*El Pajarito*" Morales Garcia. Teenage girls posed for pictures with the latter, kissing him on the cheek.

Morales got his nickname, *El Pajarito,* which means "the little bird," due to his age and speed. A boy in line, who could easily tell this was my first bullfight, explained in broken English that just when you thought the bull was going to "strike Diego, he fly away like a little bird."

BINGE UNTIL TRAGEDY

He was a favorite amongst women for his pure, boyish good looks, and amongst the men due to his skill and grace in the ring. For the oldest men, those most adamant about bullfighting's survival, *El Pajarito*'s fame was an assurance that the sport would not die with my generation.

I shuffled inside the ring, which was devoid of the extravagant advertising found in the sporting venues of the States. I bought a couple of frozen bottles of water from a lone vendor with a cart and found my seat. The ratio of pit to spectators seemed disproportionate. The pit was vast, a bright orange sand circle that appeared as pristine as Yankee Stadium on opening day. It was surrounded by wine-red boards that are supposed to protect the spectators, but too many times, pissed-off bulls would clear them with ease and go after the heaviest slob in the crowd. The seating was only two or three separate sections, which permitted those with even the most elevated seats to have an intimate experience.

I sat in the middle of two groups, far away from either aisle. In front of me was a giant calvous head whose neck rolls themselves resembled a face—if only I had a couple of googly eyes. Even though the fight had not yet started, I could see the fleshy orb lose its shine and begin to redden.

The crowd began to cheer as young men in tight teal-and-black outfits spread out across the sand. Their hats reminded me of the notorious Mickey Mouse ears distributed at Disney theme parks around the world. Each of them carried a cloth that was bright pink on one side, the other side yellow.

The heat was brutal. I put one of the sweating water bottles up to my forehead and moaned as drops dripped down my nose and onto my t-shirt. A woman, the mother of the group to my right, sat uncomfortably close to me. I was constantly moving my knee from bumping into hers, but she didn't even seem to notice. To my left was a raucous group of men celebrating a birthday, I surmised. My *compadre* on that side was beefy and smelled like my high school hockey bag doused in cheap cologne. He was fat but with a big chest and bulbous arm muscles that alleged he enjoyed working his upper body but avoided anything that resembled a sit-up. His shoulders constantly invaded my periphery, and his forearms would be the first place I'd sink my teeth into if I suddenly became a zombie.

The first bull shot out into the arena like an unguided missile and crashed into the wine-red side paneling. The crowd roared with laughter. The bull was thinner than I had thought it would be, and from my seat, I could see its ribs. The men in the tight-fitting teal outfits teased the bull with their yellow and pink capes. If the bull went too fast or got too wild, the men would jump into little cubicles built into the sides of the arena that would keep them safe from the beast.

Eventually, the bull was tired and confused. It would start a charge at one of the Mickey Mouse Club men, but then turn its attention elsewhere. The group of guys next to me disliked this and started to jeer at the bull. "¡*Venga bestia! ¡Venga cobarde!*"

I waited for the *torero*, sword in hand, to come out and kill it, relieve it of the insults. But I hadn't realized there was much more to the spectacle. A man called a *picador* rode out onto the sand. His horse was covered in padding and blindfolded. He wielded a lance tucked under his armpit like *Don Quijote*.

Immediately, the bull garnered a burst of energy and rushed at the horse. The *picador* jammed the lance between the bull's shoulders, behind his neck. It was a three-way standstill: the bull rammed into the side of the horse, the horse stood its ground, the *picador* dug the spear deeper and deeper into the back of the bull. I realized the Mickey Mouse Club also acted as rodeo clowns, distracting the bull when the main attractions needed a break. I couldn't see any blood, which didn't make sense, because a spear had been repeatedly jammed into the bull's back. I squinted for blood. I even turned to the woman next to me and said, "¿*Sangre, no?*" And she looked at me dumbfounded and said, "*Sí, hay sangre,*" and gestured to the bull. Perhaps I needed glasses, because I didn't see any blood. I was supposed to see Dr. Gehring before I left for Europe, but never got around to it.

Then I saw the blood. It wrapped around the bull's upper back and sides like a sweater. The bull was black and the blood meshed with its hide. Each member of the Mickey Mouse Club held two spears, each with their own color designation. They enclosed the bull and took turns jabbing the spears into the animal's back with simultaneous downward jabs, dodging the bull's horned thrusts. The spears stayed lodged in the flesh and bounced off the bull's expanding and deflating ribs.

BINGE UNTIL TRAGEDY

His tongue hung out of his mouth and he started to heave. "*Mira, mira, mira, que asco!*" the guy next to me shouted, his elbow drilling my arm as he pointed into the pit.

The bull stood directly in the center of the circle with a spinal rainbow of spears flopping on its back. He was too tired to chase any of the Mickey Mouse Club. The crowd yelled at it, finding any break in the action unacceptable. From what I could make out with my limited Castilian, they were demanding *El Pajarito*. He answered their call.

The young man strutted out onto the sand to a roar from the crowd—the Mickey Mouse Club clapped. He glittered in the sun in a gold outfit covered in gold sequins, and I thought to myself that this is probably how Cortés appeared to the Aztecs—not of this world.

The young *torero* acknowledged the crowd and was handed two small spears of his own, also a glittering gold. He raised them above his head and then pointed one at the heaving animal. The bull began to charge at the young *torero*, but tripped over his own hooves and crashed into the sand. The crowd laughed and jeered. The Mickey Mouse Club circled it with their capes, grabbing the animal's attention and getting it running and charging again.

El Pajarito handed his spears to his "squire" and walked the edges of the arena, waving to young girls and accepting flowers and animal skin *bota* bags filled with water or wine—he hadn't even done anything yet. All around me, young girls screamed for him, reaching out with open hands and clutching at the air. The woman next to me—her daughter, next to her, was crying from overwhelming mirth. I imagined Lucia sitting in the arena, cheering on her beast-slaying ex-lover who had girls grasping for a piece of his blood-stained cloth, like the plebeians grabbed at the severed head of Louis XVI, or Robespierre. I could tell Muscles to my left did not share the same ardor for the young *torero*, and sat, arms crossed, impatiently bopping his knee, waiting for something to happen.

El Pajarito took back his gold spears and started to run parallel to the bull, zigzagging in a backpedal to confuse the animal. Again, the bull stumbled and fell into the sand, and this time the crowd called for its head. *El Pajarito* gave the bull a chance to get its bearings and rise to its feet. The bull charged at the *torero*. He jammed the spears into its back and turned to face the crowd, arms raised. He taunted the bull by running a few feet ahead of it, placing his hand between the bull's eyes as if he were magnetically pulling the beast. The Mickey Mouse Club emerged from their cubicles and distracted the bull so *El Pajarito* could retrieve the final execution implements: the *muleta* and the sword.

The *muleta* is the stick that hides the sword, held in one hand by the matador, but the red cape that hangs from the stick is undoubtedly the most recognizable symbol of the event. Although bulls cannot decipher the illustrious color, which does not, contrary to popular belief, enrage the animal, the red has remained for tradition. I consider the practice one final taunt of the ignorant animal before its impending doom.

It was during this final round, the *tercio de muerte*, that I found myself losing any respect or admiration I might have had for the gladiatorial event. The bull had half a dozen spears jammed into its back, was jabbed repeatedly with a lance, and when it fell to its knees or rammed itself into the sides of the arena in confusion, it was heckled and considered ill-equipped. Ill-equipped to die properly, I suppose. This was the national symbol of the country, and *El Pajarito* had dropped to his knees and was bending over backward, demonstrating how such a small, young man could control the violent beast, all under the auspices of a Spanish sky.

In the States, our conception of bullfighting is largely garnered through the writings of fellow Americans who portrayed the event in a romantic, abnormal sort of way that was foreign and distinctly Iberian, but relatable to those who have experienced war or other death-defying feats—this was not my experience. I suppose I was ignorant to the order of events that took place during the fight, but by the time the *torero* dangled the red cape in front of the bull, it was already mortally wounded, with bloody foam frothing from its mouth.

Yes, in some very rare instances, if the bull fights "valiantly" and survives the *torero*'s blows, it will be relieved of its suicidal duty; but these are rare occurrences and reserved only for designated fights. Another lie we are told in the States is that the bull is revered here, but I did not witness any Native American-like admiration for the animal. Instead, if the *torero* fights well, he is awarded the ears and tail of the bull by a panel of judges—they're severed off right there in the sand. I tried to envision the American equivalent and imagined beer-guzzling fans cheering on snipers as they shot bald eagles out of the sky—the "Ace" got to keep the wings and beak, I suppose.

El Pajarito stood rigid, gracefully twirling on his implanted axis foot like a ballerina in a music box. "¡*Olé!*" the crowd cried as the bull's horns narrowly passed his knee. "¡*Olé! ¡Olé!*" *El Pajarito* grinned at the crowd, oftentimes taking his eyes off the bull. I wished the bull would make a pass at that moment. Maybe stab his thigh, something nonlethal. *El Pajarito* revealed the sword and waved it in the air and smacked the bull on its nose—*Okay, maybe something lethal.* But the young *torero* won. The bull made its final charge at the red cape, and the young *torero* leaped into the air at the absolute last possible moment in time and plunged the saber into the animal's neck, severing the spinal cord. It died instantly, a perfect kill.

The crowd erupted in violent mirth. *El Pajarito* let out a barbaric yawp, as barbaric a yawp as someone that size could release, I suppose, and soaked up the chants of praise. Everyone pulled out cloths or tissues and waved them frantically in the air. I sat alone in a sea of white. The woman next to me vigorously told me to take out my *pañuelo,* and scoffed when I didn't have one.

The young *torero* looked to the judge's panel box. The crowd sang his praises. After a few moments of deliberation, *El Pajarito* was awarded *los máximos trofeos*—both ears and the tail. Members of the Mickey Mouse Club severed them off with knives right there in the pit. The carcass was dragged by ponies out of the arena, leaving a crimson smudge in the sand.

I had no desire to watch another brutal round and contemplated leaving early. I probably would have, had I not been stuck between the family of melodramatics and gang of biceptoids. I sat through the next three fights mostly going through photos of my European trip on my phone. Right as I was scrolling through pictures of Berlin, with Kev and me and Lucky Star clanking a beer or smoking a cigarette, the woman next to me said something about my American ineptitude to appreciate a tradition of another culture, I suppose.

"Death should never be tradition," I said, not taking my eyes away from the phone screen. She didn't say anything. I didn't think she understood.

In a bullfight, three *toreros* kill two bulls each. By the time I looked up from my phone, *El Pajarito* was back in the arena, twirling around the sand, both arms raised high in the air. I hoped he would kill the poor thing quickly. I really had to piss. I wasn't sure how I would tell Lucia that I didn't like it. I didn't want to offend her or anything, but I also couldn't feign any interest—phonies did that. The crowd cheered for the young *torero* as they waited for the bull, and when he was finally released into the pit, the cheers changed to gasps that were silenced by the rolling thunder of hooves.

He dwarfed all the other bulls and stormed across the sand like a bowling ball with horns in a blurred black mass. When he slammed into the wine-red siding, the stadium rattled and quaked. His neck muscles appeared to begin below his chin and ran down into his chest, and the rest of his body rippled in the Spanish sun. I named him: GARGANTUAS.

The woman next to me held her hand over her mouth in astonishment, and her daughter began to cry. As much as I loathed the young *torero*, *El Pajarito* did not shy away from GARGANTUAS despite protests from the crowd to have him replaced. *El Pajarito* wasn't a phony. He and the Mickey Mouse Club succeeded in jamming all of their spears into the animal's back despite his muscles looking as thick and repellent as armor. But GARGANTUAS appeared unaffected by the weapons sticking out of his back and didn't seem to tire or lose a step. I liked to picture him with smoke emanating from his nostrils through a bouncing gold ring.

El Pajarito held the *muleta* and sword at his waist. Next to GARGANTUAS, the blade was the size of a toothpick. The young *torero* planted that axis foot and guided GARGANTUAS in perfectly symmetrical circles. The crowd *Olé*'d, but there was a timidity in their calls, like they were nervous to arouse the bull in any way. Throughout the event, I would scan the crowd when they waved their white tissues, a visual break from the violence. And when I saw *El Pajarito* bend at the waist, signifying the start of the final thrust to kill the bull, I again scanned the crowd, because I had come to like GARGANTUAS and did not wish to see him go. But this time I noticed another like myself, who wasn't standing or waving a white cloth in exuberance.

He wore a cloak with the hood pulled up on his head, which made only from his nose down visible. The people sitting in his row cheered and waved their *pañuelos* without giving him any attention. He remained motionless in his seat, appearing neither enthused nor disgusted by the fight. And after a few moments of staring at him without a blink, I realized I had seen him before, that he was that… thing at Cabo do Roca where that Slovakian (or were they Latvian?) couple fell off the cliff to their deaths—that thing I met in that abandoned little chapel in Sintra.

I couldn't accept that it was Death. I mean, if it was, then why had it not been sitting there for the deaths of those other three bulls? Why had he been so polite? Where was his scythe? Then my concentration was shattered by the blood-curdling scream of the woman next to me—he wasn't there for the bulls.

In the center of the pit, GARGANTUAS had *El Pajarito* flailing on his right horn. The young *torero* was stuck in his gooey middle, a goring that would make Vlad the Impaler lick his lips. The Mickey Mouse Club and others closed in on GARGANTUAS, stabbing him several times in an attempt to release the young *torero* from the terror. Medical personnel rushed to *El Pajarito*, but there was nothing they could do; the Little Bird died in the sand next to the bull.

I looked back for the hooded transient, but he was gone. The entire arena was engulfed in crying chaos. Old men cursed GARGANTUAS, who lay lifeless, bleeding out from several lacerations like a feral Julius Caesar. The future of the "sport" was gone, cut down in his prime like an American rock star.

Text from Lucia <3: 11:42 a.m.: Dios mío amor! I have heard what has happened to El Pajarito! Are you okay, my love?

I suppose news travels fast.

Text to Lucia <3: 11:42 a.m.: I'm fine Cordobesa, I decided not to fight today.

BEN D'ALESSIO

I awoke at the darkest hour of the night, my tongue and cheeks dried out. We had shared a tannic Tempranillo from up north, and I took a few shots of anis from a dusty bottle I found hidden in the cupboard when Lucia went to sleep.

I drank from the glass of water on the nightstand with floating dust and dead skin cells and tried to fall back asleep, but I couldn't. I lay in bed, scraping boogers out of my nose and combining them together to create a green meteorite, and flicked it onto the hardwood floor. I felt I had blown my chance with Death—if that's what I'm calling it—to get some answers about Adam. He was only a few feet away from me in that tiny chapel. I could always go to another bullfight and try and get lucky, I suppose, or wander the hospices of Europe.

Lucia was dreaming; I could hear the light patter of her lips. I recited pi, a trick my sixth-grade math teacher taught us for when we couldn't sleep: 3.14159, I started. I grabbed my phone. The light burned until my eyes adjusted. 26535. I had a text from Marcel. 89793.

Text from Marcel X: 4:00 a.m.: Bonsoir Joel. Ça va? How is Cordoba?

I clicked on my Facebook, went to Lucia's profile, and checked her relationship status—it still said **Single**. 23846. I wanted to change that. I wanted nothing more than to see: **Lucia is in a relationship with Joel Lupo**. 26433. When I brought it up to her, over that bloody red Tempranillo, she just giggled—83279—I don't think she understood. 50288.

I aimlessly scrolled my timeline, which had asinine statuses from people I didn't even like. I checked them anyway. 41971.

Ricky Tretola: Couldn't sleep so went to the gym. #Gym #Gymgrind #Swole #Selfie #weights #gymlife

Alexandra Marie Marcucci: SHOUT OUT to the coooolest dog of all time. Love my buddy. #bestfriend #wecute #youknowweare

THE 75 Best-Dressed MEN of all Time: From Dean to Damien Rogers

69399.

PROCESSED MEATS: HARBINGERS OF CANCER. Put DOWN the bacon America!

Clayton Wright Slams UC Santa-Berkeley, All Universities, for Liberal Agenda: "Schools like these send our youth directly into the mouth of the wolf."

Jessica Rae Goldenberg: OMG I love when Ryan randomly brings me flowers. Your the best bae! #LOVE #Boyfriend #HIM<3<3 #Ilovehim #myboyfriendisbetterthenyours Ryan Murphy

Comments:

Miguel Bautista: You're* #myboyfriendisbetterthAnyours*

Jessica Rae Goldenberg: SHUT UP Miguel! #GrammerNAZI!!

Miguel Bautista: GrammArNAZI*

Jessica Rae Goldenberg: -_____-

Riley Johansson: SPAIN why you so gawgeous?!? Loving the mediterranean life with Benjamin D'Alessio John Andrew Kingston #Spain #Andalusia #Jaen #TintoDeVerano #Tapas #Delicious

ALGERIA falls into all-out WAR: The African country is a three-headed thunderpunch. Civilians are the biggest losers. Will US? France? Come to aid?

I clicked on the Algeria link, which brought up a map of the country filled in with green, black, or red depending on the area. 37510. Almost the entire eastern part of the country was solid black except for slivers near the Tunisian border that said: *These sections are currently controlled by the Tunisian military. I checked the key: black = *al-Saif*, those crazy fuckers who were chopping people's heads off. Most of the coast, the populated part of the country, was green, which demarcated **Under regime control**. 58209. In the western corner was a red enclave surrounded by regime-controlled areas, the Moroccan border, and the

Mediterranean Sea. This area was noted as **Under rebel control**. The red extended from the Moroccan border town of Oujda to the outskirts of Oran. There was a short description for the rebels: **The rebels are made up of mostly Algerian military defectors and Algerian youth, and there have been reports of Moroccans and other internationals fighting alongside the rebels.**

I scrolled through pictures of the president from six months ago, standing below an Algerian fighter jet. The caption read: **President Hannachi is seen here at the Air Force base at Biskra–an area currently contested by al-Saif.** 74944. **This is one of the last known photographs of the president, who is rumored to be pent-up in the Presidential Palace with numerous concubines and meals delivered daily from Paris and Lyon.** 59230.

Lucia shifted violently in the bed, and half awake, asked if everything was okay. I told her I was fine and just having trouble sleeping. I asked her if we could go to Zuheros soon, that I had done some research on it and that it looked really interesting. I even tried to use some Spanish: "*Quiero ver la cueva de los... los... mur-ci-e-lagos.*" She didn't acknowledge my attempt and turned back over and said "No... no... silly American boy."

I saved the Algeria article to finish later. I hadn't dreamt about Adam in a while, and that bothered me. I didn't care if the dreams were frightening. I welcomed the darkness, remember? I wasn't afraid of being scared; I was afraid of going numb.

"I am the master of my fate. I am the captain of my soul, I suppose," I said, staring up at the ceiling.

"Go to sleep, *Americano*."

That morning, Lucia and I stared at each other in bed, half of our faces buried in the pillow. Her eyes had lost that intoxicating luster. They were green; I suppose they always had been.

I grabbed the laptop and played "Blitzkrieg Bop." She stared at me confused.

"It's the Ramones? You were wearing... never mind." I changed it to "Spring Forever." The drum pedals kicked in and I smiled and said, "This is probably my ..." but before I could finish, she cut me off.

"I don't like this, *Americano*. I don't like this music. I like Mad-Mannix. You like *'La voz de la generación'?*"

"Oh… no, not really."

She looked at me and tilted her head and said, "You are a pretty boy."

"We don't call boys 'pretty,' *Cordobesa*."

"Handsome, no?"

"Yes, handsome."

"You are a handsome boy."

"I'm a man…"

"Yes, *Americano*… of course."

She said it in the kind of way that made me feel inadequate, like the first time I saw my father's penis. She got out of bed and I watched her ass as she walked to the closet and put on a robe. She was so beautiful, and I appreciated that wholeheartedly. I never took her beauty for granted, I binged on it. But beauty can run its course, I suppose. If she had proposed marriage before that morning, I would've said yes, I swear I would've. I would've done it in an attempt to seal love in its purest form and then at least give it a chance. What is love for you? Is love butterflies or razor blades in your stomach? For the poets, love is addiction. For me, love is jealous paranoia, suffocating anxiety that is only addictive when I lack it.

So I went on loving her like one loves a flower, with admiration, with each and every sense, but with the knowledge that soon it would end, and like the flower, be buried in the layers of the soil to serve as the foundation for a love that has not yet withered. Love for me? Perhaps love was not for me. There is no love but perfect love, but love cannot stay perfect. Love with Lucia was an ephemeral love, and the flame was flickering in the gust.

She didn't have to work today, so she took me to the *Mezquita*. She had probably been inside of that giant a dozen times and mostly stayed on her phone. I tried to kiss her as we walked through the forest of columns with those red-brick striped arches, but she turned away. She never kissed me in public, not once. I tried to hold her hand as we observed the glittering *mihrab*—the arch that points to Mecca—covered in golden Arabic script on a canvas of deep-sea blue, but she pushed that away, too. She told me to go wander and enjoy "the history." She said it like I was some brute, some barbarian from the underdeveloped, uncivilized land "out there."

I sat by myself in a pew in the cathedral. The building, like so much of Europe, was layered in history. First, a Visigothic church that was split between a church and mosque, then purchased to be completely converted into a mosque, and finally, during the Christian "reconquest" of Spain and Portugal, a Catholic cathedral. The Christian kings refused to simply tear down the giant, so instead, over the years, each Christian king made his own additions, no matter how controversial. I liked the place—I mean, it was fine—but I was in no mood to contemplate the architectural creations of overly ambitious men. I was upset, dammit. I don't mean to prate on the issue, but Lucia had been perfect and to witness the perfection melt away, well, it did a number on me, I suppose.

I looked up at the hanging crucifix. I held back tears. I realized I hadn't prayed in a while, not since Adam's funeral. *Do I even remember how to pray?* Praying was like riding a bike, I suppose. So I recited the "Our Father," or what I remembered of it.

Lucia was on her phone beneath one of those thin orange trees. Before I could ask her what we should do now, she turned and started to walk, as if giving me the choice whether or not to follow. I wondered how long it would take her to realize if I just left. I remained a few feet behind as we walked through the tiny streets with artisan shops and intimate tapas bars. She stopped to talk to a man who sold hand-made pottery—she didn't introduce me. I felt like a phantom watching over her shoulder from another dimension.

We walked through the Almodóvar Gate, a medieval wall lined with perfectly symmetrical triangular points. We came upon a statue of a man in a toga, and in his hand was a rolled-up scroll. She stopped in front of the statue.

"This is Seneca. He was born…"

"I know who Seneca is," I snapped. "He died in a hot bath with slit wrists."

She turned and headed toward her apartment without saying another word. When we got back, she rushed into her room and slammed the door. I sat in the

BINGE UNTIL TRAGEDY

kitchen and poured myself a glass of Spanish brandy I had found with the anis. I waited for my phone to connect to the WiFi so I could text Riley.

Text to Queen of Campus <3<3: 1:15 p.m.: Hey… where are you?

Lucia went to bed early; she didn't kiss me goodnight. I couldn't sit and wait for her to tell me to leave, or more plausibly, make up some excuse so I had no choice *but* to leave, like she was visiting a friend in Madrid or Harry in London. So in the middle of the night, I threw whatever clothes I could find into my bag. When I was unraveling one of my button-down shirts from the bed frame, I stepped on a whimpering floorboard that I was certain would wake her up. *Squeeeeeeeak*.

Her eyes opened slightly, but they had that translucent film over them, like a cat, which gave them a harrowing, dead appearance. I took a few cans of tuna, a block of cheese, a link of chorizo, two tomatoes, and that bottle of Spanish brandy, and slinked out the front door—I would've taken that leg of *jamón* too, if it fit in my bag.

I felt like I had won this way, a preemptive strike. I wasn't going to give her the satisfaction. Hopefully she'd wake up confused and disoriented. I didn't leave anything, either, not even a note. Maybe she would think it was all a dream—we didn't even take a picture together, after all. That's when it started to hurt. The high of emotionally outmaneuvering Lucia was usurped by a draining sadness, as if something had been pulling me right from my pit, down, down, down.

I found a cozy nook on a cramped street where no one would bother me. I suppose I had become accustomed to sleeping in public, because I didn't hesitate to unpack my bag and create a makeshift bed right there on the stone. The gold glow from a front door's lantern emanated enough light so I could continue reading *Infinite Jest* until I fell asleep.

BEN D'ALESSIO

The pungent odor of spilled beer drying on a passing Spaniard's t-shirt woke me from a light slumber. I eventually found my way to the train station and took the earliest iron horse to Granada, where Riley was staying in a hostel with Ben.

Life is not a dream. Careful! Careful! Careful!
We fall down the stairs in order to eat the moist earth
or we climb to the knife edge of the snow with the voices of the dead
      dahlias.
But forgetfulness does not exist, dreams do not exist;
flesh exists. Kisses tie our mouths
in a thicket of new veins,
and whoever his pain pains will feel that pain forever
and whoever is afraid of death will carry it on his shoulders.

—Federico García Lorca, "City That Does Not Sleep"

GRANADA

THE COMPACT CAR CLIMBED THE STEEP WHITE labyrinth of tiny cobblestone streets that formed the Albayzín. Like Jerusalem, Granada was at one point divided into quadrants in accordance with religious affiliation—this was the Muslim quarter.

The cabbie dropped me off at a flight of descending steps and made the hand motions that signified "down there and to the right." I stopped at a building with a dark wood door and black iron handle that resembled something medieval. A blue sign out front bore the universal white "H" of hostels. The cramped white buildings reflected the rays of the oppressive Spanish sun, and there always seemed to be at least a sliver of shade to jump into like a puddle in the rain.

A woman of about thirty-five answered the door and welcomed me inside. She appeared more Italian than Spanish and sung her English, which was pretty to the ear. I told her I was meeting a friend, but before I could finish my explanation, Riley came bursting through a hanging bead-door that, when undisturbed, displayed a portrait of the Virgin Mary.

"Joelie!" she cried, her arms stretched out, her fingers pulling at the air. "Your beard is already starting to come back."

I hid a smile and I'm not sure why. I was happy to see Riley, and it wasn't until I saw her that I realized how much I had missed her.

"Where's El Ben?" I asked as I finally gave in to a hug.

"He's out on a hammock reading. He's always reading. Oh! Tell me you have that stupid book. He has not shut up about it."

"Yeah, yeah, yeah, I've got it."

"Okay, good. Come out back. How are you? Are you okay? Ugh, poor baby. Have some of this." She handed me a glass of cheap Garnacha. "Everything is better after a glass or three of wine!"

"Out back" was an intimate enclosure of cobblestone levels with pink and purple hammocks hanging from trees. Tables seemed to be haphazardly placed throughout the enclosure, and there was a nook or two where you could curl up by yourself and read or nap.

I followed Riley up a ladder that led to a tree house with beanbag chairs and cigarette fillings covering the floorboards. Of course, someone had a guitar.

"Yo, comrade, you have my book?" said Ben, one eyebrow comically raised.

"Riley said you were reading," I shot back, scanning for a place to sit.

"So? That doesn't mean I don't want my book."

"What are you reading?"

"Riles…" A bolt cut through me—only I called her that. "Is he serious?"

"He has your book. Joel, stop being a dick."

"Oh… okay, good. Well, I'm reading *Iberia* by James A…"

"Does anyone have a cigarette?" I interrupted.

A guy with a budding mustache and cracked lips put a hand-rolled cigarette right below my nose. "Thanks," I said.

"*De rien.*"

"*Ah! Parlez-vous français?*" I said, trying at the end to hide the excitement in my voice.

"Oh, right! Joel, this is Étienne," said Riley, exhaling a fume of smoke. "And that is Michel," she said, pointing to the guy rolling another cigarette. "And that…"—she took another drag and exhaled, and she must've eaten some of the smoke, because I could see her eyes begin to water—"is Zacharie." She pointed to the fellow slumped down in the pocket of his beanbag chair, wearing sunglasses, his head tilting off the edge. "They are from Dijon."

"*Comme c'est génial! Je l'ai attendu à utiliser mon français, mais à chaque fois...*" I started.

"We speak English as well," said Étienne.

"Zacharie is quite good at it," said Michel before dragging his tongue across the rolling paper.

"*Mais...*"

"Like I was saying," Ben started, "if we don't strengthen the gun laws in America, this shit is never going to stop. I mean, it's easier for me to get an assault rifle than my college transcripts, for Christ's sake."

"What the fuck are you talking about?"

"Americans with the 'fuck.' So cool," added Michel, bobbing his head up and down.

"The shooting… yesterday?" said Riley.

"What?"

"Joel…" she started in a soothing voice, "there was shooting at the University of Kansas yesterday. Nineteen people were killed… You didn't hear about it?"

"Kansas?" asked Étienne, letting out a plume of smoke. "That is like Texas, no?"

"What?"

Ben, who was inspecting *Infinite Jest* like an artifact, dropped the tome on the wood table with a *thud* and woke Zacharie up from his nap. "Kid walked onto campus and just started spraying. Didn't even look like he was really aiming. Had two AR-15s, one equipped and one slung across his back, a 9mm, and an Uzi. Kid got a fucking Uzi!" He took a deep, dramatic drag from a Carolina Filter. "Girl captured the whole thing on her phone from her dorm window."

"Is there WiFi out here?" I asked.

"We're in a fucking tree house," Ben snapped.

"Was he dead too?" asked Michel.

"Yeah, he put one in the back of his mouth before SWAT could arrive." Ben made a gun with his fingers and put it in his mouth, dropped his thumb like the hammer to a revolver, and snapped his head back. "Fucking pussy."

"A girl said that in order to hide, she smeared blood from her dead friend all over her face and shirt and just lay there," Riley said, shivering as she visualized it.

"Blood doesn't really bother me," I said, exhaling smoke.

"Not really the point here, amigo."

"I would've tried to tackle him," I said. "Unless I had a gun. Then I would've killed 'im."

"You would've tackled a guy with a fucking machine gun?" asked Ben.

"Yeah. Back when there was that spree of shootings…"

"The ones in Florida?" asked Riley.

"No, out in Oregon," I said.

"The farmers market shooting?"

"That was Nebraska," said Ben.

"There was a shooting at University of Oregon?" asked Riley.

"No. At like, a community college."

"I think I remember a *fusillade* in the state of Caroline, no?" said Étienne.

"They have two states of Caroline. North and South," said Zacharie.

"The *fusillade* with the racist one?" clarified Étienne as he licked the cigarette paper.

"There was a shooting in Texas, no?" asked Michel.

"There was one in Arizona, you mean that?" asked Riley.

"In Chicago, no?" asked Zacharie.

"There are always shootings in Chicago," said Ben.

"There was a shooting in Texas. I am sure of it," said Michel. "From the tower?"

"Oh! Yeah, but that was like, in the sixties," said Ben.

"So is Kansas in Texas? I mean, is Kansas *like* Texas?" asked Michel.

"There was that shooting spree in Ohio," said Riley. "You mean those?"

"I thought that was a bomb attack?" asked Zacharie.

"That was Oklahoma. Also a while ago," corrected Ben.

"I remember those shootings in Kansas," said Riley.

"Isn't that what we're talking about?" asked Ben.

"Wait… maybe I'm thinking of those shootings in Colorado. Not Columbine, the other ones."

"*All* I know is that if a shooter came on my campus, I would've fucked him up. I used to imagine it," I said.

"You used to have fantasies about a school shooting?" asked Ben.

"Yeah… but I'd thwart it before he could hit anyone. I mean, *I'd* take a bullet or two in the process, but nothing fatal."

"Most guys have fantasies about scoring the winning touchdown, chief…"

"Joel, you wouldn't even go quail hunting with my stepdad!" shouted Riley.

"That's because I was hung over! *Not* because I didn't know how to shoot a gun. You remember in Prague? I beat Kev at a shoot-off. Remember how upset he got? Because he and his dad go hunting all the time. I think we even used AR-15s!"

"Too soon," said Riley.

"You mean the friend you 'outed'?" said Ben.

"Shut up," she said, smacking him on the knee.

"What the fuck, Riles?! What did you tell him?"

"I love Americans with the 'fuck,'" said Michel. "Always 'fuck this,' 'fuck that,' 'fuck fuck fuck.'"

"*Ta gueule!*" I shouted.

I slung my backpack over my shoulder and fireman-slid down the wood ladder, a splinter puncturing the soft meat below my thumb on my way down. I popped open the wood door with the medieval iron handle and it slammed against the supporting wall. I started up the wide-spaced cobblestone steps that burned my thighs if I didn't take an extra step in between. Riley hopped up the steps like a hurdler, and when she finally caught up to me, she grabbed my shoulder and said, "Joel, wait!"

"What! What is it? You barely know this guy and you're casually telling him problems about your best friend? Real great pillow talk, Riles."

"… We're best friends?"

"Yes! No shit. I mean, you won't let me be anything else…"

After I said this, she tilted her head and squinted her eyes and started to say something but stopped herself.

"Never mind. Just drop it."

"Joel… I…"

"I said drop it." I looked around and tried to get a sense of where we were. The unrelenting sun was just as oppressive as it was in Seville. "If I stay out here for one more second, my skin is going to melt from my bones."

"Let's go grab a drink or something. I want to catch up. I want to hear all about this Spanish *mamacita* you left me for."

We turned into the first tapas bar we could find and sat at a tiny table in front of a window that faced a narrow street, and I watched as delivery trucks slowed down enough so they wouldn't pop up onto the curb. The walls were black with a glittering gold paisley design and on the bar sat three ham legs with their black hooves in the air, reminding me of cancan dancers at the Moulin Rouge.

"So… what, like… happened?"

"I don't know, Riles. For a while we were perfect, like zombies and chainsaws, I suppose."

"Interestingly put."

I wasn't in the mood to drink, but Riley insisted we order a bottle of bloody red wine. It was bold and earthy, and when I lifted my lips from the glass, velvet streaks ran down the side.

"I wanted to go flying off to paradise… and I did… for a while, before crashing down to Earth."

"You do that, you know."

"Do what?"

"You build these girls up…"

"I don't want to hear it, Riles."

"No, listen. You build these girls up and then when they can't live up to your insurmountable standards, you break them down and start to overanalyze everything."

"Into tiny cubes."

"What? Yeah, sure, but I've seen you do it." She then listed the reasons for my previous breakups, giving each one a finger on her hand. "You stopped talking to Liz because she was a Red Sox fan. You stopped talking to Ally because she likes Mad-Mannix…"

"She kept referring to him as the 'voice of our generation'!"

"Who cares?!"

"If he's the 'voice of our generation,' we should cut out our tongue."

"You randomly stopped talking to Toni for some reason…"

"She reminded me too much of my cousin!"

"…"

"…"

"Fine. But you *broke up* with Karen, who was a really good friend of mine, so thanks for making that awkward, because she had sex with some guy you got in an argument with at the bar…"

"Jeremy Rothman."

"Because she had sex with Jeremy Rothman TWO YEARS before you guys started dating."

"Yeah, well…"

"Oh! And what about Chloe? That girl is in *love* with you, Joel. Trust me, I'm a girl."

"Okay, okay, okay, holy fuck. Well, what about you, huh? You hop on different guys like a frog on lily pads."

"…You know I have trust issues."

"Yeah, well that happened, like, what? Five years ago?"

"So what?! That's fucked up."

The bartender was looking at us with a furrowed brow from behind the hanging legs of ham. I looked at Riley and then down at my wine glass, which I had been nervously swirling during the conversation. The red nectar coated the glass and the legs dribbled down like expanding alien fingers. I stopped myself from prying into the matter anymore. I was in the wrong, I can admit that.

"So you really like this Ben guy?" She sat back in her seat and began to laugh. I was confused but happy. God, I loved that laugh. I think I missed it the most. "What?" I said, starting to laugh myself.

"Oh, nothing… it's just… this isn't going to help my case."

"What?"

"You remember that artist from Prague, Miloš?"

"Yes… we *did* stay in his apartment."

"Well… he's attending an expo in San Sebastián next week and he asked *me* to be his date!"

"That's… that's great, Riles."

"And get this! After, we're flying to Dubrovnik to stay at his place on the beach. Ugh! Have you seen pics of this place? It's gawgeous. Here." She took out her phone and starting scrolling through edited photos of Dubrovnik, that gem on the Dalmatian coast.

"Looks great," I said.

"Aww, Joelie… Are you going to miss me?"

"If neither of us is married by the time we're thirty, let's get hitched," I blurted.

She was taken aback, but instead of laughing at the proposal or outright rejecting it, she sat back in her seat, nodded her head a few times, and said, "Okay."

"Yeah?"

"Yeah. I mean, thirty feels so far away. Might as well be an eternity… haha."

And I wish I had gotten up from that little table near the window and left the tapas bar right then. I wish I had taken the next flight to Newark International or JFK—I could've, there was one leaving from Madrid that night. I could've gone home and waited for the next nine years or until eternity and everything would've been in its right place, but I didn't. I stayed at the table and polished off that bottle of bloody red wine with Riley and asked her, "Hey, have you spoken to Marcel recently?"

"No… why?"

"He texts me, like, every day. He really wants me to go to Morocco with him."

"I didn't know you and Marcel talked…"

"We didn't really. I mean, not if you weren't there."

"Huh… well… what's he want you to do?"

"I can't really tell. You know him, though, always getting worked up about things but never acting on them."

"Right. Remember when he 'went to the police brutality protest' in Philly?"

"When that kid was killed walking home from school in Strawberry Mansion?"

"Yeah. Well, Marcel never went. He was in my bed the entire time."

"Oh really?"

"He made me keep the news on while we… ya know."

"Whatever gets it hard, I suppose."

"Wait, so what is he saying?"

"Just about the shit taking place in Algeria."

"It's getting really bad. Ben brings it up all the time. I try and tell him, like, what are we supposed to do? Ya know? I tell him, 'Why don't you go fight, then?' and he gets all fired up. I think it makes the sex better."

"Yeah… well, I bet we would just get to Morocco and go like, sightseeing or something. Probably go to Fez. His sister is there now."

"That's probably it then. He just has to make everything so dramatic… Hey! Let's take a reunited pic for the album." She pushed back her chair and walked around the table and rested her chin on my trap muscle so our cheeks were touching. She held her phone out in front of us and right before her thumb clicked the touchscreen button, she turned and kissed my cheek. We had probably taken a hundred pictures like that throughout college, but this one felt different, I suppose.

"So Ben wants to take me to the Alhambra. He raves about it. You want to come?"

"No, thanks. I'm enervated."

"… Never change, Joelie."

We went back to the hostel where she met Ben to leave for the red Moorish castle that overlooked the city. She gave me the key to her room and said I could stay there until I figured out what I wanted to do. She and Ben shared a private single with a tiny barred window that looked out onto the terrace where the hammocks hung like iridescent spider webs. I lay in their bed with the pale pink sheets and stared at the ceiling, counting cracks and crevices like I was back in the fifth grade, grounded in my room. The odors of balm and musk and dried sex overpowered my senses; I could taste their sin. My phone, which was on the nightstand next to my head, finally connected to the WiFi and rattled to the vibrations of incoming texts. I decided I needed to text Kev and Sal, and definitely have my mom drop some funds into my account so I could take a flight home.

I grabbed my phone, intending to message all of those people, but got sidetracked by a notification for an article on Algeria I had started and saved for later. I scrolled through the pictures of decimated buildings that had been bombarded by mortar fire and now sat in piles of smoking white silt. Everyone had blood on them, always. In every picture of a tan man with a face of pain, waving his fists in the air, he was covered in blood.

In one photo with the caption "Optimistic Algerian Youths," three boys, all who looked around my age, held AK-47s in one hand and flashed the peace sign with the other. Even if those three boys never fired a shot from those guns, they would be immortalized as freedom fighters of the Algerian Revolution. They stood for something and I wanted that. Sometimes, and I know it sounds backwards and selfish, but sometimes I wished I came from a place or time less stable, where I could make a name for myself. There are no heroes in a bull market, I suppose.

This one time, Adam and I were playing paintball up in that desolate backwoods of New Jersey known as northern Passaic County. We must've been fifteen or so, and we were the last two survivors on our team. It was five on two, and Adam and I took out all five of them using the guerilla tactics we had practiced in the backyard. I got the final kill. I purposely used red paintballs so it looked more like a kill, and on this final one, I shot the kid right in the mouth. The paint splat a pretty red and shot through the air holes on his mask. The sudden burst of vegetable oil had him bent over and heaving. The entire ride home, I imagined if those guns had been real killing machines, and that paint a hollow-tipped bullet that ripped the jaw clean off my enemy's face.

But a real fight? Yeah, there was one time for that too, and no, it wasn't with Sal. But I did get into a real fight during a hockey game my senior year of high school. Despite leading the team in scoring as a junior, I was not named a captain, and I took it to heart, I suppose.

I had already picked a college that fall, so I was usually drunk or high or some hybrid of both during the second semester. And it was toward the end of the season and we were average, so fucking average, that I didn't care anymore and skated the rink like a shark. The key bumps on the bus ride out there made me feel like a wrecking ball gone completely numb. So when one of their defensemen hit Adam late and from behind, I scorched down the rink, planning to use my skate blades as a scimitar and my stick as a halberd.

I went airborne and earholed the kid—he never saw me coming. He pulled me down with him, but my momentum carried me right into a devastating uppercut that unlocked the hockey mask from its hinges. I rained down a barrage of haymakers directly onto his exposed face, and the last ripped a cut open right above his eyebrow and blood spurted onto my mask and dripped onto the ice. I was eventually tackled by their entire second line, but the fight caused a bench-clearing brawl and I was a wanted man throughout Essex County. I thought my dad was going to erupt like Vesuvius, but on the car ride home he said, "I'm proud of you. That kid had it coming. He was throwing cross checks and slashes all game. Always fight for those less fortunate than you. Joel, you listenin'? Always fight for Adam."

I continued to scroll through photos on the Algerian article and stopped when I came to one of a boy sitting on a hospital bed covered in dirt and dried blood. He had dusty hair and was crying as a doctor put a stethoscope to his chest. The caption read: **The last words of a five-year old boy whose home was hit by a regime mortar: "I'm going to tell God everything."** I stared at the photo and couldn't scroll any further. I felt a heaviness in my chest, like I was being pressed to death and yelling, "More weight!"

I couldn't do it.

I couldn't go home and apply to graduate school or fill out job applications like some type of millennial Sisyphus who needed experience to get the job, but needed the job to get experience. The thought of sitting in a cubicle with my wrists chained to a desktop made me so anxious I thought it would give me diarrhea. I texted Marcel.

Text to Marcel: 2:19 p.m.: Bonjour Marcel. Ça va? Je suis intéressé à aller au Maroc avec tu.

I could finally get to use my French, and "Fought in the Algerian Revolution" would look good on my resume, I suppose.

TARIFA

MARCEL AND MEHDI WERE TWO DOTS IN THE PEACH sand. As I walked down the beach to meet them, the salt air bristled my hair, which had grown shaggy, and I pulled granules of sand out of my dark beard. They were in t-shirts and shorts instead of the traditional all-white *thobe* that Marcel had worn in Lisbon. They saw me trudging down the beach, sneakers in hand and jeans cuffed around the ankles, and welcomed me like I was a fellow comrade returning from the battlefront.

"*Bonjour,* Joel! Are you ready to make history?" shouted Marcel, his arms stretched out by his side. I tried to use French, but Mehdi only spoke in Arabic. When I then tried to use Arabic, the few words and phrases I had retained from my single semester, he switched to English, unable to comprehend that an American could speak more than one language, I suppose. I didn't care for Mehdi; he was a jamoke. But I still enjoyed Marcel's company enough not to turn around and head back into insular Spain.

Mehdi also rarely looked directly at me when he spoke. He dropped to his knees and grabbed two handfuls of sand, letting the grains seep through his fingers, and said, "Did you know this was where the Moors—they were Muslims—launched the invasion of Europe? The last time this continent had some civilization…"

"I thought that was Gibraltar?" I said, remembering one of Ben's lectures on Iberian multiculturalism.

"Did you know Gibraltar derives from Arabic? It derives from *Jabal Ṭāriq*, the name of an Arab general. Many places in Spain have names that come from Arabic." He picked up more sand and gripped it tight, as if trying to squeeze out any civilization that might be left behind from the footsteps of Moorish generals who walked these shores before him. "Last era this continent had some culture."

"Aren't you from Paris? The most cultured city on the fucking planet?" I said.

He threw down the sand and pulled out a circular string of beads, rubbing the tip of his thumb over each one. "Why always Americans and the 'fucking'?"

"*Mon ami*, have you checked in to the hostel?" asked Marcel.

"*Oui, je l'ai déjà fait*," I said. The receptionist had pointed down to the beach where I could find them.

"*Bien. Nous prenons le bateau tôt demain matin.*"

Mehdi started to translate, "He said, 'We take the boat early…'"

"I speak French!" I snapped, and looking back, I probably should have shouted that *in* French.

"*Je vais maintenant revenir.* Do you want to come, Joel?"

"No, thanks," I said. "I'm gonna sit here for a little."

"*D'accord.*"

I remained in the sand, knees in my arms, as they gathered their things and walked back to the hostel. I watched as windsurfers cut and crashed through waves of blended turquoise and white foam. I walked down to the cold water and let it cover my feet, and I felt the breath of Africa.

THE BATTLE OF ORAN

SALIM SAT IN A WOBBLING WOODEN CHAIR WITH HIS AK-47 draped across his lap. He had not spoken to Farah or Mohamed since arriving in Oran, and called his mother once from a disposable cell phone so she wouldn't worry—he told her he was still in Algiers. He had joined an underground network of the FLA that had ties to *La Liberté*. Salim was welcomed when he disclosed that he was from Algiers and had clandestinely traveled to Oran to fight. The government had shut down all rail lines that connected the cities to each other. The only rebel-controlled territory was the most northwestern pocket of the country, squeezed between the border with Morocco and the Mediterranean Sea.

Skirmishes had taken place on the outskirts of Oran since the rebels, who had been unifying in Morocco, broke through the border. The General had been assigned by Hannachi to guard Oran and keep order in any way possible. He formed his own secret police—an exact replica of *La Peste* in Algiers—to patrol the streets. The *Cathédrale du Sacré-Cœur d'Oran*, a Roman-Catholic remnant of French colonial times that had since become a library, was the headquarters for the General's operations. Since the institution of martial law in all of government-controlled Algeria, the General had the books torn from the shelves and burned in the streets to make room to board his personal soldiers. The library had become a hedonistic funhouse where soldiers drank shipments of whiskey and wine and took women they ripped from their homes, dragging them from makeshift rooms divided by nothing but a dirty bed sheet. If the women resisted, they were charged with assaulting a government soldier and flogged in the public square.

Salim witnessed a "dissident" receive twenty lashes in front of the library while her family was forced to watch up close—her father didn't flinch when blood spattered from the lash onto his shirt. Salim didn't understand why his leader, Farouk, a thirty-year-old defector who was hiding out in the city, refused to create some type of diversion in order to stop the flogging. Farouk urged Salim not to allow his nerves to get the better of him. If they miscalculated their attack, they could be quelled before they inflicted any real damage upon the regime, so Salim stood silent as lash struck skin.

The medical student couldn't sit anymore; his blood vessels buzzed and popped into his skin. He rose and stood by the window and ran his hand along a diagonal crack cutting across the glass from corner to corner. His stomach growled like a bubbling pot and he itched all over. He had been sleeping on a thin mattress crammed into the corner of a tiny naked room—he shared it with three other rebels from Algiers. He worried about his mother. Last he had heard, *al-Saif* had taken Constantine from the Tunisian Army, which was leaving its ally in Algiers and retreating back to their own borders. He prayed the Islamists would turn their focus to Algiers, where he would return and defend the city, and away from Tebessa in the East. That's what kept his hometown and family safe during the Olive Protests—no one cared about Tebessa.

In the distance, orange busts began erupting into the sky like dragons sending salutations to each other across the city. When one exploded close enough that it shook the floor, Salim came to. They were the signals—the battle had begun. In a frenzy, he grabbed his assault rifle and stumbled to the door. He slipped over his untied shoelace and barely broke his fall. With his cheek lying on the dusty floor, he could only see Farouk's weathered combat boots in the doorway, the commander's voice yelling at him to get up.

He followed Farouk to the underground garage where a fleet of twenty vans reinforced with armor had been sitting idle, waiting for the attack. Salim took his station in the back with the rest of his squadron. Farouk rode up front in the passenger seat. The vans burst out of the ground and screamed down the highway that hugged the coast, weaving in and out of unsuspecting traffic. There were slits in the sides of the van where a squad member could crouch and shoot. Farouk ordered his team to engage any military personnel or secret police. Their mission was to take back the library and completely rout out the General in one day.

The explosions going off around the city were coordinated bombs planted at military checkpoints and secret police hangouts. Bomb specialists who had defected from the army set out on covert missions to plant the bombs around the city. Salim hadn't known the details.

As the van pushed down the highway, some of the bombs were still going off like crashing symbols to an orchestra of car alarms. Civilians swerved to the side of the road in order to allow the roaring fleet to pass.

In beautiful coordination, different vans would turn off at different exits and head to their points of attack—their plan was to keep the General's men as thinly spread and occupied as possible. They had become drunk with vice, and Farouk had noted that they rarely performed military drills anymore. Their van headed toward the library to engage the General directly. Loud bursts popped into the side of the van, causing the metal to indent, but not rupture—the reinforcements had worked. Salim peeked through the slits in the side and saw soldiers chasing after them, stumbling into their cars.

Farouk shouted an order that Salim couldn't understand, but the guy sitting next to him told him to hold on to one of the bars welded onto the sides for support. Another soldier, a defector from the outskirts of Oran, swiped a blanket covering an object in the middle of the van and tossed it aside, revealing a light machine gun—"light" compared to heavy artillery, these guns were typically fashioned to the tops of trucks, not the insides of vans. Farouk shouted orders to open the back doors, which swung open to reveal the three secret police cars chasing after the van. The young defector unloaded on the cars while two others held him in place so he wouldn't fall from the weight of the gun. The machine gobbled the large bullets from the magazine belt and spit out the casings, which pinged and rattled around the inside of the van.

The three cars swerved and crashed into each other and the guard rails as they pulled the door closed and sped off.

Eventually, the van came to a screeching halt, forcing Salim to smash into the rebel next to him. Up ahead, regime soldiers had formed a sandbag barrier and were firing at the van. The rebels jumped out the back and hid behind pillars lining the sides of the street.

Salim took cover behind a dirty gray pillar where bullets had already ripped off chunks of the stone. Every time he peeked around to aim a shot, a bullet whizzed into the pillar or into the windshield of a car parked on the street behind him. Salim blindly turned the gun toward the barrier and fired, but his wrists weren't strong enough to handle the kickback of the assault rifle, so he dropped it in plain sight. Farouk, who was similarly crouched behind a pillar across the street, signaled to Salim that he was going to cover him, giving the young rebel a chance to retrieve his weapon.

Farouk turned out of the pillar and ripped off shot after shot. Salim watched Farouk's rippling forearm muscles contract and relax as the sun reflected off his shaved head. Farouk's beard was dark and plush, and his shoulders and chest were so built, he appeared to have natural body armor. Salim, who so much adored American cinema, couldn't resist comparing the commando to a modern-day Algerian Rambo.

Salim gathered himself and lunged for the weapon, covering his head as bullets plunged into the glass and steel of parked cars all around him. As he began his jump back behind the pillar, a blast from the middle of the boulevard shot Salim into the chain-link gate of a restaurant that made a merguez dish that reminded him of his mother's. He had always made sure to stop there when he was visiting friends and missing his mother's cooking on the other side of the country. Coughing and discombobulated, Salim looked across the boulevard to see Farouk mouthing commands, but he could not hear what Rambo was shouting over the ringing in his ears or the searing pain emanating from his leg, which punctured the adrenaline rush urban warfare had given him. Salim sat in the rubble, meagerly reaching for his gun through the dust and smoke. He touched the back of his head and looked at his hand—it was bright red. Blood never really bothered him. He was a medical student, after all. But this was his blood and his pain, so he sat in silent panic as the bullets and bombs decimated the city blocks around him.

Constantine, the City in the Sky, was a shell of its former self. *Al-Saif* had successfully breached the city to find the vast majority of the four hundred sixty thousand inhabitants gone and the Tunisian military outposts vacated. Those who decided to stay behind either sympathized with the group's message or stubbornly refused to leave their ancestral home. Regardless of their reasons for remaining in the city, all had to succumb to the strict interpretations of Sharia law that guided *al-Saif* from the desert and into the mountains. Their trucks were draped in the iconic black flag, and gunners who stood at the light machine guns fired bullets into the air to the calls of "*Allahu Akbar!*"

Four wounded Tunisian soldiers, who were accidentally left behind in an abandoned house, were pulled out onto the street. They knelt bandaged and shaking in front of a faux tribunal composed of Youssouf, Simon, and al-Maghribi—the leader sat in the center, slightly raised on a makeshift platform of scrap metal. He charged the soldiers with "crimes against Islam" and "supporting the *Kafir* State." Their punishment was death.

Al-Maghribi called out four names, and four surprised men walked out of the mass of black-clad jihadists. Youssouf ordered the camera boys to start filming, capturing the moment from all angles. Al-Maghribi addressed the president of Tunisia: "Here kneel four of your *kafir* henchmen. Enemies of Islam! Betrayers of God!" Al-Maghribi paced behind the row of kneeling soldiers with his scimitar resting on his shoulder. The camera cut. He ordered the four jihadists to each stand behind one of the kneeling soldiers. Black scarves covered their faces so only their eyes were showing, and they each held a large hunting knife. "Behind them stand four soldiers of God. Also sons of Tunisia, who have found the true calling of Islam! If the Tunisian military continues to attack the true Caliphate, their doom will be imminent!"

The camera boys crouched down to get the shot. The four jihadists pushed the wounded soldiers into the ground and began to sever their necks. Red and white fluids oozed onto the ground from their neck holes. The severed heads were placed on the smalls of the backs of the decapitated bodies—this had become their standard execution procedure. Someone set a Tunisian flag on fire and threw it in front of the headless. The camera cut to black.

Simon Turner stayed seated as the jihadists cheered and cried, "*Allahu Akbar!*" If he stood up, it would reveal his erection. Al-Maghribi led the roaring men to a white marble statue of the Roman emperor Constantine, the city's namesake. Youssouf yelled at the camera boys to run up ahead and capture shots of the group. The men wrapped ropes around the statue's neck and waist and outstretched arm and pulled it to the ground, where it crumbled into three separate pieces. Al-Maghribi handed Simon a sledgehammer. The men gathered around the American and shouted his name: "*Al-Arizona! Allahu Akbar! Al-Arizona!*" Simon stared at the head of the hammer. He flipped it in his hands, over and over, and grabbed at the handle with so much strength he could feel his palm skin tighten around the wood. He looked at al-Maghribi, who nodded with an appeasing endorsement. Simon found a camera boy and pointed into the lens. "This is a warning to the crusader states!" He continued in his distinct American English, "Your support of the apostates will not be tolerated. After we take Algiers, we will take Tunis and Rabat, and then we will take Paris and Rome." He heaved the hammer over his head and crushed the statue's skull to white dust.

She had accepted that she would die in here, in this room of hollow innocence. She had heard rumors that her father came looking for her. That he was apprehended outside the palace gates, where he was screaming through the iron bars. She had a routine now: strip naked and wait for the kind woman to come and cover her in the lavender spritz (it was the president's favorite), put on whatever brightly colored arabesque lingerie the kind woman provided that night, apply makeup—cake it on, make it look innocent, like a young girl who does not know how to apply it properly. Put on jewelry—jingling bracelets, necklaces, and earrings—her ears weren't pierced when she first arrived, so they pierced them for her. Comb her hair—the president liked hers long, he noted it every night. Stretch—she learned this the hard way. Try to smile—she never could. Breathe.

She stood around the bed with the others in the usual ring formation, emitting lavender, a smell that would be forever putrid. She didn't succumb to the president every night, especially if there was a new girl. She had gone days without doing so much as rub his chest or pick his clothing up off the floor. But it was the not knowing that still made her weak in the knees, when he would lie in the gigantic bed with his bare chest and stomach flopped out over his underwear, scanning the room for "Yasmina." He would only say "Yasmina" and point. He never knew their real names. She tried to forget hers too. Not permanently, but she kept it tucked in a compartment in the deepest depths of her brain where perhaps she could retrieve it if she ever left the Presidential Palace. But that thought had shrunk to nothing but a wisp.

A new girl was shivering at the bedside, wearing barely enough cloth to make up a hand towel. The new girls didn't bear yellow or red markings anymore, that shred of benevolence was gone. Every night there were new chains and ropes and wooden paddles. The president would make the "Yasminas" tie each other up; he liked to watch. She hated that; she hated touching the other girls. They were soft and pure and when she had to touch them, it made everything more real. She had to tie this one to the bed facedown, and her wrists were like twigs. She couldn't have been older than eleven, his youngest yet.

She got back in the semicircle, folded her hands, and looked down. Two other girls undressed him until he was a sagging naked blob. She didn't look up. He turned on his side, resting on his elbow, looked at her, and said, "Come here, Yasmina." She started to cry.

MOROCCO

WHEN THE BOAT ROCKED, IT FELT PERPENDICULAR to the water, like I was on the Titanic, sliding down the deck past the orchestra, and for much of the forty-five-minute ride across the Strait of Gibraltar, I wished it would have capsized; if only it would have relieved me of Mehdi's pestering.

"Joe, are you sure you are not of Arab descent?"

"I'm sure."

"Perhaps Turkish, no?"

"And it's Joe*L*."

"Your surname, it is Italian, no?"

"Yeah."

"You know, Joe, Arabs conquered Sicily too. Did you know that?"

"I'm not Sicilian." I felt a weird sense of pride saying this.

I was leaving Europe for the first time, and I had this itch. I didn't really know what to expect in Morocco, a decadent Tangier, like something from *Naked Lunch*? Or perhaps bustling bazaars with carpet hagglers and smoky rooms with steaming tea? But once we hit the African shores, most of my memories of Morocco were a blur. Marcel and Mehdi had a plan; there was no deliberation otherwise. We didn't even stay a night in Tangier—no deep existentialist conversations in the back room of a dimly lit café or hashish binges while wandering the meandering streets of the Medina. I got my passport ink stamp that had a little boat and a couple lines of Arabic. I couldn't read what it said. My Arabic had gone to shit. They hustled me into a van that was waiting on the street outside the port. The driver introduced himself, but I forgot his name. He didn't talk much.

We shot into the mountains, which resembled more of a Scottish green pastoral than the sandy bustling dirtiness that is so often conjured up when we think about the "Arab world." We hugged the coast, that rhinoceros spike of Africa that separates the frigid Atlantic waters from the warm Mediterranean. We passed a Spanish enclave called Melilla, a remnant of colonial Spain from when they started carving up the world a couple of centuries before the rest of Europe—besides the Portuguese, of course. You can find those guys everywhere.

"Crusader bastards!" shouted Mehdi in English, which meant he wanted me to hear it, as if I were a loyal Spanish subject. He sat in the front passenger seat and I could see his eyes peering into the rearview mirror. Then he looked to Marcel and rapid-fired a string of Arabic. Marcel seemed uncomfortable and timid about how to respond. Surprisingly, he turned toward me. "Joel, are you familiar with the word of God?" I didn't know how to respond either, so I just stared back at him. He bent down and zipped open a compartment to the bag at his feet and pulled out his pocket Quran.

"Oh... no... no, I've never read it," I said.

"It is very beautiful... here Allah says..."

"The most beautiful!" shouted Mehdi, correcting Marcel.

"Doesn't *Allah* just mean 'God'?" I asked.

Marcel and Mehdi looked at each other. The driver looked at Mehdi, then in the rearview at me, and then to Marcel, and then back to me, like a Mexican standoff with their pupils.

"What do you mean, Joel?" Marcel asked, eyes shifting back and forth from mine to Mehdi's.

"Like... *Allah* means 'God,' right? So why do you say the word in Arabic when you are speaking English?"

"I do not follow you, Joel."

"What does he mean?!"

"Jesus, man, relax."

"Jesus is NOT *ALLLAH!*"

"It is the most beautiful words you may ever read. This copy here, this is for you." He handed me the book.

I put the Quran on my lap and rested my head on the window, which gently bopped and banged over each bump we passed, and I tried to sleep.

I woke up as we approached Oujda, a city blanketed in tawny, ten miles from the Algerian border. We had been in the van for over eight hours, with only a few stops to stretch our legs, piss, and shit. At a rest stop, I had to hover my ass over a hole in the floor while trying to balance and keep my legs from going numb. I hadn't done a squat since high school, and my knees were rattling as I practically popped a blood vessel in my forehead trying to force out the turd. My ass got sore and chapped because I didn't wipe well enough—needless to say there wasn't a bidet. I was sweating and had cotton mouth. I asked Marcel why we couldn't just cross the border since the rebels controlled that hunk of Algeria right beyond the demarcation line. He told me the border had been closed to civilians and only military personnel were allowed to enter.

"Wait… so the Moroccan military is in on this?"

"Technically, no."

"What do you mean, then?"

"It is complicated. You have the Sahrawi people…"

"The who?"

"It is because of Spanish crusaders!" shouted Mehdi, looking out his window.

"So it's about those tiny enclaves up on the coast?"

"No, no," said Marcel. "In the Sahara."

"Well, what about them?"

Marcel and Mehdi looked at each other, hoping the other would take the lead. They looked at the driver—he didn't understand because we had been speaking in English.

"Well…" started Marcel.

"It is the fault of the Spanish crusaders!" shouted Mehdi. "And that is that. Because of the crusaders, *Maroc* and *Algérie*, Arab brothers, fight and kill."

"It can't be that simple," I said.

"It can be! It is!"

"So Morocco wants to protect the… *Sah-ra-wi*, or something?"

"No. They control that zone," said Marcel.

"Who?"

"*Maroc*."

"So… Algeria is helping them? Like the despot?"

"Hannachi is a demon! He does not help anyone. He will be terminated! *Allahu Akbar!*"

The driver echoed, "*Allahu Akbar!*"

I sat back in my seat and watched as we drove through the gate and entered the border city. We parked outside of a modern cream-colored skyrise and had tea with a couple of Algerian FLA fighters in an apartment on the fifteenth floor. They wore sand-colored fatigues, and their assault rifles were leaned against the wall behind them as we sat on spread-out carpets. They spoke with me in French and were nettled by Mehdi's aggression and intermittent shouts of *Allahu Akbar!*

These were the guys we'd cross the border with. I can't remember their names, but they were good men. I hope they made it through the fire.

I slept on the floor, on a thin mattress next to Marcel, up against the wall. I stunk. I was told I would be able to shower when we got to Oran. At least they gave me clean clothes: matching sand fatigues, boots, and a red beret. The shirt was a little small, but it made my arms look good. It was more official than I had imagined. There wasn't any training, though. They showed me how to load the gun and set the safety. That was about it. They told me they were grateful to have me, which was strange, I suppose. They said they were receiving more soldiers from outside of Morocco and Algeria, that they had some French and Spanish soldiers in Oran now, and even a Belgian—they were all of Moroccan and Algerian descent. However, I was "real *blanc*." I told them I had read Orwell's book, *Homage to Catalonia,* and that the FLA reminded me of the international brigades fighting in the Spanish Civil War. But war surely couldn't be *that* mundane, right? They didn't know. They hadn't fired a shot against the regime yet.

"What about *al-Saif*?" I asked, leaving the question hanging in the air.

"They are sick," said one of the soldiers.

"Really terrible," started another soldier. "They are not what we fight for. They are terrorists. But Hannachi, he make us the terrorists."

"He combine all of us together so Europe and USA don't want to help."

"*Ç'est dommage, mes amis,*" I said.

I got up from that thin stained mattress on the floor and went to the window. Outside, the city was gone, vanished overnight. There was only sand and the wisps from the gusts of wind. In the distance, I could see a tent with a shimmering light above the cloth. I stepped over the other sleeping bodies and walked down the flights of stairs and out into the sandy vastness. It wasn't even hot. I made it to the tent and threw back the sheet, and inside, on a dark green carpet, sat Adam.

I was speechless. He pointed to another dark-green carpet that was laid out directly in front of him and motioned with his hand for me to sit down. A teapot appeared out of thin air and poured its contents into a matching teacup that hovered over to me. I drank the tea, which didn't taste like much at all. I gathered myself and asked him how he made it all the way to Morocco. And did his parents know he was here?

"Mine don't," I said. "I mean, they know I'm in Morocco, but not for this reason."

"Why are you here, Joel?" he said as he put down his own cup of tea, which had also appeared out of nothing.

"What do you mean? To fight, of course. Wait, where are we, anyway? Where did the city go? Where is Oujda?"

"Where are *you*, Joel?"

"What? Cut the Absolem bullshit. Where are we?"

Adam started to laugh, but it was unlike any laugh of his I could remember. It was menacing and coarse. He leaned back and started to rock back and forth, back and forth. His eyes vanished, and then his nose and eyebrows, until all that was left was a widening smile with jagged teeth.

"You're not Adam, you fuck!" I leaped from the carpet and swung back the curtain to the tent. I started to sprint out into the orange sand and after two steps, I plunged into the grain and down into the center of the Earth. And then I woke up.

We left for Oran early the next morning. We were stopped at the border by armed FLA and Moroccan military.

"*Qui est-ce?*" asked the patrolman, looking me up and down in my seat.

"*C'est l'américain,*" responded the soldier driving the van.

"*Nous avons un américain?*"

I handed him my passport, which he seemed to look over more with genuine interest than to follow any protocol. "*Salam…* welcome," he said, and handed it back to me.

Mehdi was noticeably eager, bouncing out of his seat like a terrier pulling into a park. He kept elbowing Marcel in the side and giving him a look as if to say, "This is it. This is it."

We stopped in the mountain city of Tlemcen, the original capital and center of operations when the rebels controlled only a tiny enclave of the country. And the first thing I noticed was that spirits were high. Flags waved in the mountain wind: Algerian flags, Moroccan flags, and official FLA flags in red and black stripes. But what surprised me the most was that families carried on with their day as if everything was in its right place. They bought groceries at the outdoor markets from vendors flipping frying delights or whatever meat was on their grills.

We got out of the van to eat and rest before enduring our final chunk of road to Oran. I stumbled a little from an unexpected shot of pins and needles in the backs of my legs. I still smelled of acrid BO and used my overgrown pinky nail to scrap earwax out of my tunnel. I was hungry. I had been hungry since we arrived in Oujda, but was careful not to take more than my small portion of offered food, my "ration"—I needed to start speaking in those military terms, I suppose.

A family of three passed by the emptying van: a husband, wife, and son. The wife pushed the son in a stroller. His skull and left eye were covered in white bandages. The father looked at us and shot his arm into the air, displaying the peace sign. His other arm was missing.

"See them?" said one of our guide soldiers in French, pointing at the family. "They are from Sidi Bel Abbès, a city not far from here. It was destroyed by Hannachi. All of it was burned to the ground."

The little boy smiled when a sand-fatigued soldier handed him a big red balloon. I was surprised big red balloons were even available during a civil war.

"Why? Why was it destroyed?" I asked.

"Because Sidi Bel Abbès was the original birth of the revolution. It is small, but it was where the original students began to protest. But nobody outside of Algeria knows about this. Hannachi did it for symbolism. But it did not work. We rose from the ashes"—he started to tear up—"and fought back. But many are dead. Many are dead. We brought that family here. A rocket shot through the window and exploded in the living room of their home, releasing one hundred smaller bombs filled with needles and shrapnel."

"…"

"Their two older children were killed. The boy was a university student. A very smart boy. And the daughter was twelve and smarter than her brother."

"Is Sidi… Bel Abbès your home?"

"No, but Algeria is my home. That is why I fight."

BINGE UNTIL TRAGEDY

The little boy in the stroller let go of his balloon, which took off with the wind, over the cliff, until it was out of sight. He didn't cry, not one tear. How could he? He had already lost so much. He looked at me with a smile. I smiled back. He gave me the peace sign; his mother and father laughed and waved. I gave the peace sign back, and felt the release of everything ascend from my body and a guilty calm take its place.

We packed into another van—Marcel and Mehdi and two other Algerian rebels who were once part of Hannachi's army, and me. We took a rebel-held road practically the entire way to Oran. FLA flags were stuck in the dirt every few miles; the guards at the checkpoints were always interested by my presence. They would ask for my passport and ask why I was there. "*Pour combattre*," I would answer.

We passed signs for Sidi Bel Abbès, but there was no city, no sign of life whatsoever. The soldier in the front passenger seat let out a yawp of despair, and I looked out at the ash-covered valley of bullet-riddled buildings. It was a ghost city where nothing stood. How was this not in the news? A man firebombs his own citizens, leaving them trapped and burning like rats, and we're stuck reading coverage of people being trampled at a Black Friday sale or college students protesting the cultural misappropriation of their yoga classes and sushi lunches? It made me queasy; my stomach contracted and I let out a fart. Cars with bullet holes in their windshields littered the roads. There was rock and pieces of cement and shattered glass everywhere. And there were random bloodstains on the sidewalks and on the sides of buildings, but there weren't any bodies. It was as if Hannachi was trying to wipe the city from existence and salt the earth—a modern-day Carthage.

"You do not see this in America, right Joe?" said Mehdi.

"… No," I said, knowing full well he was not going to stop there.

"Yes. In America you have 'mental sick' boys who kill people because they is sad. They shoot up the school. How sad… Bahh! Look here…"

"I got it."

"No! Look! This is real problem. They bomb children. Hannachi bomb children and mosques and the old…"

"Yo! I said I got it. I'm here, aren't I? What else do you want?"

Mehdi sat back, mumbling to himself. The soldier in the passenger seat looked ahead and said, "I did not do this." The driver consoled him. The passenger seat soldier broke down and started to cry. Marcel and I looked at each other. "I did not do this," he said. I looked down at my boots and the butt of my rifle. "I did not do this. I did not do this. I did not do this."

We continued to Oran.

As we approached Oran, we sat up in our seats like meerkats and felt the acute jubilance emanating from the recently rebel-taken city. The passenger seat soldier had stopped crying, and kept checking his eyes in the front seat mirror. At the entrance to the city, soldiers sat in Mad Max–style pickup trucks with light machine guns welded onto the beds. Some soldiers were dressed in full military attire, while others wore t-shirts and shorts, all of them throwing out peace signs as we rode through the city. Throughout the streets were the punctured buildings and shattered glass of urban warfare—but as in Tlemcen, life carried on. Cafés and shops were up and running, and women walked with children through the markets. It was astounding.

"You will meet with your squad leader," said the soldier behind the wheel. "He is a hero."

We were dropped off before another checkpoint that was guarded by six soldiers who let us pass without question. When I saluted them before entering, they laughed and mockingly saluted back. "You do not need to do that," said the soldier with bloodshot eyes. "This is a civilian-free zone. Military only." We walked up the steps of what appeared to be a huge church. "This was the public library, but it was turned into the command center for the General."

Before we made it inside, a dozen soldiers burst out of the front doors, armed and laughing. Inside the library were hundreds of rows of identical metal cots with a path running down the center. Wooden cases of ammunition were stacked against the walls next to racks of assault rifles and pistols. It was like a gun junkie's wet dream.

We followed the path to an area filled with long desks of men yammering loudly and making colorful hand gestures that at times looked like they were about to strike each other. When we entered, a gigantic man stood up from a desk and the rest followed. He had a shaved head with a full, dark beard. When he spoke, he had a sonorous voice that was pretty to the ear—it was obscure to hear such a mass of muscle speak a delicate language like French. Again, I wasn't sure whether or not I should salute, so I waited for our guide soldier, Marcel, or Mehdi to take the lead. The behemoth gave the guide soldier three kisses on the cheek. He then introduced himself to the three of us standing in a row, spread out his arms, and said, "Welcome to the snake pit, my brothers."

We looked at each other, uncertain of how to respond. Since we'd arrived in Algeria, the usually loquacious pair had been quiet.

"*Toi.*" He pointed at me. "*Tu es l'américain?*"

"*Oui, Monsieur Hakim,*" I said, shaking, still unsure of whether I'd be accepted in North Africa.

"*Non, non, non, appelle-moi Farouk. Bienvenue en Algérie, soldat.*"

He led us to an extension of the library filled with men playing card games and smoking cigarettes and introduced us to our battalion: the 33rd a.k.a. *Les chasseurs de la mort* (the Death Chasers). They obtained their moniker from the comments on videos a few rebels had posted from their phones during the surprise attack on the city. More and more people, from all over the world, viewed these videos and praised how the vans and trucks filled with rebel fighters burst into the city to fight the General's men, instead of fleeing to the outskirts and to safety—*I'll need a* nom de guerre, *I suppose.*

They were a beat-up bunch; each and every one had bandaged eyes and skulls or was hobbling around on crutches. The smell of damp, dank, dirty laundry and smoke clogged my nostrils and eyes. And although Farouk was a colossus, the majority of the fighters couldn't have been over twenty years of age, many appearing not a day over seventeen.

I turned to ask Marcel a question, but he and Mehdi had left, or I'd lost them in the smoke, I suppose. I sat by the corner with my AK between my feet, constantly checking to see if the safety was locked. I was paranoid I'd kill myself in the dumbest way possible; hopefully they'd say I was Canadian.

"You must... how you say... rack up your gun," said a soldier sitting alone, pointing to the gun racks lining the wall. "You are the American, no?"

"Yeah, that's me," I said, beginning to accept my status as "the American." I got up to rack my rifle.

"What do you call yourself?" he asked.

"*Tu sais, je parle français,*" I said.

"You speak French? That is impressive. But I would be happy to practice my English."

"Of course you would..." I said under my breath.

"I love the American cinema."

"Yeah?"

"Yes, very much."

He was a "tomorrow baby," a term used for people who looked like a blend of everyone put together—basically, what the world's population would look like in another thousand years. My cousin Luka—yes, Luka Lupo—was a tomorrow baby. He could pass for Greek or Brazilian or Persian, or, shit, Algerian too, I suppose.

"You got a cigarette?" I asked. He pulled out an unopened carton of Carolina Filters, as if he had them on hand just for me. "Thanks, man. So what's your favorite movie?" I asked, cupping my hands to light the smoke.

"Umph! That is a difficult question for me. I very much enjoy *Doctor Jason*. I am... was... a medical student." He wavered as if he had, for a few moments, forgotten he was in the midst of a civil war.

"Oh, *Doctor Jason*. That's with Damien Rogers, right? The guy from *Punic*?"

"Yes! He is a marvelous actor."

"Ya know he's British? Well, Welsh, to be more specific."

"Is this correct? I did not know that."

"Right? British people can always do fantastic American accents, but Americans can never do British accents. We're not refined enough, I suppose."

He tied his hair back to keep it out of his eyes. When he got up, he hobbled over to a pair of crutches resting near the rifles. "And you? What film do you prefer?"

"Oh, uh... hey, *ami*, *ça va bien?*"

"Yes, but thank you for asking this to me. It is from the battle."

"Oh, man, okay. Well... you ever see *Buck and Larry Get Stuff Done*? It's stupid, but..."

"Take 'er easy there, Buck," he said, putting on a surprisingly good Southern accent.

"Holy shit, you've seen *Buck and Larry*?"

"Yes, yes, of course. It is quite funny."

"Ya know, I met Lucky Star. The kid actor from the movie."

"Is that so?!"

"Yep. In Berlin, about a month ago now..."

"How very cool. Right? *Cool*?"

"Yeah, it was cool. Hey, I'm Joel, by the way," I said, extending my hand.

"It is a pleasure, Joel," he said, stressing the "L." "I am Salim."

Al-Maghribi held a meeting with his generals at a posh house in the center of Constantine. He needed Algiers. Resistance from the National Army had been nonexistent. Tunisian forces had largely retracted from Algeria, choosing to fortify their own borders rather than pursue the jihadist group.

Youssouf and Simon were assigned brigades of fighters. Youssouf's mostly hailed from Sub-Saharan Africa—Somalians, Nigerians, Malians, and Sudanese—while Simon's were mostly Arabs, or Arabs who were European nationals, along with the South Asians. All members were required to learn Arabic, and alcohol, cigarettes, and any other "unnatural" pleasures were strictly forbidden—a Libyan teenager who was found with a carton of Carolina Filters in his duffel bag was launched from an extension bridge after a speedy trial.

"The Sahrawis are uprising in the South," said al-Maghribi. "My general in Tindouf is losing the fight. Soon I will lose Tamanrasset… Youssouf, you battled the Sahwaris in Mali. I need your battalion to leave for the desert and restore order."

"Sir… my brigade would better serve the Caliphate by attacking Algiers. My fighters are the most battle-tested…"

"I need the Black Brigade in Tindouf!"

"I deserve Algiers, not the American!"

Simon kept looking at the floor.

"We are citizens of *Allah*! Of the Caliphate!" al-Maghribi scolded.

"… Of course, sir. I will prepare the brigade immediately."

Once they were alone, al-Maghribi asked Simon to join him in a back room of the house that was decorated with crimson pillows and ornate rugs and acrid burning incense. Al-Maghribi retrieved a smoldering pot of tea and served it to the young jihadist. Simon looked around the room for the Tuareg slave girl who typically served the tea, but when he thought about it, there hadn't been a slave or servant in the home—al-Maghribi had even opened the door on his own.

"*Al-Arizona*… it has come to my attention that young men from Algiers have joined your brigade."

"Yes, sir. A few residents of Algiers have joined."

"I believe these young men can be the key to taking the city."

"They hate Hannachi with all their heart. One has told me that Hannachi requires his own book to be placed next to the Quran in all of the mosques in the city. And that it be worshipped equally."

"The pig!"

"Yes, sir. And one of the new soldiers from Algiers tells me, *every* time I see him, that he would die for the Caliphate. He was beaten by the General's secret police. He showed me the scars on his chest."

"Bring him to me."

"Now, sir?"

"No! Not now… stay here…"

The room was smoky black with flickering orange dots of candlelight. He ran his tongue up her shin to the kneecap. "More lavender. More lavender," he said as he sucked on the bone.

Yasmina grabbed the lavender spray bottle from the nightstand, accidentally bumping into the wood and jarring open the drawer. The glimmer of an unsheathed dagger caught her attention.

"More lavender!" shouted the president.

She swung her head around and sprayed—a direct shot onto the naked man's back. He sprung forward, bumping his nose on a new Yasmina' knee.

"Why is it cold?!" he shouted.

"My apologies, my king. I will have it heated at once."

After the president sprawled back onto the bed, intoxicated by the new flesh, Yasmina shut the drawer with the unsheathed dagger and left the room to warm the lavender spritz.

I followed the rising commotion coming from the front of the library-turned-barracks. Men and boys grabbed their rifles from the racks and sang chants I had not yet learned. Salim rushed to grab his crutches, hobbling on his good leg. His toes, exposed by the bandages, were dirty, the nails yellow and brittle. I carried his rifle for him, slung over my shoulder. I crammed extra rounds of ammunition into any empty pocket in my jacket or pants. I thought I was getting ready for war. I almost pissed myself. I needed a concentrated effort to stop the acute rush of urine. *What if I kill someone? It isn't illegal, I suppose.* This is war, people. This is the shit, the fray. If you don't want to know the nitty-gritty, if this is all too much for you, then go back to watching your sitcom about an incestuous group of twenty-somethings living in Manhattan or your "reality TV" show about a woman who can't stop feeding the feral cats or the couple addicted to coffee enemas. This is war, motherfuckers. Welcome to the snake pit.

    I strutted out the front door with the rifle nozzle above my head, ready to unlock the safety at any moment and fire, fire, fire. But when I made it down the steps, there was not an armada of armored vans or reinforced trucks ready to overrun Algiers. Instead, a growing group of soldiers stood in a circle around six blindfolded men.

    "The prisoners," said Salim.

    I scanned the group for Marcel or Mehdi, but couldn't find either of them. I hadn't seen them since we got to the library.

    Farouk walked into the center of the circle and quieted the crowd. He yanked the blindfold from a quivering, balding man who was wearing a decorated military jacket, but was in his underwear—an intentional humiliating juxtaposition, I suppose. The crowd jeered and hissed at the man, who didn't look up—not at the crowd, not at Farouk—as if he knew he wouldn't last the night. I could only hear bits and pieces of what Farouk was shouting at the man from the library steps. Eventually, I turned to Salim and asked who the receiver of the barrage was. His eyes grew wide and stared blankly at me.

    "That… that is the General," he said.

    I nodded my head and said "Ohhhh," as if I realized who he meant, as if I had already been informed but had forgotten. But honestly, I didn't know who the crap he was talking about. I needed to do more research, I suppose.

    "Can you hear him?" asked Salim.

BINGE UNTIL TRAGEDY

"Yeah, kinda," I said. "I'm not getting everything, though."

And as if Farouk had heard me, he grabbed a megaphone from the crowd and shouted in the General's face, causing that screeching, piercing electronic sound that happens whenever anyone uses a megaphone.

Farouk backed up from the General and the other blindfolded men and addressed the crowd.

"These are the men who bomb your homes! These are the men who kill your children! These are the men who torture your sons and rape your daughters!" The crowd roared. They launched fruit and vegetables that landed on skin and concrete with a *squish*. A date hit the General's jaw—he didn't flinch, but closed his eyes and took a breath. "This is the man"—Farouk stood next to the General, grabbed him by the collar of his fruit-covered military jacket, and made him face the crowd—"who bombed Sidi Bel Abbès! He gave the order! He attacked Algeria!"

Even from the library steps, I could see tears running down the man's face, his bottom lip quivering as he tried to keep himself together.

"What do you have to say to them?!" Farouk repeated. "What do you have to say to them? Look at them!" The crowd went silent. The soldiers put down their guns. Farouk continued to scream into the megaphone: "Look at them! Look at them! What can you say to them? You killed them! You killed their children!" And as if going off-script, Farouk pulled out a pistol and shot the General in the side of the face. The crowd gasped. Some cheered. The General fell to the ground, his body shaking. Farouk shot again, in the gut. Then again in the arm, then again and again and again in the chest, neck, and shoulder. A few soldiers from the crowd rushed the body and stabbed it with knives, hoping to inflict as much pain as possible until the man could feel no more. The other prisoners, still blindfolded, fell to their knees and began to weep. I looked on as if I was back at *Los Califas* in Córdoba, watching as men jammed their swords into a dying bull, like a mosquito stuck in the spider web, and again, I felt like nothing was in its right place. This is war, people. This is the snake pit.

BEN D'ALESSIO

"Yasmina" nodded to the soldier who stood outside the president's room, guarding the ornate ivory and gold door. The hot lavender spritz burned her hands. She grabbed at the base of the bottle and squeezed the heat. She enjoyed the pain; it kept her from going completely numb.

The soldier opened the door and she quietly slipped through the sliver of space—the president demanded that as little light as possible enter his chambers. "Only candlelight!" he would shout.

Inside, the odor of sweat and dried semen blended with the burning cinnamon apple candle, forcing Yasmina to plug her nose.

"The spritz, Yasmina!" he yelled. Yasmina, startled, pulled the spritz bottle trigger and sprayed the hot lavender directly onto the president's back. "Ahhh!" he screamed, and convulsed like a carp out of water. "You bitch! It's too hot! Too hot! Ahhh!"

"My apologies, my king!"

The president grabbed his belt from the floor and bent it in half, ready to whip her to the ground. "Please, my king," she pleaded, cowering. "Allow me to make it up to you."

The president lowered the belt, and with a menacing smile, asked, "What do you have in mind, Yasmina?"

"Allow me to satisfy your every pleasure," she said. The kind woman who helped her and the other Yasminas with their makeup and lingerie had also taught her phrases like this, and "Allow me to quench your every desire" or "Allow me to give you infinite ecstasy." She showed the girls videos, mainly American and French, with sex scenes and risqué dialogue—many were from *Punic*—at the president's request, because it showed the girls how to be "proper concubines."

She gently touched the president's arms and lowered them to his sides. She told him to get on the bed. The other girls surrounding them looked down or looked on with eyes glossed over. Yasmina straddled him and pushed his shoulders onto the Egyptian cotton sheets. She stretched out his arms and locked his wrists into the fuzzy green restraints attached to the bedposts. When he attempted to speak, she told him to relax and not say a word. "I will give you everything. Your wish is my command." She grabbed a piece of cloth that he would use to tie around the girls' mouths like a bit for a horse, and instead tied it around his eyes. She stuck his ankles in the leather straps and pulled tight, tighter than she should have, but she liked the little wince he let out when the leather pinched his skin. Her chest got heavy and she had trouble breathing. She looked around the room at the girls, at the Yasminas, and she got angry. She bit her lip to suffocate a scream. The president laughed and called, "Yasmina, little princess… I am waiting."

She took deep, dramatic breaths. "Just a moment, my king." She slid over the cotton and gingerly opened the drawer in the bedside table. A couple of the girls looked up from their trance, coming back from whatever compartment of their brain they would find solace in. Yasmina put her finger over her lips, signaling to the girls not to speak.

"Yasmina? I am waiting."

"Music, my king?"

"Music?"

She slipped the needle onto a record and turned the volume to the max. The baritone notes and pounding percussion of an Italian opera burst from the speakers.

"Too loud!" the restrained man shouted. "Turn it down!"

She threw open the drawer and grabbed the dagger with "For Our Hannibal" written in Arabic script on the blade.

"Yasmina!"

She gripped the dagger and plunged the blade into the president's exposed chest. The sonorous opera blanketed the man's blood-curdling screams. She pulled out the dagger and plunged it again into the bone, this time a few inches to the left of the original stab. "My name is Aya! My name is Aya!" she shouted, repeatedly jamming the dagger into his chest and stomach with every call: "My name is Aya! Aya! Aya!" Blood spurted onto her face and tears ran down her cheeks. No one spoke. The opera pounded on. One stepped forward and asked for the dagger, then pulled down the blindfold, looked into the bloodshot eyes of the dying man, and said, "My name is Lydia." And she rammed the dagger into his neck.

Al-Maghribi pulled shut the translucent curtain of the windowless room. Simon sat on a bed of pillows and waited for the tea. He pulled out an assault plan on Algiers from his bag and spread it across the table, illuminated by candlelight. Al-Maghribi returned with a tray of steaming tea and little cups with intricate turquoise designs.

"Why don't the Tuareg slave girls bring the tea?"

"I have them out... pleasuring the new recruits. It is pertinent to keep morale high, al-Arizona."

"I have a plan, sir."

"You do not need to call me sir... when we are alone."

"I can set up new Twitter accounts to attract girls to the Caliphate."

"Let me see it."

"Oh, no, this is for our assault on Algiers," said Simon, spreading out the creases of the paper with his hands.

"Brilliant. You are so motivated. It inspires me."

"Thank you, sir. I mean..."

"Call me Abdel."

"But Caliph..."

Al-Maghribi slid close to Simon, ostensibly to view his assault plan on Algiers, even though the plan was rudimentary and he had a far superior plan of his own.

"Explain this to me."

"My plan includes using residents of Algiers who have joined *al-Saif* and are willing to sacrifice themselves to God."

Al-Maghribi caught himself staring into Simon's light American eyes.

"We will strike from the inside!" shouted the young jihadist. The American's fervor aroused al-Maghribi, and when Simon wasn't looking, he had to tuck his erection underneath his leg.

"Yes! Go on."

"I have an adamant new soldier in my brigade who is willing to lead a strike."

"Excellent!"

Al-Maghribi moved closer still.

"He says he knows more just like him who are already nestled inside the city."

"How wonderful!"

"We will end the regime and then take Africa and then… an assault on Paris!"

Al-Maghribi leaned over the table to pretend to get a closer look at the paper, but his hand slowly crept toward Simon's knee.

"Or should we first take Spain? Like our Omayyad forefathers?"

Al-Maghribi was shaking. Sweat dripped from his palms.

A knock on the door at the front of the apartment made him yank his hand away.

"That must be him!"

Al-Maghribi knocked over the pot of tea, exaggeratingly falling to the floor to retrieve it.

"Should I let him in? I must warn you that he is loud, but his soul is for God."

Al-Maghribi remained on the floor, turned away from Simon, his erection slowly losing blood.

"Yes, sure, let him in. But be quick… we… we must finish our tea."

Simon hurried to the front of the apartment as al-Maghribi cleaned up the spilled teapot, his hands shaking, causing the cups to clatter and clank together. Simon returned through the translucent red cloth with the Algerian jihadist.

"Caliph!"

"And who is this?" asked al-Maghribi.

"Caliph, it is an honor," he said, head bowed in respect.

"Yes… what is your name?"

"Omar. I, too, hail from Algiers. The Casbah. So I can understand your struggle."

"Yes… well… al-Arizona and I were reviewing his plan to take Algiers… so if you could leave us…"

"I helped create that plan! Sir, I will be your inside man. I will be the key to taking Algiers from that pork-eater Hannachi! Please, Caliph, please grant me the position and I will not fail you."

"Yes, yes, it is granted." He made a motion with his hand as if to magically give the enthusiastic Algerian special powers.

"Thank you, Caliph," he said, bowing his head repeatedly like a Japanese salaryman. "Thank you, thank you, thank you."

"Yes, yes, go and do whatever you must do to crush the regime!"

"… Now, Caliph?"

"Yes! Go! Now! Go!"

Simon and Omar turned to leave, but al-Maghribi stopped them. "Wait!"

"Yes, Caliph?"

"Al-Arizona, remain here with me to discuss the plan in further detail."

"But Omar is crucial to the plan. He knows details about the regime and the FLA hideouts."

"Just you."

Omar bowed one last time and skipped out of the apartment with infinite mirth. Al-Maghribi locked the door behind him. Simon sat back down and spread the plan out on the table next to the stained teacups, the paper crinkling as it unfolded. Al-Maghribi crammed in next to Simon and leaned toward the table, gently placing his hand on the American's knee.

I could've used a drink; I hadn't realized it was going to be a dry revolution. I sat with Salim in the library-barracks and smoked his packs of Carolina Filters—he kept a cigarette between his lips, unlit. Salim's medical school days before the war made it impossible to actually smoke a cigarette. He just couldn't do it, even after watching the second-in-command of the Algerian government get his face blown off in a public square. But since there wasn't any whiskey or wine or beer, I sucked away.

He told me his mother was in his hometown of Tebessa, a town near the Tunisian border on the other side of the country. He worried about her constantly. He asked if my mother knew I was here. I told him I wasn't sure. I hadn't spoken to her since Spain. I'd lied to her, I suppose. But I lied to protect her. Parents always lie to protect their children, so why couldn't I lie to protect my parents? On fishing trips, my dad would tell me fish couldn't feel pain so I wouldn't cry when he jammed a hook behind the bait minnow's eye.

I didn't feel any real danger in Oran. I hadn't even fired my rifle. My only threat was chronic diarrhea—real heroic.

"You will have WiFi when we get to Algiers," he said, concerned that I had not contacted my family since arriving in Algeria.

"Another reason to take the city!" I shouted.

"You can meet my friends. I have not contacted with them either. I hope they are okay."

"What's it like there? In Algiers?"

"It is marvelous. I love it very much. And yes, I want to visit England and America, but I will always love Algiers… The city sings to you, did you know this?"

"Sings to you?"

"Yes. It is a city of song. And my friend Mohamed, he is the best musician in the city. He made a song for the revolution. Maybe you hear it?"

"Uh…"

"'Hey Algeria, Hey People.'"

"Wait… I think I might have heard that. He played it at one of those big rallies?"

"What is 'rallies'?"

"Oh… uhh… *rassemblement*? *Manifestation*?"

"Yes! That was him!"

"No fuckin' way."

"Americans and 'fuck.'" He smiled, bobbing his head.

I had accepted that I was a crass American. "Yeah, we're like the British and 'cunt.'"

"What is 'cunt'?"

"I'll explain later."

"My other friend. She makes videos. She make—*pardon,* made—'Hey Algeria, Hey People' and other videos about the revolution."

"Like the ones shot on the street?"

"Yes! 'In the shit,' as you Americans say."

"I've seen those too. She's good. A regular Stanley Kubrick."

"Joel, where are the friends of yours? The French ones?"

I still hadn't seen Marcel and Mehdi, not since we first got to the library-barracks.

"Oh… I don't know. Haven't seen 'em."

"That is peculiar, no?"

"Quite, quite peculiar. But I'm sure I'll find 'em soon. It's a small world."

"*Oui, le monde est petit.*"

Simon's SUV screamed across the Sidi M'Cid, the suspension bridge from which they used to toss Tunisian prisoners and that Libyan with the cigarettes. The SUV, with an attached black *al-Saif* flag smacking in the wind, blew through the checkpoint at the end of the bridge and traversed the mountainous terrain. Simon was shaking. He couldn't allow himself to do it.

"Sin, directly in the face of God! What happened to the Caliph? How could the leader of God's chosen say such… such vile things? Possession! That must be it. A few brief moments of satanic possession caused the Caliph to turn into a homosexual demon. Perhaps he was sick. Maybe he needed me, al-Arizona"—he loved his jihadist moniker—"more than ever?"

For a moment, Simon considered swinging back into Constantine to run his rightly deserved Caliphate. But the thought of having to confront the possessed al-Maghribi made him shiver. He could still feel the clutch of the Caliph's callused hands grab at the meat of his inner thigh and squeeze. There was no turning back. He'd start his own Caliphate. And like the taifa kingdoms of the medieval Iberian Peninsula, he would battle for legitimacy, and he knew the righteous would eventually reign supreme.

Simon drove down the desert highway that plunged into the Sahara. That is where he would begin recruiting for the new Caliphate, the righteous Caliphate. He stopped at an *al-Saif* checkpoint in Djamaa to refuel. The Malian jihadist in charge of the checkpoint didn't question his presence. Surely he knew who he was. Everyone knew who he was—the only blond-haired, blue-eyed jihadist in all of Algeria. He was loyal. Perhaps he would make the Malian his second-in-command—his own Youssouf.

After his truck had been filled, Simon sat and waited for the Malian to return so he could begin his recruiting. But it would get dark soon and Simon needed to get as close to Tamanrasset as possible, and he had already waited for fifteen damn minutes, so he took off deeper into the Sahara.

The tea was wearing off. The radio pumped out frustrating static that was unbearable to listen to, even if it did the job of keeping him awake. He started to slip. The same patterned sand dunes whisking past the truck put the American in a trance between cognizance and REM. And right as he began contemplating just how large his own scimitar would be (not comically large, he still wanted to be able to wield the thing, after all), his eyes closed. He felt the truck veer to the right and awoke, spastically jerking the wheel to left, causing it to spin in a complete three-sixty, and then pulled it back to the right, crashing into the sand and flipping onto the roof.

Simon lay in the pile of shattered glass on the ceiling of the car. The rear wheels were still spinning. He opened the upside-down door and crawled out onto the sand. Something was broken—a lot was broken. He felt a gash on the back of his head. He couldn't stand up. Any weight on either of his legs caused acute pain. He screamed. He saw lights in the distance. Two lights. Headlights!

"Praise be to God," he said, for he knew this was *al-Saif*-held territory. The lights grew closer. His saviors; they would become his first recruits. He would reward them for saving the Caliph, the true Caliph, by making them generals. The lights grew closer. Simon hobbled to his feet, wincing in pain, waving both arms above his head. It was also a truck, similar to his own but without the standard *al-Saif* flag fixed onto the rear. That was okay; these men showed they were ready for a change.

"*Al-Saif* was the faux-Caliphate, the anti-Caliphate led by a faggot with a big sword. Impure! Impure!" he shouted at the desert between coughs.

Simon waved his arms more vigorously above his head as the truck grew near and eventually came to a complete stop.

"*Allahu Akbar! Allahu Akbar!*" cried the American as he hobbled up to the side of the truck. His new generals didn't get down from the truck to help him, but he would forgive them this once. "God is great, my brothers!"

But when Simon reached the side of the truck and looked up through the driver-side window, he saw two women glaring back at him.

"Blasphemy!" he screamed, and fell onto his back. "For a woman to drive a vehicle, blasphemy! Sinners in the eyes of a just God!" he screamed from the sandy desert road. The two girls dropped down from the truck and approached the feeble jihadist. "God will smite you! With God as my witness, you will be punished by the lash in my pure Caliphate!" And as the girls got closer and the sun revealed their faces, Simon saw the traditional Tuareg speckled maroon face paint crossing the bridges of their noses and climbing up their foreheads.

Al-Saif had crushed the Tuareg insurrections in the south of the country and stolen their women. Al-Maghribi made it mandatory that all women of a "workable" age be assigned to *al-Saif* soldiers as their personal sex slaves—"For every soldier, a slave!" was a powerful marketing tool on social media to haul in spry young men.

The two girls pointed at the black flag with white Arabic script and a sword, crumpled under the overturned truck. They talked to each other in a language

Simon could not understand. "Speak in Arabic! Speak in the language of God! Black-skinned harlots!"

"We know who you are," said one of the girls, in English.

Simon realized an AK-47 and a pistol lay somewhere in the rubble of the overturned truck and shot as quickly as he could to his feet, wincing in pain, and hobbled to grab a weapon. One of the girls pulled out a large, smooth stick with a reed handle, trotted over to the hobbling jihadist, and whacked his not-quite-so-bad leg out from under him, surely shattering any damage sustained in the crash.

"You bitch!" he screamed, this time in his neglected American English. "You fucking bitch! When my Caliphate rises I'm going to tie your arms and legs to the figs trees and stick a…" But before he could finish his colorful threat, the second Tuareg girl pulled out a pistol and fired a shot that plowed through Simon's teeth and popped out the back of his head.

The girls left him for the birds. They walked over to the overturned truck, scavenged whatever suitable weapons, ammunition, and food was available, set the flag on fire, and continued on their way to Tamanrasset.

DOWN WITH THE KING

AT TIMES, I WASN'T REALLY SURE HOW TO CONDUCT myself. There wasn't any Revolutioning 101: "Look to your right. Now look to your left. One of your rebel-mates won't survive the uprising." I tried to follow Salim's lead. I was the only North American and one of the few non-Muslims. My religion (or lack thereof) didn't seem to bother anybody; at least, no one expressed any dissatisfaction to my face. About half the rebels prayed regularly, and if I was around the faithful when the call to prayer coursed throughout the city, I would usually find a quiet place to sit and be alone. I liked the *athan*; it was weirdly soothing. And the guy who did it, man did he have some range—I couldn't believe the Muslim world didn't have renowned opera stars.

After the midday prayer, Salim and I shared a pot of aromatic tea and he asked me if I was a Christian. I told him I was raised Catholic.

"I see. I have Christian friends from university, too. Do you know that Jesus and the Virgin Mary are very loved in the Quran?"

I told him that was interesting. He wanted to ask if I believed in God. I could tell it was the next thing coming out of his mouth. He was restraining himself from asking it, and I had to say yes, or something like yes—I couldn't completely ostracize myself here. Cut me some slack. But he didn't ask. Instead, he swallowed his question, and I was thankful for that because I didn't really know what I believed, I suppose.

BINGE UNTIL TRAGEDY

I finally got to shoot my gun. Not at a person or anything, just at targets. Farouk said that after taking the barracks, we had more ammunition than he knew what to do with, so he let each of us fire off a clip, for morale or release, I suppose. Back in Prague, when I beat Kev at that shoot-off, that was no fluke. I was a natural. I hit cans and empty bottles of water from far, far out. I even got Farouk's attention. "Looks like we found a sniper," he said. "Perhaps you can take the shot right through Hannachi's window." This comment didn't sit well with a few of the other rebels, and I think Farouk immediately regretted saying it. Imagine letting an American take out the tyrant who held down and raped an entire country while that American didn't receive an iota of the abuse. Talk about privilege.

I felt uncomfortable and my finger was throbbing from the trigger slap of the rifle, so I decided to go for a walk and explore a city I knew nothing about. Old men playing backgammon on the sidewalk waved to me, and a woman stopped me and asked if I wanted something to eat. Sure, I was aware there was pride in hospitality in this part of the world, but I felt like a celebrity, like Damien Rogers strolling down Oxford Street, London. I was in my fatigues, and perhaps that's how all the rebels were treated. Eventually, I did get hungry (I should've accepted whatever that lady was offering) and popped into a kebab shop where two young kids, neither of which could've been over fourteen, were slicing sweating, browning meat off a vertically rotating spit. When I placed my order, an older man, probably in his forties or fifties, came out from a back room, took one look at me, and said, "*C'est vous.*"

"*Pardon, monsieur?*"

"*C'est vous, le rebelle américain.*"

"*Oui, je suis un rebelle américain... Je ne comprend pas.*"

"*Venez ici, venez.*"

He motioned for me to come around the counter and into the back room with him. I didn't move.

"*La télévision. Vous êtes à la télé,*" he said, and continued to wave me back.

I'm... on TV?

"*Je ne comprend pas, monsieur.*"

I followed behind the counter and into the back room, where a small television with fuzzy reception was playing an American news station with French subtitles. The caption at the bottom of the screen read: "Venture Revolutioning: American Youth Fighting in the Middle East." Up to that point, I was unaware that any other Americans were taking part in the uprisings. A picture of a twenty-one-year-old named Luis Chang popped onto the screen, a second-generation Chinese-American from the City. The bleach-blond analyst described Chang, a rising senior at Williams College, as "quiet" and "introverted, without showing signs of violence or religious fanaticism." He had joined a rebel group in Aleppo, Syria.

Next, a flood of pictures of a boy named Simon Turner appeared and disappeared from the screen.

"*Ce n'est pa moi*," I said, thinking maybe the kebab shop owner had made the honest mistake of believing all of us look alike.

"*Attendez. Attendez. Vous êtes après*," he responded.

I had heard of this kid before. The jihadist kid Lucky Star was talking about back in Berlin. The bleach-blond described him as a high school heartthrob and athlete who was manipulated by foreign students at the International House at UC Santa-Berkeley. A picture popped on the screen of him holding the corner of a black banner in one hand and an AK-47 in the other. "He is believed to be operating under the alias '*al-Arizona*' and is considered a leader in the Islamist group *al-Saif*."

A clip of a pudgy, sun-beaten woman began to play: Simon's mother was being interviewed on her front porch in Flagstaff. "That don't sound like my boy. He's a good boy. He's smart. Honor roll. He ain't no damn Muslim, neither. I'll tell ya that."

Then a picture of me and Adam appeared on the screen. I remembered that picture. We both had our baseball gloves on and my mom took it before we went out for our annual first day of spring baseball catch. We were fifteen.

Another picture popped up—my cap-and-gown graduation picture. I had deep purple craters under my eyes and looked sickly pale. I *was* battling a gnarly hangover, but come on, they couldn't get a better picture of me?

BINGE UNTIL TRAGEDY

The bleach-blond began: "Joel Lupo, a recent college graduate, traveled to Europe *ostensibly* to help recover from the suicide of his childhood friend"—I froze—"but sources paint a different picture of the campus party-boy." Across the bottom of the screen the words **Freedom Fighter or Jihadist?** rolled underneath her breasts.

"Are you fucking shitting me?!" I shouted.

"Cool. Americans with the 'fuck,'" said one of the fourteen-year-old meat slicers, who had poked his head in the room.

"Sources confirm that Lupo met with two French nationals in Paris, Marcel Botende and Mehdi Zekkal, both of whom are now believed to be fighting with *al-Saif*, the gruesome Islamist group, in Algeria."

"..."

"At this time, we are unaware of Lupo's whereabouts. When we contacted the family..." *Oh god... my poor mother.* "... Lupo's mother confirmed that he *was* with Botende, but that they were visiting Botende's sister, who is studying in the Moroccan city of Fez." *Oh god... my poor mother.* "Mrs. Lupo also confirmed that she had not heard from her son in Fez, and that he had not uploaded any photos of his time in Morocco to his Facebook page."

Don't show her. Don't show her, I kept telling myself. I didn't think I could take it. If they showed her face, I would've been on the next flight to Jersey.

"Now we welcome GOP front-runner Clayton Wright to comment on the issue. Welcome, Clayton." *Come on, man, not this jabroni.*

"Thank you, Lisa, thank you for having me. Listen, I'll get right to it, we have a problem here in America, and it starts with our colleges and universities. These 'institutions of higher learning,' or 'indoctrinations of higher learning,' as I like to say..."

"Very clever, Clayton."

"Thank you, Lisa. These schools strip away the moral fibers that are sewn during their, what I like to call, 'American years of youth,' and are replaced with fibers that turn them against this great country. Take Mr. Turner, for example. He was a star athlete and student who only found the *Koo-ran* after time spent at that godforsaken campus known as UC Santa-Berkeley. I'll tell you this, Lisa, that entire faculty should be sent to Guantanamo."

"Isn't that a little harsh, Clayton?"

"Is protecting this country 'a little harsh'? Protecting the liberties of the free world—is that, Lisa, is that 'a little harsh'?"

"Well, I don't…"

"Let's take a look at Mr. Lupo here. He took the LSAT and studied French all throughout high school and college, a promising student, to say the least. He did not express any interest in the Middle East or Muslim studies until late in his college career."

What the fuck?

"His senior year, he took Middle Eastern Studies and Arabic 101. Hmm? Hmm? Something sounds off to me here."

"I wanted to bang Rachel Feinstein in Middle Eastern Studies!" I shouted at the TV.

"Then he becomes buddy-buddy with Mr. Botende, a foreigner with a less-than-stellar record, and *boom*! A home-grown jihadist."

"Fuck you!"

The kebab shop owner tried to calm me down. I came inches away from slamming my fist right through the screen.

"Mr. Botende brainwashed him. Late-night readings of that *Koo-ran*! Bahh! This is why we should revoke student visas from international Muslim students."

I've never even read the Quran. Is this clown serious? "*Je ne suis pas un islamiste*," I turned and said to the kebab shop owner, who laughed, as if to say, "no shit."

A montage of photos of me filtered in and out of the screen like it was my bar mitzvah. Lisa continued, "We have a caller who claims she is a close friend of Mr. Lupo's." Riley's voice came over the split-screen of Lisa and Clayton Wright: "Hello?"

"Yes, this is Lisa Shultz with *ANS News*, you're on the air."

"Hey! What the hell are you saying about Joel?"

"Ma'am, if you don't watch your language, we're going to have to cut you."

BINGE UNTIL TRAGEDY

"Oh... sorry."

"That's okay. What's your name?"

"Riley Johansson. I'm a close friend of Joel's and what you are saying about him is completely wrong and unfair."

"Where are you calling from, Ms. Johansson?"

"Croatia."

"Oh, that sounds nice. Are you there with family?"

"...No. I'm here with... a friend."

"A friend, huh?!" Clayton interjected. "What kind of friend? A boy? A boy you met over there?"

"What? What does that matter?"

"Ms. Johansson," he continued, "your friend Joe is a bad person."

It's Joel, fuck-face!

"It's Joe*L*!" she shouted.

"Excuse me... your friend Joe*L* is a bad person. He is un-American and an enemy of the state. Right now, he is fighting with a group that is on the US terror watch list. Did you know that?"

"*You* don't know that," she said. "Where is your proof?"

"Well, then, where is he, Ms. Johansson?"

"You can't just convict people without proof. You're un-American!"

By the look on Clayton's, face I thought he was going to have a stroke and die right there.

"... In the United States, you are *innocent* until *proven* guilty... ya jabroni."

Lisa gave a look off-camera and mouthed, "What is 'jabroni'? Is that bad? It is bad?"

"Listen here, Ms. Johansson!"

"Excuse me for interrupting," said Lisa, "but it has come to the station's attention that you *also* knew Mr. Botende, Ms. Johansson."

Pictures of Riley and Marcel taken from Riley's Facebook page began to fade in and out on the screen.

"... Well, yeah. He went to school with us."

"Is that it, Ms. Johansson? He wasn't a boyfriend of yours?"

"…"

"Ms. Johansson?"

"Ha! Will you look at that! Is that a thing with you, Ms. Johansson? Sleeping with terrorists? Is that a 'turn-on'?" He made air quotes.

"Were you intimate with Mr. Lupo too, Ms. Johansson?"

"I love Joel. He is my best friend. And he is NOT a terrorist."

"I would like some proof of *that*!"

"Joel… if you're listening… please contact me. However you can. Let me know you're okay. We're worried about you. I talked to your family. They miss you. We know you aren't doing… bad things over there. Please call us."

I stumbled out of the back room and smacked into the counter, causing the register to ring and jingle. I had lost my appetite. I felt sick and disoriented. The kebab shop owner pointed me in the direction of the library-barracks and had one of his boys walk me to the end of the street.

I had so many questions. Was Marcel really part of that terror group? Mehdi, I understood. That guy was trouble, but Marcel? Riley and I used to smoke blunts and drink wine with him all the time. And my mother… oh my god, my mother. But I couldn't wallow for long. I didn't have time to wallow, because when I was only a few blocks from the library-barracks, I could hear the shouts of jubilance bursting out of store and apartment windows.

At first it sounded like the shouting of sports fans. But then I could understand some of the screams and cheers in French.

"*Il est mort! Le roi est mort!*" a woman screamed from a third-floor apartment window.

"The king?" I said. *What king?* "*Quel roi!?*" I yelled up to the window.

"*Le tyran Hannachi, bien sûr!*" she called back.

The president? Sweet holy god, the president is dead? I took off in a sprint down the last few blocks, dodging people hugging and crying in the streets—it reminded me of those pictures of the City at the end of WWII. I launched myself up the staircase to the library-barracks and swung open the front doors—inside was a festival of smoke and musk. Random rebels grabbed me and hugged me. Many were speaking in Arabic and so quickly I had no idea what they were saying, but tears were dripping down their cheeks and they held me tight, never wanting to let me go.

"Salim!" I called out. "Saliiiim!"

"Joel!" he called, swimming his way through celebrating soldiers. "You have heard the good news, have you not?"

"Yes, of course! The president is dead!"

"It is music to my fears!"

"... What? What did you say?"

"It is music to my ears! You say this, no?"

"Yeah, yeah we do."

We left the library-barracks and went out into the ethereal jubilance of the streets of Oran. Shop doors were open, and food and drink were being given away in the squares and on the sidewalks.

"How'd he die?" I asked.

"Reports claim it was the French or American... how you say... 'commandos'?"

"Yeah, yeah, like special forces. Huh, I didn't think we were going to get involved."

"Joel... this means we can go to Algiers. You can meet my friends and *La Petite Mère*. You can remain with me. You can call your family, too. And later, perhaps we will go to Tebessa."

I should've turned around, gone back to Morocco, and taken the first flight to the States. Yeah, Salim was a good guy, but we could stay in touch through Facebook or Skype. The thing was, I wasn't finished with all this. I hadn't 'fought' at all: I came. I saw. I smoked cigarettes. Yeah, the regime stepped down, relinquished power to the rebel leaders, but there were still those crazy fuckers lopping people's heads off that we had to deal with. Maybe I'd move on, take my hired gun to Tunisia or Libya. I heard it was getting pretty bad in Syria, too. There, I could really master my Arabic. But the next stop was Algiers, the white city on the coast.

Every Friday, a line formed that began from the front door of a jewelry shop and wrapped itself around the block with itchy, antsy jihadists. Here a Saudi, simply known as the "Distributor," handed out perfectly balanced amounts of amphetamines to the soldiers. And although Omar had vocalized his opposition to the consumption of any drug, he had also witnessed the power the pills provided when battling the Tunisian forces via YouTube—they created an army of fearless super-soldiers. A Yemeni in line in front of him described the feeling as "being immortal. As if God pulled the trigger for me."

The line hadn't moved in five minutes, and given his spot at that moment, Omar was out of the shade. He was hot and sweating and tapping his foot and couldn't understand why it took so long to distribute little bags of pills.

"Cousin!" The whole line turned their heads toward the two approaching young men. "Cousin! *Allahu Akbar!* I have found you! *Allahu Akbar!*"

Omar embraced Mehdi, making sure to keep one foot in line, but embraced him nonetheless with a stiff hug and kiss on the cheek.

"My French warriors!" he shouted. "How was your trip? Where is the American?"

"We are not French, not anymore… never were! We are soldiers of God now… And the *kafir*? He is lost. A nonbeliever. He will fall with the rest of them to his vices or our sword," Mehdi responded.

"Very well then. Welcome to the land of God." He stretched his arms and took in a deep breath. "Two more soldiers, soldiers of God, thrust into the struggle between…"

"Hey!" shouted a patiently waiting jihadist a few spots behind. "They have to get in the back!" His demands were echoed by a supportive few.

"Brothers, they have traveled from Paris to join our mission of…"

"I came from Tunis!"

"… from Tripoli!"

BINGE UNTIL TRAGEDY

"... from Timbuktu!"

"Back of the line! Back of the line!" they chanted like soccer hooligans.

"Okay, okay, okay," Omar said, easing the chants. "Cousin, meet with me after I receive the pills. We have a meeting this afternoon... and Mehdi, welcome to the Caliphate!"

A lavish display of lingeried women welcomed Omar, Mehdi, and Marcel at the front door of al-Maghribi's quarters. They touched the boys' chests and whispered sexual promises in their ears—at any moment, the girls were theirs.

"Off of me, whore!" yelled Omar. "We have come solely to associate with our leader. Now back! Back!" Omar crouched down and threw out his arms like he was warding off vampires with hanging cloves of garlic. Mehdi and Marcel were silent.

"Soldiers of God!" al-Maghribi said, crashing into the foyer and licking the cheek of a scantily clad Tuareg slave. "My young... sssssupple... ssssoldiers... join us!"

"Sir..." said Omar, kneeling before al-Maghribi like a knight before a king, "these are the soldiers I told you about. They have traveled from Paris to carry out the mission..."

"Yes! Of course! The mission..." he said to himself "The mission... *my* mission!" Al-Maghribi ran into the living room and smacked his hands onto an old crumpled map of the world pinned to the wall. All the countries were shaded black with white *al-Saif* Arabic script etched onto the continents. "The Omayyads, they controlled nothing! I will take the will of God"—he dropped to his knees and raised his arms above his head—"to every corner of the world." He started to cry.

Marcel and Mehdi remained silent.

"Yes! Yes, my Caliph! But first, we must take Algiers. If you give me the order, I will carry out al-Arizona's plan..."

"Al-Arizona is a traitor!" he snapped. "He left us! In my time of… in *our* time of need!"

"He *left*, sir?"

"Yes! Yes, he left! He was a spy. Yes, that's it, he was a spy! For the Tunisians, no! For the Americans! Ahh, no, no! For… for Mossad! Yes… the Israelis, they have it out for me! Slaves!" The girls began to surround him for comfort. "No! The Israelis! We will make them slaves."

"Caliph… voice of God…" Omar began, "if you give me the order, I will carry out… the plan that will ultimately hand the white gem over to *al-Saif*."

"And then we will take Flagstaff," he said under his breath. "Burn it to the ground."

"Excuse me, sir?"

"Yes! Go! Take Algiers! Bring it to me."

"Thank you, sir."

"Go!"

Once the three young jihadists had left, al-Maghribi kicked the girls out and turned off the lights. He lit scented candles and made himself a pot of tea. He poured out two cups, drinking one while letting the other sit until it went cold. He took the cup, the one he let go cold, and threw it against the wall, where it smashed into pieces. He ran to the crumpled map and ripped it from the wall, and tore it into smaller and smaller pieces. He took out his giant scimitar, which scraped against the ceiling when he held it over his head, and began to slice the lit candles in half, spraying hot wax all over the furniture and walls. He dropped to his knees and started to cry. Then the ground shook and the tea cup and tiny plate started to clank together, and he heard the earth-shaking *zoom* of fighter jets.

ALGIERS

IT ISN'T WHAT I HAD IN MIND, ROLLING INTO THE city uncontested, barely a security checkpoint at the outer limits. I had imagined a siege, a struggle to take Algiers from Hannachi, where I would face my enemy with valor and we would come out victorious, of course. But obviously none of that was going to happen. The government surrendered almost immediately upon discovering the president's lifeless body. French commandos? I didn't buy it, but it didn't really matter, I suppose. The tyrant was good and dead. Those roving Gestapo-esque bands of thugs were imprisoned—those who weren't caught were systematically banished to the desert.

Farouk was put in charge of policing the city. He had personally asked if I'd like to ride with him into Algiers. That he was honored to have a non-Algerian, especially an American, risk his life for Algeria. I told him absolutely, as long as Salim came too.

Salim was ecstatic to return to Algiers and show off his city. He listed off every café and restaurant by name, as if they were Michelin-starred joints. He couldn't wait to sleep in his old bed again, and said I could stay with him since his roommate had left a while back. He even said there were some places I could have a glass of wine or a beer without any problems, and that he'd even have a drink with me.

"And we will meet with Farah and Mohamed. I miss them very much. You will like them, Joel. Farah makes excellent videos of…"

"Wait… Can she make a video of me?"

"Well, of course. We will have a party tonight and a video…"

"No, no, I mean like, a clip of me responding to that jabroni, the one on the news."

"Oh! I see. Yes, of course. She will be happy to do it."

Our caravan cruised into Algiers, a city built into a mountain that hugged the Mediterranean coast. We passed an imposing structure that looked like three concrete waves crashing into each other at a centered focal point. I felt like I had seen it before, in my textbook for Middle Eastern studies, but we barely covered Algeria in that class—we learned it was full of pirates.

"It looks like the Azadi Tower, in Tehran… right?" I said.

"This is more beautiful," said Farouk.

"It is called the Tomb of the Martyrs," said Salim. "It is very important to the city."

Salim filled me in on the exhaustive list of occupants who called this sliver of Africa home, from the Phoenicians, Carthaginians, Berbers, and Romans, up to the Arabs, Ottomans, and the French. He explained the Olive Protests of the nineties and the close encounter he had with *La Peste*—those guys sounded like nasty fuckers.

Farouk dropped us off at the mouth of the Casbah, where a unique mosque of blended Moorish and Byzantine architecture stood with two minarets.

"We protested here. We marched down these streets," said Salim, climbing out of the van and taking in a deep breath of the salty air. A tear came to his eye. "Come, come. You have friends to meet."

"Salim, be careful," said Farouk from the passenger seat. "My sources tell me there may be *al-Saif* fighters in the city. I will meet you later for tea. And Joel, thank you again, my friend. And welcome to Algiers."

We began our ascent into the Casbah, a white-washed part of the city where the crowded buildings seemed to be sprouting out from each other, with meandering streets speckled with the colors of hanging clothing. It reminded me of the Alfama, that magical little neighborhood in Lisbon, but more dilapidated, with more pain, I suppose.

BINGE UNTIL TRAGEDY

"So tell me about the Ketchao… Ketchaaoo… Ketch…"

"The Ketch-a-ou-a Mosque," he laughed.

"Yes, that."

"It sings."

"Yeah?"

"Yes, five times a day."

"Oh, the *athan*."

"Yes. It is quite beautiful. I think you will enjoy it."

We continued to climb the streets, weaving our way through men in jerseys of English and Spanish soccer teams and women wearing brightly colored *hijabs*. Every stand sold different foods, raw stuff to take home and cook. And in between the barbershops and cafés and shops with plastic bottles of olive oil hanging from string were intricately designed colored tiles at hip level, before turning into the white walls that helped the beleaguered residents withstand the unforgiving sun. We turned a sharp corner, where I almost bumped into a tiny table with men sitting in even tinier chairs playing dominoes. One of them called out to Salim, who stopped and gave him a hug and a kiss. As we walked, Salim would run his fingers along the tiles and look up at the sky, smiling.

We stopped briefly at his apartment so I could drop off my bag with whatever random assortment of clothes had made it with me across the strait of Gibraltar.

"Come! Farah has told me they are at the apartment of *La Petite Mère* now!"

Her apartment was only a few streets away and up a murderous flight of steps, which I needed to help Salim up, step by step. We were in a quieter part of the Casbah, away from the bustle of the market streets below.

From the front of the apartment looking up, I could see so many flowers pouring over the side of the wall that I thought I could smell them. And when there was a brief moment of silence, I could hear the little mother up there, on the roof, watering her flowers and humming.

"Salim!" cried a girl with pudgy cheeks and glasses when he entered the apartment.

"Farah! Joel, this is Farah. The incredible director!"

"*Enchanté.*"

A guy came running in behind us through the front door with an exotic-looking guitar strapped to his back and wrapped his arms around Salim with such ferocity, they almost went crashing to the floor.

"Salim!"

"Mohamed! Joel, this is…"

"The guitarist?" I interrupted.

"Yes! The best guitarist in Algiers."

"Oh, Salim. We saw videos of Oran. We are so happy that you are alive," said Farah. "We were here watching it on television."

"*La Petite Mère* got a television?"

"Yes! We finally convinced her," said Farah.

"Farah, do you have your video camera with you?"

"Yes, of course. I never leave without it."

"Wonderful. Joel is American and he…"

"We saw him on the news." She turned to me. "We know you are not a jihadist."

"Thanks."

"Joel wants to make a video telling America what he is doing in Algeria."

"Excellent."

Their French was accented and at times difficult to understand, but I enjoyed that for the most part, Farah and Mohamed did not switch over to English, and even taught me some new Arabic phrases.

"Come with me. You must meet *La Petite Mère*. This *is* her apartment anyway!"

We walked up a short flight of stairs and opened a pair of old French doors onto the rooftop—I was stunned. Green vines covered the walls, holding up flower heads of pinks, reds, blues, and violets, making the white wall barely visible.

"*Madame*, this is Joel. He is the American who fought to help free Algeria."

I didn't really like that language, to be honest. I hadn't "fought" at all. I had seen videos of the attack against the General in Oran, the bombs, the firefights in the streets, and I had not taken part in any of it. I felt… well, fraudulent. Like a cheap imitation of a rebel. Like a… a phony. I planned to take off my camouflage jacket and throw it away, or put it in a box in the attic, I suppose.

"*Bienvenue, cheri. Merci,*" she said, and touched me on the cheek and returned inside.

Salim stood with me on the rooftop, pointing out landmarks and hidden treasures of the Casbah. He told me there was a small eatery nearby that sold delicious *merguez*, a traditional sausage dish that was *almost*—he stressed—*almost* as good as his mother's.

"Soon we will go to Tebessa and she will make it for you."

"Sure thing," I said, thinking that given Tebessa's location near the Tunisian border, I could make contact with rebels there and start over: down with the next king, I suppose.

As I was looking out at the space between a set of buildings that granted me a view of the gull-infested sea, a sonorous bang of a voice enveloped me, the flowers, Salim, the Casbah as a whole—it was the *athan*, the call to prayer.

I must've jumped a little, because Salim was laughing at my reaction. "Don't worry, you become accustomed to it. I should have given you a warning. I lost the time."

"That's okay," I said, embarrassed.

"Joel, do you mind if I go inside to pray?" The question caught me off-guard and I waited for him to speak again, assuming it was rhetorical. "You see…"

"Oh, no. Of course. Yeah, of course you can. I'm fine. Don't worry about me."

"Thank you, Joel. I have so much to thank God for."

"Sure thing."

I remained on the rooftop, listening to the *athan* emanate throughout the old fortress of the city from the Ketchaoua Mosque. Below me, I could see children scampering around, chasing a soccer ball of the national colors—red, green, and white. On another rooftop, across the street, an elderly woman struggled with folding white sheets, and redid the fold until it was perfect. She saw me through the vines and flowers. I waved to her. She waved back. I looked down to the street again and saw a tall, thin black guy wearing aviator sunglasses with big mirror frames. I recognized him immediately. I would recognize those aviators anywhere.

"Marcel!" I called down from the vines. I realized I shouldn't've done that, since many residents were still probably prostrate in prayer. "*Pssstt*. Marcel." He froze but didn't look up. "Maarrrr-celllll." He darted down the street and turned the first corner on the right. *What the fuck?*

When I returned inside, Salim, Farah, and Mohamed were crowded around the small television in the kitchen.

"Can you believe this?" said Salim.

"He's really dead? It's really over…" said Farah.

"Actually over," said Mohamed.

Are they experiencing dementia? Everyone already knew that Hannachi had been killed. Why were they talking like it was breaking news?

Then I got closer to the screen and could see, through the spaces between their heads, fire and smoke and overall destruction. The caption was in Arabic and I couldn't decipher the words. "Bomb." I think I read the word for "bomb."

"Where is that?" I asked.

"Constantine," responded Salim. "It is where the terrorist group is located. They are saying that French and American planes bombed the city and killed many of the terrorist soldiers."

"And al-Maghribi, the leader," said Farah.

On the television, two French soldiers posed next to the charred remains of al-Maghribi's corpse. The French president gave a speech about how the bombing and execution of *al-Saif* was not just a victory for the West, but for *humanité*.

The news channel cut to the middle of a speech given by President Meyer, and although there was an Arabic voiceover, I could still hear the original English come through.

"And I ask that all young Americans fighting in the turbulent Middle East and North Africa at this time to please… return home. Your friends and families miss you."

BINGE UNTIL TRAGEDY

The three of them turned to me. I sat down at the table. *La Petite Mère* came over and turned off the TV—it was time for tea and snacks.

"Joel, you should call your mother now. We set up WiFi in the apartment," said Salim.

"Oh… I left my phone in my bag, back at your place."

"You can use the computer," said Farah.

I signed into my Skype account and immediately received a call from Riley. The distinct Skype ring shot me back to a nook of the campus library where I used to speak to Fantine in secret. Before I answered, she typed in the text box at the bottom of the screen: **No way Joel is that you? Are you there? Answer! Are you there????**

I clicked **Answer**.

"Hello."

"Ahhh!!! Oh my god, oh my god, oh my god! Joelie!"

Farah handed me a pair of headphones and I moved over toward the window.

"Hey, Riles."

"It's really you! Oh man… you look… tan. When was the last time you shaved?"

"Not sure."

"I can't believe I have you on here."

"Where are you?"

"Dubrovnik. Ya know, in Croatia. Oh my god, it's beautiful here, Joelie."

"You still with Andy Warhol?"

"Very funny. And yes! Miloš is super popular here. He is doing an exhibit where he gets volunteers to replace their bathroom mirror with two-way glass and puts a camera inside. He has people from all over the world doing it. He says 'we are at our most vulnerable when we are brushing our teeth or trimming our nose hairs.' He thinks it will bring people together or some crap. Anyway! How's… well… where are you?"

"Algeria. Algiers, to be exact."

"Is it… safe?"

I looked up from the screen at the three young Algerians sipping tea and holding hands and smiling. "Yeah, I'm fine. I'm with good friends." Salim pointed and smiled at me, too. "I like it here. It's amazing how different it is, but at the same time, how much we have in common. Ya know, Salim has seen *Buck and Larry Get Stuff Done*."

"Who is Salim?"

"Oh… the guy I'm staying with."

"Oh… okay. What did your mom say?"

"Well… I haven't talked to her yet."

"Joel!"

"I know, I know, I was about to call her when you called me."

"Okay… well, do it. And call Kev too. I talked to him about a week ago. He misses you. He's back in Jersey. He isn't even mad anymore."

"I owe him that. Glad to hear it."

"Mhmm."

"Hey Riles, I have to thank you for calling that show and sticking up for me. You know they're…"

"Of course!"

"And what they said about you…"

"*Psshtt*. Whatever. I can't be mad when I have this view." And she turned her laptop around, showing her balcony view of the glimmering Mediterranean dancing in the Dalmatian sunlight. "Isn't that something?"

I lifted Farah's laptop over my head, revealing the view of jumbled white buildings, but through an opening in the urban tel, you could see the Mediterranean, too.

"Isn't it cool to think that we're worlds apart, but still on the same sea?" I said.

"Huh… guess I hadn't really thought about that."

"The center of the world, I suppose."

"…"

"… So I should call my mom…"

"Yes, yeah, go, now, do."

"Okay then. Bye, Riles."

BINGE UNTIL TRAGEDY

"*Au revoir,* Joelie. Stay safe."

"*Au revoir, mon ange.*" And she disappeared from the screen.

I missed her. Oh my god, I missed her. If only she could bleed my mind.

I ended the call and shut the laptop and realized that *La Petite Mère* had poured me a cup of tea. The four of them were talking about the future of Algeria, and *La Petite Mère* was telling a story about a young man she once knew from Toulouse.

"A lover," said Farah, making the old woman blush.

We sat and talked about everything from cinema (Salim had me saying that now) to music to food—we always ended up talking about food. I told them about the Millburn Deli and about the City that has never forgiven me. I made it sound like an exotic, distant place of shimmering steel on the Atlantic, and I told them about Adam.

"We are sorry to hear about your friend, Joel. Suicide is very scary," said Salim, putting his hand on my shoulder.

"Have you ever witnessed death?" asked Farah, who I realized was a natural director, always pulling at the strings of a possible story.

I didn't tell her I had a chat with him one time—in Sintra, Portugal, of all places. I had just met this group and didn't want to creep them out. "I went to a bullfight once, in Spain," I said.

"Did you like it?" asked Mohamed.

"Not in the slightest."

Mohamed took out his exotic guitar, called an oud, and played "Hey Algeria, Hey People," and we all sang along. After, we took turns playing and sharing our favorite songs on the laptop.

"Joel, do you want to make that video now? You can be part of my documentary about life in Algiers during the revolution. It will be interesting," said Farah.

"Yeah, sure, of course," I said, and waited as she set up the camera, which sat on the kitchen table. "Hey, can I play this song? It's by my favorite band… well… kind of ex-favorite band. I met them in Prague and the lead singer was a jabroni, but this is still a special song."

"Yes, of course. We love American rock."

"Well, these guys are straight Jersey rock, kickass good stuff."

"Okay!"

I played "Spring Forever" and talked into the camera during the dark, mellow beginning.

"This is a message to the fear-mongering, emotional scavenger of a politician known as Clayton Wright." The Cavalry in the background really pumped me up. It still got me going; I couldn't deny that. "You, sir, are everything that is wrong about our country..." But before I could finish my thought, I caught a glimpse of a hooded man walk past the front door window. "I... I..."

"Joel, is everything in its right place?" asked Salim.

"What... what did you just say?"

Then I heard it, the roar of guns that had grown all too familiar. I remember the thud of falling bodies on a cement floor, the ear-splitting whiz of passing bullets striking metal pots and glass cabinets and windows. I remember Farah's scream. I remember looking out the front window one last time to see pale, hooded Death staring back at me.

I was killed instantly. I didn't have time to reflect on my life. I wasn't given that luxury. That's what those dreams were for, I suppose. I just wish my dreams were linear.

When the shooting stopped, nobody moved. Nobody spoke outside. All you could hear was the opening of car doors and the sound of wheels peeling away, back into the Casbah. And inside, the vocals of Tommy Devine continued to serenade crumbling shards of glass and motionless bodies: *I'm gonna live like it's (bump bump) spring forever! Like it's (bump bump) spring forever! Because it's (bump bump) now or never!*

Now? Now I'm here and alone and have yet to find Adam.